SILK LEGACY

By

Richard Brawer

Although inspired by true events, in no way are any of the fictional characters and fictional situations intended to depict actual people or places.

ISBN 1-58961-469-0

Published by PageFree Publishing, Inc.
109 South Farmer Street
Otsego, Michigan 49078
1-866-GO-BOOKS
www.pagefreepublishing.com

Dedicated to
Arthur Brawer and Ida Kaplan Brawer

Also by Richard Brawer

The David Nance Mystery Series

The Nurse Wore Black—Raised by a single parent, David Nance's mother has given him more love and devotion than any two parents. When David finds her murdered on the eve of her sixtieth birthday he seeks revenge and uncovers dark secrets in her past he would have rather left buried.

Diamonds Are For Stealing—Diamonds, money, power, infidelity, and revenge. David Nance pursues the theft of a quarter million dollar necklace that has vanished from a safe deposit box and is immediately confronted with the murders of the bank president and the jeweler who crafted the necklace.

Murder On The Links—David Nance roots out the murderer of a blackmailing prostitute, a penny stock con artist and the daughter of a mob boss from among the wealthy members of posh Spring Brook Golf and Country Club.

The Russell Gerrard Mystery Series

Murder Go Round—The sale of a million dollar antique carousel incites murder and exposes fraud and corruption in a decaying Jersey shore resort.

To find out where to buy these books go to: www.rbrawerbooks.com

ACKNOWLEDGEMENTS

With Many thanks to:
The Monmouth County Writer's Guild
Sandra, David, Rosalie, Bruce, Lucile, Linda, Joan, Dana
Paterson Museum
Passaic County Historical Society
Great Falls Development Corporation
American Labor Museum, Botto House Landmark,
83 Norwood Street, Haledon, New Jersey 07508
"Paterson Evening News"
"The New York Times"
Paterson Public Library
Monmouth University Library
Monmouth County Library
Brookdale Community College Library
"Voices from the Paterson Silk Mills"
by Jane Wallerstein
Arcadia Publishing, 2000

PATERSON, NEW JERSEY
A BRIEF HISTORY

In 1791 Alexander Hamilton stood on the bluffs that overlooked the Passaic River's great waterfall, and envisioned a mighty industrial city. He prophesied that the only way his new country could be truly independent from England and Europe was to develop its own resources and industry.

Wary that democracy by the masses was not powerful enough to bring about the quick development of a strong industrial economy, Hamilton lobbied Congress to appropriate one million dollars to build a government-owned and operated industrial center. Congress balked. However, through the influence of his politically connected friends, Hamilton convinced the New Jersey Legislature to charter a corporation for the sole purpose of creating an industrial city.

The corporation was named "Society for Establishing Useful Manufacturers." Its charter gave it extraordinary financial and governmental powers. SUM had exclusive control over the Passaic River and its great waterfall. Its property and the corporation were tax exempt. It had the right to create its own government within the bounds of its territory, and to condemn property bordering its lands for its own use, as well as hold lotteries to raise funds. Among the original sixty-five stockholders were two Supreme Court justices, four senators, nine congressmen, a former governor of New Jersey, and the present governor, William Paterson—the namesake of the city SUM built. This obvious conflict of interest set the tone for the operation of Paterson for the next one hundred and twenty-five years.

SUM set out immediately to build its own factories as well as to lease and sell land to other entrepreneurs. Word spread rapidly. The city became a Mecca for men with grandiose ideas such as Samuel Colt, whose six-shooter helped tame the west; Thomas Rogers whose Rogers Locomotive factory built not only one of the first locomotives in America, but Union Pacific's Engine number 119 that bumped cow catchers with its counterpart from the west at Promontory, Utah to unite the country by rail; John Holland, developer of the first practical submarine which he tested in the Passaic River; and John Ryle, who in the eighteen-forties, built a silk mill and started an industry that would dwarf all others. By 1900 there were three hundred mills in Paterson that were turning raw silk into a fabric of shimmering beauty to luxuriously adorn the bodies and homes of America's rich.

Enticed by pictures of gold lying in the streets waiting to be scooped up, immigrants flocked to Paterson, carrying with them little more than their dreams for freedom, equality and riches. A few realized those dreams and joined the ranks of the industrialists, but most soon found out they had traded their past oppression under the aristocrats of Europe for a new form of oppression, fostered on them by the powerful mill owners. The industrialists ruled Paterson as a private kingdom. They had no concern for the city or the people that inhabited it, treating Paterson and its immigrant laborers as expendable commodities needed only to create the one product that meant anything to them—money.

Nothing was built for the public without a bitter fight from the directors of SUM and the other industrialists. A cholera epidemic established an obvious need for sewers, but it took a special act of the state legislature to force SUM to build them. SUM, because of its tax exempt status, refused to pay its fair share for sidewalks, and it was not until 1907, despite numerous typhoid outbreaks, that SUM finally was forced to put proper filters on its system that supplied drinking water to the city.

Government became an industry of its own, earning its revenues from the industrialists who owned the politicians, the courts, the press and the ballot box. The working class was disenfranchised from both politics and the social order of the city. They became outcasts, treated no better than the products they produced with their labor. However, there was one factor the autocratic industrialists could not control—the flow of ideas.

During the nineteenth century, the population of Paterson increased by fifty percent every decade. The immigrants who crowded into the tenements were of the same stock as America's founding fathers and the industrialists who tried to control them. Their tongues were equally as sharp, their organizing abilities as keen, and their demands for "certain unalienable rights" as insistent. With every avenue of legal protest shut to them, they hit out at their oppressors the only way left open to them: they withheld their labor from the mills.

Their first strike came in 1794, the only demand being schooling for their children. Over the next one hundred and nineteen years, as the dictatorship of the industrialists grew stronger and their refusal to do anything for the welfare of the city became more adamant, Paterson's laborers struck their bosses an additional one hundred and thirty-six times.

Through their ownership of the politicians and the police, the bosses easily put down every strike, but each defeat taught valuable lessons to the laborers. The day was fast approaching when the masses would be heard and the power structure would shift. That day arrived on February 25, 1913. Twenty-four thousand workers walked out of Paterson's three hundred silk mills, throwing the city into chaos for five months.

Silk Legacy is the story of one family torn apart by The Great Silk Strike of 1913.

PROLOGUE

1893–1894
Dublin, Ireland

Abe stumbled out of the tenement and grasped his wagon wheel for support. Bruised and swollen from yet another fall in a dark narrow stairway, his knees barely worked. Summoning up the last of his strength, he tossed his coal sack into the wagon's empty bed and pulled his sore body up onto the seat. A drop of sweat fell from his brow and splashed on the back of his hand, washing away a circle of coal dust.

He stared at the white spot and thought, *there has to be a better job*. But he knew there wasn't. Despite twenty-five percent unemployment in Dublin, this job had gone begging. The taste of coal dust with each bite of food, the smell of oily coal with each breath, and the aches in his tortured body told him why. If only he could operate the same con here he had run in London. He quickly tossed away that thought. The Earl of Wexford may have sent word to his cronies in Ireland to be on the lookout for a tall Jew with white streaks in his hair.

Abe's blackened lips curled into a smile and his aches waned for a moment at the vision of the delightfully plump, Lady Wexford. He had met her two years ago in London, while going house-to-house begging for old clothes. That was his scam—go to the middle and upper class neighborhoods, say he was from a charity and beg for discards, "for the poor unfortunates in the orphanage," he would say. The rag merchants paid top prices for good quality clothes they could re-sell throughout the empire.

He had become an excellent actor. More often than not his pout and his eyes, saddened by drooping his lids, garnered him enough sympathy to send a servant scurrying off to the mistress of the house with his request. If he was lucky, the servant would return with a couple of garments.

When Lady Wexford opened the back door herself, she startled him. He had never met one of his benefactors before. He knew instantly she was the lady of the house. Servants didn't have painted nails or rouged lips, and servants didn't wear silk bedclothes in the middle of the day.

When she asked, "Would you like to come in for tea?" his knees buckled. No one ever invited him into the house.

She took his hand, gently tugged, and said, "Come. It's cold out. You look like you could use a hot cup of tea."

He swept off his cap and cautiously stepped over her threshold, his eyes darting everywhere.

"The servants are off today," she said, and set him down in the kitchen. She poured him tea, offered him a crumpet and slid into the chair across from him. With each movement, her loosely tied robe slipped open a little further. She made no attempt to fix it.

"I've seen you in the neighborhood," she said. "I've been waiting for you to knock on my door."

While she talked, he sipped his tea and stared at her breasts. He had seen breasts before. Besides his four brothers, he had five sisters, but none of his sisters had breasts as round, as plump, as pinky-white as this aristocratic lady.

"How old are you, young man?"

"I'll be sixteen tomorrow."

"How nice. I have a delightful birthday present for you." She parted her lips in a huge red grin. "A big bundle that will make you very happy. It's upstairs. Would you mind going up to get it?"

Still wary, he wondered, *is this some sort of trick*? Invite urchins in, give them drugged tea, kidnap them and sell them, maybe to the tsar in Russia? The tsar loved to grab Jewish boys for his army.

He balled his fist. *Let them try and kidnap me.* He was a good fighter. He had to be, growing up with four brothers. When the five of them weren't wrestling with each other, they were standing back-to-back, fending off the Christian boys who tried to gang up on them.

She rose from her chair and walked over to him. Her large, unharnessed breasts swayed with each step. Stroking her hand across his hair and down the nape of his neck, she said, "Come, young man. Let us go get your bundle."

Abe followed the lady through the house. Dark wood and thickly upholstered furniture adorned the dining room. Dishes, glass and china bowls, and figurines filled the shelves of the breakfronts. It reminded him of his uncle's house back home.

His uncle was an importer and exporter. He had a huge warehouse in the city of Libau in Latvia and agents all over the world. Before Abe left Latvia his biggest wish was to move to the city and work for his uncle. It was the only way he saw to get off the farm. But then the tsar's conscription of Jewish boys into his army started again and he had to flee.

In the living room, a painting over the fireplace of a squat, bald man in formal dress caught Abe's attention. It covered the entire wall, from the mantle to the ceiling. The immenseness of the picture and the man's erect posture were meant to make the little man look taller. Instead they enhanced his rotund belly.

"That's my husband, dear—the Earl of Wexford," Lady Wexford said. "He won't be home until late tonight. Come, follow me."

From behind her, Abe giggled at the thought of how the earl and the lady must look when they went to some fancy dressed ball. With her hair piled up and wearing a shoe with a high heel, she'd tower over him. When they danced, his head must rest on her pillowy breasts. He wondered what that would be like. Some of the boys talked about such things, but he had never experienced it.

Lady Wexford led him upstairs. Her hand—white and smooth—not rough, gnarled and red like his mother's and many other older women he knew—slid delicately along the varnished dark wood banister. Opening the third door down the hallway, she ushered him into a sitting room. It smelled like spring flowers, only there were no blooms in the room. A thick wool rug, a chaise lounge, two upholstered tub chairs and a dressing table covered with colorful bottles, decorated the room. He didn't see any clothes lying around.

"In here, dear," Lady Wexford said, and proceeded across the room into the bedroom. He followed.

Frilly lace curtains covered the windows and the bed canopy. Snow-white sheets, folded over a floral print comforter, layered the bed. Lacy white pillows were propped up against the carved head-board. He'd never seen anything like it. His mattress in his rented room in Whitechapel's East End was rag-filled. Coarse gray sheets scraped his skin when he slept. Two thin blankets, pock-marked with stitches mending the holes, offered little warmth. Even that was far better than the slat bed and straw-filled mattress he'd slept on back home in Latvia.

She sat on the bed and patted the spot next to her. "Sit for a minute."

Abe's eyes fell on a sack as big as Santa Claus's in the corner of the bedroom. A shirt sleeve and the legs of a pair of pants hung out the top. It looked like a large enough haul to bring a month's rent from the rag merchants. Not wanting to do anything that would upset her and make her withdraw her offer, Abe sat at the foot of the bed, as far away from her as he could. Quick as a lightning bolt, Lady Wexford slid down next to him, pinning him between herself and the pole that held up the canopy.

She placed her hand on his thigh and stroked him lightly. "Have you ever been with a lady before?"

He sucked in a deep breath, pulling in her flowery scent with it. He vigorously shook his head sideways.

Flashing her rosy grin again, she said, "Let me show you."

Abe flicked his eyes between the large sack in the corner and her breasts, and let her. An hour later he left with the sack of clothes and all the questions about women that had cluttered his mind since his Bar Mitzvah answered.

****

Once a week for the next two years, Abe visited Lady Wexford's house, frolicked with her in her soft featherbed and came away with a bundle of clothes, not surprisingly, all in his size. Some he kept, but others he sold to pay for a two-bedroom apartment in London's East End. He had moved to the bigger apartment when his brother Dan came to London. Abe took Dan in and taught him the trade. "But you'll have to find your own Lady Wexford," he told him. They both had a good laugh at that one.

Abe's cushy life ended as abruptly as it had begun when the Earl of Wexford came home unexpectedly one day. At six-feet-two inches, Abe towered over the short, round earl, and outreached him by almost a foot. With Lady Wexford's screams piercing his ears, Abe landed three quick blows—one to the earl's ample gut and two to his head. The earl collapsed on his padded rear, where he remained for the briefest moment before keeling over flat on his back, unconscious.

Word spread quickly through London's East End of a hundred-pound reward offered by the earl, "for the capture of a tall Jew boy with streaks of white in his hair." Premature white hair ran in Abe's family. To those who inherited the trait, it began showing up in their late teens. By thirty, Abe expected his hair to be totally white.

But white streaks in his hair would not tell the earl that, Abe was Jewish. That had to have come from Lady Wexford. When she saw that he was circumcised, she had said, "I never had a Jewish boy before."

Abe ran to Ireland, where he heard he might be able to find a haven from an English Lord. The Irish hated the English as much as he hated the tsar.

****

I could use a benefactor here like Lady Wexford, Abe thought, and unlashed the reins from the wagon's brake handle. He snapped the leather against the horses' flanks and pulled out from the row of coal wagons. "What a waste," he scoffed. They all hauled coal from competing yards to the same buildings. He delivered to two flats, someone else to three, another to a couple more.

The steel-rimmed wheels clanged through a rut in the cobblestones. He winced in pain from the jolt at the same time the idea flashed through his mind.

****

Abe hobbled into the coal yard office.

"What do ya want?" his boss asked. "Quitten' already? I knew a boyo like you wouldn't last. You ain't got the hands a no laborer."

With agonizing effort, Abe drew his soot-covered body up to its full height. His cap in his hands, he wrung it and gritted his teeth against the coal dust in his mouth to keep the word "fool" from leaping off his tongue. His objective was to get off the coal wagon, not to get fired.

"I have an idea how you can deliver more coal with the same number of haulers," Abe said.

"Yeah, smart guy, what's that?"

"Give a price break to each tenant if a whole building signs up with your yard. I'll bet a week's work with no pay you get thirty to forty percent more coal delivered without hiring more delivery men."

His idea would not win him friends among the haulers, but that wasn't his concern. All he wanted to do was wear clean clothes again, and like he did in London, make money using his *moxie* not his back.

****

At the end of five months as the coal yard's commissioned salesman, Abe had signed up twelve buildings and all but one apartment in the thirteenth. The holdout was the McGuire couple—Timothy and his pretty young wife, Katie.

Abe had called on Katie three times, bringing her a box of candy with each visit. In return for his gift, Katie insisted he stay for tea. For hours, Abe sat at her wobbly table, watched her stuff her mouth with his treats, and listened to her pathetic story.

Katie was the seventh of ten children, and the only girl. Her three younger brothers still lived at home. Her oldest brother was the parish priest.

When Katie began to develop, Timothy McGuire monopolized her, bullying any boy who got too friendly with his girl. She married him eight months ago, at the age of sixteen. Abe didn't have to ask why her parents were happy to see her wed; one less mouth to feed was a blessing.

Timothy provided Katie with a black stove, a couple of sticks of rickety furniture, an often empty coal bin, a bare pantry, and hopelessness. The only thing of value in her apartment was a pair of silver candlesticks her mother had given her as a wedding present. When Abe commented on their beauty, Katie said, "They have been in my family for two hundred years and are passed down to the oldest girl when she marries. Timothy would have pawned them long ago, but he knows my father would kill him if he did."

If it were up to Katie, she would have eagerly signed with Abe's yard, but it wasn't her decision to make. Timothy wanted a quid to agree. Others had approached Abe for a bribe, but he always let the tenants work it out among themselves. If he paid off, there would be no end to the demands. But Timothy was a hard case. He refused to budge. When he worked, it was as a collector for a loan shark. Mostly, he spent his time in the pub. Abe knew that even if Timothy relented, there wouldn't be much coal delivered to the McGuire flat, so what did Timothy have to lose by holding out.

Finally, to free Katie from the verbal thrashing her neighbors heaped on her every time she left her apartment, Abe decided to make the payoff. He figured he was a good enough salesman to convince anyone who asked that the money didn't come from him. Who were these people going to believe—that son-of-a bitch Timothy, or the charming guy who brought the candy and the lowest price for their coal?

With Timothy's quid tucked in his vest pocket, Abe climbed the narrow tenement stairs to Katie's third floor flat. The door to the McGuire apartment stood open a crack. Abe knocked on it. It swung slowly inwardly. Peering hesitantly inside, he spied Katie on the living room floor, her lip bleeding and tears running down her face. He hurried to her.

"Who did this?" he asked.

"Timothy."

That surprised him. He had thought a neighbor had done it in retribution for Katie's not signing. "Why?"

"Because I haven't been able to find a job."

"Lazy son-of-a-bitch!" Abe said to himself. The bastard wants her to work to keep him in whiskey. Abe went to the sink to hunt up a rag. Wetting it, he returned to Katie and dabbed at her swollen mouth. She didn't say a word while he tended to her, but her huge brown eyes never left his face.

"This isn't the first time," she said.

"Does your brother know your husband beats you?"

"Yes. He talks to Timothy, and Timothy stops for a few weeks. Then he starts in on me again."

"Why don't you leave him?"

"I can't. My brother says I would rot in hell. I don't know what to do." She broke into tears, and threw her arms around Abe's neck.

He picked her up, carried her to the bedroom and settled her on the bed as delicately as he would place fine Irish crystal on a table. He started to pull away. She grabbed his arm and held on tight.

"Don't go," she said and slid over.

Abe sat beside her.

Katie clung to him as if he were her only link to life itself. She was soft, and smelled of soap from a recent bath. He rubbed her back and stroked her hair. She clutched him tighter. His lips brushed her neck and ear. She pushed her head to his mouth. He didn't intend it to happen. When it was over he had no doubt that Katie's bright red hair got its color from the fire inside her.

Their ecstasy subsided, Katie said, "I never knew it could be like that. With Timothy it's over in seconds, and he hurts me."

Abe forced a weak smile. What could he say? *"I'm glad I could be of service."*

"I'm not sorry I made love with you, even if I did commit a sin," Katie said.

Lady Wexford popped into his mind. The most enjoyable time of his life was during those two years he lay with her. "Lovemaking can never be a sin. Love is beautiful."

"I'm married. I have committed adultery. God will cast me out of heaven."

"No He won't. If He casts anyone out it will be that good-for-nothing husband of yours."

"My brother would not agree with you."

"Your brother is a fool."

She pushed herself up on her elbow and drew the coarse, unbleached sheet around her. "He is not a fool. He is a servant of God."

Abe kissed her lightly, avoiding the bruised part of her mouth. Afraid her husband might appear at any moment, he said as tenderly as possible, "I should go."

She clutched his arm. "Thank you for showing me what making love can really be like, even if it means I have to spend many hours in penance."

He gently tugged free. She fell back on the bed, letting the sheet fall from her young breasts.

Abe couldn't take his eyes off her while he dressed. Oh, how he wanted to stay! He had wanted Katie from the first minute he'd seen her. He had bedded other lonely, love-starved wives since he'd begun selling coal contracts. They were cows compared to the tender young Katie McGuire.

He had known better than to make a move on her. Her brother was a priest. But he wasn't anywhere near as scary as Katie's husband, Timothy—a bull of a man. Like the thugs and low-lifes that had swarmed out of the pubs and off the docks to collect the earl's bounty, Timothy would beat Abe to a pulp if he caught him.

Leaving her apartment, his thoughts turned to her brother. What would the priest do when she told him about her adultery—and with a Jew no less, the devil himself?

For days, Abe fretted. He didn't go near Katie's building. Then a teamster from his yard gave him a note. Katie wanted him to come see her.

Before stepping across her threshold, he looked around the room. She reached out and pulled him inside.

"Timothy is gone," she said.

"Gone?"

"My brother talked to him again about his hitting me. Timothy was so mad he packed his duffle and left."

"Did you tell your brother about us?"

"Oh, no," she said, leading him to the bedroom.

****

As time passed, Timothy became a distant memory. Katie rarely talked about him. Only on Sundays, when she went to church, was she overcome with guilt from her adulterous affair. Yet she never confessed to her brother. She told Abe, "He would make me stop, and I don't want to."

Almost a year to the day after he vanished, Timothy stumbled into his apartment, clutching a pint bottle of whiskey he had mostly consumed. He confronted Katie about her affair. It seemed the only person that didn't know about it, or refused to hear about it, was her brother. The rest of the tenants in the building knew, or guessed, what was going on behind Katie's closed door. She didn't have a job, but she had new curtains on the windows, was often seen at the market buying more food than one person could eat, and the coal salesman visited her day and night.

In between swallowing the rest of the whiskey, Timothy chased Katie, swinging wildly. She ducked his first three swings, but the fourth—a backhand across her face—knocked her into the rickety table. The candlesticks toppled. One rolled toward the edge. Katie grabbed it.

Timothy approached her again, his movements slowed by the whiskey. He drew his hand back to strike her. She swung the heavy candlestick, connecting solidly with Timothy's head. A moment later, Abe walked in.

She jumped into Abe's arms, crying hysterically. Gently, he disengaged himself from her and walked over to Timothy. He leaned over the body and put his ear on Timothy's chest. He heard and felt nothing.

"Get me a mirror," he said.

Katie darted to her bedroom and returned with her looking glass.

Abe held it under Timothy's nose. The mirror didn't fog. He touched Timothy's neck. He couldn't find a pulse. "He's dead."

Katie's hand shot to her mouth to stifle a scream. "Oh, my God! Oh, my God!"

Abe grabbed her into his arms and held her tightly, but he couldn't quell her violent trembling.

"I will never be forgiven for this," she sobbed.

"Katie, darling, God works in mysterious ways. He has freed you from your yoke."

"No! God would not do this. I'll be executed. I'll go to hell. That is His punishment for my sins. Shame for me and my family."

Abe shook her. "Don't be a fool. Pull yourself together. If you keep quiet, no one will ever know what happened here."

She stared at him, trying to understand what he said.

He released her and walked over to the body. Taking a deep breath, he knelt down, pulled Timothy into a sitting position, and dug his shoulder into the corpse's gut. Clasping his hands in back of Timothy's legs, Abe rolled back on his feet and stood up.

"Open the door and check the hallway," he commanded.

Katie obeyed. "There is no one."

Pointing to the empty liquor bottle, he said, "Bring it."

Katie's apartment was on the third floor of a five-story walk-up. The stairwell was steep and dark, sometimes difficult for a sober man to negotiate. Abe quickly moved through the door to the head of the stairs. He bent down and rested Timothy's feet on the landing. With a shrug, Abe dumped him, grabbed the bottle from Katie's hand and threw it after the tumbling body. Not waiting to see where Timothy came to rest, he shoved Katie back inside.

"As far as anybody should be concerned," Abe said, "Timothy fell down the stairs. Everyone knows he's a drunk."

****

Katie maintained their contrived explanation through the wake and the funeral, but once Timothy was in the ground, she ran to her brother and confessed everything. Father Kelly sought out Abe, confronting him in the room Abe rented in Mrs. O'Conner's boarding house.

Abe acted as if he had no idea why the priest was paying him a visit. "Can I get you something to eat or drink?"

"No thank you. I came here to talk. Katie told me about your affair, about what you did with Timothy's body. I suppose I must thank you for protecting her, but I also must chastise you for seducing her."

"I didn't seduce her. I comforted her. Her husband beat her like a mongrel dog. She needed tenderness, and I gave it to her."

"You took advantage of her in a weak moment."

Abe glared at the Priest. *For the past year, this man's sister bounced around as happily as a butterfly, and he accuses me, not her husband, of ruining her.* His face flushed with rage, he blurted out, "How can a man who has never known love ever hope to understand it?"

"My love for God is deeper than any love you can experience."

"Well, I love your sister and I want to marry her."

"Impossible! You are a Jew. You both will be outcasts. We won't accept you, and your people won't accept Katie. I will not allow it."

Abe's face flushed red. "We'll run off together."

Unlike Abe, Father Kelly showed no anger, just steadfast determination. "I thought you might say something like that, so let me make myself perfectly clear. If you ever see my sister again, I will go to the police and accuse you of killing her husband in a jealous rage. There is no doubt you will be hung."

Abe's mouth flopped open. He stammered, "And . . . and then you will repent your lie?"

"Yes," Father Kelly said calmly. "Leave Ireland. It will be the best for all concerned."

****

Where could he go? He learned from his mother's letters that David, his youngest brother, was to be Bar Mitzvahed in a month. He wished he could be there, but to go back to Latvia was taking too big a chance. The tsar's conscription agents might catch him. *Damn the Tsar. He destroyed my family.*

He and his brothers had been very close. Sure they fought. How could they not get on each other's' nerves once in a while, living together in one bedroom? But they always made up, and they always stood side by side when an outsider picked on one of them. But they couldn't protect each other now. They were scattered all over Europe.

Dan was in London. He couldn't go back there. The earl might still be looking for him. Jacob and Solomon were in France, but anti-Semitism was running rampant in France with the treason trial of Captain Dreyfus.

America? He had heard so much about that classless country where gold lay in the streets, waiting to be picked up by anybody smart enough to grab it. But America was so far away from his family. What did it matter—separated by a few hundred kilometers or a few thousand?

The more he thought about it, the more he realized America was the place for a hustler like him. After he settled there, if America was as great as the stories, he would write his brothers and plead with them to come over.

****

As he lounged against the ship's rail and watched the land shrink away, he thought, *I am barely nineteen and I've been chased out of three countries. I'm through running.*

PART 1

PATERSON, NEW JERSEY
1904

CHAPTER 1

Standing under the *chuppah* as his brother's best man, reality hit Abe squarely in the face. He was twenty-nine years old, had built himself a business that afforded him a comfortable living, and he had family in town. Yet, his life was empty. He had no wife to warm his bed. No partner to share his good fortune. No children to carry on his legacy.

As he had so may times in the past ten years, his thoughts drifted to Katie and again he cursed himself for not standing up to her brother, for not grabbing Katie out of his despotic grasp and taking her to America with him. He had cavorted with many women since Katie, but none left him breathless the way she had. None left him yearning to be with them forever.

When the bride began her walk around his brother seven times to affirm this was the man she wanted to marry, Abe's eyes wandered across the gathering. He wondered if there was anyone here for him. Although most of the wedding guests were his people, he had lived away from the community for five years and recognized few of the women. Those he did know were married, or if single, did not ignite a spark in him. Then his gaze fell upon a tall young lady with silky auburn hair pulled up into a tight bun. The Rabbi's words turned into a distant drone as he focused all his attention on her.

The second the ceremony ended, signaled by his brother smashing the glass—its loud shattering meant to chase evil spirits away from the marriage—Abe wanted to rush over and meet this beautiful woman, but being a traditional old-world wedding, men and women were separated. He despised that tradition. The first time he felt its full effect was at his Bar Mitzvah, where his mother had to sit in the gallery. He wanted her in the front row of pews where he could beam his accomplishments to her. And today, because ancient sages had interpreted some verses in the Torah to mean women were to be set apart from men during both festivals and periods of mourning to avoid frivolity, Abe was not allowed to meet this magnificent girl, with a waist so narrow she would make an hourglass jealous. He muttered under his breath, "Outdated traditions should be left in the old country."

Elbowing his way through the throng of well-wishers who had rushed to surround the groom, Abe pulled his brother aside. That Abe and Solomon were related would never be discerned by anyone who did not know them. Abe towered a full head over his brother. Where Abe's pin-striped navy suit streamlined his lean body in neat lines as only a custom made suit could, Solomon's broad shoulders and powerful torso developed from years of working in the mills, made his off-the-rack black suit hike up in the back and strain against the buttons that fastened it across his chest.

"Solomon, who is that girl in the yellow dress? The one taller than the others." Abe asked.

Following his brother's stare, Solomon said, "That's Sarah Singer."

"Sarah Singer? From Libau?"

"Yes."

Deepening his gaze, Abe said, "She was three when I left home."

"Quite a few people from back home have come to live in the neighborhood," Solomon said. His voice changed to disdain as he added, "Lured by the lies the mill owner's agents spread across Europe about great paying jobs in the silk factories in Paterson."

You never quit, not even on your wedding day, Abe thought and quickly dismissed his brother's rantings. This was not the time or place for another argument about how the silk mill owners treated their workers.

"The Singers have been here six months," Solomon said. "If you came to Shul once in a while you would have known."

A pang of guilt swept Abe as he thought about his ten years in Paterson, New Jersey. Paterson was a city of immigrants—Italian, English, German, Polish, Eastern European Jews. With few deviations, like a Sunday walk over the Chasm Bridge to marvel at the Passaic River's great waterfall or a shopping trip to the new department stores on Market Street, and of course to labor in the mills, Paterson's immigrants lived their lives within the boundaries of their own distinct neighborhoods. Everything they needed was there: groceries selling their ethnic food, bars where the men could socialize in the language of the old country, and their churches and synagogues.

Abe was a rare exception to this segregated society. Not that he had planned it that way. He didn't even know the city of Paterson existed until he met Ben Goldberg on the boat from Ireland. Goldberg owned a liquor wholesale business in Paterson, and had been in Ireland negotiating a purchase contract. He offered Abe a job as a salesman. Not having any prospects at his original destination, New York City, Abe decided to give it a try.

For five years Abe lived among his own people. Then one of his Italian customers offered to sell Abe the bar and the building that housed it. Abe had been saving his money, looking for a good opportunity. Still, he only had four hundred dollars. He was elated when the owner said, "I have to get to Chicago right away. My brother is sick and he needs me to help him in his meat packing business. If you can convince the bank to let you take over the mortgage, I'll take the four hundred and you can send me the rest monthly."

Above the bar was a comfortable three-room apartment. Having lived for five years in one room in a boarding house, that apartment seemed like a mill owner's mansion. So excited at the opportunity to have his own business, Abe didn't thoroughly think through the consequences of owning a bar and living in the Italian neighborhood. Friday night and Saturday, his Sabbath, were the busiest times. Abe felt compelled to stay behind his bar rather than go to Shul.

Although his brother often frequented the bar with his Italian friends from the dye house, Abe rarely had time to sit for long. When they did talk, they chatted about a letter one of them had received from their mother or a brother or sister. Since it was the Shul where new immigrants were made to feel welcome, where news and gossip were disseminated, and since Abe had stopped going, he eventually lost touch with his own kind.

Ignoring his brother's rebuke, Abe asked, "Where is Morris?"

Solomon pointed with his chin. "There, with the Rebbe and the Cantor."

Morris Singer, his teacher until he turned thirteen, had become a distant memory, but Morris' lessons never left Abe's mind. Along with his Bar Mitzvah prayers, Morris had taught Abe English. So many immigrants didn't know the language, but because Abe did, making his way first in London, Ireland and now in America was a lot easier.

"Take me over to him," Abe said.

Having stood up as his brother's best man, Abe had already re-acquainted himself with the Rabbi and the Cantor. He nodded to them and turned his attention to Morris Singer. The past sixteen years had not been kind to his former teacher. His once dark beard was peppered with gray. His scalp, surrounding his yarmulke, was bald, with only a small ring of hair above his ears, and his stance Abe had thought of as proud and often foreboding was now stooped, as if the worries of the world had pounded down on him.

Making the introductions, Solomon said, "You remember my brother Abe?"

"I thought I was seeing things when I saw you standing next to Solomon," Morris said. "You are the image of your Uncle Isaac."

Abe smiled and thought, *not the image of my father*? Of course not! That would be an insult, not knowing me as an adult and comparing me to the town drunk.

Everyone admired his Uncle Isaac, the wealthiest member of their community back in Libau. He gave large donations to their Shul and the unfortunate. When Isaac walked through town, people addressed him with respect. Abe's greatest desire was to emulate his Uncle. Morris couldn't have offered a higher compliment.

Morris's eyes scanned Abe's fashionable pin striped suit and gold fob, draped across Abe's vest, and said, "I am happy to see you have done well for yourself here in America. What is it you do?"

Abe's smile dropped, dragging his handlebar mustache down with it. Afraid if he said he owned a saloon, Morris would change his opinion, thinking he had become his father, Abe said, "I own a restaurant."

"How wonderful! Where is it? Mrs. Singer and I would love to come and try it."

Solomon coughed and said, "I must get a drink. Can I get anyone something?"

They all declined.

"I'll catch up to you later," Abe said. Retuning his attention to Morris, he changed the subject. "I can't believe how Sarah has grown up."

"She takes after her mother."

"Mr. Singer, I would love to come by and visit you."

"That would be nice, Abraham."

"Would Wednesday evening be convenient?"

Morris bobbed his head while he contemplated Abe's request. "I think that would be good. Around seven?"

Abe grasped his former teacher's hand and shook it vigorously. "Seven o'clock Wednesday. I'll be there."

For the balance of the wedding reception, in between consuming the *schnapps* he had given Solomon as part of his wedding gift, feasting on brisket of beef, potato knishes, *kreplach,* and *schnecken*—food he hadn't eaten in a long time—and talks with his other brother David, who had come to America only last month, Abe stared across the room at Sarah and thought about a future with her and the beautiful children they could have together.

CHAPTER 2

Sarah pushed aside the muslin curtain on her bedroom window and stared at the sidewalk. She was glad her father had invited him after dinner, rather than in the daytime. The shops had closed. The streets were empty of commercial traffic. Most people had settled into their evening rituals of reading, sewing, playing a game of cards or checkers in their parlors, or sitting and gossiping on the building's stoops enjoying this splendid May evening. Even in the flickering light of the gas street lamps she would have no trouble spotting him coming down the sidewalk.

She first noticed him across the room at her best friend's wedding. When their eyes met and he smiled, her heart fluttered and she almost swooned. He was so handsome, so distinguished with his sweeping handlebar mustache. He carried himself straight and tall, sure of himself, not like the other men in the congregation who cowered when they walked, as if they were trying to draw themselves into a cocoon they thought would protect them from the outside world.

She ached to meet him right then and there, but women weren't allowed to mix with men at weddings. That Biblical edict did not stop her from discretely inquiring as to who he was. When she learned he was the groom's brother, she was overjoyed. Her father had to know him. He had taught all the Bresslers. On their walk home from the wedding she asked her father about him.

Before her father could answer, her mother cut in and said, "He's no one you are to concern yourself with, Sarah."

"Why? What's wrong with him?"

"Nothing," her father said. "He was one of my best students." Looking quizzically at his wife, he said, "I invited him to our house Wednesday evening."

Delight engulfed Sarah. But her brief moment of ecstasy crashed into desolation when her mother shrieked, "You didn't!"

Her father cowered at the rebuke, and offered his daughter no help when her mother told her, "You will be confined to your room."

"Why?" Sarah cried.

"Because I said so. That is all you have to know."

Despite her mother's forbidding, Sarah readied herself anyway in hopes her mother would have a last minute change of heart. She put her hair up, and dressed in the white linen shirt-waist with flowing sleeves and ruffled cuffs trimmed in pink satin ribbon.

"Sarah, come away from the window."

Startled by her mother's voice, Sarah withdrew her hand from the curtain as if she had grabbed the hot handle of a skillet. "Why won't you let me meet him?" she asked.

Her mother crossed to the bed, sat down and patted a place next to her. "Come, sit by me."

Sarah obeyed and fidgeted with a strand of hair that had escaped from her bun.

Taking her daughter's hand, her mother said, "He's not right for you, my darling. He's too old."

"But he's only ten years older than I. Father is twelve years older than you."

"That's true, but your father is a learned man—a scholar, a teacher. He is counting on you to carry on for him."

"And I will."

"Not if you were to become attached to Mr. Bressler."

"Why? Mr. Bressler is an educated man. He knows the value of learning."

"Does he?"

"Father said he taught him."

"But it does not mean he learned anything."

Confused, Sarah stared at her mother.

"You know all the places you read about and are aching to see—the Eiffel Tower, Rome, the Great Wall of China? You will never see them if you marry Mr. Bressler."

"How do you know that? My friend, Cecelia, Mr. Bressler's sister-in-law, told me Mr. Bressler makes a wonderful living from his business."

"Yes, a saloon."

"He's not a *shiker*?"

"His father is."

"But he's not a drunkard?"

"Not that I know."

Sarah sighed with relief. "Then why won't you let me meet him?"

"Sarah, please. You knew the Bressler family back in Latvia. The father is a carouser. The uncle is an *azes ponim*—an arrogant man. You are aware the uncle tried to get your father fired for teaching the writings of Karl Marx?"

Sarah didn't answer, thinking, yes the father did neglect his family, and the uncle lorded his riches over everyone. But that did not mean Abe was like them. Her best friend, Cecelia—Abe's new sister-in-law—said her husband was a wonderful man.

"You do know what a sow is?" Sarah's mother asked.

"Of course. *Trayf*. Not kosher."

"There is a saying I picked up in this city of silk which fits Mr. Bressler very well. 'You cannot make a silk purse from a sow's ear.' Let him go. He will stifle you."

CHAPTER 3

Declaring himself as ready as he'd ever be, Abe donned his fedora, flicked a minute piece of lint off his blue serge suit, and trotted down the stairs from his apartment over his saloon. Every stool at the mahogany bar and most seats at the round tables were taken. A waitress hustled past him, carrying a loaded tray. Steam drifted off the piping hot food. Aromas of garlic, clam sauce and fresh baked bread mixed with the ever present odors of beer and cigar smoke.

He scanned the crowd. As usually happened after a draft or two, the gloom his customers carried in on their faces from having spent ten hours standing on the floors of the silk mills had begun to lift. The player piano clattered out an upbeat tune. The click of ricocheting pool balls mingled with the din. He caught a glint of a dart flying silently through the air. The roar that followed told him its path to the corkboard had been true.

"Hey, look at Abe," one of the men at the bar called out.

"Hiya, Pietro," Abe replied.

"Where you off to, Abe?" another asked.

"Must be a lady friend," a third said.

Abe smiled. "Victorio, Carmine, is Carlo taking care of you okay?"

The two men hoisted their mugs in a salute to the bartender and Carmine said to Abe, "Give her a pat on the *culo* for us," drawing raucous laughter from the men who heard.

"She's not that kind of girl," Abe scowled.

Because Abe hired buxom bar maids and outfitted them in cleavage-exposing dresses—a tribute to Lady Wexford—his customers naturally assumed that was the type of girl that attracted him. But Abe did not fraternize with his help. The uniforms he asked his girls to wear were based strictly on a business decision. At first the girls objected, but when they saw the added tips they drew by deeply bowing to place the food and drinks on the tables, their objections vanished.

Victorio and Carmine looked at each other with raised eyebrows. "Amore?" Carmine asked.

"Si," Victorio replied.

Abe grinned. He turned to his harried chief bartender and said, "Carlo, you'll have to lock up tonight."

"I'll take good care."

"I'm in your debt." Under any other circumstances Abe would never leave when his saloon was this crowded. But for the first time since he bought the joint, he had something more important to do than make money.

Glancing at his reflection in the mirror behind the bar, Abe whisked his fingers over each side of his handlebar mustache one final time to make certain he left no built up wax. Tilting his fedora another fraction of an inch to the left, he headed out the door. He walked with long strides north on Van Houten, turned left on Curtis and passed the massive red brick buildings of the Phoenix, Harmony, and Industry Silk Mills. Paterson's dominant industry, employing twenty-four thousand laborers was dyeing, processing and weaving silk.

A Toledo steam carriage chugged by. Its steel rimmed wheels clanged on the cobblestones. White smoke hiccupped from its stack. Abe didn't slow his gait to stare at it like he usually did. He was thinking about his future with Sarah Singer.

Heading north on River Street, Abe entered the section of the city where the Eastern European Jewish immigrants congregated. It was as if he had crossed the border into another country. The language of the street had changed from Italian to Yiddish, and the men's clothes from short jackets, white collarless shirts and floppy cloth caps to long black coats and wide-brimmed black hats. The women, though, seemed to look and dress the same no matter what part of town he visited. Their shabby mercerized cotton *schmates*, sewn from fabric costing no more than eight cents a yard, hung limply on their bodies. Their hands were rough and wrinkled from the constant washing and scrubbing that took the life out of their clothes, and out of them.

Abe turned right onto Fulton, the street where the Singers lived. It was no different from the two dozen streets he traversed to get there. Not a tree sprouted anywhere. Mostly three-story frame buildings, without a crack of light between them, lined the narrow sidewalk. Here and there a couple of the wooden buildings had been replaced by a much larger five-story brick apartment house. Abe visualized the city quickly taking on the look of London and Dublin, where tenement houses cast the streets in shadows that disappeared only for a moment at noon.

The men and women, enjoying the evening air and sitting on their stoops stopped talking when Abe approached. With wary glares they studied him, trying to decide if he was a threat to them. Although he came from the same part of the world they did, he had become a stranger in their neighborhood. A stranger dressed like a landlord and walking with purpose. Eviction, maybe? Abe doubted they would ever shed their ingrained suspicion of strangers.

An aroma of chicken livers frying in *schmaltz* and onions floated across the sidewalk. Abe's mouth watered. Visions of his mother popped into his mind. Her chopped liver was the best he had ever eaten. He had written his mother often, pleading with her to come to America now that all his brothers had left Latvia and his sisters had married and moved away. Her answer was always the same—the trip was too scary. And his father was no help. No one could ever depend on him for anything. He drank at night and slept off his binge in the daytime while Abe and his brothers and sisters tended the farm. Abe's fondest memory of his father was of the man's back as his father walked down the road to a tavern in town. Abe knew the only way to get his mother to America was for him or one of his brothers to go get her.

Solomon couldn't go. He couldn't leave his new wife. And his brother David, only newly arrived in America, refused to set foot in Latvia again. He was afraid the Tsar's conscription agents would grab him. Besides, neither of them had the money for the passage. That left it up to him.

He had to get his mother. Her life would be so much easier over here. He made enough money to put her up in a nice apartment, and he certainly could keep his drunken father in liquor. But who would run his saloon while he was gone? His brothers? Lately he been thinking about the three of them in a partnership. They could open up a couple more bars, maybe even start a liquor distributor business. *I'll bet they'd jump at the opportunity to be their own bosses, he thought. Especially Solomon, now that he was married. He'd make a lot more money than working in that dye house.*

With the thoughts of Sarah as his wife, and him and his brothers in business together, Abe joyfully entered the Singer's apartment building and knocked on his future in-laws' door. When Sarah's father opened the door, Abe's gleeful expression vanished. Mr. Singer was never one to smile much, but the dour expression with which he greeted Abe made Abe feel like he had come to a funeral.

"Come in, Abraham," Mr. Singer said

Abe's knees almost buckled when he saw the living room. The décor was exactly as he remembered it in the Singer's small house back in Libau sixteen years ago. Two wing chairs, separated by the little round table, commanded the prime location in the room in front of the lace-curtained window. On the table, a short brass lamp squatted on a white doily. To the right of the lamp, a book, with the tattered black ribbon sticking out, was stationed so precisely that, when Mr. Singer sat in his chair he only had to rotate his hand a few inches to reach it.

"Sit, Abraham."

Abe hesitated, staring at the student's chair—the one to the left. A shudder swept over him as he vividly recalled that first day when he had come to Mr. Singer for instruction.

"Sit," Morris repeated. "It didn't bite you then, it won't now."

It didn't, but you did. When he had slouched into the student's chair, Mr. Singer had barked, "Up, up, up. Sloppy posture makes for lazy students."

Abe didn't slouch this time, but he didn't sit as he had after that scolding—on the edge of the chair, his knees together and his feet flat on the floor. This evening he sat fully into the chair, leaning comfortably against the back, and crossed his right leg over his left knee.

A moment later Mrs. Singer carried a tea service into the room. As she walked across the floor to serve Abe and her husband her shirt-waist dress, buttoned around her neck and curving over the swell of her breasts and the roundness of her hips, rustled. Her hostess job finished, she perched herself on the edge of the couch across from them, her teacup and saucer steadied on her knees.

Unlike her husband, her face hadn't seemed to change from what Abe remembered. Her beauty hadn't made an impression on him when he was thirteen, but it did today. It wasn't difficult to see where Sarah got her looks. But there would be no close up comparisons tonight. Sarah was not present.

"So, Abraham," Morris said in his Russian accented English, "yesterday I spoke to your brother, Solomon. He says your restaurant is also a bar and is quite the place for the Italians. You have done well for yourself."

"I can't complain, Morris."

Mrs. Singer had taken a sip of tea. She returned the cup to its saucer with an audible clink. Abe instantly realized what he had done to upset her. He was so used to greeting his customers, old and young, by their given names, he blurted out his teacher's first name. Was that really so bad? He was a prosperous businessman, like his Uncle Isaac. Of course he would be respectful to his elders, but he didn't have to defer to anyone. Why shouldn't he call a person he now considered an equal by his first name?

"And you stopped wearing your yarmulke, cut off your side-locks and grew that, that mustache to become more Americanized?"

Abe's mouth opened but he couldn't formulate words. He was accustomed to being complimented on his mustache. Many merchants sported handlebars as a symbol of their prosperity. The day after Abe bought his bar he started growing his. It was now spread as wide as the most prosperous merchants in town, and like his wavy hair, was pure white, the result of the family trait having fully matured. When he walked through town, other distinguished men of business, men who ran the city, nodded to him the way he remembered men of status nodding to his Uncle Isaac.

Thinking maybe the wax had stopped working and his mustache drooped, he gently ran his fingers over it from his nose to its tips. Finding everything in order, he suddenly realized the problem. Morris had only been in Paterson a short time and didn't know the protocol.

"And I guess you also abandoned the other things I taught you?" Morris added.

Recovering his composure, Abe said, "No, I haven't, Mr. Singer. I still remember my Torah and Talmud."

"*Fonfer*," Mrs. Singer said, barely above a whisper.

Abe glanced at her, deeply hurt. *I am not a double talker.* In Ireland, and here in America before he bought his bar, he was a salesman, and a good one. He always told his customers straight out the terms of the deal. He never conned them into buying. That way he didn't have to re-sell the product and had a satisfied customer who gave him good recommendations.

"But do you live by the Torah's teachings, Abraham? When was the last time you were in Shul on the Sabbath?"

Abe couldn't answer. His thoughts had returned to his brother. *What else had Solomon told the Singers? It's obvious he didn't build me up. I can't believe, after I sacrificed so much for him when he first came to Paterson, he would do something like this to me.*

Fighting to keep his seething anger hidden, Abe asked, "Is Sarah going to join us?"

"She is not feeling well," Esther said.

Grief stricken, he questioned, "Nothing serious, I hope?"

"No, just a headache."

He let out a sigh of relief and said, "I would love to come back to see her when she is better."

"Suppose you send us a note so we can arrange a suitable time."

"Thank you, Mrs. Singer. I will."

They fell into a strained silence, the Singers glaring at him as if he were the Tsar himself. *Sure, I have made a couple of mistakes tonight, he thought, but nothing so serious as to draw their venomous leers.* It had to be something his ungrateful brother had said to them. Since he didn't know what it was, he doubted anything he might say would placate Sarah's parents.

Tomorrow he'd confront Solomon and find out exactly what it was his brother had told the Singers. Then he could plan a new strategy to court Sarah. It made no sense to brood now. Especially since there was money to be made tonight.

Rising, he said, "Thank you for the tea. I really must be going."

"So soon?" Sarah asked as she swept into the room.

"Sarah!" her mother scolded.

"Mother, why didn't you tell me Mr. Bressler had arrived?"

"He was just leaving."

"I'm really not in a hurry," Abe said, a broad grin lifting his lips and springing his mustache upward.

"Then you will have more tea?" Sarah asked.

"Yes, thank you."

Sarah's mother seethed behind her stoic face.

Sarah said, "Please have a seat and I will get it for you."

When Sarah handed him his refilled cup, their fingers touched. Her lower lip quivered ever so slightly. She dropped her eyes and hurried back to the couch to sit by her mother.

Abe held his teacup in his lap. Sarah's fragrance lingered around him. He wanted to continue to savor it until it evaporated.

"I understand you own a pub," Sarah said.

"Yes, I do," Abe answered gleefully.

"It must be a very exciting business."

"It has its moments."

"Is it true the wives of some pub owners work behind the bars with their husbands?"

"It's true. Mostly in the Irish pubs."

Jumping up, Mrs. Singer grabbed Sarah's wrist and dragged her out of the room.

Mr. Singer stood up and said, "I think you should go."

Miffed and confused, Abe asked, "Why? What's going on?"

"It's getting late."

On his way down the stoop, his shoulders involuntarily jerked at the loud bang the door made when it slammed behind him.

CHAPTER 4

When Solomon came into the bar the next evening Abe pulled him away from his buddies and demanded, "What did you say to the Singers about me? Why did you tell them I owned a bar?"

Jerking his arm out of Abe's grasp, Solomon shot back, "Why didn't you?"

"I do own a restaurant. I serve a lot of food."

"But it's also a bar. They asked me about it. I told them. What was I supposed to say?"

"You could have told them I would make a perfect husband and son-in-law."

"I did tell them you were a hero during the fire."

"And?" Abe asked.

"And, nothing. They weren't here two years ago. It didn't mean nothing to them."

When Abe had toured the ruins of the devastating fire that had destroyed a major portion of downtown Paterson, he realized that what he had done had been the most foolish thing in his life. It also turned out to be the luckiest. Before the fire, Abe's was just another bar. After it, his saloon became the "in spot" for Paterson's laborers. They flowed in from every neighborhood to see photographs of the mayor, alderman, and ward captain, standing with the town hero lining the walls.

What should have been a manageable little outbreak that started in a trolley shed turned into a raging inferno when sixty mile per hour winds fanned the flames throughout downtown Paterson. Intent on saving his business, Abe didn't flee from the on-rushing fire like the other merchants. He remained in his bar offering it as a rest area. He handed out free food, liquor and encouragement to the firemen. The wind shifted just as the order came to evacuate. His saloon was spared. Not so lucky were four hundred and fifty-nine other buildings in a twenty-six-block area.

"What's wrong with me, Sol?" Abe asked. "What did I do? Why don't they like me?"

Before Solomon could answer him, the front door burst open, smacking back against the wall with a glass-rattling thud. A laborer rushed in—obviously a dye house worker from the looks of his clothes, spattered with colors. Spotting Solomon, he ran over.

"Segnor Bressler, hide me," the frightened man begged.

"Georgio, what's wrong?"

Georgio glanced back at the door, a desperate look on his face. "Please, Segnor, hide me, quickly."

Without consulting Abe, Solomon jumped up, grabbed Georgio's arm and rushed him toward the store-room.

"Solomon, wait," Abe said.

Solomon ignored Abe. He opened the stock room door, shoved Georgio in and slammed it shut.

"What the hell is going on?" Abe demanded.

"I don't know, but Georgio's scared to death."

The front door flew open again. A police captain, flanked by two patrolmen, stormed in. A pool player had just stroked the cue ball. The room hushed in less time than it took for the white ball to reach its numbered target. The click the balls made when they collided resounded throughout the bar.

The stocky captain planted himself in the middle of the floor and repeatedly smacked his billy club into the palm of his hand. "Where is he?" he demanded.

Abe approached the captain and asked, "Who?"

"You know who. The man who ran in here a few minutes ago."

Abe locked his cool blue eyes on the captain's. "No one ran in here."

"I was told differently."

"You were told wrong."

The captain broke eye contact. He scanned the bar room. "What's behind those doors?" he demanded.

"The stock room and my apartment," Abe answered.

"Open them."

Glancing at Solomon, Abe narrowed his eyes and jammed his lips together.

Solomon looked away.

Returning his attention to the captain, Abe asked, "You have a warrant?"

"I don't need one. This is a public establishment."

"Then look all you want in the public areas."

The captain took a step forward. His face inches from Abe's, he whispered, "You think you got friends in high places 'cause you're some kind of hero. You buck me on this and you'll see how few friends you got."

"Are you through?"

"No, but you will be when this gets out," the captain said, then pulled back and headed for the line of men at the bar. Many had turned back to their beers to avoid drawing attention to themselves.

Putting his large hand on a customer's shoulder, the captain spun him around and asked, "Where is he?"

"Who?"

"The wop who ran in here."

The laborer glanced at Solomon.

Solomon shook his head sideways.

The captain stormed over to Solomon and demanded, "Where is he?"

Solomon shrugged.

"You're the bar-keep's brother, ain't you?"

"What of it?"

"You're coming with me."

"Why?"

"Because I said so," the captain said, and pulled his hand cuffs off his belt.

Solomon braced himself. He balled his fists. His biceps bulged under his shirt. "Fuck you!"

The captain drew back his club. His two officers moved to back him up. Solomon raised his arms to defend himself.

Abe leaped between them and clamped his hand over the captain's to stop him from striking Solomon. The captain's muddy, hazel eyes narrowed and his lips turned into a scowl.

Abe said. "I told you, no one ran in here."

The captain jerked out of Abe's grasp, took a step back, colliding with his men. For a moment, the three of them were huddled together. Encouraged by Abe and Solomon, the bar patrons shuffled forward, encircling the police.

Badly outnumbered, the policemen backed toward the door. "That man was inciting a riot," the captain said.

Abe asked, "You see a riot going on in here?"

"I won't forget this, Bressler."

"You have me at a disadvantage, Captain. You know my name, but I don't know yours."

"Bimson. John Bimson. Remember that name, because I'll not forget what you did here today. It won't be long before we put you trouble-making kikes and wops where you belong."

"Where is that, Captain?"

"In jail or in the grave."

"I'll keep that in mind. Good day."

CHAPTER 5

Solomon ran to the door to check the street. Assured the police were gone, he let Georgio out of the store room.

"What happened?" Solomon asked.

"We standing around outside the shop. The police come swinging clubs. We run."

Abe whispered in Solomon's ear. "We have to talk."

"Later."

"Now, upstairs."

****

Inside his apartment, Abe pounced. "We had a deal."

"And I'm honoring it."

"Then what was that all about?"

"I don't know."

"The hell you don't! You're supposed to keep clear of the trouble makers."

"Where was I when Georgio ran in?"

Abe calmed down. "A word of caution. The mill owners are still talking about that strike you led two years ago."

"You see what they do? You gripe about your boss and they send the coppers after you."

"I don't blame them after what you guys did—beating up workers who wouldn't join your union, breaking into mills, destroying looms and silk. You turned the whole town against you. There was even talk about your union having started the fire."

"We didn't start that fire."

"You know for sure it wasn't one of your union people?"

"No."

"Be careful, brother. You stir something up again and there won't be enough bribe money to get you out of jail or to get you your job back."

"A new world is coming. The bosses will be gone. Money ain't gonna mean a thing."

"You're crazy," Abe said, exhaling sharply out of his increasing frustration with his brother.

Abe thought it was his pleas that had brought Solomon to America from Lyon, France, the silk capital of Europe. In reality, Solomon had been run out of France for fomenting labor unrest. Had his new Paterson boss known Solomon was a radical, his never would have been hired, regardless of his vast dye shop experience.

Having been forced to move to a new country did not mellow Solomon's philosophies about capitalist bosses. In the two years Solomon had been in Paterson, he had been jailed and blacklisted for inciting labor unrest, and he still couldn't get it through his thick head that the mill owners ran this town. It had been that way for over a hundred years, ever since Alexander Hamilton and his cronies formed the corporation called "The Society for Establishing Useful Manufacturers" to build and rule Paterson, and was now controlled by the city's mill owners.

Not that there was anything wrong with having good connections. Before his brother complicated his life, Abe, with a little help from a fire, had made some powerful friends of his own. He had played cards once a week with a judge, an alderman, a member of the Society's board, and a couple of mill owners. However, once the strike started with his brother in the lead, his political friends gave Abe a wide berth. They suggested he take leave from the game.

Despite his being shunned, Abe's payoffs that allowed him to keep his bar going without trouble continued. A whisper to the precinct chief, along with an extra hundred, and Solomon was released from Jail. Five hundred more to the ward captain and Solomon's name was erased from the blacklist. Despite the relative calm for the past couple of years, it still took Abe a year to be welcomed back into his card game.

"The bosses and their lackeys are not giving up their money-making machine to you or anyone like you without a fierce fight," Abe said. "If I were you, brother, I'd re-think my future."

Solomon didn't rile back in rebuttal as he usually did when Abe warned him about starting trouble again. Instead, he meandered around the living room, touching the furniture and examining the Edison phonograph. He stopped at the sideboard and stared at a piece of paper sticking out from under Mark Twain's *Double Barreled Detective.*

"It's a letter from Mom," Abe said. "Go ahead, read it."

Solomon scanned it and said, "She seems in good spirits."

"I've pleaded with her to come to America," Abe said.

"Me too, but she don't want to. Says that's where she was born and that's where she'll die."

A glint of remembering something crossed Solomon's face. He put the letter down, reached into the back pocket of his pants and pulled out a sealed envelope. Thrusting it out towards Abe, he said, "With all the commotion downstairs I forgot to give you this. Cecelia gave it to me to bring to you. It's from Sarah."

Abe gaped at his brother for barely a second and grabbed the envelope. Ripping it open, he read, "I'm sorry about last night. I will be in the shoe department of Meyer Brother's Department store Monday at one o'clock. I hope I will see you there. Yours truly, Sarah Singer."

CHAPTER 6

All day Saturday Abe drifted around his bar in a stupor, barely saying "hello" to his customers nor hearing a word they may have said in reply. His mind dwelled on Sarah. What would he say to her? After their short meeting, how did she feel about him? She must like him or she wouldn't have sent that note.

With the bar closed on Sunday, he thought the day would never pass. To keep busy, he cleaned his apartment, took stock of his liquor and food inventory, shot a solitary game of pool and tossed darts at the dart-board.

Finally Monday came. At twelve forty-five, nearly delirious from anxiety, Abe paced in front of the shoe department of Meyer Brothers. He was well acquainted with the department store, having furnished his apartment and himself from their vast array of merchandise. He shopped Meyer Brothers because he felt it was more progressive than Quackenbush's, which only had two elevators to Meyer Brothers' four. He was also fascinated by Meyer Brothers' pneumatic tube system. The clerks put money in a metal cylinder, stuck it in a tube, and whoosh, it was sucked through the pipes. A few minutes later the cylinder, carrying the change and receipt, dropped out of a second tube into a holding basket.

With the smell of rich leather punctuating the air, Abe's eyes darted in every direction searching for Sarah. Had she changed her mind? Had her parents intercepted her? At one o'clock, his anxiety turned to glee. As promised, Sarah accompanied by Cecelia arrived right on time.

****

Sarah wore a stunning afternoon dress of Copenhagen blue charmeuse. Trimmed in moiré, it had a semi-tailored waist and a smart batiste collar. In need of a new spring outfit for special occasions, Sarah had sewn it herself two weeks ago. The stores sold dresses like it for thirty dollars. She had made it for ten. It had taken her six months to save that money from her assistant teaching job.

When she stood in front of her mirror today, examining her craftsmanship, she had almost broken out in tears as she stared at her bland straw bonnet. She had longed to buy a new spring French Sailor with a wide brim and loads of silk flowers, but she couldn't afford that type of millenary. Even if she could afford the hat, her parents would have chastised her for her frivolity. Grabbing her sewing basket from her boudoir, she had retrieved the strips of fabric left over from making the dress and trimmed her straw hat.

Her original design called also for gloves, but when she her saw her old scuffed shoes, she had opted to buy oxfords instead. In keeping with her practical upbringing, she rationalized, it was spring, not fall or winter. She wore gloves to keep her hands warm, not to make a silly fashion statement.

After she had re-pinned her decorated straw bonnet to her head and surveyed herself one last time, she wished she had bought the hat instead of the shoes. Only the tips of her new oxfords protruded from the hem of her dress, but her hat still looked out of place. Able to do nothing about it now, she slipped out her bedroom door, hoping to escape the house without her mother seeing her, but as she reached the front door, her mother appeared from the kitchen.

"Sarah, where are you going?" her mother had demanded.

"I told you, shopping with Cecelia."

"Dressed like that?"

"We're going to see the new spring fashions in Meyer Brothers. I want to see how my dress compares."

"Couldn't you have done so wearing the dress you had on this morning in class?"

"Of course, Mother, but then I wouldn't have my new dress with me. I want to see how well I copied the design."

"I see," her mother said with raised eyebrows. "Well, have a nice time."

****

Before she took her leave of Sarah and Abe, Cecelia said, "Sarah, no later than three. If your parents find out about this, they'll kill me."

"I'll be here," Sarah said and turned her full attention to Abe.

"You look lovely," Abe said.

"Thank you," she answered, her hands clasped behind her back. *Maybe I should have gotten the gloves*, she thought. Her white hands stuck out like elephant ears.

Abe gently tugged her elbow, disengaging her hands, and looped her arm over his. Patting her bare fingers, he said, "And your hands are beautiful."

A warm rush flashed over her. She had extra rouge in her hand-bag, but she was sure she wouldn't need it now.

"Would you like to walk outside?" he asked.

"That would be nice."

They exited on Market Street, and he guided her toward the waterfall—the traditional courting spot in Paterson. As they passed through the mill district, the *thwack thump, thwack thump* of the looms resonated clearly through the tightly shut windows.

"I don't understand why the windows are kept closed all the time, especially on a lovely spring day like today," Sarah said.

"It's the soot in the air. If it gets on the fabric it will damage the silk."

"I didn't know that."

"In my bar, it's always easy to tell which customers are weavers."

"How?"

"Dyer's clothes are spotted with color, like a painters. Weaver's clothes are spotless because the weaving mills are kept so clean."

She gave him a questioning look. "From the stories I've heard, I thought the mills were horrible places to work."

"Don't get me wrong. No one working in those mills would think they are in paradise—ten, eleven hours a day on their feet, their ears pounded by that constant banging. And the dye houses are horrible. Acids and dyes splash all over the place, and they smell like rotten eggs."

"Yes, I can smell that noxious odor when the wind blows toward our apartment building. Sometimes I can hardly breathe."

"That's the ammonia and sulfur. It can be pretty bad."

"I'm glad I don't have to work in the mills," Sarah said. "I feel so bad for the children when I see them heading off in the morning, carrying their lunch pails."

"It is a shame, but we all did it. I drove a mule, plowing fields, when I was eight."

Frowning at the mill's windows, she said, "If I could vote, I would immediately campaign to outlaw child labor. Children should be in school, not factories. Teaching and getting the right to vote are the two most important things in my life right now."

"Do you think women really know enough about politics to cast an informed vote?" Abe asked. Seeing the stunned expression on her face, he quickly back-peddled. "I mean, of course you can. You're educated. But most women aren't. And don't women have enough to worry about with their children and taking care of the home without muddling their minds about politics?"

Sarah sighed. *Why do men think we're idiots? Why do they think that scrubbing and cleaning and bearing children are the only jobs we're capable of doing? Was he like that too? He seemed so different.*

She was about to pursue the issue when he said, "I think teaching is a wonderful profession for a woman."

That was a quick change, she thought. Maybe it's for the best. Talking about women's suffrage often led to some pretty heated arguments. She didn't want that on this wonderful day. Some other time, when she knew him better. "I like teaching very much. I'm helping my father now. With a little more studying I'll be able to have my own class."

"That's nice."

A Paterson Washing Company wagon, pulled by a team of pure white horses, rumbled over the cobblestones. It was the same company that delivered to Abe's bar three days a week. Nearing within shouting range, the teamster yelled, "Hi ya, Abe."

Abe waved and yelled back, "Hi ya, Chuck."

"Those horses are beautiful," Sarah said.

"Yes, they are," Abe answered.

"I'm glad they will be obsolete soon."

"Why do you say that?"

"The smell from their droppings is horrible. And the flies they draw bring disease."

"I never thought about that," Abe said. "I guess I'm used to it."

"It's a changing world, Mr. Bressler."

"Please call me Abe."

With a smile, Sarah repeated, "It's a changing world, Abe. Until I came to America, I only read about bathtubs with running water, automobiles, moving pictures, telephones, and—my goodness—X rays that can see the bones right inside your body! It is only a matter of time before automobiles put the horse and wagon out to pasture permanently."

"I see your point," Abe said, "but it's hard to believe some of the predictions they made at the World's Fair—airships flying across the sea, wireless telephones spanning the world, watching moving pictures in your own home, and men walking on the moon. Come now, you don't believe those will happen, do you?"

"Oh, yes I do, and I hope I am around to see all of them, and the greatest prediction of all, an end to poverty and war."

****

Abe wondered, *the scientific predictions*? Probably not in his lifetime, but maybe. An end to war and poverty? Never happen. He'd been to too many places. No matter where he went, it was always the same. Man preyed on his fellow man.

He didn't dare express his thoughts to Sarah. From the little she had said, he realized she was an optimist—a true dreamer. Trying to refute her would only upset this wonderful encounter, and he certainly didn't want to do that. Maybe some other time, when they knew each other better, they could debate that issue.

They walked along the tree-lined path that overlooked the river, and onto the chasm bridge above the waterfall. Stopping halfway across, they gazed at the foaming water. The second highest waterfall in the states that bordered the Atlantic Ocean cascaded seventy-one feet in a thunderous roar onto the rocks at the base, sending up a spray, shrouding the area below them in a silvery mist.

Sarah took a deep breath. "It smells so fresh up here, and cool. You know when I think the falls are the prettiest?"

"When?"

"In the winter when the mist freezes on the rocks, making those huge white mounds and long icicles."

"That is pretty," he said.

"When do you think the river is most beautiful?"

"When the sun is coming up. The mist sparkles like jewels in the early morning sunlight."

"Oh, I must come here one morning to see that," Sarah said.

In reality, Abe had no idea what the falls looked like in the morning. He had read somewhere that someone said the falls were beautiful in the morning sun, but he'd never seen them at sunrise. His bar didn't close until midnight. It was two in the morning by the time he finished cleaning up. He rarely rose before ten.

He'd never been with a girl so innocent. Not even Katie. Katie may have been innocent before she turned to him for help, but he would never know for sure because it had long been beaten and raped out of her by her brute of a husband.

Staring at the side of Sarah's face, as she looked trance-like at the falls, he wanted to kiss her. But how would she react? Was she really as naïve as she has led him to believe? She was studying to be a school teacher. She had to read a lot. Did she read only scholarly books? Or did she also read fiction, where love and passion were expressed so openly?

And voting! What a ridiculous idea. What could women possible know about politics? He was glad she hadn't continued to talk about that. He would have had to respond further. It would have certainly ruined the day. And what about today? Being out here alone, without a chaperone, was not something a naïve girl would do. Not that he was complaining. He couldn't have been happier.

But to kiss her? Though he ached to do so, he held off. Like not continuing to talk about women voting. He didn't want to risk upsetting her. Yes, she truly was as she portrayed herself, innocent and unworldly despite her learning. What else could he conclude from someone who only saw the serenity of the river?

Abe wondered if Sarah's outlook about the river would change if she hung out in his bar and heard his customer's gripes about the long backbreaking hours, low wages, and blacklists for speaking out against their bosses. Yes, the river that powered the mills would seem serene and beautiful to you if you owned one of the factories along its banks. It's turbulent waters provided you with a sumptuous, luxurious life.

If you were one of the immigrant laborers lured to America by the promise of a better life, the roiling river was a bitter reminder that all you had done was trade the oppression of a king or nobleman for brutal work in a factory. Behind the mill's symmetrical rows of shuttered windows you sweat in the summer and froze in the winter for meager wages that barely put food on your table, and you prayed at night that when you returned to work in the morning your boss hadn't decided he was paying you too much and replaced you with someone who would work for less.

"Abe?" Sarah asked.

"Huh?"

"You were in some far-off place like India or China, weren't you?"

"Yes. Absolutely."

"I can't wait to travel to those places—and Rome and Paris and London."

"We'll see the world together," he said, and pulled on his fob to extract his watch from his vest pocket. "We better get back."

"Can we go by your bar?"

"It's a little out of the way. We don't want to be late for Cecelia."

"Please, Abe," she said, her lips in a pout, and her round, brown eyes laughing at the same time.

CHAPTER 7

Abe quickened his pace to conserve time. Sarah, her long legs only slightly shorter than his, had no trouble keeping up. In five minutes he stopped outside the glass paneled double doors with the word "Abe's" etched in an arc on each one.

"I want to go in," Sarah said.

"I don't think that would be a good idea."

"Why not?"

"It's not right."

"Don't you have bar maids?"

"Yes."

"Why is it okay for them to work there and not right for me to go in?"

Abe nervously looked up and down the street. Seeing no one he knew, he said, "Just for a minute."

He opened the door and Sarah stepped inside. She wrinkled her nose at the heavy odor of beer and cigar smoke that hung in the air despite the lack of patrons. It was still an hour and a half before the evening rush. His waitresses lounged against the bar, chatting. Sarah's eyes fixed on their bosoms, popping out of their low-cut uniforms. Her jaw dropped for a moment. Recovering, she snapped her mouth closed.

Noticing Sarah staring at them, they abruptly quieted and scanned her from head to toe.

Uneasy, Abe said, "We better go."

She whispered, "Introduce me."

Abe walked Sarah over to the bar. As he mentioned each name, Sarah offered her hand and said, "It's nice to meet you."

These ladies were not shy, but when confronted by this smartly dressed woman, they acted as if they had been stripped bare and were embarrassed by their nakedness.

The introductions over, Sarah meandered over to the cork-board. She pulled out a dart, stepped back a couple of paces and threw it with a motion, as if she were slapping the air. The dart stuck in the wall two feet below the target.

Abe overheard a snide, "New bar girl?" from Maude, followed by muffled laughter. He wasn't going to chastise his help in front of Sarah. Later, when the time was right, he'd let them know what he expected when he brought a personal guest into the bar.

"Can I see your apartment?" Sarah asked.

Her asking such a question surprised him. He blurted out, "Oh, no! No, no, no." It was bad enough she was in the bar. He already visualized her parent's rage should they find out. He couldn't even begin to imagine what they would do if they learned she had gone up to his apartment.

"Don't worry, I won't tell anyone I was up there."

"It's a bad idea."

She headed for a closed door. "Where is it? Through here?"

"That's the store-room," he said and grabbed her arm and rushed her through the door to the back hallway and stairs. He was glad to be out of sight of his help, but wondered what they were thinking, and most likely jabbering about. None of his female employees had ever been upstairs, not even for the simple task of fetching him. Not that he hadn't had women up there, but he always brought them in through the private side entrance that led directly from the street to the stairs, never through the bar for prying eyes to see.

In his living room, Sarah stepped onto the plush wool area rug between the couch and the two wing chairs. She hesitated a moment, seeming to bask in its depth. As she moved around the room, she ran her finger tips over the silk upholstery and silk draperies, barely caressing them, as she would a delicate flower whose petals might break off if touched too hard.

"Would you like something to drink?" he asked.

"A glass of water, please."

Abe hadn't built a full kitchen in the apartment. He didn't need one with the restaurant downstairs. In a cubbyhole off the living room he had an Alaska hardwood ice chest and a sink. He opened the chest, took out some ice chips and put them in a glass. Filling it with water from the tap, he handed it to Sarah.

She took a sip and looked down into the glass. "This water tastes different."

"I run it through my own filtering system."

"You filter the water yourself?"

"Yes. I learned about it from other bar owners when I was a salesman. I installed it right after I bought the bar. Pasta is cooked in boiling water."

"I know that."

"It tastes better if the water is filtered. Keeps my customers coming back."

"When is the Society going to put filters on its water pipes?"

"I guess when the legislature forces them to, like they did when they forced them to build sewers in the streets after the cholera epidemic."

"How can the mill owners be so callous?"

Abe shrugged. The last thing he wanted to talk about was The Society For Establishing Useful Manufacturers.

Sarah stared at the Edison phonograph. "I wish we had one of those."

"Would you like to hear it?"

"Oh, yes."

Abe picked up a round, gold-colored cardboard box with the words "Edison Gold Molded Record" written in bold script. Carefully, he slid the protective covering off the two inch diameter by four inch long black wax cylinder, put it on the machine, cranked the handle on the wooden Edison box, and gently rolled forward the horn/needle device until it touched the revolving wax tube. Out of the horn a voice announced, "Billy Murray singing, 'Meet Me In St. Louis, Louis'," and a tenor voice began singing the song.

"Sounds raspy, doesn't it?" Abe asked. "Not like real singing."

"I love it. I love all the new inventions."

"The world is a thrilling place," he said.

"I want to fly in a Wright Brother's aeroplane, maybe act in a flicker," she said.

"You'd radiate off the screen and delight everyone in the audience."

She put her hand to her cheek and smiled. "You make me blush."

"When you smile your eyes sparkle like the mist from the falls that bursts up into the rays of the morning sun," he said, again recalling what he had read about the falls and the sunrise.

She dropped her eyes and reached out to the wing chair for support.

"Do you want to see the rest of the apartment?"

Raising her eyes to meet his, she said, barely louder than a whisper, "Yes."

He opened the door to the master bedroom. She looked in and absently said, "Interesting uniforms your bar-maids wear." She glanced at her chest. "I wonder how I would look in one of them?"

"All the men would want only you to wait on them," he said.

"You think I have enough to fill it out?"

He wondered, *what is she thinking?* At her house she asked about wives working in their husband's pubs. Now she begged to see his apartment and was talking seductively about his waitress's uniforms. Could she be hinting that if they married, she wouldn't have a problem living here? Of course, when they did marry, he would never let her wear one of his waitress's uniforms in front of his customers. Though it would be fun to see her model one for him up here. Besides, he would never let her work in the bar regardless of what she wore. She wouldn't have the time anyway. She would be too busy caring for their children and their home to work.

His eyes drifted over the curves of her body. *You certainly have enough to fill out any dress,* he thought, imagining her bare breasts, round and firm, their rosy nipples taut as he suckled them. He moved his head to her cheek, inhaling her essence, so fresh and clean. He kissed her ever so lightly.

She didn't jump away, but turned to face him. "Your mustache tickles."

"You don't like it?"

"No, I think it's handsome. It makes you look very distinguished."

Their lips, slowly, cautiously came together. Abe opened his mouth, drawing her lips apart with his. He touched her tongue with his. She pulled back, but only for a moment before following his lead.

PART II

1912

CHAPTER 8

Abe beamed a broad smile as he and Sarah sat on the couch in the living room of their new house, anxiously awaiting the arrival of his brothers and their wives. Eight years ago when he told them he was selling his bar and going into the silk business, they thought he had lost his mind. *When they see his mansion they'll see who the fools really were,* he thought.

Glowing with pride, Abe turned to Sarah and said, "Thank you."

"For what?"

"Everything. None of this—our children, our house, our wonderful life together—would have been possible without you."

Sliding down the couch, he gave Sarah a peck on the lips.

Funny how fate works, he thought. When he and Sarah arrived back at Meyer Brothers department store after their first outing together, they found Cecelia cornered by Sarah's parents. Sarah's mother yanked her away, saying, "I knew you were up to something. Wait until we get home, young lady."

Mr. Singer stayed behind to expel him from their lives for good. Abe would never forget what Sarah's father said that day.

"You are a gambler, a saloon keeper, a gad-about-town, a ne'er-do-well. When you were twelve, you were one of my brightest students. I hoped you would continue your education and rise to be a learned man. A teacher, maybe. Someone to make your mother proud. Instead you became a rowdy like your father. A card player. A carouser. As long as you continue on your present path, you are not worthy of my daughter."

Those harsh words made him even more determined to have Sarah for his wife. To achieve his quest he had to gain her parent's approval, and it seemed the only way to do that was to change his life. If Sarah were any other woman, he would have said, "To hell with them!" and walked away. But she wasn't any other woman. Besides her beauty, she was educated—a school teacher. Without a doubt, he was positive Sarah would be his perfect mate. The children she would bear would be handsome and intelligent. How could they be otherwise, with parents like Sarah and him?

Sure, she espoused some peculiar ideas about women needing the right to vote, about wanting to travel the world like that Phileas Fogg character in that novel by Jules Verne, *Around the World in Eighty Days*. Those were things enlightened, well-read modern girls like Sarah thought about before they found a man to take care of them. Now, having borne four boys and with another child on the way, she had forgotten all about those ridiculous notions.

He certainly showed her parents he was not a drunkard like his father, and he could do more than run a saloon. And he showed his brothers, too. When he told them he was planning to job silk yarn seconds, they stared at him as dumbfounded as they would have been had he told them he was going to run for president of the United States.

"*Nu*, what do you know by silk? How you make yet a living selling seconds?" David, his younger brother asked. Despite Morris Singer's best efforts back in Latvia, David was not a great student and had trouble learning English. Also, he was the last to reach America. As a result, his grasp of the language was a bit disorganized.

David was right, Abe thought. His saloon had been surrounded by silk mills, yet Abe knew nothing about what went on inside those factories except hearing from his customers that it was thankless hard labor. But he had two advantages other newcomers who wanted to get into the silk trade didn't. First, he knew people. His older brother Solomon and his customers labored in the mills, and David worked for a silk fabric house in New York City. They could teach him. And he was a damn good salesman! Throughout his whole life, the thought of failure never entered his mind, not in England, not in Ireland, and not here in America.

Solomon had asked a much more sober question. "You would give up your saloon for a risky business like jobbing seconds? Why?"

He shrugged and gave the only answer he could think of. "I'm tired of the night hours," which only added to his brother's lack of understanding. How could he explain to them that he was doing it to win the hand of a woman?

As it turned out, Sarah's parents did him a great favor by forcing him to change his life. As a saloon-keeper he had been the low man in the pecking order of Paterson's businessmen. Now his life was complete. He was wealthy, had a big house on the hill, four sons who would carry his name into the future, and a beautiful wife who made it all happen. When he walked through town with Sarah on his arm, silk merchants like him—the most respected men in town—nodded to him and tipped their hats to her, exactly like he remembered men of importance did to his Uncle Isaac and Aunt Sylvia back in Latvia.

Now he couldn't wait to show his brothers how wrong they were. He had never forgotten his dream about him and his brothers working together in a family business. How could they not want all the luxuries he had, if not for themselves, then for their wives and children? All his brothers needed was a little guidance to make them realize what they were missing in their lives. If his new house couldn't convince them to come into business with him, he didn't know what would.

****

Sarah stared at him. They'd been married eight years. She bore him four sons, had a fifth child on the way, and she couldn't remember the last time he thanked her for anything. Yet she had no trouble remembering how she reveled in his response to her wanting to travel. They were on the chasm bridge looking at the great waterfall when he said, "We'll see the world together."

So overjoyed was she that her dreams were almost in her grasp, the flaws her parents saw in him dissolved into the thunderous roar of the falls. The cascading water hypnotized her like Medusa. She had fallen under his spell like an empty-headed school- girl. But she wasn't brainless. She had read everything from Dickens to Marx to Balzac to Verne and Mark Twain. She had only been naïve—a naïve teacher working with her father, afraid she would never earn enough money to realize her dreams.

So seduced by his charm and sophistication, she made the biggest mistake of her nineteen years by pleading with him to see his bar. Why didn't she acquiesce when he said, "It's not a place for young ladies," and go back to Meyer Brothers Department Store? Did she want to show him that she was a modern woman, as sophisticated as he? Or, maybe subconsciously she wanted exactly what she brought upon herself?

Then, in his apartment with his flattering words enveloping her in a warm glow, she had blurted out about his bar maids uniforms, "Do you think I have enough to fill it out?" What did she think those provocative words would invoke in him? Though he didn't answer, she could guess his thoughts by the smile on his face and the direction of his gaze. She should have run. Yet she stayed in his lair that she had crept into by her own free will. Then they made love, and despite the pain from the first time, it was glorious.

After that day she ignored every derogatory thing her parents had to say about him. Whenever she could sneak away from their watchful eyes, she ran to him, and they lay together. Enfolded in his arms, he told her about the deal he made that would put him in the silk business, that he found a buyer for his bar, and the wonderful life they were going to have with beautiful children. She extolled the wonders of the world they would see. When her cycle didn't come, she cried to him. He kissed her tears away, and with feigned expressions of joy from her parents, they married. And her dreams died.

CHAPTER 9

The door knocker thudded against its brass plate. Their guests had arrived. Abe and Sarah hurried to greet them. Standing between the Doric columns rising two stories to support the portico over the landing were Solomon, Cecelia, their two children, seven-year-old Frank and five-year-old Melvin, and David and his new wife, Leah. The look of wonderment on their faces told Abe everything he wanted to know.

The hosts ushered their guests into a front hall, as big as the family room in Solomon's and Cecelia's apartment. A muffled howl from playing children filtered up through the floor.

"Your cousins are in the basement," Abe said to his nephews. "Let me hang up your caps and coats and I'll take you to them."

The children handed over their winter garments and Abe carried them to the foyer closet. They stared into the little room as their uncle put their coats on hangers and hung them on the bar. They had never seen a closet. In their apartment, all their clothes were kept in bureaus and wardrobes or on wall hooks.

On the way to the basement playroom, Abe took the children through the kitchen. Their maid had pulled a tin sheet of sugar cookies out of the oven a minute earlier. The aroma filled the room. The children eyed the cookies hungrily. Abe gave one to each of his nephews.

"Thank you, Uncle Abe," Frank said.

"You're welcome. Quick, eat them up before we go downstairs. If your cousins see those cookies, there'll be a stampede up here."

They stuffed their mouths and stood there with puffed out cheeks, grinding the cookies into bits small enough to swallow. Their eyes drifted back to the plate.

"After dinner, there will be more."

As Abe led the children down the stairs, he said to himself, "There's more than one way to show Solomon and David the errors of their lives." They needed someone to guide them so they could realize their potential. He was not going to let anyone in his family live in squalor like their father did to all of them.

His father's brother, their Uncle Isaac, was a rich businessman. His father refused to work for his brother. Why, Abe didn't know, but because of it he and his brothers had to labor in the fields of their farm. He would not allow that to happen here in America. Now that he had built himself a thriving business, his biggest dream was to have Solomon and David join him in the company. He already had decided that he would change the name from "A. Bressler Silk Company" to "Bressler Brothers Silk Company." He was sure his nephews—Cecelia and Leah too after he gave them the tour—wouldn't stop talking about this day for some time to come. How could his brothers not listen to their families? How could they not want to give their families all that he had?

In the basement, finished with paneled walls and a large wool area rug over a hardwood floor, Abe's nephews stood, frozen at his side, gaping at the array of toys scattered around their cousins. Six-year-old Isidore pushed a wooden train; Samuel, four, stuffed a jack-in-the-box back under its lid; Ira, three, and two year old Jerry had their fingers wrapped around the handlebars of a tricycle, tugging in opposite directions. Ira's face was steadfast as Jerry wailed at the top of his lungs.

Abe spotted two other tricycles nearby. *Ira's been at it again*, he thought. He only wanted a toy if one of his brothers had it. To Abe's dismay, Isidore, his first born, always gave in to his younger brother and went off quietly to play with something else, again giving that one up if Ira demanded it. Ira quickly became bored when he couldn't get a reaction from Isidore, and went after his other brothers. Samuel fought back, but rarely won. Lately, Ira was picking on Jerry, the baby.

"Ira, let go," Abe commanded.

The boy obeyed instantly, as if he were a new recruit and Abe was his drill sergeant.

Jerry fell back and sat down hard, the tricycle falling on top of him. Stunned, he stopped crying.

"Play quietly," Abe ordered. "I better not have to come down here again."

Releasing his nephews with, "Have fun," Abe rejoined his family in the living room.

"Ready for the tour?" Abe asked.

"How big is the property?" Solomon asked.

"Two full acres. It's the highest spot on the eastern side of Paterson. Across the street, the city has purchased the land for a big park. It will be wonderful for the children."

Abe showed his-awe struck family the combination study/library in back of the living room, pointing out the hardwood floors and intricate detail work of the decorative molding around the ceilings. The clock in the bookcase chimed. Abe pulled on the fob and extracted his gold watch from his vest pocket and nodded as he confirmed the time.

Next he led them to the sun-room, with its ceiling-to-floor paneled windows. The final touches had been added to the room two days ago. The odor of paint hung in the air. Heading back across the front hall, they entered the dining room. The sun's rays streamed through the windows, struck the thousand-piece crystal chandelier, and refracted into streaks of red, blue, green and yellow.

Abe winked at Sarah and said, "Looks kind of like the falls in the morning sun, doesn't it?"

She forced a weak smile.

"Your house is magnificent," Cecelia said to Sarah, "but aren't you a little scared being so far away from downtown, from the stores, and the synagogue? As we came up the hill, I only saw one other house in three blocks."

"It is a little far," Sarah answered, "but Abe bought a motor car to take us downtown. And he says the city is promising to cobblestone Broadway out here soon."

Leah asked, "Who is going to take care of this mansion?"

"Abe hired a housekeeper to help me, a nice Italian girl."

"How does she get out here?"

"Oh, she sleeps in. We have maid's quarters off the kitchen."

Astonished, Leah and Cecelia looked at each other, then back at Sarah.

On the second floor, Abe theatrically threw open the door to the twenty-five foot by twenty-five foot master bedroom. He stood back to hear the muffled gasps as his guests surveyed the mahogany, four-poster canopy bed, hand-carved high boy dressers, dressing table, chaise lounge and the billowy lace curtains on the four windows.

Abe pointed across the room. "That door leads to a private bathroom, and this is a walk-in closet."

"How many bedrooms are there?" Cecelia asked.

"Eight, and six bathrooms."

"Oh, you poor dear," Cecelia said, her eyes dropping to her sister-in-law's swelling stomach.

Sarah again forced her lips into a brief smile, but her eyes remained quietly dispirited.

CHAPTER 10

Returning to the living room, the family sat on the silk upholstered couches and matching wing chairs. Sarah reached for the velvet cord with the big tassel on the end and pulled it, ringing a bell in the kitchen.

David ran his hand over the fabric on the couch. "Give a look on these nice goods."

Beaming, Abe said, "I got the fabric from Al Rubin at Belmont Silk."

"Rubin makes only nice goods, yes?" David said.

The lining house in New York City where David worked sold silk linings for everything from mink coats to caskets. David did not hesitate to help Abe, teaching him about fabrics. Unfortunately, when Abe asked David to join him in his venture, David refused. He said it took him five years to work his way up from working in the warehouse to his management job. "Silk yarn jobbing is too risky," David had said. "I no want to have to start back lugging goods in a warehouse when we fail."

Abe was disappointed, but he shrugged off his brother's lack of faith and started his business. It wouldn't be long now before he goaded David about being so timid.

Cecelia stared at the Victor Victrola. "Can you play a record?"

"Sure," Abe answered, his pride continuing to swell. He took a Victor record—a flat black disc with grooves on one side—out of the cabinet that also housed the machine, put it on the turntable, cranked the handle and set the needle in place.

"It sounds wonderful," Leah said.

"Not like those raspy voices from the old wax cylinders," Abe said, grinning at Sarah.

She ignored him and said, "That's a symphony orchestra playing Tschaikowsky."

"It's a model sixteen," Abe said proudly.

"A sixteen!" Cecelia said. "Oh my goodness! They cost $200.00."

"Only the best for Abe," Solomon said.

"Damn right! Why shouldn't I have the best? I worked hard for it. I made it happen all by myself," Abe said, thinking, *Why the hell don't you want the best for your family?*

He was about to verbalize his thoughts when David cut in, "Abe, you have by a beautiful house. You make yet such a living from jobbing yarn seconds?"

"Nothing but. You still think jobbing is risky?"

"I tell you, the way by you do it, I not think so. But if I try to make for a living in your business, I no sleep. Your business depends by someone else. You produce nothing, no?"

Abe laughed. "My business depends on someone else's mistakes, you mean. I may not know a lot about the silk business, but I do know mill workers, and they will always make mistakes."

"*Nu*, you are not afraid if the off goods dry up? Or you buy only a lot of yarn you cannot sell? You have no worries about keeping your living to pay for all this?"

Abe tapped his index finger against his right temple. "Nope, all you need is a little *sachel* and some *mozel*.

A shriek rose up from the basement.

Sarah got up.

"Leave them alone," Abe said.

"One of them will get hurt."

"No they won't. Let them work it out for themselves. It's the best thing."

Reluctantly, she sat back down.

Their servant entered the room. She placed the sterling silver tea service and bone china cups and saucers on the low table in front of Sarah, hurried away, and returned with two plates of cookies and cakes.

"Abe thinks he's the Catholina Lambert of East Paterson," Solomon said.

"Catholina Lambert?" Leah said.

"He is a mill owner," David told his wife.

"Yeah, the richest one," Solomon said. "He built a house on Garret Mountain that looks like a castle. He wants us to think he's some kind of king."

"He doesn't think he's a king," Abe said. "He's just a good businessman."

"Who treats his workers like peasants while he bathes in riches he reaped from their sweat."

Lately, although not calling a strike, Solomon had become quite verbal in his condemnation of the mill owners, making Abe increasingly uneasy. Abe's associates he bought from and sold to had expressed their displeasure. For his own, and for Solomon's sake, Abe had to get his brother away from that Socialist rabble he had taken up with who were stirring up Paterson's laborers.

"You ever been in Lambert's Castle?" Solomon asked.

"No," Abe replied.

"I have."

"You have?" Sarah exclaimed.

"Yeah. He built this big art gallery. He opens it to the public on Sunday to gloat and flaunt his wealth. I was curious, so I took Cecelia last Sunday. I couldn't believe it. Hundreds of paintings by Renoir, Rembrandt, El Greco, Monet, and Statues by Ives."

"It really is unbelievable," Cecelia said.

"And I'm told what's in the gallery is only a small bit of what he owns," Solomon added.

Her face suddenly brightening, Sarah said, "Oh, Abe, we have to go!"

"To see a bunch of pictures? What for? I can see them in magazines."

Sarah slumped back on the couch.

Sitting on the edge of her chair, Leah asked, "What does the rest of the place look like?"

"I never been in any other part of the house. Only the gallery is open to the public, but I know a couple of laborers who built it. Want to hear what they said?"

Do we have a choice? Abe said silently.

"Yes," Leah answered, anxiously.

"The place got dozens of rooms. Each one big enough to be an apartment for a whole family of laborers to live in. I was told the entrance hall is three stories high. As large as a small apartment house. And every inch of wall is covered with more paintings. One guy told me there is a picture of Napoleon and Josephine over the mantle."

"It must be beautiful," Sarah said.

"Yeah, beautiful," Solomon scoffed. "Each of those pictures was bought with stolen wages from the men, women and children slaving in his mills. Then there are the carved moldings, coffered ceilings, marble floors and fireplaces, and gesso walls. And every room is decorated with chandeliers and massive hand-carved furniture. A laborer got to work a whole year to buy one dresser."

"Oh my," Leah said.

Glaring at Abe, Solomon continued. "Oh, my, is right. I'm sure you heard about the party Lambert threw to celebrate the completion of the place, and about the special railroad track he had built from the station to his castle to ride his out-of-town guests up there in comfort. He had two orchestras playing—one in the garden and one on the third floor walkway that runs around that entrance hall I told you about."

Abe's thoughts drifted away from his brother's harangue. He was proud Solomon compared him to Catholina Lambert. It was Lambert's Castle that had given him the impetus for selecting this piece of property for his own house.

After he and Sarah married, they moved into an apartment in Riverside. As soon as he "made it," he wanted to get away from that Eastern European rabble and live among the German Jewish mansions on Broadway, east of Madison Avenue. Who was to say he wasn't a German Jew? Latvia was controlled by the Germans before the Russians took it over. He'd just say his family immigrated to Latvia from Germany.

But land in that area where he wanted to build his house was expensive and fast becoming crowded. One day he started walking. He kept right on going after the cobblestones ended and Broadway turned into a dirt road. When he got to the crest of the hill he looked back. He knew right then that he had found the location for his house.

The land at the top of the Broadway hill was not as high as Garret Mountain on the west side of town, but higher than all the houses east of the mills, and certainly as high as his Uncle Isaac's house back in Libau, Latvia. Abe liked that feature the best, because, as he recalled from his distant memory, the richer the man, the higher up on the hill was his house. Uncle Isaac's house sat on top of the highest hill in Libau. And Abe's house sat on the highest point in eastern Paterson.

". . . Who does he think he is," Solomon droned on, "the King of France, living in the Palace of Versailles he built off the slave labor of serfs. We all know what happened to Louie."

"You going to cut off Lambert's head?" Abe asked.

"Maybe."

Abe wanted to say, "If you think the passing of time has mellowed the mill owners, you're a fool. You start something with them again and it will be your head they cut off." Instead he held his ire for now, and replied in a less argumentative tone, "You make it sound like becoming rich is a crime. Isn't that what we came to America for, to pick up the gold in the streets?"

"Nothing is wrong with being rich. It's the exploitation of the workers that is wrong."

"Be realistic. Some men are made to be bosses and others to be workers. It has always been that way and will always be. At least here in America we all have an equal opportunity to become the boss."

"I ain't arguing about opportunity. It's just that those who become bosses should have the decency to treat their workers who made them rich with respect and pay them a living wage. I own Lambert's company, that's what I would do."

"Come in with me and you'll have your chance to do that."

Cecelia moved to the edge of her chair.

"What do you mean?" Solomon asked.

"Join me in my business. We'll buy a mill and you can try out your ideas on the workers. It will be a good experiment."

Abe stole a glance at Cecelia. She was listening so hard, she was barely breathing.

"You mean it?" Solomon asked.

"Absolutely, until you fail. Then we'll run the mill like all the others."

Solomon slumped back in his chair. "Forget it. I'm not joining you so you can make a fool of me."

Cecelia was near tears.

"The only person who will make a fool of you is yourself if you try to institute those crazy ideas of yours."

"It's us laborers what run the boss's mills and makes them rich. Without us, he got nothing but bricks. It is our sweat and our broken backs, not his money—his capital he's so proud of what gives him his profits to buy his big house and fancy clothes. We're entitled to some of those riches."

"You and your friends are *eizels*," Abe said.

"We are not fools. We're fighting for our lives."

"And you're going to lose if you think you're entitled to anything someone else worked hard to get." Abe held up his hand to cut off Solomon's objection. "No one is entitled to anything. You get what you're smart enough or powerful enough to grab. From what I've seen, your people are not smart enough or powerful enough to take anything.

"When I first came here in '94, the weavers were on strike. In '99 there was another strike. Three years later you dyers walked out. In 1907 the weavers struck again. Those strikes didn't take a nickel from the boss's pocket and put it in yours. All they did was make the mill owners more powerful and more resistant."

"It's gonna be different next time."

"Yeah, how?"

"Some day we're gonna shut down the whole silk industry in this town, that's how."

Abe laughed so hard, tears came to his eyes. "That'll be the day."

"*Genug shoyn*!" David said.

David's sharp use of Yiddish to say, "Enough already!" drew everyone's attention to him. He quickly changed the subject. "*Nu*, did you hear by the latest from Latvia? The pogroms are getting worse."

"I heard," Abe said. "The Tsar is blaming all the problems he is having with the radicals on the Jews. Anytime someone throws a bomb or distributes revolutionary literature, the Cossacks attack a Jewish village."

"We Jews are always the scapegoats," Leah said.

"I was thinking about going over to bring Mom and Dad back," Abe said.

Sarah had been refilling teacups. Her grip tightened on the saucer and the cup rattled. This was not the first time Abe had brought up this subject. Sarah had told Cecelia what Abe was planning, and she asked her to get Solomon to try and talk Abe out of it.

"Why do you have to go?" Solomon asked. "Send them the money or an agent to get them."

"You don't send an agent to fetch them like some piece of baggage. Besides, I know they wouldn't leave unless one of us was there, forcing them to go."

"*Nu*, you not thinking clearly," David said. "What by your own family? What by Sarah and your children? If something happens by you, who will care by them?"

Abe reached over and took Sarah's hand. "Nothing will happen to me. The whole trip is only going to take six weeks. I'll leave March first and be back by mid-April, way before the baby is due."

CHAPTER 11

As his departure for Europe grew near, Sarah's anxiety deepened. She could not quell the fear that he would not return and she would be left with five children and the only way to support them would be to go back to teaching, an occupation that offered little money. The fact that Abe acted as if he were taking a day trip to New York City only made her apprehension worse.

Every night returning home from work, the minute Abe entered his house he bellowed, "I'm home," and was greeted by Sarah and a cacophony of stomping feet beating their way into the foyer. "Daddy, Daddy, Daddy!" his children shrieked. Their eight tiny arms wrapped around his legs.

Abe rubbed the top of each head. "That's enough now. Go off and play while Mother and I eat our dinner."

"Abe, can't they sit with us tonight? You'll be leaving soon."

"No, I've had a rough day."

From the day Isidore, their oldest, was born, Abe had insisted that, except for family occasions, the children eat before he got home. He had said, "I want peace and quiet when I eat, not the whining of children. When they get older and can control themselves, then they can eat with us."

Sarah had said no more. They hadn't been married a week when she realized that once Abe made up his mind, it was futile to try and change it. The conversation would quickly turn to an argument, ending with Abe saying, "Because I said so, that's why."

Sarah ushered the children back to the play-room. Returning to the dining room, she took her seat at the opposite end of the table from Abe. Picking up the little crystal bell in front of her dinner plate, she shook it. Frances came in with a soup tureen, served Sarah, then Abe, and retreated to the kitchen.

"The carpenter fixed the windows today," she said softly.

"What?"

The table was closed down as small as possible, but four chairs along each side still remained between them. Abe said it made him feel good to sit at the ends of the table when eating his evening meal. Sarah disliked it. She couldn't talk to him in a normal conversational voice. She always felt like she was yelling.

Yet she had no trouble hearing him. His voice had steadily grown louder over the years. She wondered if his hearing was failing, having been affected by the deafening pounding of the looms when he went into the mills to buy and sell yarn. Raising her voice, she repeated, "The carpenter fixed the stuck windows."

"Good."

She looked straight down the table so her voice would travel directly to him and said in a controlled, but heightened tone, "I thought I might have him build a gazebo in the back yard."

"Whatever you want, dear."

She stopped talking and concentrated on her soup.

****

After dinner Sarah put the children to bed, and joined Abe in the living room. He sat on his oversized wing chair, reading the paper. She picked up *Paterson Life* magazine and leafed through the pages, not really looking at them, until she came to the anti-woman suffrage cartoons. There were five characterizations on the page under a headline reading, "Visions Of Suffrage."

Three pictures showed women doing men's jobs—a fireman, a policeman, a mail-man—but dressed in outlandish uniforms. Large feather plumes protruded from their hats, and the hems of their dresses stopped at mid-thigh, with tight pants covering their legs. A fourth cartoon had women in tight pants, smoking and playing pool. The fifth depicted women in a private club setting, wearing men's tuxedos and smoking, again sporting hats with huge plumes.

Other than seething every time she saw cartoons like those, Sarah had done nothing to fulfill her desire to get the vote for women. Tears came to her eyes. She hadn't had the chance. Based on her own married life, she could certainly see why men, including her husband, spouted that argument against women voting. "Don't women have enough to worry about with their children and taking care of the home without muddling their minds with politics?"

Staring at the cartoons, she thought, *No women I know would want to do any of the jobs they mockingly show. But we could make the world a better place for our children if we had the vote. We would demand laws to outlaw children from working in those horrible mills. We would clean up those filthy orphanages, and we would insist on equal pay for equal work.*

Stop dreaming! she scolded herself. There's nothing you can do about those things. Still, you can do something about your own children.

She closed the magazine and dropped it from three feet above the table. She had hoped the smack it made would distract Abe. When he didn't look up, she again wondered about his hearing, although in reality, she knew that wasn't a problem. When he wanted to, he heard the minutest sound. When he didn't want to hear anything, he had this uncanny way of tuning everything out.

She said, "Abe, we have to talk about the children."

"Uh huh," he answered without looking up from his paper.

"They need some fatherly guidance."

"Ummm."

Frustrated, she blurted out, "I'm going to join the New Jersey Woman's Suffrage Association."

"That's nice."

She clasped her hands in her lap and bowed her head to restrain herself from yelling at him. It would do no good. He'd tuck his paper under his arm, tell her what a hard day he'd had, how he needed some quiet, and storm off to his study.

"Damn radicals!" Abe bellowed.

His outburst startled her. She looked at him. He had the paper folded in quarters and was intently reading.

"Who do those people in Lawrence, Massachusetts think they are, making demands on the mill owners?"

"Ask Solomon; he'll tell you."

This time he heard her. He smacked the paper in his lap and glared at her. "Solomon will break with those people. I guarantee it."

"How are you going to do that?"

"I will. You wait and see."

She didn't reply. She did not want to discuss Solomon and politics. He would probably get all riled up, and she would never be able to get him to talk about the children. If she ever told anyone she felt alone in her house, they would look at her as if she were crazy. She had four children, a live-in servant, and a husband. How could she be alone?

She returned her attention to the characterizations. She asked herself, "Why shouldn't I join the suffrage movement? It would make him angry, but at least when he ranted and raved, he'd be talking to me."

CHAPTER 12

In bed, with the lights off and no Victrola, newspaper or anything else to distract him, Sarah again broached the subject of the children. "You won't believe what Jerry did today."

Abe rolled on his side to face her. "What did he do?"

"Lately he's been following Frances around, watching her do housework. He drew a beautiful picture of wheels and lines and hoses. I asked him what it was? He said 'A machine to clean the house.' He has a very vivid imagination."

"Uh huh," Abe said, stroking her thigh and nuzzling her neck.

A shiver rolled through her body. "Oh, God, Abe, not now. We have to talk about the children."

"I'm listening."

"They don't know you."

He nibbled on her ear and whispered, "They know me."

"No they don't. You order them around like toy soldiers, but you don't give them more than a pat on the head for affection. Then you want them to disappear. They aren't puppy dogs. They need praise, compliments, and encouragement from their father."

He stroked her breasts.

Her body trembled. She took his hand and held it. "Abe, you have to spend more time with them. I'm worried about Isidore. He wants to show you things he's learning in school, but you never have the time for him."

"I'll talk to him Saturday," he said and kissed her nipples.

She fought the tide rushing over her. "I'm worried about Ira too. He's becoming a bully. He won't let me hug and kiss him anymore, and sometimes he won't listen to me. You have to talk to him."

"I will, Saturday."

Abe worked his hand free from her grasp and placed it between her legs. "I love you," he said.

The words, "Do you?" flashed through her mind, but were zapped away by a jolt of ecstasy as his tongue flicked around the crevices of her body.

"Oh, God!" she moaned, her back arching. *He knew just the right places to fondle and kiss to make my troubles evaporate.*

She never did get to talk to him about Samuel.

****

She lay next to him, her chest heaving and her body covered in a film of perspiration. She felt elated and deflated at the same time. As he did from that first time they lay together in his apartment over his bar, he had taken care of her physical needs with the skill of a fine craftsman, but since they married he had left her other desires empty. A tear ran down her cheek. How could he be so passionate in their bedroom and so dispassionate outside of it?

Her mother saw him for what he was. Why hadn't she? Oh, how she derided the men her mother wanted her to get to know. "Their only expectation in life is to rent a small apartment and have their wife bear many children," she had said.

"You don't want children?" her mother had answered.

"Of course I want children, but only one or two so I can travel. I don't want to end up like those wives who spend their whole day washing and scrubbing and have no bigger desire at the end of the day than to sit on the stoop of their apartments and gossip. With Abe, I won't be like them. He said we'll see the world."

"You will be nothing more than the women you mock if you marry Mr. Bressler," her mother warned.

Now, after eight years of marriage, she felt even worse off than her mother said she would be. Living way out of town, she didn't have anyone to gossip with, even if she had a stoop to do it on. The only part of the life of the women she ridiculed that did not come true was that she didn't have to wash and scrub. She had a maid for that. A tremor—not of ecstasy this time, but of fear—shook her when she thought of Abe's family. He had four brothers and five sisters. *Is that what he had planned for me*?

CHAPTER 13

Despite being angry at him for outright breaking all of his promises, both expressed and implied before they married, when the day came for him to depart, Sarah still couldn't hide her apprehension about his leaving her. At hearing the cab's horn toot, she pleaded, "Abe, please, for me. Send an agent."

"I can't. It's something I have to do."

Her ire took over as she thought, *There is something I have to do also. I'm tired of being treated as a conquest. There is more to me than being your brood mare. If you aren't going to tend to my other needs, I'll have to do it myself.*

"I love you," he said, and gave her a long passionate kiss. "You are my life."

"Then why are you leaving me?"

"It's my duty."

"It's your duty to be with me and your children."

The cab honked a long impatient blast. Abe picked up his bags, pecked her lips, and said, "Sarah, darling, I'll only be gone six weeks. I'll be back on April seventeenth. I booked passage from England on the new White Star Liner, the Titanic. It's supposed to be the fastest ship afloat."

Maybe his leaving will be a good thing, she thought. She'd learn to be independent. She could certainly get her mother to come out for a day here and there to watch the children while she took off to see the Lambert Art Gallery or pick up some books at the library. She had to do something to re-stimulate her mind. Sometimes she felt like her brain was rotting away.

"Have a good trip," she said.

She slowly closed the door, feeling as if she were closing the back cover of a book she had just finished and was about to start the first chapter of a new one.

CHAPTER 14

Abe disembarked his ship at the Port of Le Harve, France. Per his brother's letter, he caught the train to Paris. While he waited in the Paris station for his connection to Lyon, he bought Sarah picture post cards of the Eiffel Tower and the walkways along the Seine River. *She will like them*, he thought.

****

At the Lyon *Gare de Parrache* train station, Jacob greeted his bother with a bear hug that squeezed the air out of Abe's lungs.

"I almost did not recognize you," Jacob said, his English pronounced with a combination of a French and Russian accent.

"I spotted you right away," Abe said. "Your white hair, your height, just like a Bressler."

"What happened to the handlebar you had in the *Kodak* you sent me two years ago?" Jacob asked.

"It's out of style. I shaved it off."

The chauffeur loaded Abe's bags into the boot, and Abe settled into the deep Turkish cushions of Jacob's touring car. "Nice auto," he said.

"I have been lucky."

When he and his brothers had fled Libau to avoid the Tsar's conscription agents, Uncle Isaac had given each departing nephew traveling money and a letter of introduction to a business associate so they could find work. Abe and Dan had gone to England, David to Holland, and Solomon and Jacob to Lyon, France—Solomon to a silk mill and Jacob to Peskin and Dumont's factoring house.

Seymore Peskin, impressed with Jacob's quick grasp of ledgers and numbers, took the young boy under his wing, treating him like the son he never had. Besides teaching Jacob how a factor bought and financed the mill owner's accounts receivables, he took Jacob into his house and was pleased when Jacob and his only child, Naomi, fell in love and married. Two years ago Seymore Peskin had gone into semi-retirement. With George Dumont having passed away five years earlier, Jacob assumed the operation of the business.

As they passed through Lyon, Jacob gave Abe the guided tour. "The city of Lyon is over two thousand years old. It was the capital of Gaul when conquered by Julius Caesar. This section of town we are traveling through is called the *Presqu'île*—peninsula in English. It juts down from the north between the two rivers. The rivers are what allowed Lyon to become such an important industrial center."

"The Passaic River did the same thing for Paterson," Abe said.

Jacob nodded and continued. "The river on your right is the *Rhône*, and on the left is the *Saône*. If you look across the *Saône*, that hill is called the *Fourvière* Hill. Old Lyon, or Lugdunum as the Romans called it, has many Roman ruins and a Gallo-Roman amphitheatre. Also, many buildings are in Italian-style architecture from the Middle Ages and the Renaissance because we were on the main trade route between Rome and Paris during those periods of history."

Jacob hesitated for a moment to let Abe study what he had explained.

"Now we are traveling through the *Croix-Rousse*. This is the section of town that will most interest you, Abe. Many of these buildings are silk factories."

"It's so different from Paterson," Abe said. "All our buildings are fronted on wide streets and are built in symmetrical rows. These are packed together every which way."

"*Oui*, that is so. Visitors often get lost in the maze of *traboules*—passageways—between the buildings."

When they passed out of the factory district into a more quiet section of the city, Jacob said, "This is the *Quartier Tête D'or*, the residential part of the city."

There were no mansions like in Paterson, only attached town houses built in rows. The driver didn't stop at any of them. He continued out of the city for another twenty minutes and pulled into a tree-lined drive. At its end, surrounded by freshly tilled fields, stood a three-story stone house.

"My chateau," Jacob said.

"You farm too?"

"I lease out the land."

"Like royalty," Abe joked.

"No, Abe, I am not nobility. I had enough of them in Latvia and do not care to emulate them. I only ask enough to pay the taxes, if they can afford it. If they cannot, we work something out like a little maintenance work around the house."

"No wonder they elected you their representative."

"I do not need the money. Why not be charitable?"

Jacob's wife Naomi and his two daughters, Danielle and Louise, greeted them at the door. If Abe didn't know Naomi was Jewish, he would never have guessed it from her looks. She was tall and extremely thin. Her small breasts barely rippled the front of her dress. Long, straight blond hair hung across her shoulders and framed the concave cheeks of her gaunt face. Her nose was petite and her lips as thin as a pencil line. The children looked like their mother, causing Abe to wonder if any of them ever ate anything.

Naomi calmed his fears with a delicious meal, prepared by the family cook, but supervised by Naomi's watchful eye. Glazed chicken in sweet orange sauce, creamed onions, green beans sprinkled with sliced almonds, chocolate mousse and coffee.

Naomi left to put the children to bed, and the brothers retired to the study. Jacob poured two brandies. Giving one to Abe, he walked to the coffee table and lifted the lid on a silver cigar box. Abe shook his head, no, and sat down in a leather chair trimmed with brass studs.

Jacob took a cigar and passed it under his nose to savor the aroma. He snipped off the end with a gold clipper and threw the stub into the crackling, orange flames in the fireplace. Lighting it, he looked at the end to check the ash and said, "Tomorrow I want to introduce you to some important people in France's silk industry. I am sure you will be able to do some nice business with them."

"Thank you. I may need all the extra business I can get."

"I thought business was good in America."

"It is, for now. But you wouldn't believe what's going on with the workers."

"We have trouble here, too."

"I don't understand what the world is coming to. The mill workers are flocking like sheep to that Bolshevik Industrial Workers of the World labor union. In Lawrence, Massachusetts, they convinced the whole town to go on strike."

"I heard of that."

"There is some dame up there named Flynn stirring up the workers with crazy ideas."

"A woman?"

"That's right."

"*Sacre bleau*, unbelievable?" Jacob said, sitting down on the leather couch across from Abe.

"So far, the out of town radicals haven't come to Paterson, but that doesn't mean the mill owners aren't having trouble. And our brother, Solomon, is right in the middle of it."

"I am not surprised."

Abe nodded.

"He always had strange ideas," Jacob said. "He barley escaped from here with his life."

Abe told Jacob about Solomon's ill-fated strike of 1902 and how Solomon continually refused his offer of a partnership, first in the bar, then in the silk business. "I can't figure him out."

"You are a good brother, Abe."

"What do you expect me to do? He's family."

Abe rose from his chair, walked over to the bar, and poured another two fingers of brandy into his snifter. Swirling it around, he said, "Paterson is ready to explode again. Thank God it's the weavers this time and not Solomon's dyers."

"What are they demanding?"

"This fellow, Dogherty, is building a new mill in Clifton. That's a city just outside Paterson. He engineered the layout of the looms in such a way that one weaver can handle four looms instead of two. The weavers all over Paterson are grumbling about it. The mill isn't even finished yet and I hear the workers in his old mill are refusing to work in the new one, despite his offer to pay them double from the current twelve dollars to an unheard of twenty-four dollars a week to run the four looms."

"You are kidding. Why will they not do it? Our weavers have worked four looms for years."

"Who knows? But that's not all. They also want an eight-hour work day instead of the present ten."

"I do not believe it."

"I tell you, Jacob, the radicals are stirring up the whole world, and I want to be prepared if they come to Paterson. That's why I have to meet your people. If there is a strike I'm going to be able to pick up some good yarn deals that may interest the mill owners here in France."

"I will help you all I can."

"Thanks," Abe said, his eyes focusing on the painting in back of the desk. He studied the signature. "This guy Mon et does nice work."

"Monet," Jacob said, correcting Abe's pronunciation. "Yes, he does. That is one of his *Nympheas Serei de Paysage d' dau.*"

"What?"

"Water lilies and water. Interesting is it not?"

Abe nodded and cocked his head to look at the picture from another angle.

"What are you doing?" Jacob asked.

"When I look at it, I kind of feel like I'm floating in the middle of the pond, but I can't find the shore. I know it's there, but not seeing it is kind of soothing, like I'm in a dream and no one can bother me."

"It is the same feeling I get. I guess it is because there is no shore line on the horizon to get a frame of reference."

Abe took a step to the left. "Amazing, the way he painted the clouds and pieces of sky reflecting on the water. It almost looks like everything is moving and you can see below the surface of the pond."

"I bought that in a gallery in town. I think they still have one or two similar ones if you want to buy one."

Remembering that Solomon had mentioned Monet as one of the guys that did some of the paintings hanging in Lambert's gallery, Abe said, "Maybe I will. Sarah would like it."

"I am sure she will. So what do you hear from Dan? I was in London last year on business and we got together for a couple of evenings."

"Wonderful. I can't wait to see him. After I pick up Mom and Dad, we're going to stay with him for a few days before we head home on the Titanic."

"The Titanic! Well, well. From what we Frenchmen hear, that ship is *magnifique*."

"I'll write you and let you know. I booked two first-class state-rooms. I'm really looking forward to that trip." Abe sipped his brandy and asked, "Do you do much business with Uncle Isaac? How is the old man doing?"

"He is resting now. Our cousins have taken over the business."

"I can't wait to see him again," Abe said.

Jacob turned toward the fireplace, picked up a poker and stoked the logs, watching the orange embers shoot up the chimney. "He will be waiting for you, I am sure."

Naomi entered the room. "Finally, the children are in bed," she said in French.

"Darling, you will have to speak English for Abe."

"Very well, but he may not understand me," she answered her husband in French. To Abe, she said in English, "Tell me about, *qu'est-ce c'est*, how do you say, wife and children."

"You would love Sarah," Abe began, proudly taking two dozen *Kodaks* from his pocket. He broke into a monologue, showing off his children, his house, his business and his wife. "Sarah is so patient with the children. She's a wonderful wife and mother."

CHAPTER 15

Ernie, Sarah's driver, opened the rear door of the Cadillac. Sarah climbed in and settled her swelling body into the tufted leather seats.

"Where to, Mrs. Bressler?" Ernie asked.

She gave him Cecelia's address in Riverside.

Sarah had brooded for a week because her mother had been busy helping her father teach the ever-growing number of new immigrant children and had been unable to baby sit. And her maid, Frances, was unable to control the children for more than an hour, barely enough time for Sarah to get to the market and back. But today her mother unexpectedly called and said, "I haven't seen the babies in so long. Would it be all right if I come over?"

Sarah jumped at the offer and called Ernie to pick her mother up. She then called Cecelia and was overjoyed when she found out her sister-in-law was free of her children also.

"How are your wife and children, Ernie?"

"Well, thank you, Mrs. Bressler."

Ernie had been working for Abe for seven years—five as a teamster, and the last two as a truck driver. He was always the one Abe sent to pick Sarah up and bring her downtown when she had to go shopping. Now, while Abe was away, Ernie was under instructions to be at Sarah's beck and call.

At first Sarah felt uncomfortable being chauffeured around, but as she got to know Ernie, she became quite at ease with his driving. As a matter of fact, she felt more relaxed when Ernie drove than when Abe did. Ernie kept a firm grip on the wheel and never went too fast. Once, when Sarah complimented him on his good driving, Ernie had said, "Thank you, Mrs. Bressler. After all, I do have charge over Mr. Bressler's most prized possession."

Sarah had smiled at his reply, but her smile faded when she wondered which Abe considered his most prized possession—her or the car. Knowing how proud Abe was of his Cadillac, and how he must have boasted about the cost, she was almost willing to bet Ernie took such care in his driving because he was petrified he would lose his job if he damaged the auto.

****

They picked up Cecelia, and Ernie drove them to the corner of Broadway and Main, with instructions to pick them up at the same spot at three o'clock. Downtown smelled of burning coal. Soot belched from the mills' stacks and blackened the mounds of snow, cleared from the sidewalks after last week's storm. As the snow melted under the early March sun, black water ran in rivulets in the gutter and formed dark puddles on the sidewalks. Sarah and Cecelia stepped carefully to avoid getting their shoes wet.

Sarah had never gotten totally used to living so far from downtown. She loved the hustle-bustle of people moving around and seeing the displays in the store windows. Passing a ticket agent's window, posters of the Eiffel Tower in Paris and the Titanic caught her eye. She stopped to stare at them. *He promised me*, she thought, *and now he's gone off by himself as if he never said anything. If he brings me any of those picture postcards, I'll rip them up and throw them in his face.*

"What are you looking at?" Cecelia asked.

"Abe is coming home on that ship."

"Oh, my!" Cecelia said.

Continuing to stare at the picture of the Titanic, Sarah almost broke into tears. Forget Paris and London. Right now a train trip to Philadelphia or Washington, D.C. seemed as far away as the stars. Her self-pity was interrupted by a woman who shoved a circular into Sarah's hand.

"What's that?" Cecelia asked.

Sarah looked at the handbill. Taking up half the page was a picture of a man sagging in a chair, a whiskey bottle dangling from his hand. The other half showed a woman hovering over a sewing machine. The caption under the man read, "The one who votes." Under the caption was a plea, "Join us today at the First Presbyterian Church on Ward Street in a rally for Woman Suffrage. Woman's Christian Temperance Union."

"Let's go," Sarah said. "It's only two blocks away."

"Are you crazy? Into a church?"

"You afraid you're going to be converted?"

"No, of course not, but . . ."

"So, why the *shpilkes?* Don't you believe woman should have the right to vote?"

"I never really gave it much thought."

"I have, and I think women should have the vote. I want to hear what these people have to say."

"But what if they have a service for Jesus Christ, or something like that?"

"Hearing the words, 'Jesus Christ' isn't going to make you a Christian. Ignore it."

Sarah started toward the church, but Cecelia remained glued to the spot on the sidewalk.

"Come on," Sarah insisted.

When Cecelia didn't move, Sarah stepped back, grabbed her sister-in-law's hand, and pulled her along. Dragging Cecelia up the stairs and into the church, Sarah plopped them into the last pew. Despite being in the back of the church, the huge cross behind the altar still loomed ominously at them.

About fifty women occupied the pews in the front, leaving twenty rows between their backs and Sarah and Cecelia.

The woman on the pulpit stopped her speech and bellowed, "Come forward."

Cecelia stayed seated, shaking her head rapidly back and forth. Sarah let out a sigh and headed up the aisle. An instant later, as if she thought being alone would condemn her to eternal damnation, Cecelia rushed to Sarah's side. When they had seated themselves among the other women, the speaker continued.

"In 1776 the New Jersey Constitution allowed women to vote. That right was stripped from us in 1807 because of a contested election over the location of the Essex County Courthouse. There was fraud and double-voting, and the men blamed it on the women.

"John Condict of Essex County, who almost lost his seat in the New Jersey Legislature in 1797 because of women voting, was the one who pushed the law to take the vote from us. It's time we took the vote back."

Heads bobbed and a few women clapped. Sarah nodded vigorously.

The speaker went on. "Our food, our health, our play, our homes, our schools, our work are all ruled by men. It's time we also took our lives back."

Sarah thought, *My sentiments exactly.*

"We must continue to spread the word of our founders, Susan Anthony, Lucretia Mott and Elizabeth Stanton. They are looking down on us, watching our progress."

At the mention of the movement's exalted architects, many of those present bowed their heads in reverence.

After the moment of silence, the speaker said, "There is a resolution in favor of woman suffrage now before the New Jersey Senate. You must demand your husbands contact Paterson's legislators to insist this resolution be passed. Now, let us pray."

"Oh, God, here it comes," Cecelia whispered.

"Be respectful," Sarah demanded.

"Lord, give us strength to achieve our goal. Only when we have the vote will we be able to outlaw the demon rum that makes men defile and defame Your Holy Word."

****

Outside the church, *The American Suffragette* booklet clasped in her hand, Sarah asked, "That wasn't so bad, was it?"

Cecelia darted her eyes up and down the sidewalk. "Let's get away from here."

"Don't be such a Nervous Nelly. No one saw us, and so what if they did?"

Cecelia started off down the sidewalk. "You don't live in the community anymore, Sarah. You are not subject to the gossip."

"Pshaw. Pfui on their gossip."

Two blocks from the church, Cecelia finally calmed herself and slowed her gait. "How much did you give them?"

"Ten dollars."

Cecelia tripped and almost fell. "Ten dollars! That's half a week's pay for Solomon."

"It's a worthy cause."

"But ten dollars! It's so much money."

"I know, but I wanted to."

"I can't believe you gave them your name, too. They have your address. Suppose they mail something to your house?"

"That's why I gave them my name."

"What if Abe sees it?"

Straightening her back, her round belly thrust out, Sarah answered, "What if he does?"

CHAPTER 16

Cecelia walked into her apartment, closed the door and leaned up against it. The odor of cooking cabbage in the apartment next door filled the hallway and had swept in with her. Yesterday she would not have given it the slightest notice. Cooking odors, some pleasant, some that caused her to hold her breath as she climbed the stairs, always permeated the building.

Her eyes roamed from the rug, so threadbare the jute backing showed through in places, to the couch, its arms and back covered with lace doilies, not so much for aesthetics as to hide the frayed upholstery. The same battered furniture was commonplace in her friend's apartments. Until she returned from Abe's house, her furnishings seemed unremarkable.

The chauffeured car, Sarah's house, Sarah's donation—it all pounded in on her. She loved Solomon. He made a decent living as a foreman in the dye house, but if he were with Abe, they could have so much more.

At the shrill of laughter echoing in the apartment hallway, she blotted her glassy eyes and opened the door. Right on schedule, her two boys were home. She took their books and lunch pails and asked, "How was school?"

Frank answered, "School is school."

"I saw Russia on the map," Melvin said. "It's big."

"Bigger than the United States," Frank said.

"But a lot poorer," Cecelia added, suddenly feeling better about her lot in life. "Now go out and play until dinner is ready."

****

Cecelia served her family a roast, surrounded by potatoes and carrots. Food was never the problem in her household, but she wished it didn't consume so much of her budget. Taking her seat, she started the evening conversation. "I went shopping with Sarah today. Her chauffeur picked me up right outside the building. You should have seen the looks on Golda Klein's and Hannah Cohen's faces."

"What kind of auto?" Frank asked eagerly.

"I think it was a Cadillac."

"Wow!"

Chomping on a potato, Solomon said, "I hope Sarah doesn't get too used to that life. Things can change fast."

Cecelia ignored him and went on. "There were women all over the sidewalk handing out leaflets for woman suffrage."

"I think women should have the vote," Solomon said.

Cecelia was dumbfounded. She had never spoken to Solomon about the subject. She had assumed he was against it, like most men.

"Women work in the mills alongside us. Why shouldn't they vote? With all of us mill workers voting, we'd change some laws in this town. Then we'd have some justice around here."

"That is what many men are afraid of," Cecelia said.

"Only the bosses." Turning to his children, Solomon asked, "What did you learn in school?"

The boys repeated what they had told their mother.

Solomon said, "The only difference between Russia and here is the language."

"That's not true," Cecelia cut in. Addressing her children, she said, "In Russia, if you are poor, you stay poor for life. Here in America every one has the opportunity to improve themselves. We have no nobility threatening our lives or holding us back."

Solomon methodically folded his napkin and laid it next to his plate. "No nobility, only bosses. Weidmann fired six men today."

"Oh, my!"

"I told them never to discuss the union while on company property, but they forgot and were talking about it during lunch break."

"Damn bosses!" Frank scowled.

"Children, have you had enough to eat?" Cecelia asked.

Both nodded.

"Then hurry off and study your books. With a good education you can be anything you want to be here in America. That is the big difference between living here and in Russia."

With the door to the children's room closed, Cecelia said, "I wish you wouldn't fill their heads with your hatred."

"I suppose it's better to teach them they can be anything they want to be."

"You can in this country, and you know it. You just won't . . ." She abruptly stopped talking. She had never gone this far with him before. But today she couldn't hold it in. Her day with Sarah reinforced her belief that if her husband joined his brother their lives would be so much better.

"Won't what—go in with Abe? Become a boss?"

"Yes."

He slammed his hand on the wooden planked table, bouncing the dishes. "I have responsibilities to my people who look to me for help."

"You have responsibilities to your family first."

Solomon jumped up. "Are you starving? Do you have clothes?"

She rapidly bobbed her head.

"Then I don't want to ever hear again how wonderful it would be to work for Abe."

Cecelia began stacking the dishes to clear the table. She did not want to argue with her husband. Compared to others in the neighborhood, her husband was a good provider, but it would be nice to live in a house and own an auto. *If my husband worked for Abe, he could give us those things too*, she thought.

CHAPTER 17

Abe left Lyon with great anticipation. He couldn't wait to see his mother, uncle and cousins again. He wanted to show off. After all, he was a pretty good businessman in his own right.

Rather than take the railroad through Berlin, Warsaw, and up through Lithuania to Latvia, an arduous journey, Abe took the train to Amsterdam, then took a ship through the North Sea around Denmark and Sweden into the Baltic Sea to Latvia. Landing in Libau, his mood changed from anticipation to anxiety.

He walked up and down the wharf looking for his uncle's warehouse. Not only wasn't the Bressler name on any building, he didn't see a trace of anything he remembered. Then he noticed with uneasiness the name of the port on the dock master's building. Not "Libau," as it had been called when he left. Now the city was called the "Port of Lebava."

He walked into what he was sure was his uncle's old warehouse and searched out someone who looked like he was in authority. "Where did the Bressler Company move?" he asked in Russian.

The young Russian's face broke into a cocky smile. "They did not move. We took their business."

"Took?"

"Da. We own the business now."

Resisting the urge to grab this man and shake him until he stopped lying, Abe made no further inquiry. Dazed, he half staggered out of the warehouse.

It was five miles from town to the family farm. He had walked it easily when he was a boy and could still do it today, but he had luggage and the Monet, so he hired a coach to drive him.

Despite seeing the great changes in town, he wasn't a bit surprised that everything at the farm looking exactly as it did when he left twenty-five years ago. The fence was still broken and slats were still missing from the barn walls. His father was true to form.

Even his mother was right where she had been when he left—in the kitchen, wearing the same kind of shapeless dress. The wrinkles in her face were etched a little deeper, but there were no more than he remembered. Only her hair was a little different. She still wore it pulled severely back, but now it was mostly gray instead of auburn. And she seemed shorter.

Releasing her from his hug, he took a deep breath and was glad one thing remained the same. Her cooking still filled the house with delicious aromas. Chicken livers were frying in *schmaltz* and onions. They would be chopped liver soon. He salivated at the thought of it.

"Where's Dad?"

Chava wiped the tears of joy from her eyes. "In bed. He is not feeling well."

Right, Abe thought. *You mean he's sleeping off a drunk*. He didn't hate his father. "Hate" was too strong a word. His feelings were more like disrespect, disgust, contempt. The hinges squeaked when Abe pushed the wooden slat door open a crack to look into the bedroom. When he saw his father's waxen complexion, he realized the old man was more than drunk. "When did he get sick?"

"About six weeks ago. He caught a chill and has been coughing and wheezing since."

"Will he be able to travel?"

"I do not know. Some days he is better than others."

"I hope he is better in two days, because that's when we're leaving."

Abe's mother looked at him with a blank expression and said, "I know you came a long way to take us to America, but I am not sure I want to go. This has been my home for sixty years. I was born in Libau; your grandparents are buried here. I do not know if I can leave."

Abe gaped at the unpainted plank walls and dilapidated furniture and asked, "What do you have here? A drafty wooden shack! No ice-box, no electricity, no running water. Constant threats to your life from the Cossacks. In America you can live out your life as a queen."

"It is still home. It is where all my children were born. It is where your father and I have lived together for over forty years. What would be so bad if I died here?"

"Why are you talking about dying? You should be thinking about living. I am taking you to a life of leisure instead of drudgery. I am taking you to see your children and grand-children."

She hung her head. "I do not know."

"Enough of this talk. We're going in two days, and that's it." Changing the subject to one he couldn't get off his mind since he'd left the wharf, Abe asked, "Mother, when I got off the boat I went to look up Uncle Isaac and cousins Aaron and Shmuel, but the company was gone. What's going on?"

Chava's eyelids drooped sadly. "Things have gotten very bad. I did not tell you in my letters because I did not want you to worry. They confiscated the business. They took a lot of Jewish businesses."

"Why?"

"They never give reasons. They always say the Jews are the cause of all Russia's prob-lems and they do not want the Jews running important businesses like Isaac's."

"And you still don't know if you want to leave? You have to be kidding."

Chava didn't answer her son. She just stared at the floor, scrubbed so often with harsh soap that it had turned gray.

"Where are Uncle Isaac and my cousins?"

"Isaac is dead. He died of a stroke two months ago."

Abe couldn't talk. *Jacob must have known. Why didn't he tell me?* "And Aaron and Shmuel?"

"They live together in their father's big house with their wives and children. They were thinking about coming here to live on the farm. Your Uncle Isaac did own it, and now Aaron owns it."

"Yes, I know the whole story," Abe interrupted, remembering what Solomon had told him. Emanuel, Abe's father, used to work for Isaac, like so many others in the family. But Emanuel gave Isaac nothing but trouble. He was absent from the warehouse more than he was there. To get him away from the business, Isaac asked his brother to run the family farm.

"Please do not be too hard on your father," Chava said.

"Why? What has he ever given any of us? We worked the farm for him while he was off in town getting drunk."

"Abraham, please," Chava begged. "I hope you never have to find out how it is to be beholding to your brother for everything you have. It is very hard, believe me."

"Yes, Mother," he said, but he did not apologize. "Why didn't Aaron come to live on the farm?"

"They took one look and turned around and left."

"That I can believe."

"If it were not for a two hundred and fifty year tradition which dictated that the farm be transferred from father to oldest son, Aaron would have sold it like he sold everything else. I am still amazed the Cossacks have not taken it."

"Because it's too run down even for them," Abe said to himself. To his mother he asked, "And you still want to stay in this country?"

"Times change. It will get better."

"Not before it gets a lot worse. How many of the family are left in Libau?"

"The city is called Lebava now."

"I noticed that on the dock master's office. When did that happen?"

"A few years ago. The Russians are trying to wipe out all references to Latvia's Swedish and German past, so the official name of the city is Lebava. No more German, Libau, or Latvian, Liepaja."

Abe wondered how many of his mother's letters the Russians didn't send out of the country. "So, who is left in Lebava?"

"Besides your father and me, only Aaron and Smuel and their wives and children."

"Where did everyone go?"

"You know Gertrude is in America with her husband. A place called Albany."

"Yes, upstate New York. We write."

"Your other sisters are all married and gone off to Lithuania and Poland with their husbands. I still hear from Isabel and Eileen. I do not hear at all from Ruth or Hannah."

"I want to see Aaron and Shmuel before we leave."

"That would be nice."

CHAPTER 18

The five slat-beds with their straw mattresses still lay side by side in the bedroom he had shared with his brothers. Abe undressed and lay down on the one that used to be his. The stiff straw poked through the burlap fabric, pricking his back and legs. He sat up. There was no way he was going to be able to sleep. Dressing and throwing his coat over his shoulders, he wandered into the kitchen, sat in a hard wooden chair, folded his arms on the table and rested his head on his arms.

He was half asleep when he heard the pounding. Why was he dreaming about drums? He focused his hearing. Laughter and whinnying horses joined the beating. Flashes of light penetrated his eyelids. He jolted out of his seat and ran to the window. A dozen Cossack riders massed at the burning barn. Their spurs and the tips of their saber sheaths jutted out from under their great coats and glinted in the flames. Grey puffs of mist belched out of the mouths of their heaving horses. It took barely a moment for the bellowing of the cow and the plow horse to be drowned out by the roar of the fire.

His parents were awake and immobile from fright. With no time for them to change from their night-dresses, Abe gathered whatever clothes, shoes and blankets he could see and tossed them out the back window, then practically threw his parents out after their meager belongings. With the house between them and the marauders, he scooped up whatever he could and bumped and pushed his parents with his elbows and his body across the small yard to the corn-field. This was the first time he commended his father for not plowing under the corn-stalks after the harvest.

A few steps into the scraggly stalks, Abe commanded, “Get down!”

His mother dropped to her knees, but when his father didn’t respond fast enough, Abe shoved him to the dirt. He threw blankets over them and covered them the best he could with the scrawny brown stalks. As the night-riders torched the house, they lay shivering, watching forty years of memories leap into the black sky on spires of orange and red flames.

A second red glow lit up the night far off to their left. Abe patted his wallet and passport in his jacket pocket. Even in Tsarist Russia, he was sure the American dollar would speak loud and clear. Remembering that he had left the Monet in the house, he pounded the dirt and cursed this wretched country.

CHAPTER 19

Abe herded his parents to a neighboring farm. The raiders had been very selective in their burning. Not one Russian Christian had been harmed. A generous gift to the farmer bought them a warm room for the rest of the night, breakfast, and a wagon ride to Aaron and Shmuel's house in town.

"Chava, Emanuel, what happened?" Aaron asked when he opened the front door and saw his aunt and uncle huddled on the front porch.

Abe had been standing to the side, staring at the porch's broken floor-boards and the peeling paint on the siding of the house. He desperately tried to match the run down condition of this great house to the picture of the magnificent mansion he had carried in his mind for twenty-five years. Stepping into his cousin's field of vision he said, "It was the Cossacks. They burned the farm."

"Who are you?" Aaron asked, staring at Abe's muddy clothes.

"This is your cousin, Abraham," Chava said.

Aaron gaped. "Abraham!"

Abe stared back. He was stunned by Aaron's clothes, barely better than rags.

Aaron jumped through the doorway and engulfed Abe in his arms. "Abe, is it really you? I can't believe it."

"It's me, Aaron. I came to take my parents to America."

"Come in, all of you."

Abe half expected to see the uniformed maid who usually stood nearby to wait on visitors, but there was no maid. Nor was there the proper butler who always answered the door and ushered visitors into the parlor. When he entered the living room, Abe was again taken by surprise. Gone were the paintings and the tapestries. Gone was most of the furniture and all the beautifully gilded vases the company ships brought back from China. Gone were the books, replaced by dust in their shelfless alcoves flanking the fireplace.

Abe could not hide the shock that swept across his face. He had idolized his uncle. When he was a boy he couldn't wait until his Bar Mitzvah, when he would be a man and be able to work for his Uncle Isaac. He longed for that day because it meant he could get away from the farm and live in the city like his cousins. Then the Tsar's conscription of Jewish boys started again and he had to flee.

My family could use a leader like Uncle Isaac in America, Abe thought. Solomon's crazy ideas were going to land him in trouble again. And David was weak, afraid of his own shadow. *They certainly need someone to show them the folly of their ways. Why shouldn't it be me?*

Seeing the expression on Abe's face, Aaron said, "It has been a little hard around here lately. We had to sell a lot of things. But forget me, what happened to the farm?"

Emanuel coughed and answered, "What do you think happened? The Cossacks burned it to the ground. That is the reality of being a Jew in Russia. The future here has always been hopeless. You are dreamers if you think it will ever change."

"Father," Abe said, "we all know your philosophy."

"You bet you do," Emanuel said. "Live, laugh and drink to the fullest because you never know when the Tsar will take your property or your life."

For the first time, Abe viewed his father with sympathy. Maybe the man wasn't all wrong, he thought, but quickly changed his mind. His father was wrong. You don't give up and resign yourself to poverty. If they won't let you live here, you take your family elsewhere.

Aaron offered the two remaining chairs and one small sofa to his guests. "Sit. I'll get everyone. They are in the kitchen. That is the only warm place in the house these days, what with wood and coal in short supply."

Chava said, "Please do not trouble them. We will come into the kitchen."

After Abe re-united with his cousin Shmuel, Aaron introduced his wife, Matilda, his sister-in-law, Selma, his two sons and three nephews.

Abe forced himself not to stare at the women's clothes. Fine silk ball gowns had been re-cut into simple sack dresses.

"I suppose you are here to take Chava and Emanuel to America?" Shmuel asked.

"Yes, I am. We're leaving tomorrow. I hope you won't mind if we stay here the night."

"Of course not," offered Matilda. "We are happy to have you."

Abe did not expect any other answer. Family was never turned away, even if their presence put a strain on the food supply of the host.

Matilda said "I'll put on tea while you tell us all about America."

That was not the subject Abe wanted to talk about. He asked Aaron, "What happened to the company?"

"They took it. The buildings, the warehouses, the two ships. All we have left is one store in town, and that has very little merchandise in it to sell."

"Then why stay here? Come to America with me. I have a big company. You can all make a comfortable living working for me." Abruptly he stopped talking, struck by the irony of what he had said. Here he was, the one who was to be the employee, offering employment to the former employer.

Aaron straightened his back. "I do not think so, Abe. Things will be changing here soon. I know we will be able to build the business back again. We still have our contacts in England, France and Holland."

Matilda had been listening intently. Her face dropped at her husband's reply. Forcing back tears, she poured the light tan colored tea into seven cups, not quite filling them, but making sure each had an equal amount.

"You're dreaming," Emanuel said, breaking into a coughing spasm. Getting control of himself, he added, "Things are going to change all right. They are going to get worse."

"I don't think so," Shmuel said. "You of all people should know life here runs in cycles."

Using his sleeve, Emanuel wiped the dribble that had seeped out of his mouth with his cough. "This cycle is going to be a long time changing."

Matilda said, "Please sit. The tea is ready."

The family gathered on the poorly built benches, flanking an equally crudely constructed wooden table. When Abe had first seen it, he quickly realized where the six-foot high fence that had surrounded the house had gone. Selma and Matilda served the tea, making sure not to give their guests the cups with the cracks or chips.

"I'm sorry I don't have any lemon or cream," Matilda said.

"I like it plain," Abe lied and took a sip. It was so weak it barely tasted like tea. Looking at his father, he asked, "What are you talking about—cycles?"

Aaron said, "Didn't he tell you about his life in the eighteen-fifties?"

Abe tried to catch his father's eye, but Emanuel had turned his head in another coughing fit.

"I will tell you," Aaron said. "In 1852, when my father was twelve, his father, our grandfather, smashed dad's kneecap with an ax handle."

"What?" Abe exclaimed.

"That is why father walked with a limp. You never heard the story?"

Flicking his head at his father, Abe scowled, "He wasn't much on family history."

"Tsar Nicholas was intent on drafting all Jews thirteen and over into his army for a period of twenty-five years. Father told us there was not one of his friends ever caught by the conscription agents that he saw again. Grandfather would rather have his son crippled for life than to have him die in the Tsar's wars."

"How come you escaped?" Abe asked his father.

Emanuel was saved from answering by the cry of, "That's mine," coming from the corner near the stove where the children had been occupying themselves with wooden toys.

Selma went to quiet the youngsters.

Aaron answered for his uncle. "Your father and our uncles, Ruben and Moishe, were lucky. They were not yet thirteen when Tsar Nicholas died and Tsar Alexander II came to power. Tsar Alexander was a good man. He let the Jews live in peace. Father was able to expand his business."

"It did not last long, did it?" Emanuel said. "I knew it would not. These Tsars are all the same—Jew haters."

"No, it did not last long," Aaron said. "When that assassin killed Tsar Alexander in 1881, our world began to change."

"Change? That is what you call it? Ha," Emanuel said, breaking into another hacking spasm. Recouping, he roared, "Murderers, thieves, persecutors! Why don't you call them what they are? All your father's high and mighty friends in St. Petersburg abandoned him."

The vindictiveness in his voice was more effective than Selma's at quieting the children. The toys stopped rolling and their heads turned toward their great-uncle.

"You are right," Aaron said, "but they still let us live in Latvia."

"Starve here, starve in Poland. What is the difference? Our family has lived here since the middle of the seventeenth century. What did it get us? So they don't force us to move to Lithuania or Poland, where they forced others to live in confinement. Your father's economic importance to Russia did not mean a thing. They quickly found their own people to run his company."

"Yes, Emanuel, we know all that," Aaron said.

"I am not through. All your father's influence could not keep you boys in school in the University, or the government from forcing Ruben to abandon the St. Petersburg office and move back to Libau. Your father could not protect our cousins to the south who ran the business in Lithuania from being murdered in a pogrom."

"It will get better. You wait and see," Aaron insisted.

"Not this time. That stupid attempt to overthrow the Tsar in 1905 made sure of that. You boys weren't part of that lunacy, were you?"

Aaron and Shmuel would not meet Emanuel's eyes.

"If you are smart, you will leave this country with us."

Abe offered, "You said you still had your contacts in England and France. Why don't you go there and start a new company?"

"We can't, Abe. This is our base," Aaron said. "This is where we must rebuild."

Abe shrugged. It's their life, he thought. Still, he couldn't help but feel sorry for Selma and Matilda. The look of lost hope played across their prematurely-aged faces. "If you ever need anything, just ask."

"Thank you," Shmuel said.

****

The next morning, while his parents were saying their goodbyes, Abe sneaked back into the kitchen and left a hundred dollars under a plate. It was twenty times more than his uncle had given him when he left in 1888, but his cousins needed it twenty times more.

Two hours later, Abe and his parents were on their way to England. As the ship pulled away from port, Chava and Emanuel stood at the stern, watching the land slowly disappear. Abe leaned his back against the railing, letting the wind from the forward motion of the ship wash over his face.

CHAPTER 20

Sarah had been fussing for an hour. When she re-arranged the cookies on the silver serving tray for the third time, Cecelia said, "Relax, everything looks wonderful."

"Thank you so much for coming to help me. I don't know if I could have handled this by myself."

With a big smile, Cecelia said, "Thank you for sending Ernie for me."

Yesterday, Sarah had received a call from Mary Beckworth, president of the Paterson League of the New Jersey Woman Suffrage Association. She invited Sarah to come to an executive committee meeting downtown. Sarah's first reaction was excitement. Then reality set in. It was Frances' day off. She had no one to mind the children. But she wasn't going to let an opportunity to join the association slip by. She offered her house to the Committee for their meeting.

"Sarah, did it ever occur to you to ask why they want you to join their executive committee?" Cecelia asked. "You only met these women two weeks ago."

"I suppose they would like me to help with the campaign."

"Don't be naïve. I'll bet that five minutes after we left the church they were checking you out. As soon as they found out who you were, they decided to hit you up for a larger donation."

Sarah pondered Cecelia's speculation for a moment before saying, "For the past seven years I have been doing nothing but rearing my children."

"There's something wrong with that?"

"No. I love my children. But I also need something to do that's just for me. Joining the woman's suffrage movement is that something. If it takes a large donation to get me in with the leaders, so be it."

"I see," Cecelia murmured.

The doorbell rang. "That's them," Sarah said, and patted herself down, smoothing out imaginary wrinkles in her dress.

"You look fine. Go let them in."

Sarah opened the door, surprised to see only three women. She had expected six or more.

Mary Beckworth, the only one Sarah had met, introduced the others. Lillian Ford Feickert was president of the New Jersey Woman Suffrage Association. Her handshake squeezed Sarah's fingers.

Alice Stokes Paul had a much more refined hand shake, and her soft spoken, "Pleased to meet you," suggested a quiet shyness. But her blue eyes flashed an intensity that said to Sarah, that she was far from shy.

After graduating Swarthmore College in 1907, Alice Paul went to England and joined Emmeline Pankhurst's radical suffrage group. Following her mentor, Alice participated in militant demonstrations, joining Mrs. Pankhurst in prison three times. Returning to the United States in 1910, Alice enrolled in the University of Pennsylvania. Very shortly she would receive her PhD. Today she was taking a brief hiatus in her studies to help recruit new members to the cause.

Sarah introduced Cecelia, directed her guests to the living room, and served the tea and cookies. With everyone comfortable, she asked, "How can I help the association?"

Before anyone could answer, Isidore appeared and ran up to his mother. "Ira is fighting with Frank," he said.

"I'll go," Cecelia said.

"No, I'd better. Please excuse me for a moment."

Fuming, Sarah was ready to scold her children with, "Wait until your father gets home!" By the time she reached the basement, she thought better of it. Abe scared them enough already, and she didn't want them to always think of their father as someone of whom they should be afraid.

When Sarah pulled Ira aside, a glint of anticipation crossed his brother's and cousin's faces, in hopes Sarah was going to give it to Ira. She disappointed them.

"Your cousins are your guests. You must treat your guests with respect. You can play with these toys anytime, but when your guests are here you must allow them to choose the ones they want. Do you understand?"

"Yes, mother," Ira said, the others nodding.

Noticing that Frank and Melvin had triumphant grins on their faces, Sarah looked directly at them, and said, "And your guests must also treat their hosts with respect. If you really do not want to play with something, then let the others have it."

"Yes, Aunt Sarah," her nephews replied.

"Now I have important guests of my own upstairs. You must also show me respect so I can attend to them without further interruption. That means no more fighting."

They repeated, "Yes, Mother," and, "Yes, Aunt Sarah."

"Very well. There will be a treat for you if you keep your promise." Spreading her arms wide, she said, "Now come here and give me a hug before I go."

All the children jumped on her and she squeezed them tightly and kissed each on the forehead before letting them go.

Returning to her company, Sarah said, "I'm sorry for the interruption. I believe you were going to tell me how I can help."

Lillian Feichert answered, "The woman's suffrage movement is made up mostly of working women. We have the support of business and professional women's clubs, civic clubs and the New Jersey Education Association. What we don't have enough of is political clout."

"But the opposition does," Mary Beckworth said.

"Yes, their support is very strong," Alice Paul said. "Do you know Mrs. Hobart?"

"Not personally," Sarah answered, adding to herself, "but I know who she is."

Jeannie Tuttle Hobart was the wife of Garret Hobart, Vice President during President McKinley's first term. When Mrs. McKinley took ill, Mrs. Hobart filled in as White House hostess. Had Garret Hobart not died in November, 1899, he would have remained Vice President when President McKinley's was re-elected, and become President instead of Theodore Roosevelt when McKinley was assassinated in 1901. Despite not quite making it to the role of First Lady, the widow Hobart was still very influential.

"Mrs. Hobart is an outspoken anti-suffragist. She has said more than once giving women the vote will be a great injustice and a grave menace to our state and country."

"Why would she say that?" Cecelia asked.

"Who knows?" Alice Paul answered. "I have never spoken to her, but I have heard from many she was devoted to her husband. She prided herself on being a homemaker, and probably feels, like most men do, if women get the vote, they will neglect their responsibilities to their husbands and homes."

"That's silly," Sarah said.

"Of course it is," Alice said.

With a look of consternation on her face, Sarah said, "I still don't understand how I can help you."

"To date, nine western states and the territory of Alaska have given the vote to women. These states have added to our small voice in Congress on which we can build support."

Sarah nodded.

"We have heard that your husband has some influential contacts here in Paterson. We were hoping you could prevail upon him to join our cause and ask him to use his association with his friends to lend support to the resolution favoring woman's right to vote that is before the New Jersey Senate."

"Oh, boy!" Cecelia blurted out.

Annoyed with Cecelia's outburst, Sarah asked, "What does that mean?"

"Nothing," Cecelia said. "I'm sorry."

Sarah smiled feebly at her guests. She could understand Cecelia's trepidation. She knew Abe's opinions about woman suffrage and his feelings about the proper place for men and women in the world. *The world is changing*, Sarah thought. *It's time for Abe to change too.*

"Of course I'll talk to my husband," Sarah said. "I'm sure I can persuade him to help us." "I hope," she added silently.

CHAPTER 21

Memories roared back to Abe's consciousness as the motor-coach carrying him and his parents turned onto Allgate High Street and rumbled over brick pavement into the heart of the Jewish Community in the Whitechapel section of London's East End. It was there, at Tower Bridge, that Abe had landed in 1888, one day before Jack The Ripper started murdering and mutilating prostitutes.

Abe shuddered at the recollection of the fear that rampaged through the community by mid-fall. On November ninth, Mary Jane Kelly was found murdered. It was believed she had been tortured for hours. The next day a police commissioner emphatically stated, "The Ripper was a Polish Jew," even though there wasn't a shred of evidence to back up his statement. Many Jews hibernated in their homes for weeks, fearing that new pogroms from the English were about to replace those of the Tsar.

Allgate High Street merged into Whitechapel High Street. Two blocks further on, the cab turned left onto Osborn Street and inched its way through the throngs of people crowding around pushcart vendors, dickering over prices. Odors of fresh baked bread, fruit, tobacco and meat drifted through the auto's open windows.

"A *shtetl's a shtetl,*" Abe muttered.

"What did you say?" his mother asked in Russian.

"The European Jews in New York City live just like this," he answered.

Surveying what looked like a stampeding mob, Chava's eyes opened wide and her grip on Abe's arm tightened.

Abe patted her hand. "Don't worry, we don't live in New York City. We live in Paterson, New Jersey."

His words didn't seem to mean anything to her. Her frightened eyes continued to dart left and right, fixing on the mass of people rushing among the yelling pushcart vendors, trying to find the best price for what they wanted to buy.

Turning left onto Wentworth, the driver pulled to the curb two doors from the corner and stopped. The brick building looked like hundreds of others in the district, and no different from the one where Abe and Dan had rented a two-bedroom, third floor apartment so many years ago.

"Wait here," Abe said. "I'll get Dan."

He stepped from the auto onto a message chalked on the sidewalk. "Next protest meeting, April 12." At the front door he grabbed the hoop door knocker and slammed it hard against its brightly-polished brass plate.

Seconds later Dan opened the door, took one look, and threw his arms around his brother. "Abe, it's been so long."

The two brothers were almost mirror images. Dan was as tall as Abe, and his body was lean and trim. The only difference in the two was their hair. While Abe's was prematurely white, Dan's was prematurely gray.

Abe held Dan tightly. The years they were apart evaporated in a flash. Breaking the embrace, Abe said, "Dad is real sick. We have to get him to bed."

Walking to the car, Dan saw the sidewalk scribble, smudged it with his foot, and muttered, "Damn radicals!"

"What's that all about?" Abe asked.

"I'll tell you later. Let's get Dad settled first."

Abe and Dan slung their father's arms over their shoulders, hooked their hands under his legs, and carried him inside and up two flights of stairs to a bedroom. Alarmed by her father-in-law's pasty appearance, Dan's wife, Katherine, summoned a physician.

The family, except for Chava who stayed at her husband's bedside, gathered in the second-floor sitting room to hear the doctor's pronouncement.

"He has pneumonia. Keep him warm, give him soup, and pray."

Dan escorted the doctor to the door. When he re-joined his family in the sitting room, Katherine was perched, stiff backed, on the couch, holding her breath and clutching her hands together so tightly her knuckles had turned white. Her eyes were glued on her brother-in-law. Abe toyed playfully with a Chinese vase, twisting it back and forth to examine its workmanship.

"Don't drop that," Dan said. "It's very old and very valuable."

Abe replaced the vase on the round end table. Katherine exhaled, her large chest noticeable collapsing.

"Nice house," Abe said.

"I bought it three years ago."

"What's downstairs?"

"A study, snooker room, and some storage."

"All this from old clothes? It's hard to believe."

"That and a few other investments. That vase was brought over here by an importing company I helped finance, and I own a piece of Thomas's cotton mill now."

Despite twenty-four years having passed, the mention of Thomas's Cotton Mill sent a shock wave through Abe's body. His Uncle's letter had sent him there. No matter where he went in that mill, he could not escape the cotton dust that clouded the air and clogged his nose and mouth until he could hardly breathe. The thunderous thump, thump, thump of the looms pounded in his head for two hours after he left the factory. His body, wracked with pain from dragging huge bales of cotton—all he could do when he got home was fall down in bed. He had no energy left to eat dinner.

That experience had been such a horror, Abe had blocked it out of his thoughts all these years. Now that it came flooding back, he suddenly thought about Solomon. His brother was going through that anguish every day in the dye house where he worked. More than ever, he had to get Solomon out of that place.

Shaking his head to expel the horrific thoughts, Abe quickly changed the subject.

"You still collecting from royalty like I showed you?"

"With a twist," Dan said. "We let the legitimate charities scavenge the old clothes. They get hundreds of pounds more than they can distribute to the poor. We buy the excess from them. Saves us a lot of leg-work. Then we sort the clothes and sell the good ones all over the empire—India, Africa, Hong Kong, Australia, Canada.

"Very clever."

"You aren't the only one in the family with ideas, brother."

A uniformed servant appeared in the doorway. "Dinner is served, mum."

"Thank you, Edith," Katherine said.

Dan escorted Abe across the hall to the dining room, while Katherine went upstairs to get her mother-in-law.

Esther, Judith and Maxwell, Dan's two daughters and son, sat along one side of the table. Katherine and Dan assumed the ends, and Abe and Chava the other side.

Chava's face glowed with pride as she marveled at her grandchildren. "You are so beautiful," she said in Russian.

Dan translated. Esther, the oldest at thirteen, blushed and said, "Thank you, Grandma."

Dan again translated for Chava.

"Who is Lady Wexford?" ten-year-old Judith asked.

Abe choked and swallowed hard.

Dan asked his daughter, "Where did you hear that name?"

"I heard you and mother discussing her the other day when you were talking about Uncle Abe coming to visit us."

"She's just an old friend your Uncle Abe knew a long time ago," Katherine said, glancing toward Abe, her broad lips breaking into a big smile.

"Yes, an old friend," Abe repeated.

"Are you going to see her while you're here?" Judith asked.

"No."

"Have you heard from Katie McGuire?" Katherine probed, almost laughing.

It was payback time. Katherine knew Dan would never seek retribution, so she decided to deliver a few jabs at Abe. She and her parents had lived in the apartment below Abe's and Dan's. It was Katherine who had heard the commotion upstairs when the earl came looking for Abe and found Dan instead. She had gone up to investigate the noise and saw the earl's men pummeling Dan. Her screams frightened them off.

Abe's eyes narrowed when he answered Katherine. "It's not a laughing matter. A young girl's life was ruined by a husband who beat her, and a brother who buried her alive."

Esther shrieked, "Buried alive?"

"Not literally, darling," Katherine said. She looked down at her plate, her good natured ribbing ruined by Abe's somberness.

Abe stared off into space. "She was so pretty, and she loved life."

CHAPTER 22

Being married to a well-to-do merchant, Katherine had the means to be able to venture to stores outside the Whitechapel Jewish settlement. Her decorating and the meals she supervised took on a smattering of English influence. The menu she prepared for tonight had the traditional kosher brisket of beef, but instead of potato latkes she served Yorkshire pudding. For desert, instead of strudel she had strawberry short cake, but without the whipped cream.

Chava had never tasted strawberries, and she cautiously poked at it before putting the smallest one in her mouth. Her second helping was a giant fork-full, bringing chuckles from Katherine and Dan.

"I wish I had a few more days here," Abe said.

"You can't go back," Dan said. "It's over, and that's probably for the best."

Abe nodded.

Chava's head turned back and forth among the speakers. She pulled on Abe's sleeve.

"I'll tell you about it later, Mama," Abe said in Russian.

Dinner finished, the family rose from the table and split up. The children retreated to the communal bedroom they had to occupy while their guests were in the house. Chava and Katherine went to check on Emanuel and see if they could force-feed him some soup. Abe and Dan retired downstairs to the first floor study.

Accepting a brandy and refusing a cigar, Abe asked, "Why didn't you write me about Uncle Isaac?"

"I did. The letter is probably waiting for you in America."

Abe nodded, not sure whether he would have been happier to have been prepared, or to find out the way he did. He said, "It doesn't look like things have changed much in the area since I left. Except, of course, you."

"Things are changing. Remember that scrawl on the sidewalk?"

"What's does it mean?"

"It's a message to the women about the next suffrage meeting."

"You have those nuts over here too?"

"Are you kidding? Last month, this Emmeline Pankhurst and her three daughters staged a rather violent protest. They marauded the whole of Covington Street, Regent Street as far as Oxford Circus, and most of Piccadilly, smashing shop windows with hammers and stones."

"You're kidding."

"They even broke four windows at Number Ten Downing."

"Unbelievable."

"There was such a public outcry that two days later, when the suffragists tried to hold their weekly meeting at the Pavilion theatre, a gang of men retaliated by laying siege to the place. The Bobbies were powerless. Women were accosted, their signs ripped out of their hands and their hats torn from their heads."

"We're lucky we have sensible wives. Katherine and Sarah would never get involved with those radicals."

Dan refreshed Abe's brandy and the two brothers settled themselves into the large leather chairs. "Our brethren are no better than the women," Dan said.

"Our brethren?"

"Over on The Lane—you know, Petticoat Lane a couple of blocks from here. The young radicals from Poland and Russia gather there in their *Chevas* preaching anarchism. They refuse to listen to anyone. Even the Chief Rabbi has no influence over them. They call themselves 'the great visionaries of a new order in the making.' They're going to bring trouble down on all of us."

"It's happening in America, too, and Solomon is right in the middle of it." Abe told Dan about their brother's union activities.

****

Returning to the living room, Dan and Abe found Katherine and Chava having a conversation in Russian and Yiddish.

"How is he?" Abe asked.

"He's sleeping," Katherine answered. "I think the steam is helping him."

"It'll be a shame if he has to spend the crossing in his cabin," Abe said.

"What do you mean?" Dan asked.

"The Titanic sails in four days and I'm not missing it. It's supposed to be the most magnificent ship ever built."

"But Abe, if father is still too sick to travel?"

"He'll be fine. What's the difference if he lies in bed here or in a first-class cabin on the ship? I'll hire a nurse to sit by his side."

"Why don't we wait a couple of days before making a final decision?" Dan suggested. "What would it hurt if you took another ship."

"I can't."

"Why not? Katherine and I saw this fellow, Charlie Chaplin, at the Music Hall on Mile End Road. He's the funniest little guy. Why don't you delay your trip a couple of days and I'll get tickets. We'll take Mom."

"Does he talk in Russian or Yiddish?"

"No."

"Then she wouldn't understand him. My decision is made. I have to get home to my business. We're sailing on the Titanic, and that's final."

CHAPTER 23

Tears stained Sarah's cheeks and dropped onto the newspaper in her hand. She crumpled it and threw it across the room. "I know he's dead. I know it. I asked him not to go. Why wouldn't he listen to me?"

"We do not know by anything for sure," David said. "All the news is rumors, no? I am sure more have lived than reported."

"It has been three days since it sank. If Abe was alive he would have gotten word to me. He's dead. I know it."

David's wife went to Sarah's side and put her arm around her sister-in-law's waist to stop her from pacing the floor. "You must calm down," Leah said. "Come, sit on the couch."

Solomon picked up the paper, smoothed it out and folded it so the headline of the Titanic's sinking was inside. "You know Abe is a lucky guy. He'll make it through this. You have to believe that. You must rest now."

Sarah pulled away from Leah. She began pacing again, each trip across the floor faster than the one before. As she walked, she wrung her hands—left over right, right over left. "I pleaded with him not to go. What are we going to do? How will we survive without Abe? I won't let my children work in those mills," she said a moment before she let out a shriek, grabbed her stomach and collapsed to the floor, shaking violently.

Leah and Cecelia fell to the floor and grabbed her. David ran to the telephone to call the doctor.

Two hours later a six-week premature baby was delivered to Sarah and her missing husband. With Sarah in bed resting and Cecelia by her side to watch over her, David, Leah, and Solomon huddled quietly in the living room with the doctor.

"He's quite fragile," the doctor said. "Only God can help him. If he survives, you'll know he's a fighter."

Leah went to Sarah's bedroom and motioned Cecelia to come out. "How is she?"

"Sleeping fitfully. She keeps mumbling, 'I'm going to name him Abraham.'"

Leah gave Cecelia a feeble smile, bowed her head and crept silently into Sarah's room to take her turn at her sister-in-law's bedside.

Suddenly Sarah bolted up. "Abe, is that you?"

Leah pushed gently on Sarah's shoulders to make her lie down. "It's me, Leah."

As soon as Leah removed her hands, Sarah jerked up again. "I want a newspaper. Why won't any of you get me a newspaper?"

"Sarah, please lie down."

Giving Leah a weak push, Sarah said, "Get out of my way."

Leah resisted, and though shorter and lighter than Sarah, it was not hard for her to hold down her exhausted sister-in-law.

The bedroom door burst open. Waving a piece of paper, Solomon flew into the room, rushing to Sarah's side. "Abe is okay. He didn't sail on the Titanic. He missed the boat."

Leah exclaimed, "How do you know?"

"This wire just came. It's addressed to Sarah and says, 'Missed the boat. Will be in England another week. Love, Abe'."

Sarah snatched the paper. "Where did you get this? You made this up. You know Abe is dead and you won't tell me."

"No. This is real."

"Why? You tell me why. He was so set on sailing on that boat and Abe never changes his mind."

"I don't know why. All I know is this wire is real."

She crinkled the paper into a ball and threw it at him. "I don't believe you. Why are you hiding the truth from me? Where is my baby? Bring me my baby."

Leah consulted with Cecelia and they decided to bring in the baby, hoping he would calm Sarah down.

Sarah hugged him to her breast, rocking him gently from side to side. "My little Abraham. You'll listen to your mama, won't you, darling? You won't be stubborn like your father was."

Cecelia left Leah alone and conferred with Solomon. They decided he should take their children home. The noise from Sarah's own herd was bad enough. No sense in adding more voices to the chorus.

At his apartment, Solomon found another wire wedged between the door and the frame. He tore it open, read it, begged a neighbor to watch the kids and ran back to Sarah. "This is why Abe missed the boat. My father died before they were to sail."

CHAPTER 24

The past two weeks had been filled with both sadness and elation for Sarah. Sadness for Solomon and David. Euphoria for herself that her husband had been saved. On the day of his arrival home, she was up and about, making sure the house was in readiness.

"What are you doing out of bed?" Cecelia yelled.

Sarah clutched the banister as she made her way down the stairs. "My Abe will be home today. I have to prepare for him."

Cecelia ran up the stairs to help her. "You're such a *balboste.* I give up. Go ahead, rip up your insides."

Sarah kissed her sister-in-law on the cheek. "I will never forget how you helped me, but now I have to make everything ready for Abe's arrival."

Sarah pushed her tired, wounded body around her house, making sure all was in order. Everything had to be just right for her love, who was returning to her by the grace of God. Her own health was not important. Only her husband mattered.

****

Solomon paced the floor in the great room of the Jersey City railroad terminal, waiting for Abe and their mother to arrive on the ferry from Ellis Island. He had been prompt in getting there because he knew there would be no hold up at immigration. First-class passengers were given special treatment, skipping the medical and oral examinations the steerage passengers had to endure at Ellis Island before they were cleared to enter America. And with Abe to guide their mother, the time would be cut even shorter.

Spotting them, Solomon rushed to his mother and wrapped her in his husky arms. He said in Russian, "I'm so sorry about Dad. But don't worry, you are in good hands now."

"Solomon, it was unbelievable," Abe said. "All of London was in a panic over the sinking. I didn't even know if my telegram would be sent. When did you get it?"

"Three days after she went down."

"Three days! How is Sarah?"

Solomon turned his head and fumbled with the luggage. "We took care of her. Everything is fine."

"What is it?"

"Sarah delivered the baby early," Solomon said. Looking up at Abe he added quickly, "But she and your son are doing fine."

"Thank God," Abe said for what must have been the fiftieth time in two weeks.

When his father died the day before they were to sail, Abe had cursed him for being true to his mother to the end. When he vented his anger, his mother had said, "Abraham, do not speak ill of the dead. He was your father."

"You call him a father? What did he give any of us besides the choice of starving or working the farm for him while he was off gadding about town? And what did he give you? Ten children you had to bring up by yourself in that run down shack he called a house? Now, in death, he still denies you. He took away your one chance to sail on the finest luxury liner in the world."

The family was observing the traditional seven days of mourning when they heard the news of the Titanic disaster. Suddenly, Abe realized he had not sent Sarah a cable telling her he missed the boat. He ran to the telegraph office, only to find the lines hopelessly overburdened with the disaster news. He left his messages, his fee, and a bonus for the clerk, and received a promise that the telegrams would be sent as soon as possible.

On his walk back to Dan's house, Abe had raised his head to the heavens and asked his father, "How did you know? Were you given a message?"

That night, during the *kadish*—the mourner's prayer—Abe tried to make his peace with his father by saying an extra prayer in his memory.

****

Seeing the taxi arrive, Sarah ran from the house, threw herself on Abe and kissed him ferociously. Oblivious to her mother-in-law, she clung to him as if she was a passenger on the Titanic and he was her life preserver.

Kissing the tears from her cheeks, Abe said, "I love you. I missed you every minute I was away."

"I missed you so much," Sarah said.

"Solomon told me about the baby. How is he?"

"He's doing well."

"Thank God."

"I know its not tradition, but I wouldn't allow the *bris* until you came home."

"I'm glad. I want to name him Emanuel after my father."

"Of course," Sarah said, and kissed him again.

David, Leah and Cecelia had followed Sarah out of the house. While Sarah greeted Abe, they showered Chava with hugs, kisses and condolences. When Abe saw the opportunity for him to jump in, he freed himself from Sarah's bear hug and said, "Mama, this is Sarah."

"Da, I guessed," Chava said in Russian.

A blush on her cheeks from embarrassment at the way she had pounced on her husband, Sarah regained her composure and said in Russian, "Mother Bressler, I am so sad about Father." She leaned forward and kissed her mother-in-law. "But you have no worries now. You are with your family and we will take care of you."

Tears flowed from Chava's eyes.

Abe pulled a handkerchief from his pocket and blotted his mother's face. "Mama, you're home now. You're safe. There are no Cossacks here. Only people who love you."

Sarah took one of Chava's arms and Abe the other and they escorted her into the house.

"You must be hungry," Sarah said. "I have prepared a wonderful meal to celebrate your arrival."

A playful shrill of laughter drifted up from the basement.

"Are those the children?" Chava asked.

"Yes," Abe said.

"Can I see them?"

"Of course," Sarah said, and went to call them.

A moment later, six pairs of running feet—four from Abe's and Sarah's brood and two from Solomon's and Cecelia's—trooped up the stairs and into the foyer. As each was introduced, Chava kissed her fingertips and tenderly touched the child's cheek.

Isidore accepted his new grandmother's affection by reaching up. When Chava bent down, he hugged her neck and kissed her cheek. Ira wiped Chava's kiss off with a swipe of his hand. Samuel and Jerry ran back and wrapped themselves around Sarah's legs. Frank and Melvin followed Isidore's lead and kissed their grandmother, but without the hug.

"They are all beautiful," Chava said.

The greetings over, Abe ordered, "Back to the playroom."

"They are not eating with us?" Chava asked.

Sarah's eyes sprang wide. She glanced at Abe, and thought, *Maybe bringing his mother here will be a good thing and not another chore for me*. Smiling at Chava, Sarah said, "I didn't know what time you were going to arrive so I fed them earlier. Come, let me show you to your room so you can freshen up before dinner."

The entourage followed Abe, Sarah and Chava up the stairs. The bedroom Sarah had prepared for Chava had a four-poster bed, lace curtains, damask wallpaper, a rocker, an upholstered easy chair, a dresser and a private bathroom.

Overwhelmed, tears came to Chava's eyes again. She had been to her brother-in-law Isaac's house many times for Passover seders and Rosh Hashanah dinners, but she never thought she would ever live in such a palace. The only luxury she had back in Latvia was a pump in the kitchen so she could draw water without going outside.

Sarah took Chava in her arms and said, "I know how you feel. I felt the same way when I first came to America. Don't you fret. We're all here to help you get adjusted."

****

By eight o'clock, Sarah had put her mother-in-law and her children to bed and was in her own bed, propped up against the padded headboard, waiting for Abe to emerge from the bathroom. As he slipped under the covers, she draped herself over him and said, "Now I can welcome you home properly."

****

Lying next to him, sucking in deep breaths, a nagging thought flashed through Sarah's mind and veiled her happiness with a touch of trepidation. With all his repeating many times over, "I missed you, I love you," he never did say the words she wanted to hear the most: "I'll never leave you again."

CHAPTER 25

The sun shone brightly in a cloudless sky on this first Sabbath in June. Cradling baby Emanuel in her arms, Sarah stood at the window, watching her children play on the swings and slide the carpenter erected as a coming home present from their father.

"You're getting stronger everyday," she said to her baby. "Soon you will be out there playing with your brothers."

She lay Emanuel in his bassinet and covered him with a light cotton blanket. Abe would be home from Shul soon. He had been going religiously since his trip. She thought, *I would too, if what happened to him had happened to me.*

Sarah's mother-in-law spent the Sabbath at Cecelia's and Solomon's. Sarah missed her. At first, Sarah had thought a sixty-year-old woman would be another burden to cope with. She soon found out how wrong she was. Chava loved the children and she quickly became a live-in nanny. Feeling as if she had been released from jail, Sarah attended every Paterson League suffrage meeting, visited the library, and browsed the new fashions in the department stores at her leisure. She had never felt so free.

The idea hit her out of no where. Maybe it came because it was such a beautiful day, or maybe because Abe had been in such a good mood these weeks since he returned. It didn't matter where it came from. It was a good idea.

****

Sarah served Abe lunch on the porch. A few lilac and dogwood blossoms still hung from their branches. Wild flowers popped up in the woods across the street, filling the late spring air with their sweet fragrance. Birds flitted gleefully among the trees.

Sitting in the white wicker chair next to him, she smiled and nibbled on her corned beef sandwich. Swallowing, she inhaled deeply to bolster her courage. "Did you know there is a resolution before the New Jersey Senate in favor of women voting?"

"It'll never pass."

"It would if enough pressure were put on the senators."

"Who is going to do that?"

"The New Jersey Education Association, for one."

His mouth half full, he replied, "That group is mostly women. They can't vote. Why should the senators listen to them?"

"If some influential men, like a judge or some big mill owners, talked to the senators, they might be inclined to be in favor of the resolution."

"Why would the mill owners do that?" He turned to look questioningly at her. "Do you really think you need to vote? Don't you have enough to worry about with the house and the children to take care of?"

She had heard that argument so many times in the past few months it no longer angered her. What bewildered her was Abe carrying on such a low-key conversation about a subject he scorned. She translated that to mean business was good. She could always tell by Abe's mood how things were going at the shop. *Business must be exceptionally wonderful*, she thought, and pressed on.

"Did you know over twenty percent of women work out of the home?"

"And you're one of the lucky ones. You don't have to."

"What about those who aren't so lucky? They bring money into their house and put food on their table. Shouldn't they have a vote?"

"What would they do with it? I know something about this issue. Women want the vote to use it to control men."

"That's ridiculous."

"Is it? Why are the Woman's Temperance League and the Anti-Saloon League so mixed up with the suffrage groups?"

"Is that bad? Liquor makes men do some awful things."

"I like a *schnapps* now and then. Are you going to deny me that?"

"Of course not."

"But a lot of women would."

Sarah didn't reply. The conversation had gone too far a field. She was well aware that many of the woman's suffrage leaders were devout moralists. Susan B. Anthony was a Quaker. So was Alice Paul. Their trumpeting their morality was a major reason why men had their backs up so strongly against the vote.

Staring out over her front lawn, she saw a couple of robin red breasts pecking the ground for worms. She tore a piece of bread from her sandwich and threw it toward them. They fluttered away for a moment, then came back and attacked the morsel. She said, "This is the time of year I like living so far away from downtown. With no noise from the factories, no soot or noxious odors, it's almost like living on a farm in the country."

"It is peaceful," Abe said. He followed her lead and threw some crumbs to the birds.

Thinking him still receptive, she said, "Nine states have given women the right to vote. Why can't New Jersey? In the original New Jersey Constitution women had the vote."

"I didn't know that. What happened?"

"A hundred years ago some man almost lost an election. He claimed fraud and deceit by women, and since the legislature was all male, he was able to have the constitution revised to allow only white males to vote."

"Doesn't seem fair, does it?"

Did he really say that? Encouraged, she was ready to press on when he added, "But I think it's for the best."

Her excitement evaporated. Almost in tears, she demanded, "Why do you say that?"

"Think about who these suffragists are. I play cards with some very important people . . ."

I know that. That's why I'm trying to persuade you to talk to them.

". . . Some of these women have approached my friends and offered a deal. They said they would be willing to accept literacy tests for voting, and if they were given the vote, they would be in favor of limiting immigration. Of course that backfired on them because my friends need immigrants to run the mills."

"And they need immigrant women and children, too, for the menial jobs so they can pay them half what a man makes. I can see why they're afraid. If women vote, that part of their labor force would be in jeopardy of being made illegal, and their profits would disappear."

"It's unfortunate some children have to work, but it's not my problem."

"It was almost mine."

He spun to face her.

His attention in her grasp, she pushed on. "When I thought you had died on the Titanic, I was petrified our children would have to go to work in the mills to keep us from starving."

Taking Sarah's hand, he said, "I never thought about that. It must have been horrifying for you. First thing Monday, I'm going to look into life insurance."

With that said, Abe gave her hand a reassuring squeeze, then a pat, picked up his newspaper from the floor and opened it.

A little miffed that he had ended their conversation so abruptly, Sarah thought about continuing, but quickly changed her mind. Abe had showed her he was done with this discussion. Trying to pursue it would only ruin this beautiful day.

At least something good came from this talk, she thought. If he buys life insurance, she and the children would be taken care of if something happened to him. As far as trying to help the rest of the unfortunate children in town who slaved in the mills, she'd think of something. She hoped business would remain good to keep Abe and his friends in a receptive mood.

PART III

1913

CHAPTER 26

January 27

Solomon and two fellow union organizers, Ewald Koettgen and Adolf Lessig, sat at a corner table in the Nag's Head Bar, a meeting place for laborers since before the present owner, Ben Goldberg, had bought it from Abe. Other than changing the name and Goldberg running a bookmaking operation out of the upstairs apartment, everything in the bar was exactly as Abe had left it. Piping hot food still flowed out of the kitchen in ample serving, and the waitresses still wore low-cut uniforms.

Solomon sipped a beer while he scanned the sports page of the *Paterson Evening News*. "I can't believe they took Thorpe's Olympic medals away," he said.

Ewald snatched the paper from Solomon and turned it back to the front page. He jammed his finger at the headline, "Strike At Dogherty's." "We didn't come here to talk about Thorpe's troubles. We got our own problems."

Taking back his paper, Solomon folded it and laid it on the table. "Sorry."

"If we don't shut down Dogherty's four-loom system, thousands are going to be put out of work," Ewald said. "We got to stop him. We got to get others to join our strike."

"How we going to do that?" Adolf Lessig asked.

Solomon shrugged. "So far, the other mill owners are holding to their word. Dogherty's mill is the only one to break the agreement not to put a weaver on four looms."

Ewald smacked his hand on the table, the loud bang drawing eyes in their direction. "We had a deal. No four looms. We're right back where we were fifteen years ago."

"That little change from one loom to two looms to a weaver killed my father," Lessig said. "He was out of work for six months. We almost starved to death."

"We're not falling for that scam this time," Ewald said. "A lot of people still remember what happened. The generous bosses paid twice the going rate to run the two looms. The only problem was, half the weavers were fired, and wages soon sank back to what they were because the unemployed weavers begged for a job at any pay, and the bosses quickly accommodated them."

"It's gonna be the same this time," Solomon said.

"Only worse," Ewald said. "There are double the number of mills today than fifteen years ago. Many more of us will be out of work. We can't let Dogherty get away with it."

Solomon's face took on a worried look. "He will if no one else breaks the deal."

"I don't suspect your dyers will help us," Lessig pleaded.

"My people are still angry about you weavers not helping us in '02 when we asked you to join our strike."

"You dyers refused to join our strike in '99," Ewald said bitterly.

"Stop it," Lessig said. "When are we going to end this stupid feud?"

Solomon raised his hands in surrender and fought hard to control a grin as he thought about what it must have been like four hundred years ago in Florence, Italy. During a celebration to capture the Queen's favor, the silk dyers and weavers staged a mock battle, with the dyers winning by tossing the weavers into the Arno River.

Ewald acknowledged Lessig's chastisement with a nod and said, "Some union officers we are. Out of twenty-four thousand silk workers in this town, we've recruited nine-hundred to the Industrial Workers of the World. And most of them work with me at Dogherty's."

"I'm through being a slave to the bosses and their lackies," Adolf spat out. "I'm through being scared he'll fire me if I look at him the wrong way or say something he don't like."

"There's nothing you can do about it," Ewald said.

One of the men who had been watching the pool game walked over and asked Ewald, "How's it going out at Dogherty's?"

"We got him beat, Kurt. How about you guys from Diamond Silk joining us in a sympathy strike?"

"I don't know, buddy," the shop steward at Diamond Silk Company answered. "You do have our sympathy, but there's no way I can talk my men into a strike. The winter's a tough time to be without money for coal."

Kurt wished Ewald luck and returned to the pool table.

"See what we're up against," Ewald said. "As long as no more mill owners join Dogherty's with that four-loom system, we're alone. But if Dogherty wins, every weaver in this town is dead. We have to get more people to join our strike."

A roar from the area of the dart board cut off their conversation. Looking over, Solomon saw a dart planted dead center in the bulls eye. His eyes drifted around the room. His fellow workers were in high spirits, drinking and giving the waitresses a little good-natured abuse by pushing nickel tips into their cleavage.

"These men are not in a strike mood," Solomon said.

"Then we'll have to put them in the mood," Ewald replied. "I'm going to write the IWW headquarters in Chicago. Maybe they can send us some help. If Dogherty fills his mill with scabs, the Industrial Workers of the World union is through here."

"Maybe Elizabeth Flynn will come," Solomon said. "Look what she did in Lawrence last year. She shut down the whole town tighter than a drum. Got the workers good raises from those American Woolen Company bosses."

"And violent, too," Lessig said. "Children beaten, people killed. They had to call in the State Militia."

"We don't need that here," Ewald said.

"Sometimes it's the only way," Lessig countered.

"No!" Solomon insisted. "Look what happened to us in '02 when we were violent. I won't be a party to violence."

"Okay," Lessig said, trying to make his voice sound convincing. "Maybe if Elizabeth Flynn, 'Big Bill' Haywood and some of the other leaders of the IWW come here, we can spread this strike." He raised his glass in a salute. "All power to the workers."

"All power to the workers," Solomon and Ewald chimed in.

CHAPTER 27

February 12

Sarah looped her arm around Abe's and felt him squeeze her hand as he escorted her across the gilded lobby toward the ballroom in New York City's Astor Hotel. As he brushed some imaginary lint off the lapel of his tuxedo jacket and ran the palm of his hand over his hair, Sarah thought she had never seen him this anxious. Tonight was the annual Silk Association of America's charity ball. Weeks ago, when he told her they were going and "to buy a smashing dress," she was ecstatic. She had never been to a formal ball.

As heads turned in their direction, Sarah could feel Abe's chest puff out with pride. She was draped neck-to-toe in a blue and gold evening gown with an irregular hip yoke and the skirt was laced up with gold silk cord. The dress puffed at the shoulders, tucked at her waist, and fell to the floor in flattering lines that slimmed her hips and hid her slightly rounded belly.

"You are beautiful," Abe said, taking her hand. "You certainly will be the belle of the ball tonight."

"Thank you, darling. And you are very handsome."

Abe had been unusually attentive to her since the Titanic sank, and it wasn't only in their bed. Suddenly he was talkative at dinner, he asked about the children, and he even listened when she complained about the prices in the market. He still didn't agree with woman suffrage, but at least he heard her out before rebuffing her. Did that narrow escape really make him open his eyes and see what he almost lost, or was he still numb from realizing how close he came to dieing? She didn't care, as long as he kept on this path.

Entering the wide ballroom doors, Abe and Sarah hesitated, bedazzled by the chatter from the huge crowd and the glitter from the eighteen crystal chandeliers. Irving Pincus, Abe's mentor and closest associate in the trade, had been keeping an eye out for them and rushed to greet them. Abe introduced Sarah to the older, stoop-shouldered man.

Pincus took her gloved hand gently in both of his and said, "All the women will be jealous of you tonight, my dear."

Sarah's creamy white complexion took on a slightly red glow as she graciously accepted Pincus's flattery with a smile. "Mr. Pincus, I am so happy to meet you. Abe has told me so much about you."

"Only good things, I hope."

"Only," Sarah said. "After all," she added silently, "how much could he say about anybody on the train and ferry ride in from Paterson?"

Of all the people Abe met in the silk trade, it was Irving Pincus, more than anyone, including his brothers, who had put him in the business.

****

After his lambasting by Sarah's father, Abe vowed to change Mr. Singer's mind. To do that, he had to change his occupation. He thought about buying a dry-goods store and becoming a merchant, but that life seemed so boring. That left the silk industry. After calculating the money he could get from selling his bar, he realized he didn't have enough to buy a mill. Even if he did, he didn't have the knowledge to run it.

Discussing his plight with his brother, Abe learned that jobbing silk yarn overages and seconds could be highly profitable for an enterprising person. Little money was needed to get into that end of the business.

"The mill owners don't want to sell their overages to their own customers," Solomon had said.

"Overages?"

"From weighting and stretching."

"What's that?"

"Weighting is treating the raw silk with metal salts like tetrachloride of tin mixed with tungstate of soda. It bulks up the yarn. Makes it denser. If you weight it, you can use less yarn when you weave fabric."

"And stretching?"

"The raw filaments can be stretched up to twenty percent."

"Doesn't everyone know that?"

"Sure, but there's also a working loss the dye houses insist on."

"Working loss?"

"Breakage. And spoilage. Say the deal to dye a batch of yarn calls for a twelve percent stretch—theoretically you can get twenty percent, but that's tough to do under factory conditions—and a five percent working loss. You following?" Solomon asked.

"So far."

"With a thousand yards you should get eleven hundred twenty less five percent loss on the original thousand, ending up with a thousand seventy yards. If the mill owner has less working loss or more stretch, he keeps it and sells it off to jobbers."

"Why jobbers? Why not sell it to their own customers?"

"Because they don't want their customers to know how much stretch they actually get. If they sell the overages to a jobber, it gets mixed in with all the other odd lots and seconds the jobber deals in."

"I get it," Abe said, and realized right then that all it would take was a little ingenuity and salesmanship ability to become a jobber. He also quickly learned that it took one more thing: the ability to get goods. That was taken care of by something he also knew a lot about—bribery. He had been paying off the precinct chief, ward captain and alderman for years to keep his bar running smoothly. When he was approached with a proposition by a patron in his bar, Frank Lucano, master dyer at National Silk Dyeing Company, Abe knew exactly how to handle it.

"I heard you talking to your brother about the jobbing business," Lucano had said. "If I owned this joint, I'd never give it up for no jobbing business. Why you doing it?"

"I have my reasons," Abe had said.

"Yeah, well, I hope they're good ones, 'cause jobbers come and go in this town."

"I plan to stay around for a while."

Lucano shrugged and came to the point. "If I can get you the seconds and some of the first quality overages my boss sells off, you want 'em?"

Abe studied Lucano for a minute, wondering why this guy was being so magnanimous. He didn't care for Frank Lucano. The man got loud when he had a couple of beers. "Sure, I want them," Abe said.

"The only way I can get 'em for you is to offer the boss a little more than he's getting now. And you got to give me an additional five percent of what you pay him. It'll mean less profit for you, but it will put you in business fast. You want the deal?"

"Absolutely," Abe said without hesitation.

"Stop by the shop tomorrow morning. I got a good deal for you."

The instant Abe opened the dye house door, the chemical-laden air pricked his eyes and glazed them with tears. A few breaths and his throat felt as if he had swallowed nails. The opened awning-style windows and whirling fans did little to remove the caustic odors. He fought back the urge to flee. His mission was too important. He had to prove to Sarah's parents he could be more than just a saloon owner.

Men, their clothes spattered with colors, leaned over vats filled with hot colored liquid. As they stirred the contents with large wooden sticks, steam drifted up and enveloped their heads in a thin gray fog. Bare lightbulbs, screwed into sockets at the ends of double strands of black cords, dangled a few feet over the vats. Pipes and valves were everywhere. The few rays of sun that dared to penetrate the streaked windows to pass through the humid air refracted into shafts of dingy light.

Up until that moment, Abe had thought his customers exaggerated many of their gripes, like their boss making them taste the dye bath to see if it was acidic enough. Seeing it actually happening, he garnered new-found sympathy for his customers. Although this wasn't the dye house where Solomon worked, he assumed his brother's working conditions were similar.

Without knowing what he was looking at, Abe bought a batch of tender sewing thread from Lucano. When he tried to sell it to garment manufacturers in New York City, the kindest welcome he received was a laugh. The rudest, "You idiot, get out of here with that junk!"

What little Abe knew about the silk business, he knew even less about garment manufacturing. He soon learned that the women sewers were paid by the number of pieces they produced. The faster they sewed, the more money they made. If their thread continually broke because it was tender or weak, causing them to stop sewing to re-thread their machines, they would howl at their boss and maybe even walk off the job.

Abe cried his woes to Solomon over a beer in his bar. "What a jerk I was letting that guy rob me like that."

"Yeah, you were. You should of discussed the deal with me first," Solomon said. "I would of told you tender goods are worthless."

While they talked, Abe peeled off a long strip of thread, doubled it and doubled it again, then twisted in around and around. In his frustration he gave his hank of sewing thread a yank. It didn't break.

"Look at this," Abe said.

"So what?" Solomon answered. "That wad is too think to sew with."

"Where can I get this stuff twisted together?"

"You'll be throwing more good money after bad."

"I don't care. Give me a name."

Solomon directed Abe to Irving Pincus's processing plant. Pincus was a contractor for small weavers. While a few large silk manufacturers were able to do all the operations, from turning raw silk into woven goods, many of Paterson's three hundred mills, as well as the mills in Allentown and Scranton, Pennsylvania only had looms and needed a processor to ready the silk for them to weave.

Pincus gave Abe a tour of his mill, explaining how silk-worms make their cocoons by extruding two, five-one-thousandth inch thick filaments from holes in their heads in unbroken lengths that can stretch up to three thousand feet, and stuck the filaments together with a gummy secretion.

"Once dried, that secretion becomes so hard it could scratch polished steel," Pincus had said. "We take the raw silk skeins and wash them in saponified soap, with little or no alkali, for up to five hours to remove the gummy stuff and separate the two filaments. That's why Paterson is so good for silk processing. The Passaic river-water is soft. It has very little minerals."

In showing Abe the washing process, Pincus pointed out, "It doesn't take a lot of skill to open the burlap bales from the silk-worm farms and put the skeins in those big vats, then ring them out and hang them up to dry. That's why we use boys for this operation. I only have to pay them three dollars a week.

"After the skeins are washed and dried, they go to the winding, room where they are wound onto octagonal reels called 'swifts,' which are then mounted on racks and the yarn wound onto spools," Pincus explained. "When you see a slub in silk fabric, it's from where the filament broke and had to be spliced. The neater the splice the smaller the slub. That's why we use women in this operation. They have daintier, more nimble hands than men. And we can get away paying them five to seven dollars a week less than a man."

Pincus next led Abe to the doubling and throwing processes. "Doubling is combining filaments. Throwing is actually twisting the yarn," Pincus said.

Abe shook his head. *These names are ridiculous*, he thought. You throw a baseball, not yarn. Why didn't they just say "twisting"?

"The spools from the winding room are stacked on those pegged racks, and two or more filaments are combined on one spool, depending on what type of yarn we are making. For tram—that's filling yarn, the crossways yarn in the fabric—we double it first, then we take it to the throwing section and give it two or three twists to the inch. For warp yarn we throw it before we double it, giving it twelve or more twists to the inch, depending on the end use."

"Why do you twist the warp yarn before you combine it?" Abe asked.

"For strength. The twisting gives it strength. The more twists, the stronger it becomes."

"Doesn't the filling yarn need strength?"

"Not as much. There can be up to two to three times as many warp yarns than filling yarns to an inch of woven fabric."

"I see."

"After throwing the warp yarn, we take it to the doubling area, combine two or more filaments, then take it back to throwing and give the combined yarn another ten or twelve twists to the inch."

Pincus walked Abe down the length of the building, pointing out the doubling and throwing sections. Abe watched the throwing process for a moment, and asked, "Aren't those octagonal reels taking up the twisted, sorry, thrown yarn the same ones I saw the washed silk being placed on after it was dried?"

"You've been attentive. They are. Before we can put the yarn on bobbins or warp beams, it has to be dyed, and it's dyed in skeins similar in size to the ones that we washed at the beginning of the operation. After dyeing, we again wind the yarn on spools. From there we put the finished yarn on bobbins and beams."

Pincus led Abe to a room where colored spools hung on pegged racks that stretched from ceiling to floor and for couple of hundred feet down the mill floor. The yarns coming off the spools were so numerous they almost looked like a piece of fabric. "How many spools are in here?"

"Thousands," Pincus said. "Each one of those racks can hold up to five hundred spools. The yarn is pulled off those spools and is slowly wound up on the metal cylinders you see over there. The narrow cylinders, three to four inches wide, are beams for the ribbon weavers. The wider ones—thirty-six to forty-eight inches wide, and weighing up to five hundred pounds when full—go to broad silk weavers.

"This is the most expensive operation in the mill. A thirty-six-inch wide beam with four hundred warp yarns to the inch takes over fourteen thousand individual yarns. They have to be kept strictly parallel and under the same tension. These men are highly skilled and can make up to twenty-five dollars a week."

The tour over, Pincus took Abe's weak thread, doubled it to four strands thick and twisted it for strength.

"My brother tells me it's too thick for sewing," Abe said.

"Garments, yes. Take it to the cheap luggage and satchel manufacturers. For the right price, they'll take all you have."

Pincus' little bit of creative processing turned Abe's first venture in dealing with silk yarn seconds from a potential two hundred dollar loss into a hundred and thirty dollar profit and a vast amount of knowledge.

****

As Pincus guided Abe and Sarah through the crowded ballroom toward their table, the two men nodded and said hellos to business associates and acquaintances. Sarah tried not to seem obvious in her scrutiny of the women's jewelry and dresses. In turn, the women glanced back at her, some down their noses, others as curious as she, and still others glaring at their husbands, who smiled at her.

They stopped at a table, one short of the rear wall. "It's a little far from the dance floor," Pincus said. "With that thirty-piece orchestra, you don't want to be too close. You won't be able to hear yourself talk."

Sitting at the table with the Pincuses and the Bresslers were Horace Belmont, owner of Belmont Silk, and his wife, Abigail, Arthur Gross of Paterson Silk and his wife, Sadie, Nathan Diamond, owner of Diamond Silk Mill, and his wife, Florence. During the introductions, Sarah let her eyes linger an extra moment on Florence, wondering where she had seen her before. Florence held Sarah's eyes and almost imperceptibly shook her head in a warning to Sarah not to say anything.

CHAPTER 28

"Delicious," Abe said, popping the last piece of his filet mignon into his mouth. He put down his fork and pushed his plate a few inches forward. Shifting in his chair, he glanced over his shoulder into the depths of the room for what must have been the tenth time.

He and Sarah had been the last of their party to arrive. The seats left for them placed Abe with his back to the room, making him uncomfortable. With the band on a break, the boisterous conversations, accompanied by the soft clinking of gold flatware against bone china, had dropped to a more moderate level.

Returning his attention to the table, Abe said, "Nice party."

The red-jacketed waiter emptied the champagne bottle into the glasses, turned the bottle upside down in the ice bucket and removed the stand.

Pincus lit a cigar, blew the gray smoke toward the haze hovering around the chandeliers and said, "I read the memorial to Abraham Lincoln will cost two million. That's going to be something."

"I don't know why it has to look like a Greek Temple," Horace Belmont said. "Why can't it look American."

"What do you mean, American?" Pincus asked.

"Like a log cabin," Abe joked.

"I think Mr. Bacon's design is perfect," Arthur Goss said. "Lincoln was a great man and should have a stately shrine."

Sarah turned to Abigail Belmont and said, "Abe and I went to see *The Sunshine Girl* at the Knickerbocker. Did you see it?"

"Not yet. Was it good?"

"Hilarious. Don't miss it."

"You think Taft will send the troops into Mexico?" Nathan Diamond asked.

"I doubt he'll do anything," Pincus offered. "Wilson gets inaugurated next month. Taft will let the problem fester and dump it in Wilson's lap."

"The whole world is going crazy," Horace Belmont added. "Revolutions in Mexico. The Servians, Bulgarians and Greeks fighting in the Balkans."

"It's the radicals," Nathan Diamond said. "We have to get rid of the radicals like that Elizabeth Flynn woman stirring up trouble all over the country. First she causes those riots in Massachusetts, then she gets the hotel workers here in New York all riled up. It's about time someone put her in her place."

"She's only trying to help poor people improve their lives," Sarah said.

An eerie quiet enveloped the table. The men directed icy stares at Sarah and the women sat in shocked silence at one of their own interrupting a man's conversation.

Arthur Gross broke the silence first, but he did not address Sarah. "Abe, does your wife side with these radicals?"

His hand hidden by the table, Abe squeezed Sarah's leg, signaling her to keep quiet. "Of course not, Arthur. What Sarah is trying to say is, she's a little concerned that some people don't have the where-with-all to make it on their own and they need help. The problem, as I see it, is, they're turning to the wrong people for that help."

Horace Belmont glared at Sarah and said, "That's why we have this annual ball. To help the poor. Tonight's affair will raise hundreds of dollars to feed and clothe the less fortunate."

A slow boil simmered inside Sarah. She hadn't been lectured since she had left her parent's home. Ignoring Abe's signal, she said, "If instead of this lavish party, we each took a hundred dollars and donated it directly to a worthy cause, it would do much more good. I almost cry when I go downtown shopping and see those poor children with no warm clothes and worn out shoes. I thank God every day they aren't my children."

Waiters descended on the table. The diners sat in stone silence while the dishes were removed and replaced with coffee cups. When the attendants left, the broad beamed Mrs. Gross tried to change the subject. "How many children do you have, dear?"

"Five boys."

Through a weak smile, Abigail Belmont said, "You certainly are lucky to have kept your figure."

"Thank you," Sarah replied, and pressed her point. "I feel that we who have so much could be more charitable to those not as fortunate."

Nathan Diamond scowled. "What do we have here, one of those Red's who are running around saying the workers have a right to own our businesses?"

"I am not saying that. I just think everyone should have enough to eat."

Belmont asked, "What do you mean by more charitable—pay them more? I pay my people a fair wage. The same as every other mill owner."

"If it's so fair, why are there so many strikes?" Sarah asked.

"Because of radicals like you stirring up the workers," Belmont said.

"I beg your pardon, Horace," Abe cut in. "Sarah is not a radical. She does not go running around the country advocating violence. What she means is, she can sympathize with the motives of those who are trying to help the poor and unfortunates like that Elizabeth Flynn girl. But she certainly does not approve of the way they are going about it."

Having defended her, Abe glared at Sarah, his eyebrows cinched in and lips tightly pursed, silently ordering, "Don't say another word."

"Harumph!" Belmont snorted. "And I suppose she thinks women should have the vote, too."

"I do."

Abe leaned over and commanded in her ear, "Not now."

Infuriated, she ignored him. "If women had the vote, those poor girls would never have perished in the Triangle Waist Company factory fire. One hundred and twenty-three women, more than half of them teenagers, died because the exit doors were locked to prevent theft the owners admitted amounted to a maximum of fifteen dollars a year. And for what? A lousy seven dollars for an eighty-four-hour work-week." Sarah's face reddened, and her voice rose when she said, "Did you know the owners of that factory collected sixty thousand dollars from their insurance company, but the families of those that perished were forced to settle for seventy five dollars each?"

Unmoved by Sarah's passion, Belmont asked, "What would you have done?"

"We would have passed safety laws requiring open exits and proper fire escapes, and restricted child labor long before there was a devastating fire."

"I suppose you would have voted for Roosevelt and his Progressive Party?"

"Roosevelt should have been the Republican party nominee over Taft," Sarah said. "In the twelve Republican primaries he won nine outright and got over a million votes. Taft only got seven-hundred thousand."

"So, what? Those primaries were experiments. They didn't count," Belmont retorted.

"This time they didn't, but the people have spoken. They no longer want back room cigar-smoking grafters on that Republican National Committee selecting their candidates. Those that don't listen are in for a hard fall."

"Well! It's people like you that got that Democrat, Wilson, elected."

Abe glared at Sarah and said, "Ladies, gentlemen, you made your points. We're here to have fun."

Sarah refused to yield. "Me, hah! I couldn't vote. It's your ilk that forced Roosevelt to start his own party because you wouldn't listen to the people."

"Socialist!" Belmont shot back.

"If you mean I am a Socialist because I want to do settlement work to help the poor and less fortunate with basic social services like Jane Addams of Hull House in Chicago, then I am a Socialist. Unlike you men, Roosevelt respected women's intelligence. His Bull Moose Party mandated that at least four women sit on the party's national committee. Women are doctors, lawyers, teachers like me, leaders of civic movements. We have the right to vote and to be elected to political office."

A grin plastered across his face, Nathan Diamond said, "Could you imagine women in the legislature? Why, the minute two of them showed up with the same bonnet, they'd declare war."

The men laughed. Even Abe chuckled.

Sarah was about to retort when Florence Diamond sprang on her husband. "And you men have done such a wonderful job running the world . . . ?

That's it! That's where I saw her, Sarah thought. *At a suffrage meeting last week. In the back of the audience, keeping to herself. Good for you, Florence.*

". . . It's about time you men showed some compassion for your workers. The fire escape in that Triangle Company building was only eighteen inches wide. It collapsed, dumping the girls down nine floors, skewering them on an iron picket fence. I want to cry when I think of those poor girls tumbling to their deaths, and the others who jumped from window ledges or down open elevator shafts. You'd think you men grew up in a vacuum. Women were not put on this earth for the purpose of pleasing you and propagating the species. Who raised you? Who tried to teach you right from wrong?"

The men drew back in their chairs, aghast at Florence's vehemence. That left the door wide open for Sarah to jump back in. "It's obvious they didn't learn much. That's why we need the vote to clean up the mess they made."

"Like outlawing alcohol?" Belmont spat out.

"And prostitution, and child labor and separate pay for women despite their doing the same work," Sarah said.

"Bolshevik!" Belmont roared, slapping his napkin down on the table. "Why aren't you out there marching to Washington with Rosalie Jones and her so-called Army of the Hudson?"

"If I could, I would. But I am going to the National Woman's Suffrage meeting at Carnegie Hall next week." Turning to Florence, she asked, "Would you care to accompany me?"

Before Florence could answer, the orchestra started playing again.

"Shall we dance, dear?" Pincus asked his wife. "Join us on the floor, Abe."

Abe grabbed Sarah's hand and yanked her off her chair. Weaving through the tables to the dance floor he asked, "What's this about going to some suffrage meeting in New York?"

"I've made all the arrangements. Your mother is watching the children."

"You're not going."

After eight years of marriage, she had learned that when Abe gave an order it was best to agree with him, whether she was going to obey or not. That way there was no pre-issue argument, and she only had to listen to his ranting and raving after-the-fact.

"Yes, Abe."

"And no more suffrage talk. You're upsetting everyone."

"Yes, Abe."

Taking her in his arms, Abe twirled Sarah into the midst of the circling waltzers. This may have been the first ball she attended, but it was not the first time she had danced with Abe. When he told her they were going to the ball, he also told her he had hired an instructor to come to the house and teach them the latest dances.

Like everything else he did, Abe had learned quickly. For that hour or so once a week when she floated in his firm but gentle arms, she drifted back to the time when they courted. Back then he always wanted to hold her hand when they walked. After they married, he rarely touched her outside their bedroom. Until his return from Europe with his seemingly new attitude toward her and the children, the euphoria of those courtship days had become oh so fleeting. If he hadn't been so amorous in bed, she didn't know how she would have coped these past eight years.

As they spun to the music and she relived those bygone days, a sudden tinge of anxiety crept into her bliss. Her biggest worry was not the day trip to New York, which would have her home before Abe knew she was gone. What troubled her most was how to broach the subject of her planned three-day trip to Washington, D.C. next month to march with the Paterson League in the delegation from the New Jersey Women Suffrage Association. How was he going to react to that?

CHAPTER 29

The music stopped. The dancers ceased their whirling and daintily applauded the orchestra.

"I hate the waltz," Abe said. "Why don't they play a Turkey Trot?"

"They would never play that kind of music here."

"Yeah, yeah."

Pincus worked his way across the dance floor to Abe and asked, "There are some people I think you should meet. Sarah, would you mind going back to the table with Edith?"

Abe drew her aside and whispered, "Talk about the children."

"Yes, Abe."

Motioning to the left, Pincus said, "See that group over there? Those are the men, if you can get in with them, who can really help you."

"Who are they?"

"The man dominating the conversation—the big, heavy set man with the bushy mustache—that's Catholina Lambert."

"I thought I recognized him from his pictures in the newspapers."

"It doesn't matter who the president of the Silk Association is, Lambert sets policy."

"So I've heard."

"If he likes you, you travel with the in crowd. If he doesn't, you'll always be on the fringes of this group."

"And he likes you?"

"I bailed him out of a potentially costly mistake his people caused. A little innovative processing. Like what I do for you."

"Who are the others?"

"The tall, bald fellow is Melvin Dippel of National Ribbon Company. He's the chairman of this year's banquet. The fellow with the part in the middle of his head is William Skinner of William Skinner and Sons. The distinguished-looking man is Judge Joseph Congdon. He owes his judgeship to Lambert. And the one who is on the wrong side of Lambert's lecture is none other than Henry Dogherty himself."

"He doesn't look happy."

"You wouldn't either if Lambert was dictating to you."

"How do you know what Lambert is saying?"

"Because we had a mill owner's meeting yesterday. Take my word for it. Lambert is giving Dogherty a strong warning."

Abe and Pincus approached the group and listened.

"You said your workers would be back in a week," Lambert growled. "It's now two, and they're still out on strike."

Henry Dogherty was not a short man, but the way he was cowering before Lambert's chastising, he looked almost dwarfish. "I know, Mr. Lambert," Dogherty replied. "but believe me, they will be back to work next week. They can't hold out."

Tapping his index finger on Dogherty's chest, Lambert said, "Let me tell you what I see. Your weavers are holding a very tight picket line around your mill. No one is crossing it. And there is a lot of sympathy for them all over town."

"But no other mill joined them in this strike," Dogherty answered. "And look at the laborers at Scranton Textile in Pennsylvania. Their strike failed. They went back to work on four looms. Take my word for it, my people will be back to work this week."

"You're making us nervous, Henry, and we don't like it."

"Don't be . . ."

"Don't interrupt me," Lambert ordered, his nostrils flaring. "We can't afford to gamble. From all the early signs, business is going to be very good this year. We don't want to give the laborers an excuse to cause trouble. I think you should put off this experiment until next year. What's the big deal? We're all making plenty with two looms to a weaver."

"Mr. Lambert, let me have one more week. Two at the most," Dogherty pleaded. "I designed that whole mill for four looms to a weaver."

"A warning, Henry. The first sign your strike is spreading, you'll have me to deal with. Is that clear?"

"Yes, Mr. Lambert," Dogherty said, and fled as if running from a charging bull.

Pincus, with Abe at his side, moved in to fill the vacancy in the circle of men. Shaking Lambert's outstretched hand, Pincus said, "I would like you gentlemen to meet a friend of mine." As he introduced each man, Abe shook hands and said, "Pleased to meet you."

Lambert asked, "You work with Irving?"

"I'm a jobber of yarn seconds," Abe answered proudly.

The smiles on the faces of Lambert and his pals vanished. Lambert glanced at Pincus disapprovingly, turned to Melvin Dippel and said, "Damn seconds jobbers. Nothing but parasites praying on other people's misfortunes."

Pincus's mouth hung open. He was too bewildered to say anything.

Abe answered for him. "I don't deal in misfortunes, Mr. Lambert. I deal in problems, and solve them to everyone's best interests."

"You're scavengers," Lambert said.

"That may be so, but scavengers clean up messes made by others. That's what I do best. I turn mistakes into the smallest possible loss," Abe said, whirled on his heels and walked off, with Pincus scurrying behind him.

"I'm sorry, Abe. I had no idea they felt that way."

"Forget it, Irving. It's not your fault they're a bunch of fools."

"I wanted to help you, and I ended up making you some enemies," Pincus said. "I don't understand those guys. Just because they're big operators doesn't mean they don't make seconds. And they all have overages and need jobbers to get rid of them."

"Don't worry about it," Abe said. "Unless they're ready to buy up all the overages and seconds in every dye house in Paterson, and in Scranton and Allentown too, they can't hurt me."

"I hope you're right."

Weaving through the tables, Abe unexpectedly came face to face with Jacob Weidmann, Solomon's boss. Weidmann was a bulky man with a barrel chest and an even bigger gut.

"Hello, Bressler," Weidmann said, his alcohol-laden breath forcing Abe to pull back.

"Jacob," Abe acknowledged.

"That brother of yours has been pretty quiet lately, but we all know he's cooking up something. Why don't you tell us what it is?"

"I don't know, Jacob, but if I were you I'd be very careful," Abe replied, and elbowed Weidmann out of his way.

Arriving at his table, Abe took one look at the frigid faces glaring at Sarah and asked, "Ready to go?"

"With pleasure."

CHAPTER 30

On the train-ride back to Paterson, Abe barely said a word. At home, he clomped up the stairs. Sarah hurried after him. "Abe, please. You'll wake the children."

In their bedroom he shrugged off his tuxedo jacket and threw it toward the chaise lounge in the corner. It missed and landed on the floor. Spinning around, he pounced on her. "What was all that drivel you prattled on about tonight? Who put those crazy ideas in your head?"

Sarah picked up his jacket, and said, "I have joined the New Jersey Woman's Suffrage Association and the National Child Labor Committee."

"Are you crazy? You'll quit them right now."

"Yes, Abe."

"Don't, 'yes Abe' me. You practically destroyed me with my associates. Those are the people I buy from and sell to." He waved his hand around the room in a frenzy. "Without them, we wouldn't have all this."

"I'm sorry. I didn't know they would be so offended," she said and disappeared into the walk-in closet.

Despite her apology, he wouldn't let it go, and yelled, "Since you have so much time on your hands, you don't need a housekeeper. I'm firing Frances."

Sarah stayed in the closet a long moment to give him time to cool down. She shrugged off her dress and undergarments, put on a robe and released her hair from its bun.

When she didn't answer, he demanded, "Did you hear me?"

His selfish arrogance infuriated her. Emerging, she hollered back, "Then you can make your own dinner when you get home from work."

"You fool! Can't you see what those radicals have done to you. They're home wreckers. Look how they've changed you."

Being called a fool didn't phase her. She had grown numb to the word, having heard him use it on so many people. The rest she had to respond to. "The only one who has changed me is you. I need a useful life."

"You have a useful life here."

"Ohhh," she spat out on a long exhale of breath. "You'll never understand."

"I understand this. There are a bunch of unhappy, degenerate women running around out there wanting to be men, and they're trying to change the way the world works."

She thought, *Why fight him?* Crossing to the bed, she folded down the bed-clothes. Still, she felt she couldn't let him have the last word. "Do you really think, because I want to vote to clean up the slums, take care of the orphans, and give everybody a decent wage,

I'm going to start playing pool, or get drunk in saloons, smoke cigars and wear pants? Maybe you think I'm going to take a job as a fireman or a policeman."

"I wouldn't be surprised, the way you're talking."

"You're the fool, Abe."

In two quick strides he was on her, his powerful hands clamped on her arms. These were not the gentle hands she felt when they danced or when they made love. They were hands she had never felt before. Afraid he was going to strike her and unable to raise her hands to cover her face, she turned her head sideways and pulled her chin into her shoulder.

"Don't ever call me that," he said.

"I'm sorry," she whimpered.

"Look at me."

"Please don't hit me."

"Hit you? Is that what you think of me?" he said and shoved her away.

Sarah bounced off the side of the bed and sprawled onto the floor.

Chava appeared in the doorway and asked in Russian, "What is the commotion?"

His eyes filled with rage, Abe grabbed the afghan off the bed and stormed downstairs.

Chava helped Sarah up. "The Bressler men have a temper sometimes, my dear. You have to remember not to upset him."

Through her sobs and thoughts of *what have I done*, Sarah said, "Everything was going so well these past months. I was so looking forward to a nice evening. I was going to tell him I'm pregnant again."

CHAPTER 31

In the morning, Sarah told her mother-in-law she wasn't feeling well and asked Chava to please tend to the children and Abe's breakfast. She was not ready to see him yet.

As the night wore on, Sarah's focus had changed. *He's the one with the problem, not me. I cater to his every whim. I walk on eggs to please him, and he still abuses me. I'm not going to take it anymore. The mill workers are not the only ones who can go on strike.*

****

Abe was still scowling as he drank his coffee.

Putting a plate of toast on the table, Chava said, "You should not be so cruel to Sarah."

"Stay out of it. It's none of your business."

"This is the way you talk to your mother?"

He grumbled under his breath.

"Sarah is pregnant," Chava said.

Astonishment replaced his grimace. He jumped up from the table, climbed the stairs two at a time, opened their bedroom door a crack and peeked in. Sarah was lying on the bed on her side, facing away from him.

He tiptoed to the bed and sat down. She rolled onto her back.

"I'm sorry," he said.

"Are you?"

He hugged her gently to himself.

How could he be so rough one minute and so gentle the next? she thought before saying, "I'm not a slave."

"I know, I was out of control. Why didn't you tell me?"

She bit her tongue, keeping it inside, *Would it have changed anything*? She'd had her fill of arguments. "I wanted to surprise you last night."

Actually, she had known for a couple of weeks, but had tried to deny it. She prayed it wasn't so, but when her cycle didn't come a second time, she resigned herself to it.

Babies were blessings from heaven. But she had enough blessings. She didn't want this one. What choice did she have? The Comstock Act of 1873 labeled all birth control devices obscene, and outlawed them. Contraceptives could not be sold through the mail or transported across state lines. And with many states passing their own version of obscenity laws, birth control devices were no longer sold over-the-counter. Still, condoms were available in the underground market. Cecelia told her Solomon wore one.

Even if she did break the law and ordered those "rubber goods for gents," as they were clandestinely advertised, Abe would never wear one. And she was afraid to order chemical suppositories, vaginal sponges and medicated tampons touted as "married women's friends." She wasn't about to put something like that inside her without knowing what it was.

Sarah had whispered her anxiety about continually getting pregnant to her doctor and asked, "Can you fit me with a 'womb veil'?"

"I can't, Sarah. I'm sorry. Comstock spies are everywhere. If they learn I even discuss birth control devices I could lose my license and possibly go to jail."

She had discretely tried to find a doctor who would ignore the law, but none of her associates in the movement admitted to knowing one, or were keeping his name to themselves for fear that too many people knowing would put their doctor in jeopardy. And since Cecelia used the same doctor she did, she was no help.

Her only other solution was to do what her parents did—abstain until that time of the month when she knew she couldn't get pregnant. Not only was that a hideous solution, it would never work. The enjoyment of coupling was the one aspect of their lives she and Abe truly had in common. There were no disagreements in their bed, only one objective occupied one hundred percent of their minds; seeking pleasure.

Yet she was distraught at the thought that she would continue to get pregnant year after year, like her mother-in-law, until the changes set in. She loved children, but enough was enough. This pregnancy had to be her last.

"Forgive me?" Abe asked.

She threw her arms around him and thought, at least one good thing would come from this baby. She could enjoy Abe's amorous ways without fear of getting more pregnant. With seven months to solve her problem, she repressed her thoughts about the future and took delight in letting her husband make up for last night's spat.

****

An hour later, her anger with Abe had become a distant memory. Everything was back to normal. Except, she thought, how was she going to tell him about her trip to Washington next month? More than ever she had to take that trip. Thousands of women would be there. Many from New York City. The Socialist newspapers Solomon read and Cecelia passed on to her had vehemently condemned the Comstock Act for years. Someone in the movement from New York City had to know a doctor who was not intimidated.

CHAPTER 32

Seated from left to right across the stage of Turn Hall, the Ribbon Weaver's Guild meeting place, were local union organizers Solomon Bressler, Ewald Koettgen, Adolf Lessig, Louis Magnet and their invited guests from the Industrial Workers of the World National Union headquarters: Patrick Quinlan, Carlo Tresca, Elizabeth Gurley Flynn and Elizabeth Flynn's red-haired assistant. They talked quietly to each other while the crowd filled the rows of backless wooden benches.

Solomon glanced at the strikingly beautiful woman seated to the right of Elizabeth Flynn, at the far end of the row of dignitaries. His eyes traced her body, pausing to concentrate on the curve of her hips and fullness of her breasts. "Who is she?" he asked Ewald.

"She's Flynn's aide."

"What's her name?"

"Katie. I don't know her last name."

Louis Magnet, leader of the Ribbon Weaver's Union, moved to the podium. He was a broadly built man with powerful arms. "May I have your attention please," he said.

Within seconds the thousand silk workers ceased their squirming. Magnet's presence had always commanded that kind of immediate respect from his fellow ribbon weavers, but not from his bosses. He had emigrated from England twenty years ago, at the stern request of his employer. His boss's exact words were, "If you ever want to work again, you better move to another country." Magnet chose Paterson. Within one year he found himself embroiled in a ribbon weaver's strike. He had been the ribbon weaver's spokesman ever since.

"For those of you who are not ribbon weavers and don't know me, my name is Louis Magnet. We ribbon weavers have been involved in many strikes . . ."

Whistles, shouts, hand-clapping and foot-stomping erupted from the crowd, vibrating the wooden-planked floor and rattling the windows. When the noise quieted to a low murmur, someone yelled out, "But you snobs never supported us."

"Yeah!" echoed from a dozen people.

Magnet patted the air with his large hands in a signal to quiet down. "We have always been a tight-knit group. Maybe our closeness has created some misunderstandings."

Raising his voice to be heard over the grumbling, he said, "That is why when Mr. Koettgen came to me and asked me if I could help with his problem, I agreed to allow him to hold this meeting in our hall. I hope we can clarify some of the misconceptions you dyers and broad silk weavers have about us ribbon weavers, and we have about some of you."

Solomon bobbed his head up and down and mumbled, "You can say that again," his words muffled by the constrained laughter from the audience.

"Without further ado" Magnet said, "let me introduce the shop steward at Henry Dogherty's Silk Company, and the organizer of tonight's rally, Mr. Ewald Koettgen."

Ewald took the podium. His stature was slight, and the lectern seemed to overpower him. "I am glad to see so many of you here tonight. I know you didn't come out in the cold to hear me . . ."

"You said it, Ewald," a voice yelled out.

He straightened his back, but it only added an inch to his height. "Let me present to you one of labor's foremost spokeswomen—a young lady who, seven years ago at the age of sixteen was nicknamed 'Comrade Elizabeth Flynn, The East Side Joan of Arc' by *Broadway Magazine* because of her fight for child welfare in New York and equal opportunity for every human being. A young lady who last year brought the American Woolen Company of Lawrence, Massachusetts to its knees and got huge pay increases for its workers. A young lady who helped the shoemakers in Brooklyn win their strike and the bakers win theirs, and who just finished fighting for better pay for thousands of striking waiters and cooks in New York City's finest hotels and restaurants. I present to you Comrade Elizabeth Gurley Flynn of the Industrial Workers of the World."

Elizabeth released her grip on Carlo Tresca's hand. Before she stood up, she turned her head. Hiding her face from the audience with the wide-brimmed French sailor hat she wore, cocked at a rakish angle, she flashed Carlo a playful look from her sparkling blue eyes. "Wish me luck," she said.

He blew her a kiss.

Elizabeth Flynn walked to the front of the stage. She never spoke from behind a podium. She had learned early in her organizing career to use all her assets to hold her audience. Not everyone came solely to hear her speak; some came to ogle her shapely body. To make sure she kept on attracting those people too, she wore form-fitting dresses that outlined her curves.

When the whistles, hand claps and stomping feet quieted, she began in her powerful but pleasing voice. "I have learned a lot since my last visit to Paterson, six years ago. We lost that strike because we were not of one mind and the bosses were united against us. If we are to defeat the bosses who steal our labor and get rich off our toil, we must work together. We are in the middle of a fight for our very existence. We are waging a class struggle that is just beginning to pay off for us."

"What do you know about struggling?" a voice yelled.

"Shushes" and "Be quiet" were directed toward the heckler.

Striding across the stage to the side the jeer came from, she focused directly on a man she thought might have been the heckler. "That is a good question. What right do I have to talk to you? You are the ones being starved by your bosses, and I don't work in the mills."

"You said it, doll," the man yelled.

This time Elizabeth spotted the heckler and concentrated her gaze on him. She elevated her voice a trifle—not shouting, but making it slightly more imposing. "From the day I was born, and I was named after the woman doctor Elizabeth Kent, who birthed me . . ."

At that shocking revelation a few hushed "Oh's" gushed from the crowd and many women's hands covered their mouths to hide their horror. Female doctors were as rare and held in as much disrepute as woman labor leaders.

". . . I was taught about struggling. My father slaved in a quarry, losing an eye for his boss. Because he could no longer see well, his boss fired him. We moved to Adams, Massachusetts, where for six days a week my mother dragged herself to the textile mill as the sun began to rise." Redirecting her attention to a woman, she said, "And she didn't get home until after dark. Even with all her hours of work, she still couldn't afford a hat or a warm shawl. But the boss's wives had plenty of hats and beautiful shawls. Like you, we had little heat in our home in the winter, but we had plenty of rats and roaches for company."

Pointing to a girl in the audience, with golden hair draping her shoulders, she continued, "I was six years old then. About your age. A year too young to work. But I wasn't too young to listen. I'll never forget the day I walked by a mill and heard piercing screams from a young girl who had forgotten to put her beautiful long blond hair up. It got caught in a machine. She was scalped alive, and later died."

The girl screamed and grabbed her head. Her mother quickly comforted her with a hug.

Many of the women openly cried.

Elizabeth bowed her head in prayer, the audience joining her.

Solomon used the moment of silence to gaze out over the hushed audience. He marveled at how quickly Elizabeth Flynn took control of the crowd and quieted the hecklers.

Lifting her head, Elizabeth walked across the platform and zeroed in on individuals as she talked. "From that moment on, I decided to fight for myself. I knew if I didn't, no one else would. It is time we—the wage earning class—stop being victims of society. We must unite, skilled and unskilled alike, if we are to beat the bosses."

She paused to take a sip of water from the glass on the speaker's stand behind her. Louis Magnet approached and asked, "Miss. Flynn, if I may ask you a question?"

"Certainly."

"As you know, many of us ribbon weavers are members of the American Federation of Labor Craft Unions. The president of your union, Bill Haywood, has called our craft unions 'stooges of the bosses.' He has accused us of collaborating with the bosses to keep the wages of unskilled workers low so we can keep our wages high."

Solomon bobbed his head in agreement. The fifty dye-house workers he brought to the meeting followed his lead.

"If Mr. Haywood berates us, why should we join you?"

"Because you are losing your fight with the bosses, aren't you, Mr. Magnet? But if you listen to me, I will show you how to beat them."

CHAPTER 33

The Hamilton Club was the gathering place for the silk mill owners. In rebuilding and re-decorating their hide-a-way after the fire had destroyed their original club eleven years ago, Paterson's business elite overlooked nothing that would enhance their comfort and enjoyment. Every room had brass-studded deep leather chairs, marble fireplaces and mahogany tables matching the color of the rich dark molding around the ceiling.

Meeting in a second floor room were Catholina Lambert and his guests, Police Chief John Bimson, Mayor McBride and Judge Congdon."

"Cigar, gentlemen?" Lambert asked. "They're direct from Cuba."

The only one to accept was Chief Bimson. Plucking one of the inch-thick dark Chavanas from the humidor, he bit off the end, removed the trash from his mouth and dropped it into the crystal ash tray on the table next to him. Lighting the cigar, he exhaled a mouthful of gray smoke. Content, he sat back in his chair and waited for Lambert to begin.

In contrast to the chief, the stout, short-legged Mayor McBride sat uneasily on the edge of his seat.

The distinguished Judge Congdon warmed himself in front of the fire, waiting patiently to hear what his friend and mentor had to say.

The small talk ended after the waiter brought their beverages and exited the room.

His brandy snifter in one hand and his cigar—the end snipped with a gold clipper—in the other, Lambert remained standing in front of the mayor. Fixing his eyes on the rotund politician, he said, "At this very minute there are three outside agitators speaking to our laborers. I want them stopped."

Craning his neck to look up at Lambert, Mayor McBride asked, "How can we do that? They have broken no laws."

Lambert's face reddened. "They're inciting a riot and insurrection. They're trouble makers. They're advocating a strike. They have to be arrested."

The mayor retorted, "Talking strike is not illegal."

"What about unlawful assembly, inciting a riot and advocating violence? That is what they're doing."

"Do you have proof?" the mayor asked.

"I'll show you the proof after they're arrested."

Judge Congdon asked, "You have witnesses attending the meeting, am I correct, Catholina?"

Lambert thanked the judge with his eyes. "That is correct."

"I would like to speak to these witnesses," The Mayor said. "I cannot authorize the chief to arrest visitors to our city without proper evidence."

Lambert put down his brandy and picked up the *Paterson Evening News* from the drop leaf table next to the chair he had yet to occupy. In two steps he was before the cowering mayor. Smacking the newspaper into Mayor McBride's chest, he said, "Didn't you read Harry Haines' editorial? He says emphatically, 'A strike is not in the best interest of our city.' If you want my support in your next campaign, stay out of this and let us handle the troublemakers."

Addressing Judge Congdon, Lambert asked, "How long can you keep them in jail?"

"They won't be brought before me. I don't handle routine police arrests, but I'll pass the word to Police Recorder Caroll. He's the one who will hear their arraignment."

"You tell him to throw the book at them."

Judge Congdon smiled.

"Okay, Bimson, you know what to do. Get on with it."

Springing from his chair, the chief said, "Yes, sir. Consider it done."

CHAPTER 34

Solomon leaned forward and listened intently to Elizabeth Flynn. He had been trying to beat the capitalist bosses, both in France and America, for twenty years, with no success. Hearing this confident, self-assured woman speak, a glimmer of hope flickered in his mind.

"The bosses are using you, Mr. Magnet," Elizabeth Flynn said. "They are keeping one group of workers happy at the expense of others so you won't unite. How can you condone what is going on at Bamford Ribbon Mill?"

"What do you mean?" Magnet asked.

"I know what she means," a woman yelled. "My daughter works there. They rob her."

Elizabeth Flynn turned sideways to face Magnet. "You do know the boss at Bamford keeps up to half the wages of the girls that work for him?"

Magnet bowed his head sheepishly, an unusual act of contrition for him.

"He supposedly gives that half back to them at the end of the year. But he only gives it to those that are still employed. Any that quit or get fired do not get the withheld wages. The boss calls it a 'Christmas bonus' for staying on the job. I call that 'thievery.' What do you call it, Mr. Magnet?"

When Magnet didn't answer, Elizabeth Flynn turned back to the audience. "Is there anyone here who works at Bamford?"

A girl stood up.

"Am I telling the truth?"

She dropped her eyes to her chapped hands, folded in front of her sack dress. "Yes," she said, barely loud enough to be heard.

"How much do you take home from Bamford?"

"A dollar eighty-five cents a week," she said and sat down quickly.

"A dollar eighty-five cents a week," Elizabeth Flynn repeated. "Mr. Magnet, how can this happen?"

Louis Magnet shook his head and hurried back to his seat.

Elizabeth Flynn looked over the gathering again and asked, "And how many of you have been robbed by the boss for what you Jewish weavers call a *mispeek*—a flaw?"

A man and woman raised their hands.

"Tell us what the boss does about a flaw," Elizabeth Flynn said.

The man poked the woman with his elbow. She rose slowly. Her shabby cloth coat hung open over a shapeless dress.

"Where do you work?" Elizabeth Flynn asked.

Her chin down almost to her chest, the woman answered, "Gold mill."

"What do you weave?"

"Broad silk."

"Tell us what the boss does to you."

Keeping her chin down and talking in a barely audible voice she said, "Each time I stop the loom to yet tie on a *mispeek*, the boss, Mr. Gold, he call me in the office and he say, 'That *mispeek* will cost you a dollar from your pay' even if the *mispeek* is caused by the not good yarn he buy."

"Even if the flaw is caused by yarn seconds the boss buys, he takes money from you?"

"Yes," the woman said and quickly sat down.

Tossing Magnet a quick glance then refocusing on the crowd, Elizabeth Flynn said, "The bosses are very smart and you ribbon weavers are not going to escape their scheming and thievery. The same thing that happened to many low-skilled workers is now happening to you.

"Your fathers and grandfathers were proud men because they were independent. They wove fabric on hand-looms with great skill. They were tradesmen. They were able to sell their services to the highest bidder because they owned their tools, their looms. They were their own bosses. But the power-loom changed everything and made all of us slaves to the bosses."

She paused for a moment, allowing her words to sink in. Older workers bobbed their heads in agreement.

"The power loom replaced all the skilled craftsmen who wove fabric on hand-looms in their homes. The power-looms became the tools of production. But who owns the power-loom?" With thunder in her voice, she answered her own questions. "The capitalist boss, that's who."

"You said it," Solomon blurted out. The crowd echoed his sentiments with, "Down with the capitalist boss."

Having captured full control of the crowd, Elizabeth pounded her point home. "You weavers who learned your trade from your fathers no longer own your own tools. The capitalist who owns the power loom now owns those tools. You no longer have a trade, because you have no tools.

"It didn't take the capitalist boss long to realize what he had." Pointing her finger from man to man, she bellowed, "And what he had was you. He owns you and treats you like his mindless machines, paying you what he wants and discarding you at his will.

"You ribbon weavers have been luckier than others. Your skills are still needed to run the looms that make the fancy jacquards. Until recently you were able to fight your bosses alone because he couldn't replace you so easily. But things are changing, aren't they? With the latest improvements in the power-looms, even your skills are fast becoming unnecessary to the capitalist bosses. Women and children are running the new jacquard-looms at wages a fraction of yours." Glancing to those behind her, she demanded, "Isn't that so, Mr. Magnet?"

He nodded in agreement.

"All your hard fought gains are disappearing, aren't they, Mr. Magnet?"

Again, he nodded.

"All the uniform wages you fought so bitterly for in your strikes over the past twenty years are vanishing. Am I correct, Mr. Magnet?"

"Yes," he answered.

"When Bill Haywood made his remarks about craft unions in 1905 he didn't explain it correctly. What he should have said was, the capitalist boss was using you and your craft unions to keep skilled and unskilled workers separate while he developed his machines so he could get rid of all you skilled workers. Soon the capitalist boss will have all workers at his mercy to hire and fire solely because he doesn't like the way you look or what you say."

She spread her arms wide, as if she were embracing the far reaches of the crowd. "That is why you must unite with the Industrial Workers of the World. The IWW represents all workers in their class struggle against the capitalist boss. You cannot beat the boss in a shop-by-shop strike. Unite with us in the IWW, and together we will throw him out of his factory and take back our tools of production. Join us, and together we will throw off capitalist bondage and slavery. Skilled, unskilled, men, women, children, you all work together for the benefit of the boss. It is now time to unite together to fight for yourselves."

Solomon jumped to his feet. He twirled his outstretched arms around and around, urging the crowd to jump to their feet. "Unite, unite, unite," he screamed.

Instantly the crowd followed his lead. "Unite, unite, unite," they yelled, and stomped the wooden floor with their feet.

Carlo Tresca came to Elizabeth's side, took her hand and squeezed it. The crowd didn't seem to care when he brazenly gave her a kiss, and only those at the back of the stage saw him pat her behind.

Solomon whispered in Lessig's ear, "Isn't she married?"

"Sure is. Has a two-year-old child my wife is taking care of while she's giving speeches in town."

"Where's her husband?"

"Somewhere out west working with the United Federation of Miners."

Elizabeth left Carlo's side and walked back and forth across the front of the stage. She smiled broadly and leaned over to shake the hands of the people who had crushed up against the platform. After a few minutes she stepped back and raised her arms for silence. "Thank you. Now, Carlo Tresca has some words he wants to say."

Tresca stood silently at the podium, waiting for the audience to settle down. He was five-foot-ten and thin. Bushy black hair topped his narrow head. A mustache curled around his mouth, covering a scar he had received from a knife wielding boss's goon during a union organizing fight. A pointed goatee sprouted from his chin, giving his face a long, triangular appearance.

Speaking in Italian, the native language of the majority of Paterson's weavers and dyers, he began. "How many of you were lured to the United States by the posters put up in your home-towns, showing the mills on one side of the street and the bank on the other, with the workers marching from the mill to the bank loaded down with bags of money?"

"Si, si," many in the crowd yelled, shaking their fists.

"But when you got here you found only the capitalist bosses carried the money to the bank."

Those that understood him roared their agreement.

"You found out fast what the bosses wanted from you—to work like their machines and be paid nothing. How many of you are dye-house workers?"

Solomon, having understood Tresca because he had learned Italian from having worked with so many Italians over the years, stood up and motioned for his fifty dyers to do the same.

"How many of you have had your mouths blackened because your boss makes you taste the dye bath to see if it has enough acid in it?"

"Si, si" yelled the dyers.

"And your eyes burned and your lungs seared by the chemicals, your skin scalded when the hot dyes from your tubs splashes on you when you stir the silk, and your backs broken from hauling the wet silk around?"

Tresca screamed at the top of his lungs, "And for what, eleven dollars a week, barely enough money to put food on your table? Join with us and stop being wage slaves to the bosses. Join with us and we will take over the factories. Join with us and we will reap the profits from your labor."

He thrust both arms over his head. Balling his hands into fists, he pumped his arms into the air, and yelled first in Italian then in English, "Power to the workers!"

Solomon ran forward. Stomping back and forth across the stage, he mimicked Tresca, beating the air with his fists and yelling, "Power to the workers!"

The dyer's voices erupted in loud support of their leader.

Patrick Quinlan, the national secretary of the Industrial Workers of the World moved to the podium. Using his foot, he pulled a small box out from under the speaker's stand and stepped up on it. Parted in the middle and slicked down, Quinlan's hair enhanced his protruding ears, but his black, deep-set compelling eyes kept attention away from that flaw in his appearance.

"The Paterson silk mills are slaughter-houses where your blood is used to dye and weave the silk that decorates the backs of the aristocratic women of the United States. Every silk worker—skilled or unskilled—must join together as a class if we are to defeat the boss and take back our tools . . ."

The front door burst open. Chief Bimson stormed into the building, followed by rifle-toting policemen.

As Bimson marched up the center aisle, his men dropped off at intervals, standing back to back, rifles at port arms, facing the crowd. Climbing the stairs onto the stage he turned to the mill workers and yelled, "This meeting is over. Go home."

Louis Magnet jumped up from his chair. "You can't burst in here. Get out!"

A sadistic grin crossed Bimson's fat lips an instant before he cracked the back of his hand across Magnet's cheek.

Magnet towered over Bimson. The ribbon weaver's leader could have crushed the chief with one blow. What restrained him from tossing Bimson off the stage into the hands of the shocked mill workers was the Colt 45 Bimson had received as a gift from the Sam Colt Gun Mill and now held inches from Magnet's gut.

"Easy, Magnet," Bimson said. "You've been begging for trouble a long time. You make one move and you're going to find it."

Bimson pointed a stubby finger at Elizabeth Flynn, Quinlan, and Tresca, and ordered, "You, you and you, you're under arrest for inciting a riot." Waving his gun toward the door he said, "Move."

Before he left the stage, he addressed the crowd. "The rest of you, go home. And in case you have any other ideas, this hall is surrounded by fifty men."

With Quinlan, Elizabeth Flynn and Tresca in front of him, he marched down the aisle, his men falling into ranks behind him. The invasion and exit didn't take two minutes, but the shock of its quickness froze the audience for an additional two. As the men on stage and the audience slowly recovered, murmurs turned to denouncements.

"How can they do that?"

"Let's stop them!"

"Yeah! Let's get them!"

The crowd pushed toward the door.

"No!" Solomon yelled. "They have guns! Getting yourselves killed will not help anyone." He turned to Magnet, Adolf and Ewald. "This time they have gone too far."

Magnet nodded his agreement and said, "This insult will be made known to every mill worker in this city."

As the four Paterson labor leaders turned to descend the stage, Solomon suddenly realized someone was missing. The red-haired beauty had vanished.

CHAPTER 35

The next day, at the same time Solomon and his fellow union leaders were meeting to plan a protest against the arrests, Sarah stood at the pulpit of the First Presbyterian Church ready to give her acceptance speech at being elected a Vice President of the Paterson League of The New Jersey Woman Suffrage association. Cecelia sat in the front pew smiling up at her. Mary Beckworth, President of the Paterson League, sat behind her, under the large cross.

"Ladies, please take your seats," Sarah urged. "We have a lot to talk about."

As soon as the shuffling of feet and rustling of skirts ceased, Sarah launched into her talk. "The day is fast approaching when we will again have the vote. But we are not there yet. We must work harder to get the New Jersey Senate to enact the woman suffrage bill."

She paused for a moment, until the heads stopped bobbing up and down.

"When we get it, we will elect politicians, many of them from our ranks, who will vote for child labor laws, equal pay for women, and to abolish the Comstock laws."

The applause bounced off the stone walls.

"Overturning the Comstock laws is one of my major causes. Those laws claim that contraceptives are the main reason for the proliferation of prostitutes, pornography, lust and lewdness. That is ridiculous. Men will be men, with or without contraceptives. And, as our courageous sister Margaret Sanger writes in the *New York Call,* it is the Comstock laws that are responsible for the rapid spread of venereal disease . . ."

The two men seated in the back row stood up and left. Sarah had noticed them, and wondered who they were. Reporters, maybe? She shrugged them off and continued with her speech.

". . . If men are roamers, wives have to demand they use contraceptives to prevent them from passing disease onto us. We must reclaim our bodies. We have the right to use contraceptives . . ."

****

Abe entered his house with his usual bellow, "I'm home."

His mother and children greeted him in the foyer.

Shooing his sons back to their play-room, Abe asked, "Where's Sarah?" She never missed greeting him when he came in. "She's not ill with the baby?"

Chava clasped her hands tightly in front of her and glanced into the living room at the clock on the mantle. "She will be here soon. Come, I will give you dinner."

His mother wanted them to sit in the breakfast nook in the kitchen, but Abe insisted they sit in the dining room and be served by Frances, as was done in his house every night. Chava sat to his right, but Abe barely looked at her and said nothing to her during the entire meal. His eyes were fixed on the empty chair at the other end of the table.

Why isn't she here? I need her. Where is she?

This will not happen again! He scowled to himself. He'd had a very profitable day, and during his drive home he had thought about how he wanted to celebrate his good fortune with Sarah.

As Frances served him coffee, the front door knocker banged against its brass plate. Slamming his napkin down, Abe went see who was disturbing his dinner. He flung it open to find his brother panting on the stoop.

"Solomon! What's wrong? Is it Cecelia?"

Working hard to catch his breath, Solomon gasped, "It's Sarah. She's been arrested."

"What? Where? Why?"

"She was giving a speech to her woman's group and they arrested her."

"Fool!" Abe grumbled. He stormed into the livingroom and made a telephone call to his friend and weekly card-playing crony, Police Recorder James Caroll.

****

Abe drove in a frenzy down the Broadway hill. Solomon, holding on for his life, told Abe what he thought had happened. "Lambert and his lackeys have gone mad. They're arresting everyone in this town for giving a speech."

Abe gritted his teeth and held his tongue. His and Sarah's disagreements were none of his brother's business.

"These illegal arrests have to stop," Solomon said. "This is not Russia. Tomorrow we're rallying in front of City Hall to demand they release Elizabeth Flynn, Carlo Tresca and Patrick Quinlan. We'll show Lambert and the rest of them they can't arrest people for talking."

Roaring around the corner onto Ellison Street, Abe screeched to a halt in front of City Hall. "Fools!" Abe said and leaped out of his car.

****

Police Recorder James Caroll escorted Sarah out of the holding cell to the lobby of the police station. Weeping, she ran to Abe and fell into his arms. "All I was doing . . ."

"Shhh," Abe barked. Lowering his voice, he whispered in her ear, "We'll talk about this later. You've humiliated me enough for one day."

Pulling away from Sarah, Abe said, "Jim, I don't know how to thank you."

Caroll shook Abe's hand and answered, "I had the charges dropped."

"I appreciate it."

"What did you do to get Chief Bimson mad at you?" Caroll asked. "He was more than happy to do the Comstock Agent's bidding."

"We had a run-in years ago. To tell you the truth, I had forgotten all about it."

"What happened?"

"Bimson burst into my bar with two of his men, searching for someone."

"Who?"

"I don't know. Some guy he said was inciting a riot."

"Was the guy there?"

"Yeah."

"Why didn't you turn him over?"

"We never got that far."

"Why?"

"He started rousting my customers, pushing them around, threatening to arrest them. I stopped him."

"How?"

"When he raised his billy to strike one of my patrons, I stepped in between them."

"Did you hit Bimson?"

"No, I just put my hand over his."

"And that stopped him?"

"That—and the sudden courage my customer got at seeing someone defending them for a change against the coppers. We all kind of surrounded Bimson and his men and backed them out the door. Now that I recall it, he didn't leave quietly."

"What did he say?"

"Something like he couldn't wait to put all kikes and wops in the grave."

"You may have forgotten the incident, but I'm sure Bimson didn't. He wasn't overly-anxious to release Sarah. I had to lay the law down to him. When it comes to outsiders asking for favors we, decide who gets arrested here."

"Bimson is a bad cop, Jim. You should get rid of him."

"Yeah, well, that's not for me to say."

Abe nodded, shook his friend's hand and said, "Thank you again."

****

Sarah kept her silence until Abe dropped Solomon off at his apartment. With her brother-in-law gone, she started to explain. "I was giving a talk to a group of women in the First Presbyterian Church . . ."

"You were in a church?"

"Yes. We meet there."

"In a church?" he repeated.

"Yes. These two men were sitting in the last row. I didn't know they were Comstock agents."

"Who did you think they were—angels?"

"I thought they might be newspaper reporters."

"They weren't, were they?"

"No. What right do they have to arrest me? All I was doing was talking about an article Margaret Sanger wrote in *The New York Call*."

"Where did you get that Socialist rag?"

"Cecelia has it. Solomon reads it."

"I should have guessed. What did I say? Didn't I tell you to stop seeing those radicals? And that Sanger woman, she's a trollop."

"She is not. She's a progressive."

"A tramp is what she is. All those Bohemians in Greenwich Village are nothing but radicals, stirring up trouble, going around spewing all that talk about sex and contraceptives and men spreading disease. See what happens when you listen to her?" He abruptly stopped his verbal thrashing. With all that had happened, he was still strangely in the mood, and he needed her in a good mood also. He glanced at Sarah. Tears flowed down her face. Pulling out his handkerchief, he thrust it at her.

****

It was after eight when Sarah shoved aside her barely eaten cold dinner. Abe suggested they go to bed. She certainly was agreeable. She thanked her mother-in-law for putting the children to bed and trudged up the stairs.

In bed, she lay on her back staring at the ceiling. When Abe snuggled close to her, she said, "That jail was horrible. It smelled of urine, and the police were so mean. They put manacles on my wrists. They wouldn't let me call you. I was so scared. If it weren't for Elizabeth Flynn . . ."

"She was at your meeting?"

"No. She was in the jail cell next to mine. She was very comforting to me."

"Shhh," he cooed in her ear. "It's over. I'm here to protect you."

When his hand slipped between her thighs, she tightened and thought, *not tonight. Please, not tonight*. Yet she couldn't deny him. She never denied him. *Let me get this over with*, she thought.

She did her best to respond, but her body wouldn't cooperate. She was tired. Exhausted. Her ordeal had sapped her energy. She couldn't find a rhythm. Finally he came and rolled off her.

Why is it always about his needs? Why doesn't he ever think about my needs?

Her trip to Washington, DC to take part in the woman suffrage parade popped into her mind. She trembled at the thought of telling Abe about it. He was not going to like that at all.

CHAPTER 36

Abe parked his Cadillac in the lot on the corner of Curtis and Van Houten. He slammed the door and headed down the sidewalk. Laborers had gathered in small groups in front of the Industrial and Harmony Mills. In their faces, Abe could see they were still angry at the arrests of the outsiders two days ago, and probably had a right to be. But he couldn't worry about them; he had his own problems. Sarah's embarrassing arrest last night and her lack of attention to his needs hammered in his head. From the moment he started, he knew it wasn't right. There had been times he came away unfulfilled, but not for her lack of trying to please him. Last night she hadn't even tried. It had to go down as one of the worst nights they had spent together. Even that first time in his apartment over his bar, where he taught her what he liked and she absorbed his lessons like a fresh-faced eager student, was better than last night.

Look what those radicals have done to you, making you neglect your family. What kind of nonsense are they filling your head with? Don't I provide you with everything you and the children need? It's over. Tonight I will demand you quit those lunatics, or else.

Heading for his warehouse in the Phoenix Mill complex, Abe crossed the bridge over the water canal—the system designed by the great architect, Pierre L'Enfant—to bring water from above the Passaic River's great waterfall racing through a series of spillways and dumping it back in the river below the falls. The "Raceway System," as it was called, opened up much more land for mills to be built than would have been possible, had factories been built solely along the banks of the Passaic River.

The Phoenix Mill was a group of buildings surrounding a courtyard. The first was erected in 1815. The last, an unheated wooden storage structure, was thrown up in 1900. It was that building that Abe had talked his friend, William Hammil, Phoenix's owner, to first rent and eventually sell to him. As his business grew, Abe fixed the leaky roof, added a coal furnace and electric power originally provided by the Edison Company, soon to be taken over by the Society For Establishing Useful Manufacturer's hydro-electric plant that was being built at the top of the great waterfall.

Entering the courtyard Abe saw hundreds of workers crowded near the entrances to the buildings. *What the hell was going on*? he wondered. *Not another damn strike*! That was all he needed right now. Spotting a familiar face, he asked, "Harry, there a problem in the mill?"

"Get lost," Harry said, and turned his back to him.

Abe was in a hurry, but he couldn't let that slight go by. "Harry, what did I do to deserve that?"

Over his shoulder Harry said, "You're one of them."

Abe maneuvered around until he faced Harry. "One of who?"

"The bosses."

"Since when do I own a mill?"

"You deal with them; you're one of them."

Abe glanced at another face he recognized. "Did I ever do anything to you? Or you," he asked a third, "except give you guys an occasional beer on the house?"

"That's a long time ago, Abe," Harry said. "Times change."

"I haven't changed. I'm still the same guy that owned the bar across the street." He stuck out his hand. "Come on, Harry. You got a gripe with your boss, lay it on him, not on your friends."

Harry looked around at his buddies, who were staring at the ground. He hesitantly took Abe's hand.

"Thanks, Harry."

Walking across the courtyard, Abe sympathized with his old customers. They'd had their meeting broken up the other night for no good reason. He cursed under his breath, "Whoever ordered that is a damn fool!"

He unlocked the door to let his workmen in, gave a few quick instructions and headed for the office. Rolling up the top of his desk, he scribbled a note, shoved it in the pigeon-hole on the right, grabbed the Paradise Silk Company file from the ledger rack and rushed out.

His long legs, taking deep strides toward the corner of Ellison and Curtis, he passed a seemingly ceaseless flow of laborers headed in the other direction. It is another strike, he thought. *Damn that Bimson and who ever had the stupid idea to arrest that Flynn dame*! "Fools," he muttered.

Entering a narrow three-story office building, Abe climbed the stairs two at a time to the second floor. Glancing at the room number on the front of the file, he found the office with "Gillman and Scott, Attorneys At Law" written in gold letters on the door. He announced himself to a secretary and was ushered to an inner office.

The only introduction needed was to George Scott, the attorney for Paradise Silk Company, a mill now in bankruptcy. Abe knew everyone else. "Bernie, Phil, Duane," he said somberly to each of the partners of Paradise Silk Company. He did not shake their hands.

Turning to the others, Abe did cordially shake hands with Russel Murray of Russel Murray Company, Al Rosenthal of A. Rosenthal Silk Company, Herb Coleman of Standard Silk Dyeing, and John Dunlap of John Dunlap and Sons.

"Gentlemen, if we may begin," said George Scott. He lifted some papers, shaking the cigarette ashes off them. The ashtray on his desk was filled with tamped-out butts. The air in the closed office reeked of their rancid smoke.

Abe disliked those tiny cigars. They looked silly in a man's hand. Not that he liked the big cigars either, but at least when a man smoked a regular cigar he looked like he had stature. And their aroma was powerful, not puny like those cigarettes.

Everyone sat in the wooden armchairs arranged in a semi-circle around Scott's desk. Except Abe. He was too upset to sit.

"As you know by the papers you received from the court," Scott said, "Paradise Silk Company is in bankruptcy. As attorney for the bankrupt, I am instructed to gather in all outstanding obligations. I'll start with you, Mr. Bressler."

Abe handed him the file. Scott examined it and said, "Seven hundred eighty-nine dollars. Is that correct?"

"Correct."

Scott repeated the same procedure with the other men. "John Dunlop and Sons, six fifty-seven, A. Rosenthal Company, two sixty-six, and Russel Murray and Company, two twenty-four. That makes A. Bressler Silk Company the largest unsecured creditor."

"Wonderful. What does that mean?"

"It only puts you at the top of the list," Scott said. "It carries no more weight than do the amounts owed the others."

"It means you were a bigger sucker than the rest of us," Al Rosenthal said.

"How much will we get back?" Abe asked.

"About twenty cents on the dollar," Scott answered.

John Dunlop pointed a finger at the Paradise owners. "Twenty cents? That won't come near covering the cost of the goods I sold you."

"That looks like it," Scott confirmed.

Abe's vision of himself seated behind the wheel of that new roadster evaporated. He had spent weeks studying the Hudson, Franklin, Chalmers and Maxwell before settling on the Stutz. "When do we get the money?"

"The auction of the assets should occur in about six weeks," Scott answered.

"You'll call me when you have my money?"

"Yes, Mr. Bressler."

Abe glared at the owners of Paradise and said, "Fine. If there is nothing else, I'll be leaving."

Abe stormed out of the office, grumbling to himself. This was the first company to go bankrupt and owe him money. He'd had some slow payers before, but he always managed to get his money eventually. "How the hell could those bums do that?" he asked himself. A deal was a deal. A debt was a debt. No matter how long it took to pay it off, it had to be paid.

Al Rosenthal followed Abe out the office and said, "Wait up, I'll walk with you."

Heading down the stairs, Al added, "The whole town is pretty tense."

"I know. I got a taste of it on the way to my shop."

"What happened?"

"Nothing serious. A couple of guys I know from the old days gave me the cold shoulder."

"That was pretty dumb of Bimson, arresting those people."

"Bimson doesn't strike me as having any brains," Abe said. "I'm sure it wasn't his idea."

"I have a terrible feeling something is going to bust wide open around here," Rosenthal said.

Abe stepped out of the building onto the sidewalk. He stopped so abruptly that Rosenthal bumped into him. He pointed west down Ellison. "Already has. Take a look at that." He turned to look in the opposite direction. "And that."

Al Rosenthal glanced left and right and said, "I'll see you, Abe," and ran across the street.

CHAPTER 37

Ellison Street was shaped like a boomerang. Abe stood at the bend. To his left, spread across the street from curb to curb, an endless procession of mill workers marched toward him. To his right, a flow of police, their shiny brass buttons gleaming on their blue jackets, hustled into ranks. From his position he could see both groups, but neither of them could see the other.

Solomon, Ewald Koettgen, Adolf Lessig and Louis Magnet headed the parade of laborers. Abe ran to intercept them and tell them about the police. He fell in step next to his brother and asked excitedly, "What's going on?"

"We're marching to police headquarters to demand the release of Elizabeth Flynn, Tresca and Quinlan," Solomon said.

"And what happens if Bimson doesn't release them?" Abe yelled to be heard over the stomping feet.

"Then we are prepared to strike until he does."

"The only thing that's going to get struck around here is you guys. Bimson is waiting for you and he has plenty of men with nightsticks in hand."

"Enough to beat up two thousand of us?"

"Sol, you're crazy! Why are you sticking your neck out for those troublemakers?"

"It's not for them. It's for all of us. This time they went too far. They can't just bust in and arrest someone for talking."

"Let them get a lawyer and fight it out in the courts."

"Like you did with Sarah last night?"

When Abe didn't answer, Solomon said, "We don't know any judges. And there is no court in this town that ain't owned by the bosses. At eight o'clock this morning a lawyer for Elizabeth Flynn, Tresca and Quinlan came over to the Nags Head Bar, where we was meeting. He told us he was denied the right to see his clients, and that his clients had already been before the judge and are being held on one thousand dollars bail each. You call that justice?"

"No, but it's still no reason for rioting."

"We are not rioting. We're marching in protest. We have the right to peacefully assemble."

"Let me talk to Judge Caroll."

"It's too late. They played their cards. Now we're playing ours."

"We don't need your help," Adolf Lessig said. "Go back to your boss friends and tell them this time it's going to be different."

"How's that?"

"Every shop in town is going out on strike. You bosses won't be able to work one shop against the other. We're going to get what's due us."

Rounding the bend, the marchers came face to face with over a hundred policemen stomping toward them, their solid oak clubs drawn and at the ready.

"You're going to get a lot more than that, little man," Abe said.

Chief Bimson led the police force, his chest puffed out and his round head topped with that funny sawed-off stove-pipe hat held high. Coming within two feet of each other, the two forces halted and glared.

Bimson repeatedly smacked his nightstick into the palm of his hand, each whack sounding like a mallet hitting a wooden peg. He snickered with delight at the sight of Abe and Solomon. "Disburse. Go back to your homes and your jobs," he bellowed. His breath condensed into small gray clouds in the cold morning air.

"We want Elizabeth Flynn, Tresca, and Quinlan released," Louis Magnet answered in the same demanding voice.

The crowd behind him raised clenched fists and echoed his words in a chant, "Release Elizabeth Flynn, release Carlo Tresca, release Patrick Quinlan."

"They are awaiting trial for inciting a riot, and you are going to join them if you don't disburse this instant," Bimson yelled.

"Bimson, whoever is pulling your strings is making a big mistake," Abe found himself saying, almost to his disbelief. But he kept on. "If I were you, I'd back off and let these citizens march around the jail a few times. Once they get their anger worked out, they'll go back to work. You use those clubs and who knows where it will end?"

"Bressler, are you the spokesman for this unlawful parade?"

"No, I'm a concerned citizen who was passing by and thought I would try to stop something before it got out-of-hand."

"Then shut your mouth and get out of here or you will end up in the same jail with the rest of them."

Solomon said, "Go, Abe! This isn't your fight."

Abe turned his head slightly toward his brother, but kept Bimson visible out of the corner of his eye. "You're right, it isn't my fight. You, of all people, know I'm not in favor of strikes or unions. But I dislike loud-mouthed Cossacks who pick on women even more."

Bimson locked his eyes on Abe's. "That's it. Either you disburse or you spend the rest of the day in my jail."

No one knew who threw the rock, but an instant after it hit the policeman in the head, all hell broke loose. Abe fended off Bimson's club with his left forearm, and turned his body slightly to block the left Bimson threw at his midsection. His own right never reached Bimson's head. A sharp blow from behind landed just above his right ear. He only felt it for a split second. It was when he woke up lying on the cold concrete floor of the city jail, that the pain set in.

"He's coming around," Solomon said.

"What hit me?"

"A nightstick and a boot or two," Solomon answered.

Abe sat up and winced at the shooting pains in his side and shoulder.

"We tried to cover you the best we could, but Bimson likes to kick. After one of his men conked you from behind, Bimson kicked you in the side and the back before we forced him off you."

Abe looked at the twenty men in the crowded cell and similarly jammed cells next to his and across the aisle. "How many of you did he arrest?"

"Got about sixty before we scattered. We couldn't fend off the nightsticks. They are still bringing in people from shops all over town. Got twenty-seven from Geering Dye Shop and another group form Passaic Silk, and who-knows-where else."

"We're from Dexter, Lambert," a voice yelled out, followed by others from throughout the jail proclaiming their mill: "Commercial Silk, Newark Silk, National Ribbon, Charm Silk, American Silk Dyeing."

"Hey, Bressler, it's nice to hear you're finally awake. It's me, Harry Coughlin."

"Harry, you should have gone in to work," Abe joked, then let out a long, "Ohhh," as the pain shot through his body.

"No one is going to work in this town for a long time after today," Harry said.

Solomon sat next to his brother. "This is it, Abe. The whole town is out. The men that got away from Bimson's goons ran to every mill, spreading the word. When one shop walked out, the men ran to another, urging their comrades to follow. Bimson was looking for a riot and he got it. But he can't control it. It's a complete shutdown."

"Congratulations! You finally got what you wanted. Now how do we get out of this dump?"

A policeman entered the lock-up. Clanging his club along the bars, he said, "All right, you jail birds. It's time to see the judge."

CHAPTER 38

A squad of armed policemen ushered the prisoners up a flight of stairs and into rows of hard benches in the courtroom. The American flag, a picture of President Taft—soon to be replaced by President Elect Wilson, and a clock were the only decorations in the austere room. A faint smell of furniture oil used to polish the judge's bench to its bright sheen hung in the air.

A few minutes after they were seated the bailiff yelled, "Hats off. All rise." The mill workers swept their caps off their heads and shuffled to their feet as the gray-haired Judge Caroll, his black robe flowing around him, entered the courtroom through a side door, followed by Chief Bimson. The judge walked rapidly up three steps to his seat behind a high platform where he could peer down on those being paraded before him.

Abe spoke out, "Your honor, may I have a word with you?"

Chief Bimson quickly said, "Your honor, that man . . ."

Judge Caroll banged his gavel. "You will have your chance, Chief Bimson. Follow me, Mr. Bressler."

Walking into his chambers, Judge Caroll spun around, his cloak flaring out from his body like the skirt of a whirling dancer. "What the hell is going on? First your wife, now you. Why are you here with this rabble?"

Abe ignored the questions. He wanted to calm his friend down first. "I didn't have a chance to ask you last night, how did you make out at the game last week?"

Judge Caroll's anger deflated. "With you not there, I did very well. It's a nice feeling to rake in a few pots. Maybe you should sit out more often."

"Not on your life. You think the silk business is so great?" Abe joked. "I need the extra *glicken* you guys provide to pay for that house on the hill."

Motioning Abe to a chair, Judge Caroll sat behind his desk. "How did you get caught up in this?"

Abe gingerly sank into the hard chair and shook his head. "It happened so fast, I don't know. I was coming out of a meeting at Scott and Gilman's law offices. One of my customers went bust on me."

"You get stuck for much?"

"Almost eight hundred."

"That's rough."

"You're telling me. I had my eye on this new Stutz."

"Nice auto. So, how did you get from there to here?"

"I walked out of the building and saw the mob marching up Ellison from Mill Street, and the police running out of City Hall. Like a *schmuck* I stepped in the middle and tried to mediate."

"One of these days you're going to stick your head out and get it cut off."

"Do I have a choice? My brother was marching at the head of the parade."

"You really have your hands full with him."

"True. Anyway, when I saw Bimson leading the police I knew there was going to be a fight."

"I think you've reason to be prejudiced."

"That does not change the fact that he is brutal and sadistic, looking for any excuse to bang heads with his club."

"I can't believe that."

Abe attempted to rise, winced at the pain in his side and sat back down. "I've got the bruises to prove it. Want to see?"

"I'll take your word for it."

"I tried to talk Bimson into letting the workers march around City Hall a couple of times. I figured they would get tired and go home. But the Chief started swinging first."

"The way Bimson tells it, the workers were rioting."

"That's crap!" Abe said with such vehemence a pain stabbed him again. When it subsided, he continued. "I know a lot of these men. I've heard their complaints about their bosses every day for five years." Calming his voice he said, "These are good people. They may get a little loud and rowdy, but riot? If they were going to riot, they would have brought their own clubs and sticks and maybe a few torches. Does your report show any of them had weapons."

"No."

"They weren't rioting."

"They were parading without a permit."

"They were walking down the street. Maybe they were a little over-zealous in their chanting, but they have a reason to be upset. Two nights ago they had their meeting broken up. For what? Someone giving a speech?"

"I sympathize with them, but . . ." Judge Caroll said.

"But what?"

"I'm going to tell you something in confidence. It goes no further. Do I have your word?"

"Absolutely."

"There is a lot of pressure coming down to break this strike fast."

"From who?"

"Do you have to ask?"

"I met Lambert only once. He struck me as a pompous ass. Too impressed with his own importance."

"Yeah, well right now he has the power, and he's using all of it."

"And using it wrong," Abe insisted. "This strike will never be won by breaking heads. Not this time."

"How do you know?"

"A feeling. I've never seen the workers like this before. Big parades, meetings outside the mills, all the dyers and weavers sticking together."

Judge Caroll nodded, his face taking on a thoughtful expression.

"What are you going to do with them?" Abe asked.

"I have my orders. Twenty-five dollars fine per man."

Abe jerked up straight in his chair and winced again at his foolish sudden movement. "Twenty-five dollars? That's two weeks pay for a lot of these men. You'll starve them out."

"From what I understand, that's the idea. Then they will go back to work."

"Or rot in jail."

"We aren't going to leave them in jail. We'll make them sign a promissory note and warn them if they don't pay off the fine in a reasonable time they will be back in jail for thirty days."

"You'll have most of them back."

Judge Caroll stood up. "Maybe, maybe not. They've already gotten a taste of it. My bet is they'll go back to work and pay up."

CHAPTER 39

Abe walked down the courthouse steps with Solomon and Solomon's friends. "We have to talk," Abe said to his brother. Glancing at the others, he added, "Privately."

Solomon turned to Lessig and Koeltgen and said, "I'll meet you there."

Abe led the way across the street. "I thought we had an agreement. No more strikes for you."

"I stayed out of strikes for eleven years. You didn't hear my name mentioned in '07 or last year, did you?"

"But now you're back in the middle again."

"Every agreement's got a time limit."

"Not as far as I'm concerned," Abe said, exhaling sharply. "I don't understand you. You could give your family everything I have, but you refuse to do it. Why?"

"Somebody has to help these people."

"Why does it have to be you? Leave it to the charities and the churches."

"They ain't no help. They can't change nothing."

"Now you're a social worker?"

"No, but I think everyone is entitled to earn a living wage from his labor. Look at you. How much did that suit cost? Five dollars?"

Abe looked down at his clothes, smeared with dirt. "Right now it's not worth much, but when I had it custom made, fifteen."

"Fifteen dollars! A dyer's apprentice got to work a week and a half to earn that. A coarse cotton work-shirt costs thirty-four cents. Most guys I work with don't own two."

"That's life, brother. There will always be haves and have-nots."

"The world is changing, Abe. The have-nots are going to rise up in a revolution and throw off the yoke of the bosses."

"Talk like that will get you killed."

"You do understand. We talk and we're the ones murdered. Despite what that judge said a few years ago, we ain't commodities to be used up and discarded at no boss's whim. We got rights too."

Abe glared at his brother. "The only rights anyone has in this town are the ones he can buy."

"We're done being treated like outcasts because we're poor. This ain't the middle ages. We're not serfs, and we're done making the bosses rich off our labor for the crumbs he tosses us."

"You don't have to be poor. Come in with me."

Solomon looked at Abe with a glint in his eye, as if Abe had just given him an idea. "And do what?"

"Build a business."

"What would be my job in this business?"

"We'll be partners."

"Where am I going to get the money to buy my partnership?"

"From the money we make."

"Until I get the money to buy in, who will own the business?"

Abe stared at his brother, recognizing that cocky look. He knew from past arguments that Solomon was goading him and he should cut off the conversation. He didn't. His dream of him and his brothers working together forced him to go on. "Since I started it, I'll own it at first. But we'll have an agreement where you can buy shares from me."

"How many shares you gonna sell me?"

Abe couldn't hide his annoyance anymore. "Why are you making such a big deal out of this? We'll sit down and work it out."

"But until I own my shares, you're the boss?"

"Since it's my money that started the business, I'll be the boss. Is that what you want to hear?"

Solomon's lips turned up into a leering grin. "The money. The capital. You put up the capital and you're the boss. It's so familiar."

"Okay, Sol, let's have it. What's eating you?"

"The mill owners, they have the money so they're the boss. And us laborers with no money are sweated until they use us up. Then they throw us away like a piece of old machinery."

"Sol, we're family. We don't do that to each other."

"We don't?"

"What are you driving at now?"

"You'll be the boss and dole out jobs to the rest of the family, letting us know everyday where our job came from, just like Uncle Isaac did to dad. What do you really want? To be the family patriarch here in America like Uncle Isaac was in Latvia?"

"I don't want to be any patriarch," Abe insisted. "All I want to do is care for my family."

"You sound like Isaac already. I don't need you to take care of me."

Abe thought, *Don't you? You can't even see how the world works. You keep tossing around that word "entitled." No one is entitled to anything in this life.* "You're going to lose again," he said.

"Not this time. This time we're all together. We've shut down every mill in town."

"For how long?"

"For as long as it takes. There's no worker who ain't getting robbed by his boss. New machines are replacing the ribbon weavers. The four-loom system's gonna put half the broad-silk weavers out of work. We dyers now see our chance to join in and get what we want. We control this strike."

"How's that?"

"The weavers can't settle without us. If they don't get dyed yarn they can stand by their looms all day, but they won't have nothin' to weave. My people are calling the shots, and we ain't goin' back to work for a crummy one dollar a week raise."

"You feel powerful. That it, brother?"

"Yeah."

"Don't let it go to your head. However united you think you are, the mill owners are more united. And they own the police, the mayor and the judges."

"We vote too. There are twenty-four thousand of us. How many of you are there?"

"Damn it! Why does everyone align me with the mill owners?"

"Because you make your living from them. You deal with them everyday. You ain't a laborer—you're a boss."

"From now on, I'm neutral. Go ahead and strike. I'm going to be making a lot of money while you people keep the mills closed."

"Yeah? How?"

"The big mill owners all have operations in Scranton and Allentown, Pennsylvania. Your strike isn't going to hurt them that much. But the smaller guys with only one mill here are going to need cash. They'll be dumping yarn. I'll be there to buy it and peddle it in Pennsylvania."

"Always out for the buck. That it, Abe?"

"That's life. Someone's misfortune is someone else's good luck, and this time it's going to be mine."

"You got anything else to say?"

"No. I wanted to see if I could talk some sense into you. It's obvious I can't, so you listen good. I'm not a mill owner, and I'm not a laborer. I'm neutral. I buy and I sell. I don't take sides. You get blacklisted again, don't look to me to buy you off. Understand?"

"Yeah, I hear ya."

Engrossed in condemning his brother, Abe hadn't realized they had walked to his old bar. Solomon pushed open the door.

"This where you're meeting your chums?" Abe asked.

"Yeah."

"I can use a beer myself."

CHAPTER 40

When Abe had put his bar up for sale, word spread fast. There were a lot of bidders, but by some coincidence their offers were all a little bit lower than Ben Goldberg's bid, and Abe knew why. Having worked as a salesman for Goldberg for five years, it didn't take Abe long to learn why his boss always walked around town accompanied by body guards. Goldberg's secondary business was as a loan shark and those big oafs were his collectors.

Abe never put two and two together as to why the guy he bought the bar from gave him such a fabulous deal. He figured it was his good fortune to be in the right place at the right time. He wasn't behind the bar two days when a couple of hoods came in and asked for the owner. When Abe said he was the new owner and the former owner had gone to Chicago, they demanded he pay the gambling debt owed them by the skip. When Abe refused, one of the thugs grabbed his shirt and pulled him halfway across the bar. Lucky for Abe he had long arms and was able to reach the sawed-off pool cue on the shelf under the bar. He whacked both men on the head and threw them out.

The next day, Goldberg's bodyguards and the two hoods he threw out returned and would have beaten Abe to a pulp had Goldberg not been with them and called off his men. Goldberg left Abe's saloon that day without his money, but with all debts past and present considered paid. Goldberg owed Abe. The two men had met on the boat from Ireland. Abe was watching a card game between Goldberg and a dandy dressed in a shirt with a ruffled front and ruffled sleeves sticking way out from the cuffs of his cutaway coat. He saw the dandy slip a card from his sleeve into his hand. Goldberg couldn't see it, but Abe could from his vantage-point, looking at the game from a low-slung easy chair on the side. Normally, Abe wouldn't have stuck his nose in something that was none of his business, but he hated cheats. His father had cheated his mother all her life.

After the game, Abe told Goldberg about the cheat. Abe never saw the dandy again. There was a rumor that someone had fallen overboard during the night, but the ship never slowed.

Knowing intimidation was Goldberg's way of conducting his business, Abe had no doubt the other bidders for his bar were visited by the loan shark. Abe paid his own visit to Goldberg and said, "You want the buy my place, this is the price." It was a thousand higher than Goldberg's offer.

"And if I won't pay it, who you going to sell to?"

"I'll keep it and mortgage it to get the money I need. Take it or leave it."

Goldberg paid.

Walking up to the bar, Abe slid between two men and watched Solomon receive pats on the back and words of encouragement as his brother worked his way to the table in the corner. Already seated were Adolf Lessig, Ewald Koeltgen, two other men Abe didn't know, a woman with a big black hat cocked at a rakish angle, and another woman with bright red hair, her back to Abe. When Solomon took his seat between the redhead and Lessig, Abe turned to the bar and caught the eye of his old bartender. "Carlo, beer."

Carlo placed the mug in front of his ex-boss, eyed Abe's ripped and dirty clothes, and said, "I hear you have trouble this morning."

"Yeah, the city owes me a new coat and a hat." He took a sip. "Big crowd for this time of day."

"It going to be crowded like this until the strike over."

"I'll bet Goldberg isn't complaining."

"He all smiles. The men using this place as the strike headquarters."

Abe glanced back at the table where Solomon sat. "Who are the broads back there?"

"I not know the redhead, but the one with the hat is Segnora Flynn."

"How'd she get out of jail?"

"I hear bail money, it come in from Chicago. She here an hour with those other two she arrested with, and the redhead."

As Abe stared at the redhead's back, a chill rippled through his body. He attributed it to the weather and the cold cement floor of his prison cell.

Two of his old customers came up to Abe and shook his hand. The word was out. Abe may be a boss, but he's an okay guy for trying to intervene with Bimson and Judge Caroll. Turing back to Carlo, Abe said, "Three more beers for me and my friends."

CHAPTER 41

"Sorry I'm late," Solomon said. "My brother wouldn't shut up." He addressed the redhead. "We haven't been introduced. I'm Solomon Bressler."

She stared at him so hard he wondered if there was something wrong with his face. He wiped his mouth with the back of his hand.

"Bressler?" she asked. "I knew a laddie named Abraham Bressler a long time ago, in Ireland."

Now it was Solomon's turn to gape. "I have a brother Abraham. He lived in Ireland for a while." Pointing across the room, he said, "That's him at the bar. The guy with the white hair."

Katie stared at Abe's back for a long moment. Pushing back her chair, she stood up.

"Where are you going?" Elizabeth Flynn asked.

"To see an old friend."

Looking at the smirk on Katie's lips, Elizabeth asked, "Are you sure he's a friend?"

"We'll see," Katie said and headed for the bar.

Men stumbled over themselves, clearing out of Katie's way as if she were royalty riding through the streets of their old countries. But unlike what they would do when their former rulers passed, they did not drop their eyes. As Katie marched with purpose in a straight line toward the bar, they couldn't take their eyes off her. Her red hair glowed under the electric lights. The pale mounds of her breasts bounced above the scoop neckline of her dress that clung to the curves of her lithesome hips and outlined her slender legs with each step.

Stopping behind Abe, she put her hand on her cocked hip and glared at his back with blazing green eyes. Whistles and calls of, "Come to me, my sweet face" in English and Italian erupted from the men.

When Abe turned around to see what the fuss was about, his eyes opened wide and his jaw dropped.

"Hello, laddie."

"Katie!"

"Miss me?"

"I . . . How . . . What . . . ?"

"You used to be such a smooth talker, boyo. Maybe this will help unstick your tongue." She took his head in her hands, pulled herself up on her toes and smothered his mouth with hers, her tongue shooting between his lips.

The whistles and shouts bounced off the walls and the floor shook from foot stomping.

For the briefest moment, Abe stood like a statue, then swept his arms around her and pulled her body against his and returned her kiss.

Breaking the kiss, Abe asked, "Katie, where did you come from? How did you get here?"

"Walk me home, laddie, and I'll tell you."

Like a child with his tongue hanging out at the anticipation of receiving his bag of rock candy from the shop owner, Abe followed Katie through the crowd to get her coat. More hoots and hollers of, "I'll take you home, lassie," and "You can take me home, darlin'," followed them.

At the table, Katie said to Elizabeth, "I'll be at Mrs. O'Neil's."

"I had a couple of people I wanted you to meet when we broke up here," Elizabeth said.

"Ring me up later."

Solomon jumped up, pulled Abe aside and said, "What are you doing?"

"I'm walking an old friend home."

"You have a wife and kids."

"So what? Katie's a friend. I want to talk to her."

"Abe, she's a *nefkeh.* She entertains men."

Abe shoved Solomon. If the guys behind him hadn't caught him, Solomon would have fallen to the floor.

"You're crazy," Abe said. "Get away from me."

"You're the one who's crazy."

CHAPTER 42

The sun had set. The temperature had dropped into the twenties. Flurries and coal soot swirled through the air on a brisk north breeze.

Katie pulled her cloth coat around her to ward off the cold. "It was quite a shock seeing you," she said.

"I missed you."

"Did you now? Not a word from you in nineteen years."

"I wrote you six letters. I begged you to come over. I told you I'd send money for your passage."

"My brother. He must have kept them from me."

Abe drew her hand from her pocket, slipped it through his arm and covered her cold fingers with his hand. "You're here now, and we're together again."

Katie nudged closer to him, letting her hips brush against his as they walked. "You look like you made something of yourself. What do you do, boyo?"

"I buy and sell silk yarn."

"A boss, eh. Elizabeth doesn't like bosses."

"I'm not a boss. I'm just a middleman. How did you get tied up with her?"

"I was a bar maid in a pub in Boston. Cheerful place, like the one we just left. Elizabeth was holding a rally, trying to organize the hotel and us pub workers into her union. I talked to her after the meeting. She told me all about the Industrial Workers of the World. We hit it off. She was going down to Lawrence to lead a strike against the mill owner and asked me if I would like to tag along. I wasn't goin' nowhere in my job and she said she'd pay all my expenses. We've been together for about a year."

"What do you do with her?"

"I'm kind of like her entertainment director. Try to get laddies to help out with the union organizing. What about you? Any wife and wee ones?"

"I'm married and have five sons."

"Five! And all laddies. That could have been us," she said. A distant look enveloped her face and a glint of moisture filmed her eyes. "I waited for you. Why didn't you come for me?"

"I wanted to, so badly. You brother threatened to accuse me of killing your husband. He said he would see me hung if I tried to see you again."

Her somber expression turned into a scowl. "What a bastard he was. Sent me off to another parish to tend to a priest friend of his. Cook for the man. Do his washing. Clean his house."

"I'm so sorry."

They crossed Oliver Street, the unofficial dividing line separating the Italian neighborhood from a neighborhood the Irish nicknamed "Dublin." Stopping in front of a three-story brick building, Katie said, "This is my rooming house. Want to come in, laddie?"

"Of course."

Katie directed Abe past the parlor. On a settee in front of a crackling fire, two young women snuggled close to two men.

"Looks like a nice rooming house," Abe said. "Homey."

"Mrs. O'Neil's is a bit more pricey than other places, but it's comfier."

Katie's room was on the first floor, the third door down the carpeted hallway. She unlocked the door with a long key and hit the switch inside, turning on a small brass chandelier. The smell of cigar smoke hit Abe as he followed her into the room.

Red velvet drapes, trimmed with gold tassels and topped with crescent valances and jabots, decorated the windows. A wool rug adorned the floor. A tufted couch with tasseled fringe and claw feet, an upholstered armchair, a double bed with carved mahogany head and footboards, a matching armoire and dresser, and a desk and wooden chair rounded out the furnishings.

Katie took off her coat and threw it on the arm chair. She picked up a bottle of Irish whiskey from the dresser and asked, "Drink?"

Abe shrugged off his coat and threw it on top of hers. "Absolutely."

She filled two glasses and handed Abe his. Raising her glass in a salute she said, "Here's to cheating, stealing, fighting and drinking. If you cheat, may you cheat death. If you steal, may you steal a woman's heart. If you fight, may you fight for a brother, and if you drink, may you drink with me."

"Where'd you hear that?" Abe asked.

"It's an old Irish toast. Kind of fits, don't ya think, laddie?" She reached out and clinked her glass against Abe's. "*Sláinte*, to your health."

"*L'chaim,* to life," Abe said

Katie plopped down on the couch. Abe sat beside her, and asked, "How did you come to America?"

"That priest friend of my brothers turned out to be a no good bastard, too. A week after I was there he came to my room and forced himself on me. Night after night the bugger came."

"Oh, Katie. I'm so sorry."

"You're sorry a lot, bucko."

When Abe didn't answer, Katie said, "I stole money from the poor box and ran off to London. I worked in a pub there. Didn't like it, though. British are bastards, too. Cheap buggers. I saved my money and went to Boston. I heard there was a good Irish crowd there."

The steam radiator under the window clanked as the boiler in the basement pumped a fresh batch of hot air hissing through the pipes. Katie unbuttoned her dress down to her waist. "It's getting' warm in here, don't you think, laddie?"

Abe's eyes rested on her breasts, flowing out from her undergarment. Her lilac perfume swirled around his nose. "Yes," he said, and slipped off his suit jacket and vest.

"That bar we were in, I owned it before I went into the silk business."

"That so? I worked in a pub in London and Boston."

"Yes, you told me."

"Right, boyo, I did. You know, if it weren't for you I wouldn't have been able to do that kind of work."

"Me?"

"Yes, laddie. You taught me the skills."

"Skills?"

"How to please the men I sold myself to to keep from starving."

Abe jumped up and stared down at her.

"Why ya so upset? Ya should be proud of yourself. I make a good living. Look at this room. Ain't it lovely?"

Abe's eyes blazed. "Oh, God, Katie, I loved you! I never treated you like a whore."

She leaned forward and picked up a brown Phillip Morris box off the coffee table and shook out a cork-tipped cigarette. Sticking it between her lips, she lit it with a wooden match and exhaled a plume of gray smoke. She slumped back against the cushions and said, "Elizabeth tells me God is a tool of the bosses. A slick invention to give false hope of a better life after death so the workers won't complain too much about their life here on earth. I believe her."

"What are you talking about?'

"Ya said, 'Oh God!' I was commenting."

She braced her feet against the edge of the coffee table and raised her knees. Her dress slid down her legs, exposing her bloomers. She patted the couch and said, "Sit down, laddie. We have a lot of catching up to do."

Abe sat on the edge of the couch. Her dress was almost off. His eyes drifted to her breasts, then down her shapely thighs and legs. Her body was a bit rounder now, but it made her all the more comely.

Katie stubbed out her cigarette in the ashtray on the end table. Seeing where his eyes focused, she cupped her hands under her breasts and pushed them up out of her undergarment. Teasing her rosy nipples between her thumbs and index fingers, she said, "Ya always liked these. Do they still look the same to you?"

****

The bedspread and blanket hung tossed over the footboard of the bed. Katie lay on her back, naked on top of the sheets, trying to control her breathing, but she couldn't stop herself from sucking in deep breaths. When he grinned at her broadly, she cursed him silently. "Damn you, you bastard! You know what you did to me."

She had planned to have him all along, but not to give him an ounce of satisfaction. When he mounted her, she fought her feelings, but they quickly overcame her. As he plunged into her, her fingers involuntarily dug into his back and her legs clamped around his. In seconds she went from hating him to delirium at being with him again. The past nineteen years evaporated like a bad dream.

Abe left the bed and reached for his clothes.

With the warmth of his body gone, her ecstasy quickly cooled. The past flooded back like a tidal wave. She still wanted to hurt him like he had hurt her so many years ago. "Just like the first time we did it, right, laddie? Hit and run."

"We can bring those days back. We can be together again."

"We can be together anytime ya want. The price is five dollars. Leave it on the desk before ya go."

His face hardened into a scowl. He dug out his money roll, peeled off a five and flipped it toward the bed. As it fluttered to the floor, he spun on his heels and yanked the door open.

"Come back anytime," she said.

"I'll not be back. I don't frequent whores."

Abe slammed the door and Katie buried her face in a pillow to muffle her sobs.

CHAPTER 43

Sarah replayed last night over and over in her mind. Granted, every time they coupled wasn't pure ecstasy, but she couldn't remember an episode quite as bad as last night's fiasco. Usually when she wasn't in the mood she could fake it to give Abe his pleasure. She liked pleasing him. It added to her excitement, and many times it changed her mood.

There was no doubt that last night was totally her fault. She couldn't even make believe. She had absolutely no desire. It had to rank at the very bottom of their coupling.

They were having a lot of disasters lately in the only part of their life they still eagerly shared. The night of the Silk Association Ball was the first time he walked out of their bedroom. Then last night's catastrophe.

Even the time he seduced her in his apartment over his bar was better than last night. She knew nothing. But he was patient and tender, and taught her. And she learned, and she reciprocated. And the more she reciprocated, the more joy she received.

For nine years, despite his aloofness, despite their arguments, they always had their togetherness in bed. Now that was slipping away.

"No, I won't let it," she said out loud.

She thought of the morning after the Silk Ball when he returned to their bed to make up. A warm wave passed through her. It was her turn to make amends.

****

Sarah sat in the kitchen, staring at the clock. He was two hours late. A delivery man had told her about the trouble downtown. Abe couldn't have been caught up in that, could he? It wasn't near his warehouse. It was over by City Hall.

She walked to the stove to re-check dinner. She had made Abe's favorite: brisket of beef cooked with potatoes, and carrots in tomato soup. It had cooled and she had turned on the gas burner to re-heat it. Now she was trying to keep it from sticking to the bottom of the pot and burning.

Hearing the sound of an auto pulling under the portico, she ran to the side door and sighed with relief when she saw it was Abe. She rushed across the porch and down the stairs. Opening the car door, she said, "I've been so worried!"

For a moment he stared at her as if he didn't recognize her. Coming out of his stupor, he said, "I'm coming. Get inside before you catch your death."

Seeing his torn and soiled coat, she shrieked, "What happened?"

"I tried to stop it, but no one would listen."

"You were in that riot downtown?"

He didn't answer until they were in the kitchen. Shrugging off his coat, he let it fall to the floor. "I was on Ellison Street. Solomon and his people were marching to the police station to protest the arrests."

Her own arrest flashed back to her. "The police are going too far."

"The police wanted them to disburse. I tried to reason with everyone. Someone threw a rock."

"How horrible. Is Solomon hurt?"

"He's all right."

"Thank God," she said, picking up his coat.

"I'm through with him. He's on his own."

"You don't mean that."

"Damn right I do, and I told him." He gazed at his coat in her hands. "Throw it away."

She studied the damage. The odor of cigar smoke clinging to it was familiar. The faint lilac smell mixed in did not register. "It's only the seams. I can mend it and I'll have it cleaned. It will be as good as new. Come, I have your dinner ready."

He shuffled toward the back stairs. "I'm not hungry. I need to lie down."

In the bedroom, he shed his clothes, exposing the bruises on his torso and the scratches on his back. Sarah cried out, "I'm calling a doctor."

"Don't bother. Nothing's broken. I just need to rest."

"In a hot bath," she insisted.

Sarah scurried to the bathroom and drew a tub of steaming water, threw in some bath salts and helped him in.

He leaned his head back on the edge and rambled, "After all these years, she's here. I can't believe it."

Placing a fluffy towel behind his head, she asked, "Who?"

Rolling his head, he gazed at her. "What?"

"You said, 'After all these years, she's here.' Who's here?"

When he didn't answer for an agonizing few seconds, she anguished that he might have some kind of brain damage, but a moment later the light returned to his eyes.

"That Flynn woman. She's nothing but trouble."

"Yes, Abe, I heard," she said, wondering how he knew Elizabeth Flynn.

Her earlier desires set aside, Sarah doted over Abe, feeding him dinner in bed, smoothing liniment on his bruises and keeping the children quiet so he could rest. When he fell asleep, she repaired his coat. As she sewed, the lilac aroma chipped a small notch into her unconsciousness.

CHAPTER 44

March 1

Saturday, five days after the melee, Sarah revealed her plans to go to Washington, D.C. She would have cancelled her trip if Abe had not recovered from his ordeal. If she had any doubts that he hadn't, he quelled them by his reaction.

Abe was getting dressed for Shul. He abruptly stopped tying his tie and asked, "You're going where?"

"To Washington, D.C. for the suffrage parade Monday."

"Have you lost your mind?"

"No, Abe, I haven't. This is something I must do. It's the biggest demonstration for woman's right to vote ever assembled. We picked Monday because so many dignitaries will be in town for President Wilson's inauguration on Tuesday."

"You're not going." He said it as if he were giving instructions to one of his workers.

"Why is it you can go off to Europe for six weeks and I cannot go two hundred and fifty miles for three days?"

"Because you have responsibilities here."

"This household will not fall apart. Your mother and I had a long talk. She can handle things very well. She certainly has the experience."

"You're pregnant."

"What does that have to do with it? Women work in the mills until their time."

The calmer and more reasonable she was, the more his face reddened. He waved his hand at her as if he were making a big X across her body. "You are not other women. You have no right to risk the child you're carrying."

"That's exactly the purpose of this trip. We have no rights, and we demand them."

"You demand? Who earns the money to keep this house? Who puts clothes on your back and food on your table?"

His tirade was oh so predictable. It was the reason she waited until the last moment to tell him. She hadn't wanted his rant to go on for days. "You think you work so hard," she said. "Try toting laundry up and down these stairs. Or moving furniture to clean, or running from the second floor to the basement to break up a fight then back up again because the baby is crying. All, while I'm making sure your dinner is on the table when you get home. How come I can do that while I'm pregnant—a situation, by the way I didn't want, but you created."

Abe's face turned the color of the town's new fire truck. Before she knew what happened, he grabbed her by the arm, pushed her out of the bedroom and slammed the door so hard the crystals in the dining room chandelier hanging below their bedroom clinked. She stood on the landing, dazed, wondering if she should charge back in.

A few seconds later he stormed out. "You dare desecrate the Sabbath by not wanting God's blessing?" he asked, then left for Shul without waiting for her to answer.

Shaking, Sarah returned to her bedroom. She slumped down on the bed and hugged her stomach. Through her tears, she said, "I didn't mean it. You're a *simcha*—a joy. I do want you."

Her oldest peeked in and asked, "Mother, what's wrong?"

Despite his young age, Isidore always seemed to be able to pick up on her troubles and tried to comfort her. "Nothing, darling."

"Why is father angry?"

"Nothing for you to worry about. Come, let's go play."

Still unnerved at Abe's intimation that she wasn't a good mother, Sarah went to the basement playroom. She hovered over her children, joining in their games until she sensed her presence was disrupting their fun.

Leaving them, she went to the kitchen. As she set out lunch for her family, she watched the clock tick toward twelve-thirty, Abe's usual time for arriving home from Shul.

What was he going to say? How would he demean her to try and stop her from going? It didn't matter, she told herself. She was going, regardless of what he said.

She fed the children and sent them back to the playroom. By the time the clock struck twelve twenty-five, she had steeled herself for his harangue.

One o'clock and Abe still had not arrived, nor had her mother-in-law. Chava had been spending Friday's at Solomon's and Cecelia's, going to Shul with her sons on Saturday to say *kadish* for her husband, then returning home with Abe.

By two her nerves itched. At three, her pacing had practically worn a path in the floor. She called the number of the common pay telephone in Solomon's building. No one answered. She wasn't surprised. The tenants were all orthodox. None would pick up the telephone on the Sabbath.

At six-thirty she panicked. Her train departed Newark's Pennsylvania Station at eleven PM. Since there was no direct route from Paterson to Newark, she had to go to Jersey City, change trains and backtrack to Newark's Pennsylvania Station. If she didn't make the connection, there wasn't another train to Washington until the morning. A whole day wasted. She might as well not go.

That's it! That was his plan. He had coerced his mother to reveal my time schedule and purposefully delayed her so I would miss my train.

Her suitcase standing by the front door, Sarah collapsed onto the foyer stairs in tears. "How could he do this to me?" Her sobs muffled the sound of the back door opening. She wasn't sure she had heard it. Holding her breath, she listened.

Relief swept over her when Chava yelled out, "Sarah, I am here."

She hurried to the kitchen.

"Abe tried not to bring me," Chava said, "but I made him. I promised you I would be here."

"Thank you so much."

From behind his mother, Abe said, "You leave, you don't come back into this house."

"You're not serious," Sarah answered, bracing herself for another verbal assault.

"Leave and see how serious I am."

"Abe," Chava said. "Don't be a *zhlub* like your father. This is important to Sarah."

Stupefied, it took him a moment to respond. "How dare you say that! I'm not like my father. I am a responsible husband. She's the one who's abandoning her family."

Sarah stomped her foot. "I am not abandoning my family. I'll be gone three days. I don't see why I can't take a short trip once in a while."

"Because it's not natural for a wife to do that."

"What is your idea of a natural wife, Abe? Someone who subjugates herself to her husband's precious needs and has no life outside the home?"

"Yes."

A horn blew. Her cab had arrived. She had barely a minute left. Looking at Chava, with sympathy in her eyes as if to say, "I'm sorry for what is coming," Sarah answered, "My parents pleaded with me not to marry you. They told me how your father treated your mother, how your uncle treated your whole family. They warned me you would stifle me. You know what she called you?"

Abe smirked but didn't answer.

"A sow. Her exact words were, 'You cannot make a silk purse out of a sow's ear'."

"Hah! She was a fool."

"My mother wasn't a fool. I was the fool. I wouldn't listen. I thought you would be different because you were so supportive of my aspirations. Were they all lies? I'm going, Abe. I'll be back Tuesday evening." She stepped forward to kiss him goodbye.

Abe turned his back and stormed toward his study. Sarah picked up her bag and walked toward the front door.

"Mothers are never fools, dear," Chava said. "Don't worry about the children. They will be fine."

And I'll be fine too. I've been looking forward to this trip for a long time, and I won't let him ruin it for me.

CHAPTER 45

With her yellow gardenia pinned to the lapel of her coat and her yellow "VOTES FOR WOMEN" sash bedecked diagonally across her chest from shoulder to hip, Sarah shivered on the platform of Newark's Pennsylvania Railroad Station. The Paterson contingent had left on the morning train. Sarah didn't go with them because she would not travel on the Sabbath unless it was a dire emergency. With many of the meetings and practice for the parade tomorrow, she knew she could catch the night train and still get there in plenty of time.

Out of the corner of her eye Sarah caught a couple of men staring at her. She was the only woman on the platform. The blackened ceiling muted the light that spewed from the weak bulbs overhead. Despite a breeze blowing through the station, the air smelled of urine and burned coal. She leaned out from the platform and looked down the tracks into the night. *Please come.*

When she had arranged her trip, she never gave a second thought about traveling a mere two hundred and fifty miles. Ten years ago she had crossed the ocean and she'd been to New York City with Abe a number of times. But now, standing on the platform being stared at by strangers, she realized she'd had companions on those trips.

Reaching up, she touched her pearl-tipped hat pin. The sharp pointed four-inch needle was a formidable weapon, but it gave her little comfort. Suddenly the bright white head-light of the approaching train broke out of the darkness. She breathed a sigh of relief.

Seconds later the train screeched to a halt. Steam hissed from under every coach, the last two of which had yellow banners pinched in the top of every closed window. Sarah was about to show the conductor her ticket to find out where her compartment was when a voice yelled, "Sister, over here."

A lady wearing a hat bursting with yellow gardenias hung out the doorway from the second to last car. "Join us," she said.

Sarah eagerly accepted.

Her escort took her hand and guided her into the car. The women wore sashes of violet, green and white, which surprised Sarah. She thought all participants were to wear yellow sashes.

Continuing to hold Sarah's hand, her host introduced herself. "I'm Eleanor Hewitt. Welcome to the private cars of New York's Political Union."

CHAPTER 46

The train pulled into Washington's Union Station at eight. Joined by scores of yellow-sashed women, disembarking trains from Illinois, Georgia, Missouri, even Canada, Sarah and her newfound friends walked through the vaulted glass-ceiling waiting room. As the porter put their bags at the taxi staging area, Eleanor Hewitt asked Sarah, "Where are you staying?"

"The Willard Hotel."

"How wonderful! So am I. We'll take a cab together."

Turning to her traveling companions, Eleanor told them she was going with Sarah and would meet them at the Columbia Theater for the rally. Commandeering a taxi, Eleanor pointed out hers and Sarah's luggage.

"I didn't tell the other girls," Eleanor said, "but I have a date with some dignitaries at the hotel. You must join me."

"Thank you, but I can't. I have to meet up with my league. They're supposed to be having parade practice at ten this morning."

"Pshaw! What's there to practice? You know how to walk, don't you?"

Sarah laughed. "Yes."

"You'll learn more and do more in the Palm Court at the Willard than you will standing around in the cold. The Willard's the place to be today. Everybody who's anybody will be there. You must join us."

"If I don't find my associates, I will."

Before sliding behind the steering wheel, the taxi driver asked, "Do you want me to put up the canvas top?"

The air was cool, but the sun felt warm on Sarah's face. "I don't mind it down. Do you, Eleanor?"

"It's fine. Besides, we can see the sights better."

"Here we go," the driver said. "Keep them hats pinned on tight."

"This is so exciting," Sarah said, grasping Eleanor's leg.

Eleanor patted Sarah's hand, and said, "Washington is an exhilarating city."

"You've been here before?"

"Many times. Lobbying for the cause."

"I envy you."

"You don't travel?"

"Not since I came to America. That was a scary trip, not fun like this is going to be." Sarah smiled at Eleanor. "I want to meet new people and take in the sights."

Eleanor took Sarah's hand and affectionately squeezed it. "Then you're lucky we met. We'll have great fun together."

Sarah bounced in her seat. "Oh, look! There's the Capitol."

The taxi turned onto a broad avenue. "This is Pennsylvania Avenue, Washington's main street," Eleanor said. "It connects the Capitol to the President's house."

Despite its being Sunday, the city hummed. Autos carrying people to church zipped up and down the Avenue. Pedestrians, clutching newspapers and brown bags from bakery shops meandered along the sidewalks.

Sarah wished she had retrieved her Kodak from her luggage. But then she thought she was probably lucky she hadn't, because she'd waste her film. The ride wasn't bumpy like bouncing over the cobblestone streets in Paterson, because these streets were paved with asphalt like New York City. Still, the pictures wouldn't come out if they were taken from a moving car. Tomorrow she'd get all the pictures she wanted.

A policeman, standing under an umbrella in the middle of the street, had twisted a pole that had signs on it in the shape of a plus. The one now facing them said, "Stop."

The taxi halted abruptly. Sarah and Eleanor pitched slightly forward. Sarah's left hand flew out to brace herself against the driver's seat. Her right hand, still in Eleanor's, tightened.

"Sorry about the sudden stop," the driver said. "Gotta have the coppers directing traffic or it'd be a mess around here what with the Center Market over there on the Mall to our left."

Sarah stared down the cross street.

"That Mall was supposed to be for foreign embassies and grand mansions and such," the driver said. "Didn't work out that way. What happened was the farmers and merchants set up shop there 'cause it was near the Capitol building. It's a real mess. Even got that Smithsony Building there with all them arty-facts in it."

"I would love to see that," Sarah said.

"I'll take you after the parade," Eleanor said.

"You will? Oh, thank you so much," Sarah said and craned her neck to look in all directions.

Sensing a break in the conversation, the driver said, "Mall was even worse before the railroads was forced out."

"How so?" Sarah asked.

"The Pennsylvanny Railroad, the Baltimore and Ohio and the Baltimore and Potomac all had their terminals down there between the Capitol and the market place. Charles Guiteau shot President Garfield in the Baltimore and Potomac terminal while the President was waiting to catch his train to Elberon, New Jersey—wherever that is."

"It's a section of Long Branch, a resort city on the Atlantic Ocean," Sarah said. "I used to summer there with my parents before I married."

"That so," the driver said.

Actually, she worked there. Her father received a commission to teach children of wealthy families a couple of hours a day in the summer, and she helped him. They roomed with the servants on the third floor of the house of her father's benefactor. The owners called their summer retreat a "cottage," but it was as big as a mill owner's mansion.

Two men sidled off the curb and approached the taxi. They were neatly dressed in suits and ties. The one with the bushy mustache doffed his derby and said, "Hello, ladies. How about we get in there with you and show you lovelies the town?"

Sarah slid away from the door and pushed against Eleanor.

"Go away," Eleanor said, draping a protective arm over Sarah's shoulder.

"What's the matter? You those kind of ladies who don't like men?"

The policeman twisted his sign post to "go." The driver stepped on the gas.

The speaker hit the rear fender of the fleeing cab and yelled, "Go on, go home, you freaks. We don't want you here."

"Don't pay no mind to them boys," the driver said. "Lot of them work for some senator or congressman and think they is important and can do anything they want."

Eleanor rubbed Sarah's shoulder and tried to lighten the mood by saying, "Look at all the decorations."

Yellow bunting, the color of the suffragist cause, intermixed with bunting of red, white and blue, flapped in the breeze on many houses and buildings. Although not yet nine o'clock, street vendors hawked little yellow flags with "Votes For Women" inscribed on them.

"Those is for you ladies tomorrow and the president on Tuesday. This ole street's seen a lot of parades. Want to hear 'bout them?"

Away from their tormentors, Sarah relaxed, but she didn't move back to the door. Eleanor's arm across her shoulder gave her a feeling of safety. "Oh, yes," she said.

"First parade wasn't much," the driver continued. "It was in 1805 for President Jefferson's second inauguration. After he was sworn in, he rode back to his house with a group of friends, some congressmen and a bunch of other well wishers. But that was the start of the inauguration parades. Jackson's was an unruly mob. I'm sure you heard about that."

"Of course," Eleanor said. "My family has been in America since before the Revolution."

"That so? Mine too," said the driver. When Eleanor didn't respond, he went on with his speech. "It was so cold during ole President William Harrison's parade, he caught a chill from tipping his hat so many times, and a month later there was a funeral procession for him.

"Lincoln's first parade was more like an armed escort to protect him, but his second, after the war, that was something. I was ten then, and I seen it. The Grand Army was parading in a victory march and Colonel Custer, his yellow hair flowing out from under his hat, rode a horse covered with flowers. When someone threw some more flowers at him, his horse reared up and almost run off with him.

"Then, of course, there was President Buchanan, riding in a float shaped like the USS Constitution ship.

"And McKinley's parade was four miles long.

"But I liked Teddy Roosevelt's gala in O-five the best. He had the Rough Riders marching, and Indian chiefs in war paint, and the bands played 'There'll Be A Hot Time In The Old Town Tonight'."

"It must have been wonderful!" Sarah said.

"Yes, ma'am. But I think your parade's gonna be another first. Only women marching. That's gonna be somethin' to see."

Eleanor said, “It most certainly is. I hope most of you men are not like those boors that accosted us, and will cheer us.”

“We will, ma’am,” he said, honking and waving at an observation bus going the other way. The seven rows of benches mounted on a flatbed truck, each one elevated slightly higher than the one in front like an open air theater, were occupied by wide-eyed gawking tourists.

“Up to your left,” the driver said, “you can see the top of the Washington Monument. Was supposed to be Washington on a horse, but that one never got built. And now, just south of it, they’re gonna build a monument to President Lincoln. Gonna look just like him, beard and all, sitting in a big chair inside a Greek temple.”

“It’ll be beautiful,” Sarah said, recalling Abe and his friends talking about Lincoln’s monument at the Silk Ball.

“After Washington, I think Lincoln was the greatest President. I still remember it plain as day when he was shot. I was sleeping, and was woke up by all the uproar in the streets.”

A block later, he pulled up in front of the Willard Hotel.

Exiting the cab, Sarah didn’t know where to look first—at the hotel with its exquisite mansard roof with the inset port hole windows, or the columned building a block away.

Pausing from his task of unloading the baggage to the curb, the driver pointed and said, “That there’s the Treasury building. There’s seventy-four of them columns, all made a granite. Took thirteen teams a’ horses to haul each column through the streets here.

“There’s supposed to be an open line of sight from the Capitol to the White House, but I heard that Ole Hickory—that’s Andy Jackson’s nickname—picked that there spot for that Treasury Building so as to block the view a the White House from the Capitol ’cause he done had a tiff with Congress.”

Eleanor opened her purse.

Sarah said, “Let me get it.”

“I won’t hear of it.”

Eleanor paid the driver, gave him a fifty-cent tip and said, “That’s just a rumor, Sarah. Don’t go believing everything you hear from these taxi drivers.”

Sarah ignored her and stepped into the street for a better look. The blast of an auto horn made her jump back.

“Easy there, ma’am,” the cabby said. “Drivers in this town can be a mite crazy. Now where was I? Oh, yes. The president’s house is just around that corner on the other side of the Treasury.”

Placing the last suitcase on the sidewalk, the driver removed his cloth hat and crumpled it in his hand. “There you are, ma’am. All set.”

Sarah slipped him another dollar.

He plastered a big grin on his face and said, “Thanky ma’am,” as he backed away.

“Oh, Sarah, you over-tipped him,” Eleanor said.

“Pshaw!” Sarah answered.

CHAPTER 47

The lobby of the Willard Hotel bustled with activity. Fashionably-dressed men huddled close to the two-story marble columns and chatted discretely. Women with yellow gardenias emblazoned on their hats checked in at the front desk and sat in groups on the plush leather and velvet chairs and settees.

A silly thought popped into Sarah's mind. She had visited Catholina Lambert's art gallery while Abe was in Europe. She wondered what Solomon would say when she told him Lambert's Castle could probably fit in the Willard's lobby, and his art gallery in the lavish arcade.

Before departing from Eleanor, Sarah promised she would try to join her for the early lunch. Although tired and in need of freshening up, she sought out a telephone and called home to tell everybody she had arrived safely.

Chava said, "Abe is sleeping. He was out very late last night. I did not hear him come in until three in the morning."

Probably out playing cards with his cronies, Sarah thought as a feeling of relief at not having to speak to him swept her. She didn't need another argument. "Mother Bressler, it's so exciting here! It's going to be a wonderful festival." Hearing a child, she asked, "Who is with you?"

"Isidore."

Of course, Sarah thought. He was the most needy and would be missing her the most.

"Let me speak to him," Sarah said.

A quiet, barely discernible voice came through the receiver. "Father says you are not coming home."

Stupefied, Sarah did not know what to say. In the background she heard Chava say, "No, darling, that is not so."

Picking up on her mother-in-law's comment, Sarah said to Isidore, "No, no, that's not right, darling. Listen to Nana. You didn't hear correctly. I'll be back Tuesday night."

"Why did you go away?"

"An important trip for mommies. I'll tell you all about it when I get home. And I'll bring you photographs, too. I love you. Let me speak to Nana."

When Chava came back on the line, Sarah asked, "Did he really say that to the children?"

"Yes, and I scolded him." She did not tell Sarah that Abe had come home with his coat reeking of that horrid lilac perfume. Chava knew what that meant. Her husband often carried that same cheap perfume smell into their house on his clothes. The whores in Libau soaked themselves in it.

"Thank you, Mother Bressler. Thank you so much."

Despite her efforts, she couldn't wipe Abe from her mind. Tears welled in her eyes as she hung up the receiver. "How could he be so cruel?" she mumbled. "I read to my children every day. I bandage their cuts and scrapes. I hug them. I solve their problems. Where is he? He's the absent parent. I'm surprised he spared the time to talk to them at all. I'm a good mother. I'm a good wife."

Noticing people staring and shying away from her as if she were a loony woman, Sarah bowed her head and scurried across the lobby to the bell captain's desk to advise him she was ready to go to her room.

Forcing back tears as she waited for the elevator, she thought, *My life is ruined. Why didn't I listen to my parents?*

The doors slid open and Sarah started forward before letting the passengers exit. She collided with Mary Beckworth, her chapter president.

Seeing Sarah's distress, Mary asked, "What's wrong? It's not the baby, is it?"

"No, I'm fine. The trip was tiring."

"Well, you just lie down. Forget about the practice. I've taken care of reserving you a spot on one of the floats so you can ride tomorrow."

"Thank you."

"If you feel up to it later, we're going to a rally at the Columbia Theater around three." Mary reached in her purse and pulled out a bunch of name tags. Finding the right one, she held it out. It read, "Sarah Bressler, Vice President, Paterson League, New Jersey Suffrage Association." "Pin this on and you'll be ushered right in."

Sarah's face brightened.

"Now you go up to your room and rest. You have to take care of that baby, you know. We're all sure it's going to be a girl this time, and an ardent supporter of the cause."

In the elevator, Sarah stared at the name tag: Sarah Bressler, Vice President. At least someone acknowledges me.

CHAPTER 48

The cheery décor of her suite further heightened Sarah's spirits. Lovely chairs and settees bordered a Persian rug in the sitting room. Two vases, filled with flowers, graced the cherry wood desk and coffee table and filled the room with their perfume. Out her window she could see the top of the Washington Monument. She heard it was lit up at night. She couldn't wait to see it.

Months ago, when Sarah made her reservation, the hotel offered her various priced rooms. She had already decided she wasn't going to pinch pennies on the trip. Abe had gone first class to Europe and she was going first class to Washington.

For six months she felt like a thief, asking Abe for a dollar here and two there, which she squirreled away. "For household expenditures," she told him.

He gave her the money without question. At least that was one thing about him that was okay. He was always generous.

She no longer felt guilty about taking Abe's money. After what he had put her through, she figured she earned it. Raising her head in mock defiance to him, she said, "I know my children love me. Your mother loves me. You're not going to ruin this trip for me."

Sarah shed her clothes, washed her face and applied a bit of rouge to add color to her cheeks. Her tear-reddened eyes stared back at her from the mirror. She couldn't do anything about them, but she could easily explain their condition away by saying the trip was fatiguing. She donned her afternoon dress and laced up her sturdy walking boots. Plucking a couple of fresh yellow gardenias from the vase, she stuck them in her hat, pinned it to her head and walked out the door, ready for practice.

In the lobby, Eleanor Hewett intercepted her. "I'm so glad you could join us."

"But I'm off to meet my league."

"No buts. You'll have a much better time here."

Eleanor took Sarah's hand and escorted her toward Peacock Alley. "Did you know the word 'lobbyist' was coined in the lobby of the Old Willard when men seeking influence bent President Grant's ear over a Chavana Cigar?"

"No," Sarah said as they entered the plant-filled restaurant. Waiters hustled overflowing trays of Sunday brunch fare to the tables. Sarah inhaled the aromas of eggs, sausage and French toast.

The Palm Court was even more exquisite close up. A row of arched windows stretched from front to back and filled the room with bright sunlight. In every nook, around every column, near every table, green palms rose from marble planters. Some tables were tucked behind the flora for privacy. Others were out in the open for those patrons who wanted to see and be seen. Eleanor guided Sarah to a table, smack in the middle of the room.

Sarah recognized Alice Paul, walked over to her, shook her hand, and said, "Nice to see you again."

"Oh, you know Alice?" Eleanor asked, a bit flabbergasted that Sarah should know someone of such importance.

"We met in Paterson."

Eleanor asked Alice, "Do you want to do the honors?"

"You go ahead, please," Alice said.

Eleanor introduced Sarah to the rest of the party. "My good friend, Harriet Stanton Blatch, President of New York's Political Union. Dr. Anna Howard Shaw, President of the National Woman's Suffrage Association . . ."

Sarah's knees buckled, making her look like she had done a slight curtsey.

". . . Carrie Chapmann Catt, President of the International Suffrage Alliance . . ."

Sarah grabbed the back of a chair to keep from falling.

". . . Inez Milholland. Inez is the Herald for the parade and is riding a beautiful white horse. This is my friend, Sarah Bressler. Sarah, what is your maiden name?"

In awe of these great ladies, Sarah struggled to answer. "Singer," she finally said, barely above a whisper.

"Sarah Singer Bressler," Eleanor said.

Sarah moved around the table, demurely shaking each gloved hand as she went. When she reached her empty seat, she practically fell into it, having called up all her resolve not to swoon.

"Sarah is Vice President of the Paterson league, and a marvelous fund raiser," Eleanor said.

"Congratulations," Alice Paul said. "You've done well since we met."

Sarah was not sure why Eleanor had latched on to her. Maybe it was because Eleanor needed someone her own age to talk to. Whatever it was, Sarah didn't care. She was going to have the most wonderful stories to tell when she got home.

"Sarah has five children and one on the way," Eleanor said.

Inez Milholland gasped.

Harriet Blatch said, "If you learn one thing from your trip here to Washington, it is that you must take control of your own body. It's your body. You give it and you withhold it as you see fit."

But what if I don't want to withhold it? Do I have to have a baby every year just because I like coupling?

Her anxiety must have shown on her face, because Harriet patted her hand, and said, "Are there no doctors in Paterson you can turn to?"

"None that I have found." She continued to stare at Harriet, her mouth partially open.

"Yes, dear. What is it?"

Did she dare ask a stranger? Did she dare not to? She licked her lips and whispered, "Do you know of a doctor in New York City who practices in these kinds of women's problems?"

The other women quickly busied themselves, talking or fiddling with their silverware, making like they had no interest in what Harriet and Sarah were discussing. They all knew someone who was fined or went to jail for disseminating birth control information. It was best not to be a witness to such activities. They couldn't testify to anything they knew nothing about.

"I'm afraid I don't, dear."

Sarah studied Harriet's face. *She knows a doctor. I know she does.*

Under the table, Eleanor patted Sarah's thigh and said, "I'll ask around. If I hear of such a doctor, I'll acquire a name for you."

Her face breaking into a huge grin, Sarah said, "Thank you so much."

Harriet glanced at Eleanor with what seemed to Sarah to be a disapproving look—maybe even an admonishing leer.

A man strolled up to their table.

Extending her hand, fingers curved slightly down, Harriet Blatch said, "Hello, Congressman."

He nodded and replied, "Ladies, I have good news. Friday, by a vote of 199 to 51, Congress passed the resolution to ban all traffic and the trolley on Pennsylvania Avenue for your parade."

"Yes, we heard. We are appreciative," Harriet Blatch said.

Alice Paul asked, "What about my request for a military escort?" Alice was chairwoman of the parade committee, and had a meeting with Secretary of War Stimson, asking for an escort to keep the streets clear for the parade.

"I don't believe the Secretary will approve that, Miss Paul. But Retired General Johnson, the D.C. Commissioner in charge of the police, has been instructed to keep the parade route clear. He has been in charge of many large parades and should know what to do."

"Thank you," Harriet Blatch said.

"I must tell you, ladies, it got a little uproarious on the House floor. Several of my colleagues—not me of course—made suggestions about women wanting to wear pants, and it was even offered that the House should give Captain Hobson—the Congressman from Alabama, you know—a frock and a bonnet so he is properly dressed when he marches with you."

With her face set as sternly as any of the monuments around Washington, Dr. Shaw said, "I don't think that will be necessary."

"Yes, yes, well, have a nice day, ladies."

When he was out of hearing range, Harriet said, "Boor. If I ever get the vote, he's going to be the first one I vote against."

"Condescending little man, isn't he?" Inez added.

"That he is, but we need him now," Dr. Shaw said. "Once we have the vote, we can pick candidates who will be more respectful."

Carrie Catt said, "Let's order. We have to be at the Columbia Theater in an hour."

During the meal, Sarah listened as these esteemed ladies joyously talked about how the parade was going to impress President-Elect Wilson, about strategy to catch a congressman's ear, and what to say to their husbands to turn them in favor of woman's suffrage.

"If each wife can convince her husband, the battle is won," Harriet Blatch said.

Sarah nodded and smiled. *I will get you to support us, Abe, if it's the last thing I do,* she thought, and then wiped him from her mind. She didn't want to think about him for the rest of her trip.

CHAPTER 49

After lunch, Sarah walked with her exalted associates to the Columbia Theatre on the corner of F and Twelfth Streets. Inside, Eleanor said, "Harriet, Inez and Anna are speaking. Won't you join me in the front row?"

Sarah spotted Mary Beckworth waving at her. "I must join my party, thank you."

Eleanor had been holding Sarah's hand. She patted it and said, "Later then."

"Yes, of course."

Sarah joined her Paterson League and told them about her chance meeting on the train, luncheon and the congressional resolution.

Mary Beckworth said, "My, my, you have been a busy little bee, haven't you? And all this time I thought you missed practice because you were tired."

Carole Davis whispered in Sarah's ear, "Don't let her get to you. She's very protective of her position."

"After the rally I want to take you up to the stage and introduce you," Sarah said to Mary.

Mary's face quickly brightened. "Thank you. I would like that."

"There's Harriet Blatch, getting ready to speak. Let's take our seats," Sarah said.

Harriet pounded her gavel on the speaker's stand. When the crowd quieted to a low murmur, she said, "What better time to gather here in Washington than on the eve of the inauguration of a new president? Unfortunately, Theodore Roosevelt, the candidate we favored, a standard bearer for our cause, is not the President-Elect. But that does not mean we are defeated. Tomorrow we will show President-Elect Wilson and the nation how determined and how united we women of America are in demanding a new amendment to the Constitution to correct the glaring omission of the Fifteenth Amendment which granted, all men suffrage."

Mrs. Blatch waited for the foot-stomping to subside, spoke a few minutes more, then introduced Dr. Anna Shaw. It took five minutes for the applause to abate.

Holding up a bound booklet, Dr. Shaw said, "I have here the message signed by thousands of women and carried in her hand from New York by General Rosalie Jones during her relentless march to Washington. The message is clear, President-Elect Wilson. You must recommend equal suffrage in your inaugural address and insist on a Constitutional Amendment to allow women to vote."

Hidden behind the uproar of approval, Carole Davis leaned in toward Sarah, and said, "Did you hear what Rosalie Jones' mother said?"

Sarah shook her head, no.

"She is planning an anti-suffrage march around the eastern states to thwart her daughter. Would you believe it?"

"When did this happen?"

"Last night at a banquet in Rosalie's honor."

"How embarrassing."

They returned their attention to the front, because Rosalie Jones, dressed from head-to-toe in her standard-issue brown, stepped forward on the stage and introduced her band of hikers.

Mary Beckworth said, in her best sarcastic tone, "It seems all is forgiven between Rosalie and Dr. Shaw."

"What do you mean?" Sarah asked.

"Rumor has it, Dr. Shaw was all in a tizzy when Rosalie started organizing her Army of the Hudson for her march. Afraid she might lose control, I suspect. She went as far as to say she wasn't responsible for Rosalie's actions."

"I'm sure it was a misunderstanding."

"Sure it was, my dear."

Inez Milholland took over the podium and asked for quiet. She spoke, then did Maude Younger of California, re-asserting that women in California—like nine western states—could vote in state elections and demanded the right to vote in national elections.

Harriet Blatch re-claimed the speaker's stand. "Our cause cannot fulfill its function without money. Please reach deep, ladies, and give the ushers your donations."

Mrs. Champ Clark, the wife of the Speaker of the House, stood up in her box seat to the right of the stage and yelled, "One hundred dollars to the war fund."

A roar erupted from the crowd.

John Barrett, Director of the Pan American Union, followed suit and also offered one hundred dollars. When the usher came in the box to collect the money, John patted the pockets of his jacket fumbling for his wallet, while ogling the girl out of the corner of his eye. Luckily for him, few noticed the leer on his face.

Mary Beckworth did, and said, "They knew there would be men here favorable to our cause. That's why they picked the girls they did to be ushers. The most prettiest group I've ever seen. Not a plug among them."

Sarah, and all the ladies within ear shot, laughed.

A woman in the middle of the orchestra stood up and yelled, "A contribution in the name of Theodore Roosevelt." That sparked many from all over the audience to rise and offer donations by proxy for President Taft, President-Elect Wilson, William Jennings Bryan, and Eugene V. Debs.

A woman in the gallery yelled, "I give five dollars from an anti-suffragist in the memory of Florence Nightingale, who did great work without wanting a vote."

"We'll take it," Harriet Blatch said.

An usher quickly snatched the bank note.

When the laughter subsided, Harriet added, "Any woman who says she is not for equal rights is a liar and knows it in her heart."

Thunderous applause filled the auditorium.

Exhilarated by the show, Sarah settled back in her chair. She was having the best time of her life.

CHAPTER 50

Sarah awoke with a start. Realizing where she was, she snuggled under the covers, savoring the richness of her hotel room for another moment. Telling herself she would be late, she forced herself out of the cozy bed, ordered room service and hurried to get ready for a glorious day. An hour later, her breakfast consumed, her gardenia-covered hat pinned to her head and her yellow sash draped across her chest, she joined her group and boarded the trolley for the ride to the parade-staging area.

Hundreds of gardenias worn by the suffragists filled the air with the smell of spring. "What a beautiful day," Sarah said, inhaling deeply. "I love it brisk."

"As long as the wind doesn't pick up any more," Mary Beckworth said.

The trolley stopped at Twelfth Street to pick up passengers from the Raleigh Hotel. When it started up again someone said, "Would you look at that?"

All eyes turned to where the speaker pointed. The trolley driver clanged the bell, offering his comment on the poster filling the store window. It depicted a woman in a suit and derby hat, carrying a cane, and a man slung over her shoulder, a bottle of whiskey falling from his pocket.

"Ignore them," Mary Beckworth said. "You've seen them all in the magazines. We have twice as many posters for us, and look at all the yellow flags and banners flying."

Once noticed, it was hard for Sarah not to see the other anti-suffrage posters, especially since the trolley bell clanged as they passed each one. All were typical of what she had seen over and over. A woman standing over a crib, next to her a woman in a suit and derby hat with the caption reading, "I feel two natures struggling inside me." And the most often displayed ones of women garbed in men's uniforms, all goofing up the job. The firelady, cutting the hose with her axe. The policewoman being bopped on the head by the hoodlum. The postal woman, spilling her mail all over the street.

To avoid having a pall cast over the lovely day, Sarah stared straight ahead out the front of the trolley. She noticed that the police had already cordoned off the street with ropes strung on flimsy posts along the curb. Despite its being over an hour before the parade was to begin, spectators—mostly men—were gathering.

Her spirits lightened a bit when she spotted a lady, her hat covered in yellow gardenias, toting a sandwich board sign. "Look!" she said.

As the trolley passed, its bell silent, the passengers craned their necks to read the message.

Jack and Jill have equal will
And equal strength of mind.
But when it comes to equal rights
Poor Jill trails far behind.

"You tell 'em, honey!" someone yelled out the window.

The trolley stopped at the Peace Monument by the Capitol Building. Carved in Rome in 1877 as an ode to the Navy's dead of the Civil War, the woman crying on a man's shoulder, depicted America crying on history's shoulder.

As they disembarked the trolley the driver said, "Have a nice march, ladies."

"I hope your trolley jumps the tracks," one of the women said, followed by cheers.

"What a lout," Carole Davis said.

"You should be used to his type by now," Mary said, gathering her group around her. "That's why we're here, to show them we won't be bullied into silence." Referring to the sheet of paper she had taken from her purse, she said, "Sarah, you'll be riding on the Education float. You see it over there?"

Sarah followed Mary's outstretched arm. She nodded when she saw the truck decorated with huge cardboard books and big letters of the alphabet. In the bed of the truck were desks and chairs. Signs reading, "In Education" draped the sides almost to the ground.

To Sarah, the area seemed a mass of confusion. Women milled in groups by the Peace Monument, Grant's Statue, and on the Capitol grounds. Floats were parked along every curb. Besides her float, she saw ones labeled "1840," "Today," "In the House," "In Patriotic Service," "Sweat Shop."

"Carole," Mary continued. "you're on the 'Today' float. You did bring your costume?"

Carole raised a bag. "Right here."

"Eloise, you're with the business women. Did I tell you I like your suit?"

"Thank you."

"The rest of us will be in the Sixth Section with the New Jersey State Delegation, but any of you who want to march in the housewife section are welcome to do so. Any questions?"

When no one answered, Mary said, "Let's show 'em, ladies."

"Wait," Sarah said. "Gather together in front of the monument. I want to get a picture."

She snapped one, wound the film, and said, "One more, just in case the first didn't come out."

Her photography done, Sarah walked over to her float. There were three desks and chairs—two side-by-side in back of the driver's compartment, and one in the rear. Two other riders, she thought, and took a picture.

With a bit of time before the parade was to step off, Sarah decided to look over the other parade sections. Being in it was fun, but she wouldn't be able to see much from her float.

Inez Milholland had just ridden up to the Peace Monument on her white horse. She looked splendid. Unfortunately, she also sent a shiver through Sarah. Her outfit—a white Cossack suit with long white kid boots and a pale blue cloak embroidered with a golden

Maltese Cross—reminded Sarah of harsh times back in Latvia. Accompanying Inez were three other horsewomen in more demure corduroy riding habits and wide-brimmed plumed hats, and the person Sarah guessed must be Mrs. Burleson, the Grand Marshal.

Mrs. Burleson was decked out in yellow from head toe. One side of her western-style hat was pinned to the crown and a huge yellow plume spired up from it. She set her horse in regal fashion, back straight, hands caressing, but not grasping the reins.

Sarah strolled First Avenue to the corner and headed down B Street. The cacophony of bands tuning up, auto engines sputtering, and women talking amplified her excitement. Flags of every state hung on their staffs, stuck in the ground and ready to be grabbed up by their standard bearers at a moment's notice. Banners calling out slogans for all women to join the cause rippled in the breeze. Some were serious,

Women of the world unite
We want to protect our children
We demand an amendment to the United States Constitution
enfranchising the women of the country.

Others were humorous. One made her chuckle aloud. Printed over the picture of a large boat, it read,

Here's to the baby of five and fifteen,
Here's to the widow of fifty,
Here's to the flaunting extravagant queen
And here's to the hussy that's thrifty.
Please take note
They are all in the same boat;
They have not a chance of recording a vote.

Sarah continued her exploratory tour and picture-taking. Contingents of women, each group wearing a different color sash across their chests, announced their occupations.

The *business* group wore blue,
The *writers* in white,
Musicians in red,
Lawyers, gray,
Physicians, pale green,
Teachers, yellow,
Librarians, orange,
Social workers, violet,
Clergy, black.

And there were scores of women in everyday street clothes with the word, "wives," proudly displayed on their sashes.

Gleefully snapping pictures, Sarah thought, *We certainly will show the men who we are this day. They'll see there's nothing they can do that we can't.*

Shouts of, “The parade is ready to start,” relayed down the line of marchers. Sarah hurried back to her float. She climbed on and got the shock of her life.

CHAPTER 51

Helen Keller and her companion Annie Sullivan waited on Sarah's float. Recovering from her stunned stupor, Sarah didn't think, pushed out her hand, and spoke as if Helen could see and hear. "It is a pleasure to meet you, Miss Keller. I'm Sarah Bressler."

Realizing how stupid she was, Sarah quickly dropped her hand as Annie Sullivan relayed to Helen what Sarah said by scratching the palm of Helen's hand. Helen replied in a slightly marbled, but certainly discernible voice, "Nice to meet you, Sarah."

"This is going to be a delightful day. Can I take your picture?"

Again, Annie coded Sarah's words into their sign language, and Helen said, "Yes."

Rather than ask her subjects to re-position themselves, Sarah shifted around until she had them both centered in her view-finder. Snapping the button, she asked, "Are you going to the allegory at the end of the parade?"

After the message was relayed, Helen nodded and Annie said, "Helen is the guest speaker at the allegory, and she will also be speaking tonight at Constitution Hall. Will you be there?"

"I wouldn't miss it."

Their conversation was cut off by Mrs. Burleson's command of, "Fall in!" which was repeated by the Herald, Inez Milholland, and echoed from section to section.

The parade began with the Grand Marshal in the lead, and Inez and her horsewomen just behind. Following the cavalry was a truck with a banner on each side, reading,

WE DEMAND AN AMENDMENT TO THE CONSTITUTION
ENFRANCHISING THE WOMEN OF THE COUNTRY.

Next marched the national and international leaders. In the center was Dr. Anna Howard Shaw, wearing the hood of her degree and her college gown. Carrie Chapman Catt and Harriet Stanton Blatch flanked her, both wearing yellow dresses and sashes, designating their positions.

Following their leaders, two women also dressed in yellow, carried the "WOMEN OF THE WORLD UNITE" banner. Behind them, in snappy blue uniforms, stepped the thirty-five-piece Marysville, Missouri band. Then came floats of countries where women were also fighting for suffrage.

Sarah's float jolted and rolled forward. She had been sitting, but now that they were moving, she wanted to view the extravaganza and stood up. The sky was bright blue, temperature about fifty-five, and just enough breeze to flutter the banners, standards, flags and bunting.

She heard the spectators roar, but she had no clue it was the first sign of trouble until they rounded the corner of First Street and turned onto Pennsylvania Avenue. Way out in front, flying their white and blue police flags and moving at a pace too fast for the parade to keep up sped the nine autos of Commissioner Johnson. Their wedge formation effectively held the spectators before them off the street. But when the autos passed, the crowd surged, tearing down the rope barriers as if they were paper streamers. Yelling and screaming, they adulterated the music from the band to the point where no tune could be recognized.

"Oh, no!" Sarah blurted out.

"What's wrong?" Annie Sullivan asked, rising to stand next to Sarah.

The solid mass of humanity that lined the parade route from the Treasury to the Peace Monument swallowed the marchers.

Annie Sullivan dropped down in her seat and signed to Helen what was happening. Helen became agitated, snapping her head to and fro and squirming in her seat. Annie hugged her, trying to calm her.

Keeping an eye on the head of the parade, Sarah said, "Don't worry, the floats are doing fine."

The crowd avoided Mrs. Burlson, Inez Milholland, and her three outriders. The horses reared a couple of times and no one wanted to be under their hooves when they came down. Sarah was amazed that the riders managed to stay in the saddles.

But the crowd hemmed in the walking suffrage leaders and squashed the musicians shoulder-to-shoulder, forcing them to stop playing. No longer hearing the band, Inez Milholland, turned in her saddle to review the goings on behind her. Seeing the melee, she quickly wheeled her horse and rode into the crowd. Her three mounted compatriots followed her lead.

"Good for you!" Sarah shouted.

With two horses on each side of them, the suffrage leaders were protected. The other marchers, their ranks destroyed, huddled in behind the floats, letting the autos act as rams to push through the rioters. General Johnson, in the lead of the police caravan never looked back.

Sarah's float had not yet reached the melee, but she heard it. The bellow of voices melded into one loud howl. What Sarah couldn't distinguish above the din were the screams of terror from the marchers as hands shot out from the males in the crowd and pinched the women's thighs and rear ends. The few policemen standing along the parade route made no attempt to maintain order.

Somehow, the parade inched forward, the horsewomen managing to open a path. Sarah's float reached the free-for-all and the mob quickly besieged it. Annie clutched Helen, fear on both of their faces.

Sarah yelled, "Stop that!" as the banners were torn from their truck, spat on and stomped.

Her float edged forward, nudging people out of its path. A policeman came into Sarah's view. He laughed and joked with the molesters.

"Help us, please," Sarah yelled.

His hands clasped behind his back, he bellowed back, "I'm doing the best I can."

"Do you know who is on this float with me?"

"If it ain't the President, I don't care."

"You boor!" Sarah screamed.

The policeman elbowed his way past a few men and drew up beside Sarah's truck. "If you was my wife, I'd knock you down," he said.

"I pity your wife having you for a husband."

The policeman pulled his club from his belt. The hoodlums nearby cowered back, thinking they were his target. But his target was Sarah. He swung his club and yelled, "Go home."

Sarah jumped back as his club struck the truck with a resounding clank. Whether he had tried to hit her or not, she wasn't sure, but he scared her almost to death. Clutching her stomach to protect her baby, Sarah, along with Helen and Anne, cowered by their desks, afraid to move until the policeman was no longer in view.

Twenty feet further on, her float came near a troop of Boy Scouts. True to their creed, they tried to hold back some of the mob, but to no avail.

"Can you help us, please?" Sarah begged.

"What can we do, ma'am?" the one who looked to be the eldest asked.

"This is Miss Helen Keller. Can you young men please come up here and protect her?"

"We would be honored," he answered, and the six boys climbed up on the float and flanked Helen and Anne.

Having stripped Sarah's float of its decorations, the crowd lost interest in it and focused its attention on the next contingent in the parade.

Sarah looked to the rear. The hoodlums swarmed on float after float, defrocking them of their signs, banners and flags. The marching women who had hoped to spread out from curb to curb were hemmed in behind the still-moving trucks. As they had done to the forward contingents, many men molested the women.

A liquor bottle in his right hand, a man latched his left on the tailgate of Sarah's barely moving truck. Holding up his bottle, he said, "Join me in a drink, sister?"

As Sarah retreated from his foul breath, he hoisted himself up.

"Do something!" Anne Sullivan screamed.

Sarah snatched her hat-pin from her flowered bonnet and jabbed at his hand. He fell back, dropping his bottle. It smashed on the bed of the truck, splattering Sarah's new dress with whiskey.

"Oh, no!" she cried, swatting at the spots as if she were on fire. She accidentally stuck herself with her pin and cried out. The pain focused her attention on what she had just done to the drunk. She yelled at the women being accosted, "Hat-pins, ladies," and poked another hand grasping onto the side of her truck. He howled and let go. Moments later, similar howls wailed from the rowdies.

Most of the louts retreated, but some men, intent on as much destruction as possible, punched at the women.

Just as Sarah feared all was lost, the Thirteenth Regiment of the Pennsylvania National Guard, in town to march in the inauguration parade tomorrow, trotted double time down the Avenue from the Treasury Building. With their weapons at port arms, they took up positions along the route from Ninth to Fifteenth Streets. They were augmented by a troop of cavalry from Fort Myer. The commanders of both contingents had been watching the parade and took it upon themselves to rescue the women.

As each beleaguered section of the parade reached the safe zone, the suffragists gathered what was left of their pride, raised their heads and marched on to the finish, disbanding at President's Park to the south of the Treasury and the Executive mansion.

The parade was to culminate in an allegory on the steps of the Treasury. With the huge white columns in the background, actresses robed also in white were to depict Justice, Charity, Liberty, Peace, and Hope in a review of the woman's suffrage movement over the past decade. It should have been a marvelous zenith to the parade with the band beginning the show by playing "The Star Spangled Banner," and an actress dressed as Columbia in velvet robes of red, white and blue emerging from the pillars to introduce the other players. Sadly, it was not.

Although performed without a hitch before hundreds of spectators surrounded by a military guard, its beauty and meaning were marred by the destruction of the parade. And the guests of honor, Mrs. Howard Taft and her daughter, Miss Helen Taft, had been ushered from the grandstand and back to the White House when the riot erupted. Helen Keller, who was to be seated next to Mrs. Taft, also decided not to attend. So did Sarah.

CHAPTER 52

Disillusioned, Sarah had climbed down from her truck and walked halfway back to the Willard before she realized she had forgotten her camera. Practically running, she returned to where she had left the float. The truck was gone.

Will this nightmare never end?

In the hotel lobby, she bumped into Eleanor Hewitt. Eleanor had an ugly bruise below her right eye.

In an offer of sympathy, Sarah asked, "Does it hurt much?"

"A little. But it could have been a lot worse if we hadn't used our hat pins."

Sarah smiled weakly. "That was a good idea."

"It was disgusting, the way the police just stood by and let those ruffians spit on us and . . ." She broke down, weeping.

Sarah took her in her arms and led her to the settee.

Eleanor gazed into Sarah's eyes. "Please come to my room with me. I don't want to be alone."

"Where are the others from your group?"

"At a meeting with the Suffrage Association's Congressional Committee. They're drafting a vigorous protest to deliver to Congress and a telegram to send to President Wilson after the inauguration."

"Good. That horrid Commissioner Johnson took off and left the parade stranded."

Eleanor took Sarah's hand. Begging with her eyes, she said, "Please come with me."

Sarah nodded. Draping her arm around Eleanor, they boarded the elevator.

In her suite, Eleanor offered Sarah a drink.

"Water will be fine. Thank you," Sarah said.

Eleanor fixed herself a brandy, wrapped a handful of ice chips from the ice chest in a bar towel and carried the drinks and the ice pack to the coffee table in front of the couch. Before sitting down, she went to the desk and jotted a note. Returning to the couch, she handed Sarah the piece of paper and said, "If you've decided you're having your last child, that is the name of a wonderful doctor in New York City who might be able to help you. He studied in Europe. They're much more enlightened over there."

Sarah stared at the note.

"Don't tell anyone about him," Eleanor said.

Sarah clutched the note to her breast and thought, *My biggest wish has been fulfilled. Meeting Eleanor had to have been divine intervention.*

"Would you mind if I rested my head on your lap so I can lay this ice pack on my cheek?" Eleanor asked.

"Of course not," Sarah said and adjusted herself to make her legs more comfortable for her friend.

As she stretched out to lie down, Eleanor brushed her lips across Sarah's breasts, causing Sarah to flinch slightly. Positioning the ice pack, she grasped Sarah's hand and placed it on her midriff. Stroking the back of Sarah's hand, forcing Sarah's fingers to massage her belly, Eleanor moaned and said, "That feels good. A man hit me here."

"Does it hurt much?"

"It's better now," Eleanor said, adding a bit more pressure to Sarah's hand.

More out of reflex than conscious thought, Sarah stroked Eleanor's hair. A strange feeling rippled through her. She wished she and Abe would lie like this once in a while, with either her head on his lap or his on hers, listening to a Victor record and talking about their day—or about nothing at all.

To balance the ice pack on her cheek, Eleanor had her head turned in toward Sarah's slightly swelled stomach. She opened her mouth and pinched Sarah's dress and a bit of her flesh with her lips.

"That tickles," Sarah said.

Eleanor did it again.

"Stop it," Sarah giggled.

"You don't like to be tickled?"

"It's silly."

"You don't like being silly?"

"No, I do. It's just that . . ." Sarah said and giggled again.

"What?"

"Nothing," she said and thought, *Wouldn't it be nice if Abe played like this now and then out of the bedroom?*

"Would you mind if I changed into something more comfortable?"

"Of course not."

"And you can too, if you want. You know, undo your buttons. Free yourself."

"Okay."

"Let me help you."

Sarah turned around and Eleanor undid her buttons all the way down to Sarah's waist.

"There, doesn't that feel better?" Eleanor asked.

"Much," Sarah said with a sigh.

Before entering the bathroom, Eleanor said, "Why don't you take off your dress? You'll be more comfortable."

"It's fine like this," Sarah said and flopped back onto the couch.

When Eleanor emerged, Sarah's mouth popped open.

Eleanor had changed into a sheer nightgown. With the light coming from the side and the rear, it looked like no more than a shadow covering Eleanor's ample breasts, curvy torso, and her legs all the way up to the dark triangle at their crest.

Eleanor quickly crossed the floor and fell onto the couch. Before Sarah knew what was happening, her hand was in Eleanor's grasp and was thrust flat on Eleanor's breast, and Eleanor kissed her full on the mouth.

Sarah yanked herself away, jumped up and gasped, "Are you crazy? What are you doing?"

Eleanor looked stunned. "But you accepted my flirtations."

"What?"

"We held hands. You patted my belly. You stroked my hair. You said you liked the tickle I gave you."

Backing away, Sarah's eyes opened into wide ovals and her jaw quivered. She grabbed her coat and fled toward the door.

Looking hurt, Eleanor said, "I gave you the name of a doctor. You said you were grateful."

Sarah yanked the door open. She flung her coat over her opened dress and ran down the hall to the elevator. Retreating to her room, she packed her bags and hovered behind her locked door until it was time to leave for her train in the morning. She couldn't wait to get back to Paterson, where she would be safe.

CHAPTER 53

Dour of body and spirit, Sarah fought her way through the boisterous crowds exiting Union Station. She was going home. They were arriving for the jubilant occasion of the inauguration of a new president.

On the train, the porter showed her to her compartment—a feature of the train she now wished she had used on her way down. She settled in to read the Washington newspaper, trying to take her mind off what could be a nasty homecoming.

The front-page headline blared the story of the disastrous parade. Every leader of the suffrage movement vehemently denounced the police. The United States Senate passed a resolution to investigate, with Senator Nelson of Minnesota the Spokesman. "The failure of the police to preserve order and clear the Avenue was a most disgraceful affair, discreditable to the police and the National Capital."

"Whoop-de-do," Sarah blurted out. Three hundred women taken to hospitals and the great, wonderful men of our government passed another resolution. Their report should make a nice trash-can liner, along with their other resolution that was supposed to have cleared Pennsylvania Avenue.

Sarah thought, *I'll bet there'll be no complaints today about how the police protect the inaugural parade. I'm sure they'll shoot anybody who even thinks about disrupting it.*

She came to the quote from General John A. Johnson, commissioner of the District in charge of the police.

"The police did as well as they could under the circumstances. I myself was at the head of the parade in an automobile. Stopping at the corner of Fifteenth Street and Pennsylvania Avenue, I noticed the faces of the marchers and saw no sign of distress indicating that they had been subject to insults. It was a big, typical good-natured American crowd and I witnessed no rowdiness."

Sarah crumpled the paper and threw it on the floor in disgust. "So much for an honest investigation."

To calm herself, she closed her eyes and leaned her head back, letting the sway of the train soothe her. She had barely slept a minute last night. No matter how hard she tried, she couldn't wipe Eleanor's attempted seduction out of her mind. She had read about lesbians. How could she have been so naïve that she didn't recognize what Eleanor was doing? The more she thought about it, the more she wondered if subconsciously she didn't push Eleanor away earlier in their encounter because she liked the contentment Eleanor's affection gave her. It was only the kiss that nauseated her, not Eleanor lying on her lap, not the petting. That didn't make her uncomfortable. Oh, God, what had she become, finding solace in the arms of another woman? What had Abe driven her to?

That was last night. Today, other thoughts twisted and churned her stomach. How was Abe going to react to her arrival? What if he wouldn't let her back in the house? What would she do? Where would she go?

****

With heightening trepidation, Sarah walked through her front door at six in the evening. Her sons ran to her from their lookout position on the stairs and wrapped their arms around her legs, yelling, "Mommy, Mommy!"

Feeling a slight bit of relief at not seeing Abe, she dropped to her knees and hugged each of her children until they cried out, "You're hurting me." Releasing them, she hustled them up to their beds, tucked them in and kissed each one on the nose, the forehead and both cheeks.

Chava waited for her on the second-floor landing. "I'm sorry," she said.

"You heard what happened?"

"Abe told me."

Sarah thought, *I'm sure he only told you the brutal parts and not the intended beauty of the parade and allegory.* "Where is he?"

"In his study."

Barely able to control herself from shaking, Sarah made her way down the stairs and across the living room. She softly tapped on the door. Seconds later—it seemed like an hour—Abe opened it. With a big smile on his face, he stared at her for a moment, then grabbed her in his arms and gave her a long, loving kiss. Relief swept over her.

"I tried to warn you," he said. "It's a harsh world out there."

He led her to a chair, poured her a glass of water and asked, "Hungry?"

"Yes."

With him gone to get her dinner, she slumped in her chair. Her taut muscles contracted like a rubber band, hastily removed from a bundle.

Returning, Abe said, "Frances will be right in."

Pouring himself a brandy, he sat across from her. "I hope you realize now you're never going to win."

Her ire flared again. She didn't know which was worse—having him yell at her, or having to put up with his smugness.

"Abe, you weren't there. The police just stood around. They would have given more protection to a drove of pigs being herded through the street than they afforded us."

"Yes, dear. I'm sorry," he said with a frown. But it wasn't a real frown. It was a complacent, laughing, upside-down grin.

She knew if she continued talking it would only bring on more of his holier-than-thou attitude, but she couldn't stop herself. "Even with the fiasco, we did accomplish one thing."

"What was that, dear?"

"The movement acquired new friends. Many anti-suffragists were outraged. Sometimes it takes something like this to bring attention."

"Absolutely," he said, and stood up. "Come here, I want to give you another hug."

Captive in his strong arms, she had no choice but to listen. "I forgive you for leaving us. I realize it was something you had to experience yourself. I hope you learned your lesson."

His words echoed in her ears like the noontime whistles at the mills. *He is so self-righteous*, she thought. Yes, she certainly learned something. The fight for suffrage was all about control. Men coveted their domination over women like sacks of money, and weren't going to give it up without a long, dirty fight.

Was she strong enough to continue that fight? If someone in her group touched her, how could she tell if it was an innocent brush or a deliberate act? If she found out it was intentional, would she be repulsed? Or, if Abe continued to demean her, would she respond the same way she did to Eleanor, desperately seeking the tenderness Eleanor gave her? Was it possible she could turn into a lesbian? Could another woman's affection actually entice her into becoming . . . No, it couldn't happen, could it?

PART IV

APRIL–JULY 1913

CHAPTER 54

Sarah braced herself with her outstretched arm against the auto's dashboard as Abe raced down Vreeland Avenue and skidded to a stop at the same moment the train pulled into the station. Pulling Sarah out of the car, he hustled her across the platform, pushing her up the steps as the conductor yelled, "All aboard!"

Sarah fell hard onto the cane seat and gasped at seeing her reflection in the window. Her hat hung precariously on her head, and a speck of soot smudged her chin.

"David and Leah will certainly be surprised when they find out where we're going," Abe said with a grin.

Still unnerved from the hair-raising drive, Sarah fumbled in her purse, recovered her handkerchief, wet it with her saliva and rubbed the black spot away. Re-pinning her hat, she was finally able to fill her lungs with air and asked, "Are you sure it was a good idea not to tell them? I hope Leah is dressed properly."

"She'll be fine."

"I wish Solomon and Cecelia could have joined us."

As soon as she said it, she wanted to suck the words back into her mouth. She glanced at Abe out of the corner of her eye. His face was bright red. She was positive, if they weren't on this public train he would have exploded into another tirade about his brother and Paterson's ungrateful laborers. She was not about to be the blasting cap that set him off and ruin what she hoped would be a wonderful evening. She certainly could use one.

Since she returned from Washington, she had purposefully avoided mentioning Solomon, or the strike, or suffrage. Within a few days, life had returned to normal—at least normal from Abe's viewpoint. He went off to tend to his business. She stayed home as the dutiful wife, caring for the children and the house.

But to her, life was not normal. She thought she had seen every side of him over their nine years of marriage. However, since her return, he had shown her yet another face—withdrawn. In the past four weeks he had barely touched her. It was so unlike him. Coupling was as important to Abe as breathing. It was important to her, too. She needed his strong arms holding her, his lips caressing her skin, him inside her to dispel those recurring visions of Eleanor. She couldn't seem to banish Eleanor from her mind. Every time she craved affection from Abe and he didn't give it to her, the warmth of Eleanor's petting came flooding back, and she hated it. She thought about it long and hard. She wasn't a lesbian. She didn't want to lie with women. She wanted Abe.

She stared out the window at the passing factories so he wouldn't see the tears welling up in her eyes. What kept him from her? She refused to believe it was that one failure the night of her arrest. It had to be the strike. That's all everyone talked about on the street or in the market. It was killing everyone's business—merchant and silk man alike. How long would their money hold out? she wondered. This was going to be an expensive evening, yet he was excited about it. Still, he had to be worried wondering how long the strike would last.

And all those late night meetings with the mill owners, trying to no avail to arrive at a solution to end the strike had to be tedious and frustrating. Coupling surely had to be the last thought on his mind. So why couldn't she get the gnawing feeling out of her head that it was something more than the strike that was keeping Abe from her? She prayed, "Please let it end soon," hoping her anxiety would go away with the mills re-opening.

CHAPTER 55

From Jersey City's Pavonia Avenue Station, Abe and Sarah took the ferry across the Hudson to the Chambers Street terminal in lower Manhattan, where they met the chauffeured car Abe had hired for the evening. "One fifty-seven Hester Street," Abe told the driver.

"Yes, sir," the chauffeur said, and shut the window between himself and the passenger compartment.

Settling back into the plush leather seats of the four-passenger Franklin Torpedo Phaeton, Abe thought about this evening. He had made the reservations a couple of weeks ago, when he still had a business. Now it was an extravagance. The laborers in Pennsylvania's mills had joined their Paterson comrades in a sympathy strike. The country's entire silk industry was shut down. Still, he had promised a night out to David and Leah to celebrate their anniversary. He didn't want to disappoint them.

The driver pulled up in front of David's building. As Abe exited the car to fetch his brother and sister-in-law, a whiff of rotting garbage attacked his nose. He glanced at the trash in the alley and shuddered at the thought of what must be running around among the rubbish.

When Abe re-appeared with David and Leah, three shabbily dressed boys hovered together on the sidewalk, staring at the car. They kept their distance because the six-foot-four-inch driver held a position on the curb next to the back door of the auto. Seeing his employer approach, the driver opened the door for Abe and his guests. Hustling back to the driver's seat, the chauffeur asked, "Where to, sir?"

"Delmonicos," Abe said.

As the car pulled away from the curb, David exclaimed, "Delmonicos! I thought we go by the chop house on Fourteenth Street."

Leah's eyes dropped to her plain turquoise smock, and she reached up to touch her simple hat. "I'm not dressed properly."

"You look lovely," Sarah reassured her. She leaned forward to give her sister-in-law a kiss on the cheek and suddenly realized the bulge in Leah's belly was part of her and not the poor fit of her dress.

"Leah, are you *shvengern?*"

"Yes, I'm due in July."

"Me too, in September," Sarah revealed.

"Congratulations," Abe said. "Now we really have something to celebrate."

****

At the restaurant, the white-gloved, red-uniformed doorman opened the car door. A second, similarly-dressed doorman swept open the massive glass-paneled restaurant door. The two couples walked into the dining room, Abe and Sarah confident, David and Leah in awe.

Abe announced himself to the Maître d, and discretely tipped him with a five-dollar bill.

"Yes, sir, Mr. Bressler. Follow me."

Arriving at their table, Abe assisted Sarah while the Maître d held the red velvet, gold-leaf armchair for Leah.

David's eyes roamed around the room. "This is is . . ." He couldn't find the word he searched for and left his sentence incomplete.

Abe winked at Sarah and said, "I'm glad you like it."

Leah, too wonderstruck to speak, tried to take in all the opulence at once. Ten huge, layered crystal chandeliers sparkled with what seemed like a hundred light bulbs. Red velvet drapes, trimmed with gold braid and topped with yards of fabric swooped into festoons and jabots, adorned the windows. White Irish linen tablecloths, English bone china, hand-blown and hand-cut crystal stemware and sterling silver flatware graced the table.

The head waiter arrived. Lifting the napkins from their plates, he opened them with a flourish and placed them in each diner's lap. He handed them a red leather folder. The eight-page menu was so tall, if stood up on the table, the diners would not be able to see above it.

"Please send over the wine steward," Abe said.

Another red-jacketed man appeared. Around his neck hung a silver dipper he used to taste the wine. Abe ordered champagne.

A few moments later the wine steward reappeared and placed a floor stand, holding an ice bucket and a bottle, next to Abe. Withdrawing the bottle, he showed Abe the label. When his patron nodded, the wine steward popped the cork. Leah let out a short squeal and covered her mouth in embarrassment. With the champagne bubbling in their glasses, Abe raised his and said, "To the children."

Leah took a sip and giggled as the bubbles tickled her nose and cheeks.

The toast complete, they placed their orders, and the waiter bowed and backed away. Abe asked David, "How are things going at Ribbicoff's? He give you the raise you asked for?"

David took another sip of champagne. "Everything is fine."

"What's the strike doing to your business?" Abe asked.

"Like everybody, we have no goods to sell. What are they doing to settle?"

"Nothing. The bosses refuse to talk terms as long as the IWW people are in town, and your brother and his locals refuse to kick the radicals out."

"Abe, please," Sarah said. "No more talk about the strike."

Abe glared at her.

Leah cut off his admonishment. "Men!" she said. "If women ran the strike, it would be over by now."

"There is one woman on the striker's side, and she is as stubborn as any of them," Abe said, triumphantly continuing the conversation.

As stubborn as you? Sarah thought, but bit her tongue. "I met Miss Flynn. She is a very nice person."

"You met Elizabeth Flynn?" Leah asked. "Where?"

"In jail."

"You visited her in jail?"

"No, she was there when I was arrested."

Leah's mouth dropped open. Her lips fluttered, but she couldn't speak.

"You were arrested?" David said.

"Sarah, not now," Abe commanded.

Sarah turned away from Abe and mouthed to Leah, "Later."

The table fell silent. The festive atmosphere had turned somber, exactly what Sarah wanted to avoid. Why couldn't she keep her big mouth shut?

Having recovered from her shock, Leah rescued her. "Tell me about the children. What kind of trouble are they getting into lately?"

"The boys are great," Abe said.

"They're growing so fast," Sarah added.

The waiter arrived with their steaks. The juices sizzled on the plates as he placed them in front of the diners. David deeply inhaled the aroma and snatched up his knife and fork. Even though the meat wasn't kosher, he savored each morsel as if it were his last meal.

The entrees eaten, Sarah and Leah excused themselves and went to the powder room.

Having risen with the women, Abe and David reseated themselves, and Abe asked, "You think Wilson will keep us out of the disputes brewing in Europe?"

"This is something I do not know," David said, his mind seemingly off somewhere else. "Abe?"

"Yes?"

"Do you still keep your offer open?"

Abe stopped gandering at the surrounding tables and focused on his brother. "What offer?"

David swallowed hard. "To come by you to work?"

Momentarily caught off guard, Abe asked, "Why the change of heart?"

"Ribbicoff closed his doors until the mills reopen."

"I'm in the same boat as Ribbicoff," Abe said, trying to buy some time while he thought about what he could do. For nine years, he had held onto the idea of uniting with his brothers in a family business. Now, at the worst time possible, it was happening.

When the strike started, Abe had contacted his brother Jacob. Jacob wired back with a nice order. Abe had just made a deal with a Pennsylvania mill for a job lot that would fill that order and a couple more when that mill closed. His warehouse was empty and his cash reserve was vanishing fast to cover his personal expenses. But he couldn't let this opportunity slip away. He'd find some way to pay David

"I understand," David said.

"Let me finish. I was going to say, but I haven't been stopped yet. Will thirty-five dollars a week be okay with you?"

Exalted by Abe's generous offer—ten dollars more than he was making at Ribbicoff's—David couldn't speak for a moment. When he recovered, he said, "Thank you, thank you," as if he were a serf expressing his gratitude to his sire for a small handout.

A big grin on his face, Abe said, "You're welcome."

Sarah and Leah returned to the table. "What are you grinning about?" Sarah asked Abe.

Raising his champagne glass, Abe said, "A toast to a new partnership. David and me."

Leah's mouth fell open. "What is this all about?"

"David is coming in with me," Abe replied.

Gaping at her husband, Leah asked, "What about Ribbicoff?"

"He shut his doors yesterday."

"And you didn't tell me?"

"I didn't want by you to worry."

"But what about . . . how will you get back and forth to Paterson?"

"You will move," Abe said, his comment more a command than an offered solution.

"But my parents, my family . . ."

"Leah, don't worry," Sarah said. "Paterson is only an hour from New York City by train and ferry. You can visit your family any time." Picking up her champagne glass, Sarah said in a subdued, almost apprehensive voice, "Congratulations."

Abe beamed and thought, *Now that I have David's life on track, all I have to do is work on Solomon.*

CHAPTER 56

Abe hurried his steps past the gangs of workers gathered outside the mills for their daily shop meetings and thought, *That bunch of IWW thugs know how to organize even if they are damn fools.* Abe purposefully avoided looking at the men and women. Infuriated at what he heard last night, he was afraid if he caught the eye of a familiar face, unpleasant words would erupt into a confrontation. On Mill Street, Abe passed Peter Ryle's house. Peter was one of the last mill owners still living across the street from his mill. Most others had moved out to the east end of town across Madison Avenue. Peter couldn't give up the house his father built. "It would be bad luck," Peter was often heard saying. Peter's father, John, had opened the first silk mill in Paterson seventy years ago and was revered as the founder of Paterson's silk industry.

Abe turned right on Market Street. He took that route because Rogers' locomotive factory covered half the block. Rogers' workers weren't on strike. The fire from the hearth, reflecting in the windows, and the clanging hammers molding and fitting steel reassured Abe there were still some sane laborers in town. He couldn't help but wonder what Alexander Hamilton, Paterson's founder, would have thought of all this foolishness.

Turning right on Spruce, he proceeded half a block to the entrance of the mill owned by his friend, Saul Rosen. Saul, and every mill in the city, flew the American flag over the entranceway to their shop. A hastily-painted banner hung next to Saul's flag.

For God and Country!
The Stars and Stripes forever!
The red flag never!

Last night Solomon's gang tried to get the workers to abandon the American flag and pledge allegiance to that idiotic red flag of theirs. Thank God no one was dumb enough to fall for that. The great majority of the workers proudly displayed American flag pins on their jackets and dresses. Abe was willing to bet not one of them had forgotten what it was like living under the boot of a king or tsar. He didn't care what country they came from, they all came to America for one reason: to get away from brutality and oppression often fostered on them by a nobleman.

So why are they following that bunch of liars? he thought. Despite dozens of strikes, the workers still couldn't understand that it was hopeless to fight the mill owners. But at least they did learn one thing from their battles with their bosses: violence only makes matters worse. He was surprised how peaceful the strikers were. But for how long? he wondered. If the police kept up their brutality, the laborers were bound to retaliate. He knew he would if he were in their position. Spying a worker's banner, he paused to read it.

We wove the flag
We dyed the flag
We live under the flag
But we won't scab under the flag.

"Damn fools!" he muttered.

A paddy-wagon with four policemen leaning against its side idled in the street in front of Saul Rosen's factory. Rosen stood on the steps of his mill, pad and pencil in hand, talking to another cop as he pointed and said, "That man there, and that one, and that one." As he wrote the worker's names on his pad, the police at the paddy-wagon came to attention, grabbed the men who had been singled out and threw them into the back of the truck. His identifications finished, Rosen quickly disappeared inside.

Ignoring the hoots and obscenities hurled at him, Abe muscled his way through the crowd to the door Rosen left wide open in case anyone changed his mind and wanted to return to work. As he crossed the dust-free wooden floor, the sound of his clicking heels echoed eerily throughout the empty mill. A haunting feeling crept over him. There hadn't been a worker in the place for six weeks, yet the looms looked as if they were waiting for the weavers to return from lunch and start them up.

The shed of warp yarn in the harnesses yawned wide open. Abe fully expected to hear the whack of the picker stick as it banged the shuttle through the shed so the bobbin could dole out the weft yarn, and the beater thump as it pounded the weft into place, and the harness thud, reversing position to form a new shed. But of course he wouldn't hear that rhythmic *whack, thump, thump*. Rosen's looms, like all the other looms in Paterson, stood idle.

When he got two steps from the door marked "Office," it opened. "Oh, it's you, Abe," Saul Rosen said, a baseball bat clutched in his hand. "Come in."

The mill office was austerely furnished. A table, cluttered with scraps of fabric, stood against the wall, below a high window. A few black-framed photographs adorned the walls, and one leather and two scarred wooden arm chairs sat before Rosen's roll-top desk.

Rosen leaned the bat against his desk, motioned his visitor to a seat and slowly lowered himself into the leather chair. Rosen's back seemed to curve a little more than usual, and the wrinkles in his face looked to be etched a little deeper than when Abe had seen him a few weeks ago.

"You need that bat?" Abe asked.

"I'm not taking any chances. They're peaceful so far, but who knows what will spark them?"

Abe nodded. "What was that all about outside?"

"The men they hauled off threw rocks through my windows."

Abe nodded and asked, "You see any break in the strike?"

"Not yet. Those trouble-makers really have them organized this time. Every day two men from each mill go to a meeting at the Guild Halls. They listen to the IWW rabble tell them what monsters we mill owners are. Then they run back to their mill and regurgitate that rubbish to the rest of the laborers, blocking the doors with their picket lines."

"So I've noticed. I didn't see one silk mill working. I can't believe the crap those outsiders are filling our workers' heads with? Calling the American flag the symbol of the bosses' oppression and murder. That bunch of odd-balls probably never held a job more than a week in their lives."

"Unbelievable!" Rosen said.

"What's that red flag they're waving around supposed to mean?" Abe asked.

"They say it's made from the blood of oppressed workers all over the world."

"More crap," Abe said and asked, "How's the mill association handling them?"

"We're as united as they are. We aren't going to deal with the strikers until they get rid of the IWW trouble-makers. Then we're only going to talk shop by shop."

"And if they don't agree?"

"The mills will stay closed until they do. How long can they last without money to buy food?"

"How long can you last?" Abe asked, thinking the same thing about himself. He had the orders from France's weavers and Jacob's letter of credit financing their purchases. All he had to do was buy the yarn at the right price.

For a moment, Rosen lapsed into a far away look. "I don't know. There are a few workers who want to come in, but the pickets won't let them. I'm thinking of going in with some who are hiring private detectives to protect them. At least I can get some production."

"Maybe you can convince President Wilson to send the troops here instead of to Mexico."

"We've been in touch with the governor. He won't send the militia unless there's violence. So far, those outsiders are keeping the lid on."

Abe nodded.

"Why did you want to see me?" Rosen asked.

"I'm open to buy yarn."

"What are you going to do with it?"

"I have my markets."

"Where? There isn't a silk mill operating in the whole country."

"Here and there."

"Afraid I'll contact them myself?"

Abe shrugged.

"How much are you offering?"

"Four dollars a pound."

"Are you crazy? Fifty cents on the dollar."

"I know, but if this strike lasts for a long time, I'll have to sit on the inventory."

"I thought you had a buyer."

"They may be bought up by the time I get to them."

Rosen leaned back in his chair. "I got a call from Lambert the other day. He said he's contacting all the mill owners to warn them not to buy or sell anything to you. He's claiming you're aligned with your brother to keep the strike going so you can buy yarn cheap, and you're going to use the profit to aid the strikers."

"That's crazy."

"Is it? Fifty cents on the dollar, Abe."

"Lambert and I had some words at the Silk Association banquet. It seems he doesn't like jobbers."

"But he has to deal with them, so they take his abuse."

"I didn't."

"Not smart, Abe."

"Lambert's a fool."

"Maybe so, but he runs this town."

"So, you don't have any yarn to sell me?" Abe asked.

"I didn't say that. I just told you what Lambert said."

"So you do have yarn to sell?"

"I didn't say that either."

Abe lifted his eyebrows and gestured with his hands in a silent, "Well?"

"I never did like that pompous ass, and I don't think he is too partial to us Jewish mill owners. Besides, he never said he would pay my bills. I'll accept your price, for cash only."

Abe stuck out his hand. "Deal. When can I pick up the goods?"

"Send your truck by at ten o'clock tomorrow. I'll notify the police to have a few men here. Chief Bimson has been very cooperative that way, sending over officers when we need help with the rock throwers."

"I'll bet he has," Abe said cynically. "I hear the hospitals and his jail are full, and they're sending prisoners over to the county lockup on Clark Street."

"If that's the way the workers want it, that's the way it's going to be. Some people out there want to work, but they're afraid of the mobs blocking the mills. We can't allow that. The police are helping us clear our doors. Anyway, whoever gets locked up deserves it."

Abe rubbed his head behind his ear. "Is that so?"

"You shouldn't have been anywhere near that mob."

"There was one problem. My brother is mixed up with that bunch of fools."

"I sympathize with you, but when do you stop being your brother's keeper? At some point, you're going to have to pick sides."

"Like Rabbi Mannheimer did at our Shul?"

"Yes," Rosen said defensively.

"All he was doing was trying to be a mediator."

"It's us mill owners that support the congregation. We weren't happy when he denounced us in his sermon."

"He's a Rabbi, not a laborer or a mill owner. It's his job to preach understanding and charity."

"Maybe it is and maybe it isn't, but I, for one, don't need my Rabbi telling me I'm not a good Jew because I'm trying to starve people into submission."

"I wasn't crazy about the sermon, either, but his intentions were good. He was reminding us that being a Jew extols forgiveness, not vindictiveness. His sermon was no reason to fire him."

"We felt otherwise. The Rabbi is dismissed, and he stays dismissed."

"I still don't have to like the decision."

"No, you don't, but sooner or later you're going to have to take a stand. No one can be neutral in this strike. It's too big."

"We'll see."

****

Abe drove the truck himself. Even though his workers weren't on strike, they refused to go with him. They told him they were not going to be called "scabs."

Arriving at Rosen's, he found the entrances blocked by a much larger mob of workers than was there yesterday. Unable to enter his own factory, Rosen paced back and forth in the gutter.

"Saul, what's happening? Where are the police?"

"They're not coming."

"Why?"

"Lambert has spies everywhere. Word got out you were here yesterday. Your name is mud in this town, Abe, and now mine may be too. What am I going to do? I can't even get into my own shop without police help, and I've been told the police aren't coming to me anymore."

"How about private bodyguards?"

"I called the Pinkertons. No one was free today. They said try them again tomorrow and they'll see."

Abe took a step toward the gang of laborers guarding the door. The workers tightened their ranks and balled their hands into fists. "Ain't nothin' moves in or outta this mill," one of them said.

Abe backed off and said, "I'll fix this, Saul. I promise you."

"Leave it alone, Abe. You've done enough for me already."

CHAPTER 57

Solomon and Adolf ran like thieves along East Twenty-Sixth Street. The modest wood-frame houses with their tiny front lawns flashed by in a blur. Stopping on the corner of Broadway, Solomon sucked in deep breaths and demanded, "Where did you get that gun?"

"Did you see those Pinkerton men duck for cover?" Adolf asked.

"Damn it, we went to throw a few stones at Cooke's house to scare him a little, not kill him. I won't abide with any killing."

"Relax. I shot high. But I'll bet Mr. Cooke got the message. He won't try to hire any more scabs to work the dye house."

"You get rid of that gun or I'm through."

"Okay. Take it easy.

"I mean it, Adolf."

"I said I'd get rid of it."

"I'm late," Solomon said.

"Yeah, your Passover. There's no room in our fight for religion. When are you going to realize that?"

Dodging the question, Solomon said, "I'll see you at the meeting at Turn Hall tomorrow."

****

A moment ago Abe had made the decision not to wait for Solomon any longer and gathered the family around the dining room table to begin the Seder. He opened his Passover Haggadah and was about to start the service when Solomon walked through the front door, which had been left open for the Prophet Elijah to enter for his cup of wine.

Cecelia leaped from her chair, almost knocking it over, and ran to him. "Where have you been?"

Solomon pushed past her, heading for the downstairs powder room. "I had an unexpected meeting."

"On Passover? Isn't anything sacred to you anymore?"

He ignored her wailing and closed the bathroom door. A minute later he emerged, lifted the traditional white robe worn by the leader of the Seder off the chair where Abe had tossed it, put it on and took his place at the head of the table.

The dining room table was spread to its maximum fifteen feet. Sarah's finest linen tablecloth, which she had embroidered herself and reserved exclusively for Passover covered it. Her special Passover bone-china dishes, cut-crystal wine and water stemware, and sterling silver flatware gleamed brightly under the glittering chandelier.

Abe sat at one end of the table with Sarah to his left. Next to her were their five children: Isidore, Samuel, Ira, Jerry, and one-year-old Emanuel. Chava sat next to Emanuel's high chair to help him and keep him quiet when necessary.

Tradition called for the oldest family member to conduct the service. Solomon occupied the head of the table designated by the Matzoh, covered with another of Sarah's elegant embroidered cloths, and the Seder plate. Next to Solomon was Cecelia, then their two children, Melvin and Frank, followed by David and Leah. Abe's in-laws, Morris and Esther Singer, filled the remaining seats to Abe's right.

With indignation flaring in his eyes, Abe nodded for Solomon to begin. Having calmed down from his escapade with Adolf, Solomon went through the ritual service with practiced ease. The highlight was four-year-old Ira, chanting the four questions, a job traditionally performed by the youngest male member who could read. Morris had taught Ira the prayer, and he beamed with pride as his grandson went through the passage without a mistake.

Just as Solomon finished the third blessing over the wine, the doorknocker banged. Throwing his napkin on the table, Abe shoved his chair back and stomped toward the foyer. Passing Solomon, he scowled, "Who could that be?"

Chief Bimson, flanked by three policemen, stood in the open doorway. "Is Solomon Bressler here?" he demanded.

"What do you want? Don't you know tonight is Passover?"

"I want your brother."

"What for?"

"There were shots fired at William Cooke's house and your brother was spotted running away. I want to question him."

"Do you have a warrant?"

"I don't need one to question him."

"But you need one to come into my house," Abe replied and slammed the door in Bimson's face. Elijah would have to knock if he wanted to come in for his cup of wine.

"Who was that?" Sarah asked.

Solomon refused to meet Abe's eyes.

"Now we know why Solomon was late. He was out with his Socialist friends, defiling the Passover, trying to kill someone."

"What?" Sarah exclaimed.

Cecelia gasped, fighting for breath.

"I was not trying to kill no one," Solomon said.

"Were you at Weidmann's boss dyer's house today?" Abe asked.

"We had a rally there in retaliation for Cooke's calling the police and having two-hundred pickets arrested yesterday."

"The way I heard it, your pickets were threatening and terrorizing men who wanted to go inside to work."

"Stop," David demanded.

Abe drew his bushy white eyebrows together and glowered at David, but he said nothing.

With the pre-meal prayers over, the mood should have been festive. It was not. Their faces cast down at their plates, they ate the gefilte fish and matzoh ball soup without a word. Only one-year-old Emanuel broke the strained silence babbling nonsense and banging the spoon he held in his tiny fist on his highchair tray. Ignoring Abe's scowl, Chava refused to chastise him.

By the time the servants—Frances had enlisted two of her friends to help in the kitchen—removed the first course and served the chicken main course, they had all calmed down. Sarah restarted the conversation. "I understand the Shul is bringing Rabbi Mannheimer back."

"It's about time," Abe said. "But it really doesn't matter. I have decided to quit B'Nai Jeshurum and join Temple Emanu-El over on Van Houten."

Sarah shrank back into her chair in shock.

Morris recovered faster than his daughter. "You wouldn't! You can't! That is not an Orthodox Shul."

"I know, Morris. It's conservative, and it's more in tune with modern thinking. Separation of men and women in the Shul is old-world and outdated. It doesn't belong in America. I wanted my mother in the front row when I was Bar Mitzvahed, but she had to sit in the gallery. That is not where Sarah is going to sit when our children are Bar Mitzvahed. She is going to sit with me."

"But how are the children going to learn their Torah?"

"They'll learn fine. Temple Emanu-El has a fine school. And if you want, you can still teach them at home."

"Abe, how could you?" Sarah finally said.

"Because the Orthodox Shul is out-of-touch with reality. Men and women should be able to sit together and pray." He looked at his mother. "Orthodoxy is not for me or my family. They are trying to keep the old country alive, and I don't want that for my children."

"I'll never set foot in the place," Morris said adamantly.

"I think you'll be right there in the front row with Sarah and me when your grandchildren are Bar Mitzvahed."

CHAPTER 58

Solomon conducted the closing prayers in rigid formality. Barely a second after the word "Amen" had fully left everyone's lips, Abe announced to his brothers, "I'd like to see the two of you in my study."

They dutifully followed, with David bringing up the rear and closing the door behind him.

At the sound of the latch clicking, Abe whirled and pounced on Solomon. "Bimson said someone fired gunshots at William Cooke's house."

"It wasn't me."

"But you know who it was?"

When Solomon didn't answer, Abe said, "And you strike leaders say you're against violence. Hah!"

"We're not the ones who start the violence. It's the police and the hired thugs who taunt us."

"Just like tonight," Abe said sarcastically.

"That was a mistake. It won't happen again."

"This whole strike is a mistake. You can't win."

"We are winning," Solomon insisted.

"Winning what? Starvation, deprivation, broken heads, police records. You haven't gotten one concession from the mill owners. They won't even talk to you."

"You'll see. With the mills in Allentown and Hazelton, Pennsylvania joining with us, the bosses will be talking soon. We'll get our demands."

"Rumor has it those Pennsylvania strikes are folding. Scabs are showing up there everyday to take the jobs of those strikers. Even some of your Paterson workers have gone there to look for work."

Solomon paced the floor. He stopped behind the wing chair and crossed his arms on top of it. "We don't need Pennsylvania. We hear rumors, too. The word is, the small mill owners here in Paterson are willing to talk to us. They want to settle."

"That's a false rumor. Lambert controls the mill owners and he has no intention of negotiating as long as that IWW crowd is in town. Get rid of them and maybe you'll have a chance."

"We run this strike, not the IWW," Solomon insisted.

"Nobody would ever guess it. You local boys do nothing but follow Tresca, Quinlan and that Flynn dame around while they give speeches."

"That ain't so."

Abe went to the bar and held up a brandy bottle. David and Solomon nodded. Handing out the glasses, he said, “That Flynn girl isn’t a bad looker. What she needs is a good *shtup* and she’ll forget all about this Socialist foolishness.”

“You are disgusting,” David said.

“Elizabeth Flynn is not Katie McGuire,” Solomon shot back.

Abe’s eyes locked on Solomon’s, daggers leaping out at his brother.

“*Nu,* who is Katie McGuire?” David asked.

“A *nefkeh* Abe knows.”

“You bastard!” Abe yelled and stepped toward Solomon.

David jumped between them. The look he gave Abe silently asked, “You visit whores?”

Abe withdrew to the bar and refilled his glass.

“Elizabeth Flynn is one of the most intelligent people I ever met,” Solomon said. “She and Tresca are visionaries. They’re going to change the world and get the working man what is due him.”

“You’re a fool. You and your bunch of radicals are never going to change the fact that some people are made to be bosses and others to be workers. Just like bees.”

“We’re going to try damn hard.”

“By killing anyone who doesn’t agree with you? It was a Socialist who murdered the King of Greece, wasn’t it?”

“We had nothing to do with that. Haywood is against violence.”

“Sure he is,” Abe scoffed. “You keep saying ‘we,’ but you’ll never convince me you have any control over what’s going on.”

“I’m the leader of the dyer’s union,” Solomon insisted.

“Then act like one. The smartest thing you can do for your people is tell them to get back to work before it’s too late.”

“What’s the matter, you beginning to feel the pinch? I heard about your trouble at Rosen’s mill.”

“What trouble?” David asked.

“Abe went to Rosen’s to pick up some yarn. The pickets wouldn’t let him in the mill.”

“Why did you not tell me?” David asked.

“I didn’t have a chance, what with you moving into your new house yesterday, and Passover.”

“*Nu*, how do we send . . .”

“Be quiet,” Abe scowled.

David gaped at his brother’s sharp rebuke and plopped into a chair.

Turning to Solomon, Abe said, “Face facts. You’re beaten. I’m told by a reliable source the mill owners will talk to you as soon as you’re back on the job.”

“What happened to the ‘I’m neutral’ you spouted last month?”

Abe smiled and said, “As you’re so fond of saying, things change. If I were you, brother, I’d chase those outside agitators out of town. That dribble they’re preaching about taking over the mills and throwing out what they call the ‘Capitalist boss’ can never happen.”

“It will happen,” Solomon said.

"Not without a blood-bath first, and your people will be on the wrong end of Bimson's guns."

"And you'll back Bimson?"

"If I have to."

Solomon stormed out of the room.

David started after him.

"You better tell him to slip out the back and run through the woods," Abe said. "Bimson's men are in the street out front."

David returned in a few minutes, and said, "He got away."

Abe nodded.

"Sarah wants Cecelia and the children to be the night here," David said.

"Fine. Another drink?"

"No," David said, and finished the question he had tried to ask when Abe rudely cut him off. "Where by we get the goods to ship to Jacob's people?"

"Don't ever let the enemy know your business," Abe said.

"Solomon be not our enemy. He be our brother."

"Now he's the enemy and I don't want him to know our problems or where we're shipping goods."

"Where by we get the goods?" David asked, again.

"I'll figure something out."

"What?"

"Stop worrying. You're getting paid."

"For how long by you pay me? I moved to Paterson because you give me a job. Now I have no job. What am I going to do?"

Abe stormed to the door and flung it open. "I can't stand your sniveling. Go home."

It was David's turn to spin on his heels and storm out. Interrupting his wife's conversation with Sarah and Cecelia, he said, "Leah, we go."

Sarah escorted her guests to the door, then hurried to Abe. "What's going on?" she asked.

"Nothing," Abe said and slammed the study door in her face.

CHAPTER 59

Adolf Lessig skipped up the steps and into his rented row house on Godwin Street in Riverside. He was still excited about the way he had scared the pants off those guys with his gun. *It's about time we got in some licks of our own,* he thought.

Entering the kitchen, his nose filled with aromas he hadn't smelled in weeks. Elizabeth Flynn had brought meat, bread, potatoes, and vegetables to feed the guests that would be arriving shortly.

"We eat good tonight," he said to no one in particular, even though his wife was standing in front of the stove, fussing over a large black pot.

Adolf's wife Gretta wore a plain cotton smock, giving her thick body a square appearance. Her short gray hair flopped in every direction. Her eyelids, jowls and mouth drooped from the strain her husband had subjected her to by insisting their house be used as a combination guest house and meeting place for the out-of-town strike leaders.

Gretta pointed her chin toward the ceiling. "Do you hear that?" she asked.

Adolf listened to the rhythmic *thump, thump, thump* coming from the bedroom above the kitchen. Only one thing could make that noise—the bed bouncing on the bare wooden floor.

"He came by an hour and a half ago," Gretta said in disgust.

"Tresca?"

"Who else? I want that woman out of this house. I take care of her child all day and all she does is lay with him."

"Now, Gretta."

"Don't 'Gretta' me! She has no shame. She parades around here half-dressed, bosom exposed, legs exposed. I want her out of here."

Adolf turned his back on his wife's rantings and went to prepare himself for his visitors.

****

As her husband greeted his arriving guests, Gretta set the dining room table. Having no cloth to adorn her knotty-pine planked table, turned grayish white by repeated scrubbings with a harsh cleanser, she placed six settings of her silver-plated tableware on the bare wood. She returned to the kitchen for a wicker basket of bread and six porcelain bowls, which she stacked in the middle of the table, then brought out the stew pot. Her task done, she went to the living room and announced, "Dinner is ready," to her husband's guests and disappeared into the kitchen to eat her meal in solitude.

William Dudley "Big Bill" Haywood, President of the Industrial Workers of the World Union, held Carlo Tresca back as the others left for the dining room. At six feet-six inches tall, Haywood towered over the smaller man. Putting his beefy arm over Tresca's shoulder, Haywood asked, "How is your wife, Carlo?"

"We are separated."

"I see. You are aware I have known Elizabeth since she was seventeen? We met in 1907 at an IWW convention in Chicago."

"She told me."

"Did she tell you I watch over her as a father? No, of course not. She wouldn't say that. But I do. Her father and I have a lot in common. Elizabeth told me he lost an eye working in the rock quarries. I lost my eye working in the western mines."

Tresca tried to lift his face from Haywood's chest, but he could not bring himself to look at Haywood's glass eye and the droopy eyelid that covered it.

"Elizabeth and I have been working closely since that first meeting. We have talked a lot about her father and what he taught her about Socialism. Our philosophies are identical."

"She told me about her father, too."

"He was a good man, but he was weak. He couldn't put his thoughts into actions. Elizabeth can. With me guiding her, we will become unbeatable."

"What are you getting at?" Tresca asked.

"Elizabeth is a natural leader. Did she tell you we met Lenin at the International Socialist Congress in Copenhagen in 1910?"

"Yes."

"Lenin took quite a liking to her. Elizabeth is destined for big things in the IWW. I don't want anything to interfere with her work."

"It won't."

"I hope not. What are your intentions toward her?"

"We love each other. We have since we met last year in Lawrence."

Haywood slapped Carlo on the shoulder, buckling the slight man's knees. "That's wonderful. Treat her kindly."

Wincing, Carlo said, "I will," quickly adding, "I do."

****

Ewald Koettgen and Patrick Quinlan sat along one side of the small table. Carlo Tresca sat next to Elizabeth Flynn on the other side. As host, Adolf Lessig occupied one end. Bill Haywood, the guest of honor, took his place at the other end.

"Where is Bressler?" Tresca asked.

"Tonight is Passover," Lessig answered.

"Oh, yeah, I forgot. Bressler's a Jew," Tresca scoffed. "If he wants to remain part of this council, he better learn that the IWW comes first. We have no master, not even God."

"Carlo, talk like that will hurt us," Haywood said. "The people we are trying to reach are not ready to give up their God. Let's win the strike for them first. Once they see what the IWW can do for them, then we can show them God is nothing more than another of their boss's tools to keep them in bondage as slaves to the Capitalists."

Elizabeth Flynn smiled at Tresca and squeezed his hand. "He's right, Carlo," she said. "Our enemies would love nothing better than to revive the Spanish Inquisition to rally the workers to their side. Whether or not we believe in God is not the affair of Police Chief Bimson."

"Thank you, Elizabeth," Haywood said and asked, "How many new members did we enlist this month?"

"About ten thousand," Elizabeth Flynn said.

"Out of twenty-four thousand strikers? Fourteen thousand are getting a free ride."

"This town isn't like Lawrence," Elizabeth Flynn countered. "Up there we had one boss, —The American Woolen Company—and most of the workers were unskilled. It was easy to enlist them."

"Aren't the workers here just as poor and exploited?" Haywood asked.

"For one thing, there are three hundred mills in Paterson, not one."

"Which means?"

"We have three hundred bosses to deal with. Three hundred shops where scabs can work. And yes, many of the workers are being exploited, but there are also a lot of skilled workers, and they belong to the American Federation's craft unions."

"That bunch of grafters," Haywood muttered. "They dare call themselves the labor movement of this country. They don't represent the unskilled laborers like we do. Some of their chapters won't let the colored man join. Some keep foreigners out. They sold out to the bosses long ago."

Quinlan said, "You convince Louis Magnet of that and we'll bust the A F of L in this town."

"Before this strike is over, he and all the A F of L craft union members will be flocking to the Industrial Workers of the World."

Quinlan's face turned somber. His ears seemed to stand out from his head farther than ever. "Right now I would settle for winning the strike."

"You have doubts?" Haywood asked.

"The bosses are solidly united."

"So are we," Elizabeth Flynn said. "We have our daily meetings. Our pickets are out surrounding all the mills, keeping scabs out."

"And Chief Bimson keeps arresting our people," Quinlan said.

Haywood scraped the bottom of his bowl and looked toward the pot.

"There's plenty," Lessig said, sticking out his hand for Haywood's bowl.

Receiving his refill, Haywood said, "This is very good, Adolf. Please convey my appreciation to your wife."

Lessig grinned at the compliment from his leader and from the warm feeling the hearty meal gave him. It had been a month since he had tasted meat. "I will. Thank you."

"We should thank the police chief for doing us a favor," Haywood said. "The workers see the police as an arm of the boss. The more the police beat and arrest, the more determined our people will be to win."

"And we must not let that spirit subside," Elizabeth added, looking around the table at her associates. "We are very lucky Mayor Bruechmann across the river in Haledon is a Socialist and favorable to our cause. Those Sunday rallies he allows us to have are important. We must keep the strikers occupied every day. They can't be left to sit around a stove that has no fire or a table that has no food and think about their hungry children running around in threadbare clothes."

Haywood smiled at his protégé. "You are so right. With a victory here we will emancipate all the workers of the United States—and the world—from the tyranny of the Capitalist bosses."

CHAPTER 60

If it weren't for the difference in their ages, Ben Goldberg and his son Marvin could have been mistaken for twins. Both were stocky, with round faces and short legs. Both had receding hairlines, although Ben's was a few inches farther back on his head than his was his son's.

The Goldbergs ran their businesses from three offices in Paterson. Their main location of the Goldberg's only legitimate operation—a liquor distributorship—was in the mansion on Broadway that Ben had taken possession of a couple of years ago from a mill man who ran himself into bankruptcy from gambling. The office at *The American Loan Company* was where they conducted their pawn brokering and loan sharking business. The third office, where they maintained their bookmaking enterprise was over the bar Ben had bought from Abe.

It was in the Nags Head office that Marvin Goldberg now sat quietly, half listening as his father gave orders to their lieutenants about what to do with a delinquent payer. The fledgling idea that had been germinating in Marvin's mind for a week finally took shape. Now all he had to do was convince his father that it was a good one.

As soon as his father dismissed their subordinates, Marvin lifted his stocky body from the overstuffed armchair, paced the floor for a moment and said, "Dad, if we play our cards right, we can be sitting pretty when this strike is over."

"We're sitting pretty right now. The Nags Head is full, day and night. Somehow the men always seem to have a couple of nickels to spend on a drink."

"It's dumb luck the mill workers picked our place as their central relief point to hand out the food donated by those charity people."

"Yeah, isn't it great? What are they calling our joint, 'The Striker's City Hall'?"

"This strike isn't going to last forever. If we act now, we can take advantage of our good fortune."

"And do what?"

Marvin stared out the window at the people coming and going along the sidewalk. "I've had my ears open downstairs. The mill workers have a lot of complaints and they aren't all about their bosses. Many of them don't like those IWW people and are not members of that union."

"What's it to us? We take bets, sell beer and whiskey, and make a loan now and then. What do I care about some damn union?"

"Hold on a minute and listen. Something big is coming with these labor movements. Look at that American Federation of Labor, sucking in all those small unions into one big one. Do you really think that Sam Gompers guy who runs that union is in it for love?"

"I never met a man who was in anything for love unless it was some broad." Ben chuckled at his joke. "But so what? How is that guy gonna help us? We don't loan to laborers. Our clients have always been businessmen. It's easier to lean on them should they decide not to meet their loan commitment. They got roots that keep them in place."

"I think it's time we took a closer look at laborers and labor unions. Unions collect dues. But that's penny-ante. Suppose you were a labor leader here in Paterson with all these workers looking to you for guidance? How would you handle this strike?"

Ben thought for a second. "I don't know, how would you?"

"I wouldn't do it like that crazy IWW crowd, thinking they can take over the mills. That's the stupidest thing I ever heard. What I would do is go to the big guys, Lambert and his crowd, and ask them what they would give me to settle this thing."

Ben's eyes lit up.

"Then, when I got my fee I'd say, 'You give my people some kind of token raise and I'll get them back to work.'" Ben thought for a moment and added, "And maybe we don't even have to call a strike, just kind of hint at it and they'll pay off."

"Right," Marvin said.

"But how do we get the laborers to follow us instead of that Gompers guy or those IWW idiots?" Ben asked.

"That's my idea. It will take an investment of a few thousand, but I'm sure it will pay off ten times that in the future."

"Let's hear it."

"I go down to the bar and pass out some money. Those guys are starving. They'll do anything for a few bucks. We'll keep a record of who borrows from us. When the strike is over, we'll cancel their loan if they join our union."

CHAPTER 61

Sarah paid the taxi driver and went up the front walk to her house. She missed Ernie. With no business, Abe had to lay him off, along with all his other employees. Without her driver, the only way to get downtown was by cab. She fretted about spending the money, but she had to bring food to Cecelia. Cecelia never told her they needed it, but how could they not? She owed Cecelia for all Cecelia had done for her last year when the baby was born prematurely.

Finding Chava outside the study door, holding a tray of food, Sarah asked, "Is he still in there?"

"Da," Chava answered.

Sarah tapped softly on the door to Abe's study. For the past two days since the end of Passover, Abe had locked himself behind the closed door. He hadn't come to their bed, and he only emerged to relieve himself or grab a tidbit of food. She was growing increasingly worried.

"Go away," Abe said.

"Abe, please. Talk to me. I can help you."

"The only way you can help is to leave me alone and keep the children quiet so I can think."

Chava said, "Abraham, I bring food."

"Go away."

"I leave it here on a table." Putting the tray down, Chava draped her arm around Sarah's shoulders and gently turned her away from the door. "Come, we play with the children. He come out soon as he can."

"Why won't he let me help him?" Sarah asked.

"Bressler men, they not like to trouble women with their problems."

****

Abe sat in his leather chair, staring out the window. *She wants to help me*, he thought. *Ha! What can she do, organize another parade calling for an end to the strike*? There's nothing anyone can do as long as Lambert is in charge. "Fool! Make a deal," he muttered out loud. "Give them a couple of cents raise and they'll run back to the mills. But no, Lambert says he's not dealing with the outsiders. Damn him! He's destroying my family with his stubbornness."

Abe's thoughts returned to his finances, where they had dwelled for the last two days. He had twenty-four hundred dollars in the bank. Supporting his household and his whining brother ate up three hundred and fifty dollars a week. In a few weeks the bank would be knocking on his door, demanding he pay his mortgage or get out.

If he had that yarn he'd sold those welshers at Paradise Mill . . .Paradise! That yarn!

He whirled his chair around and grabbed a piece of paper and pencil. He scribbled what he thought he remembered was owed him and the others who had sold yarn to Paradise. "If I had their entire inventory . . . But how would I move it out of the mill with the pickets surrounding it?"

Get their yarn first then worry about moving it, he thought. *I'll hire my own thugs if I have to. There are plenty of men out there who'd do anything for a couple of dollars to buy food. And their ranks are growing by the day. And if you get in my way, Lambert, I'll turn them on you.*

Yanking the receiver off the hook, he gripped the thin round body of the stick telephone in his other hand and bellowed George Scott's telephone number into the mouthpiece at the operator. The telephone number for Paradise's lawyer was burned into his memory.

"Mr. Bressler, what can I do for you?" Scott asked.

"You said I'd be lucky to get twenty cents on the dollar for my Paradise debt?"

"Yes, that's correct."

"Call Murray, Rosenthal, Coleman and Dunlap and tell them I'll give them thirty cents for their debt if they want to sell it to me."

"That's very generous, Mr. Bressler, but I don't believe it will do you any good. The bankruptcy court will not allow you to take the yarn, if that's what you're thinking."

"Why not?"

"Because the bank has a lien against the mill and everything in it. They hold the mortgage and the notes on the machinery."

"How much is the lien?"

"Let me get the file."

Abe held the silenced receiver to his ear for an agonizingly long moment.

"Here it is," Scott said. "Fifteen thousand dollars."

Abe slumped in his chair.

"Mr. Bressler, are you there?"

"I'm here. How much would the bank settle for to be rid of those liens?"

"A figure of eleven thousand was batted around."

"Draw up the papers transferring ownership to me. I'll be at your office tomorrow with a check for eleven-thousand six-hundred for the liens and the yarn."

"Don't forget my fee, Mr. Bressler."

Abe exhaled sharply. "How much?"

"Four hundred."

"I'll see you tomorrow," Abe spat out, slammed the receiver onto the hook, and raced out of the study. He grabbed his hat and coat from the hall closet and roared through the kitchen toward the back door.

"Where are you going?" Sarah asked.

"I'll be back in two hours."

****

Sarah thought about calling Cecelia to put her plan in action, but she quickly realized there was not enough time. Well, at least he was out of that room. Maybe tomorrow he'd be gone longer and she could get things moving.

CHAPTER 62

Solomon leaned his back against the bar and watched the procession of laborers go hat-in-hand to the table where Marvin Goldberg sat, sign a book, get money and hurry off. One of the men sidled up to the bar. Solomon asked him, "What's going on?"

"Goldberg's giving out money."

"What's the vig?"

"Ain't none. Says we don't gotta pay it back 'til the strike is over."

Solomon knew the Goldbergs. They all belonged to the same Shul. And he knew what they did for a living. Why the sudden charity? What were they up to?

He thought about approaching Marvin and asking him, but now wasn't the time. Behind Marvin was one of the bar's bouncers, and another one stood nearby, kibitzing the pool game. Some other time, when there wasn't a pile of money on the table.

Chugging down his beer, he left, heading for the picket lines in front of the dye houses.

****

Five minutes after Solomon left the bar, Abe walked in. He asked Carlo, "Is Goldberg in?"

Carlo pointed to Marvin.

"Ben," Abe said.

"Upstairs, I think."

Abe took the stairs two at a time. He was met at the top by two bodyguards.

"I have to see your boss," Abe said.

The door to Ben's office, formerly one of the bedrooms, was open. Abe could see Goldberg peering out at him.

"Bring him in," Goldberg said.

Ben Goldberg sat in an oversized chair behind his desk. His short round stature made him look almost like a dwarf in it. Resting his elbows on the padded arms, he raised his hands and pressed his fingertips together tent like and studied his visitor. "You look like hell, Bressler," he said.

"It's been a rough few weeks."

"I guess it has. What can I do for you?"

"I need thirteen thousand dollars."

"How you going to pay it back?"

"When the strike is over, you'll get your money."

"What about the vig? That's two hundred a week."

"Two hundred a week? Are you crazy?"

Goldberg smirked. "If you could get the money from a bank, you wouldn't be here."

"Okay, it's a deal."

"You know what happens if you don't pay?"

"Yeah, yeah, I'm familiar with your boys."

Goldberg nodded, stood up and went to his safe. He removed stacks of banded greenbacks and piled them on the desk. As he shoveled them into a paper sack, he said, "Don't be late. I don't like it when people are late with their payments."

****

By three, Solomon had finished his pep talks to his strikers and headed home. Cecelia greeted him with, "Sarah was here this morning."

"I'm sorry I missed her," he lied.

"Sarah told me she wants to help."

"Hasn't she helped enough?"

"What?"

"Never mind." Lately Sarah's visits to their apartment came more and more frequently. Each time she came, she brought something with her. It was tradition. Never visit empty-handed. He knew her visits were excuses to bring food. He began to resent her unasked-for charity.

Cecelia shook off her husband's sarcasm with a shrug. "She says she stashed away a lot of food and she wants to give it to the strike relief fund."

"Is she crazy? What if Abe finds out?"

"He won't if you're careful."

"Me? What can I do?"

"She'll call when Abe is out of the house. It's up to you to get someone to keep tabs on him. When you're sure he's in his shop, you get a couple of men with wagons or wheelbarrows and get up to Sarah's to get that food."

"I'll take care of it first thing in the morning."

Solomon grabbed a towel and headed for the bathroom. He felt guilty about his unkind thoughts for his sister-in-law. Sarah was taking a big chance. If Abe found out, he'd kill her.

CHAPTER 63

All the marble-topped tables and walnut sideboards had been cleared out from the main sitting room on the ground floor of the Hamilton Club to make space for more chairs to accommodate the gathering of the mill owners, newspapermen and politicians for this Sunday's meeting. Despite the windows being thrown wide open to take advantage of the warm end of April day and the fans spinning rapidly to aerate the room, a gray haze hung near the ceiling from the multitude of lit cigars.

Behind the long table placed across the front of the room were Paterson's leading mill owners. Catholina Lambert sat in the middle chair. Its hand carved back towered a foot and a half above his head. To his left and right, in smaller, simpler chairs were Jacob Weidmann, Monroe Dippel, William Skinner and Peter Ryle. Peter was present mainly because of his family name.

Picking up the gavel he had borrowed from his friend, Judge Congdon, Lambert banged it three times. "Order, gentlemen. Come to order."

When the din ceased, he said, "Yesterday I received news the strikes in Allentown and Hazelton collapsed. The mills in Pennsylvania will be running full force tomorrow."

The roar was so great, David had to yell to make himself heard. "Is good news, no?"

Abe leaned close to David's ear and said, "We're back in business."

"Now we no have to ship to Jacob's people, yes?" David asked. "Let us return the letter of credit and tell them we have no goods."

"That yarn goes out on schedule."

"*Nu*? In Pennsylvania we can make yet three times what we earn shipping to France."

"A deal is a deal. I don't go back on my agreements, no matter what the circumstances."

David slumped in his chair and stared straight ahead.

Harry H. Haines, editor of the *Paterson Evening News*, leaped from his front-row seat and waved a pad at Lambert. For weeks he had been lambasting the mill owners in his editorials for their refusal to negotiate with the strikers.

"Why did they end their strike?" Harry asked.

"We made a few wage concessions and they returned to work," Lambert replied.

"Does that mean you are ready to negotiate with the strikers here?"

"Never!" Lambert yelled, his broad chest heaved out. Many in the gathering burst out in cheers, echoing their approval of Lambert's defiance.

"But you said you gave concessions in Pennsylvania. Why not here?"

"Write this in big headlines in your paper, Mr. Haines. We will never deal with the strikers as long as that IWW rabble is in town."

"Lord knows I don't agree with their philosophy, Mr. Lambert, but those people did not start this strike."

"They're keeping the laborers stirred up. If they weren't here, this strike would be over already."

"But they are here," Harry said, "and it looks like the only way to get them out of town is to negotiate with them and settle the strike."

"Never! This is our city. We run it. No one is coming to this town, dictating to me."

"They are nothing but a bunch of anarchists and Socialists," Jacob Weidmann concurred, drawing more confirming hoots from the audience.

"Did you hear what that Flynn woman said?" demanded William Skinner. "The only purpose of this strike is to take possession of our mills."

Harry Haines gave up trying to answer. Many in the gathering had jumped to their feet and shook their fists at him.

"Run her out of town on a rail!"

"Tar and feather her!"

"Arrest her!"

"Kill her!"

Buoyed by the howls of approval, Lambert said, "You think these laborers are the only ones who know hard work, Mr.Haines? When I was ten I worked seventy-two hours a week. We built this town, and if it weren't for the men in this room there would be no place for those laborers to work."

"You're damn right," William Skinner offered. "We provide the money for the charities. We pay for the schools. And we do it under our God-given rights as Capitalists. My mill is open to any worker who wants to return to work under the terms he left. I am not ashamed, Mr. Haines. I can look at any worker directly in the eye and tell him he is getting a fair deal from me—something he'll never get from that bunch of atheists leading them."

"Do we make ourselves clear, Mr. Haines?" Lambert said. "The workers would not still be out on strike if it weren't for that bunch of Socialist revolutionaries directing them. No, Mr. Haines, we will not negotiate with the strikers. We will crush them."

****

Five thousand mill workers gathered around the Lafayette Oval. They came to hear "Big Bill" Haywood speak. While they waited for the speeches to begin, they joked and jibed about his influence with the weatherman. The sun shone brightly on this delightful Spring Sunday. The smell of flowering trees perfumed the air.

Haywood had rejected the safety of Haledon for this rally. He purposefully wanted to defy Paterson's laws against Sunday meetings and chose the Lafayette Oval because it enabled him to maximize his audience. Formed where Straight Street crossed the river, the Lafayette Oval was easily accessible to the workers from Paterson and Haledon, and thus a perfect place for a rally. A speaker standing in the small park in the middle of the intersection could confront an audience of thousands who were sitting along the curb on River Street and on the wide grassy river bank.

Mounting a stepstool, Carlo Tresca raised his hands for silence. When the crowd quieted, he said, "I am not going to speak to you today. Instead, I want to introduce a friend of mine, a true believer in our cause. Here from New York City is Frederick Sumner Boyd."

Boyd should have brought a ladder to stand on. Stepping up on the stool, his narrow set eyes barely poked above the people in front of him. "You and I and people like us all over the world are right in the middle of a revolution," he said. His voice boomed out over the crowd, surprising those near him, who expected to hear a timid squeal matching his stature. "We, the wage earning class, have been victims of 'boss law' too long. 'Boss law' is more oppressive than martial law. Our flag, the flag of the workers of the world, is the red flag because it has been soaked in the blood of our oppression under the boss's boot. The boss's flag is the American flag, the flag of the rich and privileged. It is time we dip their flag in their own blood and turn it red like ours. It is time to make the bosses victims of the worker's law."

Adolf Lessig stood next to Solomon, Tresca and Haywood. Lessig raised his fist in the air and let out an uproarious cheer. Some in the crowd followed his lead. Most, including Solomon and Haywood, remained quiet, shifting their bodies and shuffling their feet. Many had brought their children and had not expected to hear this kind of speech.

"The Industrial Workers of the World will show you how to sabotage the bosses and their AFL scabs. When we win this strike and you go back to the mills, take a club steak soaked in vinegar and rub it over the reeds of the looms where the scabs worked. The stench will keep them from their machines. Or take a piece of sandpaper and rough up the spindles so the silk will be torn. You dye house workers, put shodenaime in the tubs to spoil the silk . . ."

Haywood turned to Tresca and asked, "Where did you find this man?"

"In New York at a Socialist rally. He's good, isn't he?"

"He's a jerk. He'll get us killed and he'll get the state police called to Paterson. All the bosses need is an excuse to go to the governor, and this guy is giving it to them."

"But the bosses . . ."

"Shut up, Carlo," Haywood ordered, and walked over to Boyd.

Though Boyd was on a stool and Haywood stood on the ground, the top of Haywood's Stetson was aligned with the top of Boyd's head. Clamping a large hand on Boyd's shoulder, he forced the little man off the stool in mid-sentence. Taking Boyd's place, Haywood rose a full head higher than the tallest man in the crowd.

"Thank you, Mr. Boyd," Haywood said, and clapped politely.

He let the crowd adjust for a moment before speaking. "My fellow workers of the world, violence is not the way to defeat the bosses. Civil disobedience to the boss state, that is how to overthrow him. Ignore the boss. Ignore the boss's laws. Do not damage his property. That will only bring the militia and martial law, directed by the bosses. Fold your arms. No, don't fold them; keep your hands in your pockets so the police can't put a bomb in them."

A sputtering of laughter swept the crowd, relieving the tense silence that had overcome the gathering during Boyd's talk.

"By ignoring the boss's law and doing nothing you will keep the mills shut. By staying out of the mills, you will be taking the profits from the boss. This is the harshest way you can treat the boss. The boss prays to his god of profit. By not letting him reap those profits, you will defeat him."

Loud applause sprang, out along with hoots of approval.

"I urge all of you to join with your fellow workers of the world in the IWW. We formed our union in 1905 to represent all oppressed and exploited workers. That first convention we laborers of the world held in Chicago will go down in history as the 'Continental Congress of the Working Class'."

He paused to remove a piece of paper from his pocket. Unfolding it and holding it over his head he said, "Let us show you to a better life. I read to you our goals from our manifesto. 'The growth and development of the IWW will build up from within and create an industrial democracy, a worker's cooperative republic, which must finally burst the shell of capitalist government, and be the agency by which the working people, you people, will operate the industries and appropriate their products to yourselves.'"

The thin applause told Haywood that very few understood his words. He folded the paper and put it away. "This is what I see in your future: huge mills run by the workers, with big clean dining rooms filled with music and tiled bathrooms. Each of you will have an ownership in the factories where you work."

A tug on his pants leg interrupted him. He looked down. A little blond girl, wearing a frilly white dress, stared up at him through wide blue eyes. She held out a bouquet of lilacs. He stepped down, picked her up, and climbed back on his perch. Cradling her in his husky arm, he said, "This is your future. This is why you must throw out the boss. For your children."

Hollers of approval and thunderous applause rolled from the gathering. He couldn't have planned it better. Children always brought forth the right emotions.

"You are in a fight for your survival, for your children's survival. The bosses say they won't talk to you as long as we are in town. They want to divide you. They demand a mill by mill settlement. You know what will happen if you give in to that—the same thing that happened in the past. Anything you win will soon disappear.

"We are not here to deal with the bosses for you. Your strike committee must do that. We will guide you wherever we can, but we will not sit on your committee. Only you can deal effectively with your own bosses. But you must do it as a group. Do not back down. Stand firm. Stand together. Stay out of the mills until the bosses recognize you and deal with you as one. Do not compromise. Do not surrender."

****

Rising from the center of the room, his hat clutched in his hand and his legs wobbly as if he were a vassal addressing his lord, a man said, "That's easy for you to say, Mr. Lambert. You have mills in other areas of New Jersey and Pennsylvania. I have only my one tapestry mill here in Paterson. This strike is ruining me."

Lambert glanced left and right to see if any of his colleagues knew the speaker. Peter Ryle scribbled a note and shoved the paper across the table.

Lambert read the note and said, "Mr. Fulton, I truly sympathize with you, but we must stand united if we are to beat this strike. Otherwise, we will be at their mercy."

Calling on some inner courage, Fulton said, "I beg to disagree. There have always been strikes here and there always will be. We offer them a little more money and they go back to work. After a few months things settle back to where they were before."

"This time it's different," Lambert said in an uncharacteristically patronizing voice. "In other strikes, our workers didn't have this bunch of riffraff leading them. We must destroy them or our whole way of life will be threatened."

Jacob Weidmann jumped in. "I agree with Mr. Lambert. I have no apologies to make for the wages I pay. They are more than fair. Nine dollars a week for learners to twelve dollars for helpers and strippers, thirteen for shakers and whizzers, fifteen for finishers all the way up to twenty-one dollars a week for a dyer, handling three boxes. What is wrong with that?"

"And I pay my broad silk weavers up to sixteen dollars a week," Peter Ryle said. "That's two dollars a week more than they are making in Pennsylvania, and they went back to work out there."

Lambert took the floor back. "You let that rabble win this strike and you will no longer be boss in your own mill."

Murmurs of approval rumbled through the room.

"No one is going to tell me who to hire and fire," Lambert said. "If I don't like the looks of a man's face, I'm going to get rid of him."

Heads bobbed in agreement.

"I say we keep the mills shut all the way to July if we have to, and starve them back to work," Weidmann said.

"I don't know if I can hold out that long," Fulton said.

"You need any help, you come to me," Lambert said. "I'll see you get the loans you need. Now, let's put our heads together and see how we're going to chase those out-of-towners back to where they came from so we can break this strike."

From far back in the audience, Abe spoke up loudly. "Busting heads is not going to win this strike."

Lambert scanned the crowd. "Who said that?"

Abe stood up.

"What are you doing here, jobber? This meeting is restricted to mill owners." Lambert turned to Chief Bimson, the meeting's sergeant-at-arms. "Chief, show him to the door."

Abe started to thread his way through the haphazardly placed chairs. "I am a mill owner, Mr. big shot. I own the Paradise Mill."

Reluctantly, Lambert waved the chief off.

Arriving up front, Abe wagged his finger at Bimson. "First you have to stop that man from his violent attacks on the workers."

Lambert's face broke into a cocky smile. "I think the chief knows his job, and he's doing it correctly. He's providing a service to this community and the honest working man by offering protection to us and anyone who wants to return to work."

In his own defense, Bimson said, "I'm told there are many workers who want to work, but they're afraid of the pickets. We're clearing them out from in front of the mills so the good workers of this city can get in."

"You're a fool, Bimson, and anyone who agrees with your tactics is a fool."

"Now just a minute," Lambert said.

Abe ignored him and went on. "If those workers wanted to, they could take this town apart brick-by-brick and all your police would be powerless to stop them. Lay off before you create a real riot."

Weidmann stood up. "You wouldn't be sympathetic to the strikers, would you, Bressler, what with your brother being one of their leaders?"

"My brother already knows he is on his own in this. What happens to him is no longer my concern."

"Hah!" Weidmann scoffed.

Harry Haines jumped up. "I agree with Mr. Bressler," he said. "Chief Bimson's arrests are unlawful. They show a weakness in our police force, and with you mill men, if you back him."

Lambert replied, "The mayor must be agreeing with Chief Bimson or he would have removed him long ago."

"You seem to be the only one who knows what our illustrious mayor is thinking," Haines answered. "Where is he, anyway? Nobody has seen or heard from him since this strike began."

"I've seen him, and he approves of the way we are handling this strike," Lambert said.

Haines asked, "Can I quote you when you said the mayor approves of Chief Bimson?"

"I don't care what you quote. You'll distort it anyway. I've read your editorials, and I don't like the way you defend these strikers."

"And I don't like the way you mill men are treating the strikers."

Thomas Quigley, Alderman from the Eighth Ward, jumped up. "Gentlemen, please. This bickering will get you nowhere."

"What do you suggest?" Lambert growled at Quigley.

"I would like to arrange a meeting between we aldermen, clergy, merchants, bankers and any other interested party, and the strikers. I think if we all sit down, we can solve this thing."

"I'm not meeting with any strikers," Lambert said.

"Now, Catholina," Peter Ryle said. "I don't see where it can hurt if we send a representative to the meeting."

"Why don't we send Bressler?" Weidmann suggested. "His brother is one of them. I'll bet he is friendly with a lot of those radicals."

"Yes, I am. I met many of them in jail," Abe said, shooting an angry glare at Bimson. "I accept. When is the meeting?"

"We'll let you know," Quigley said.

The front door burst open. All heads turned to the police officer who rushed to Bimson's side. He whispered in the chief's ear and left as fast as he had come.

Bimson slipped behind the table, leaned close to Lambert, and said, "I have to go arrest some wops, kikes and Socialists."

****

Chief Bimson left the meeting and took his position in the front of the hundred policemen, his aid, Captain McBain, had assembled outside the Hamilton Club in anticipation of what the chief would want. "Follow me," he commanded, and marched rapidly up Ellison Street. Turning left on Straight Street, the police force broke into a trot. They covered the ten blocks to the Lafayette Oval in less than two minutes.

The human jam fleeing the police created a blockade on the bridge which led to sanctuary in Socialist Haledon. This time, Bimson's target was not the common laborer. His men surrounded Haywood, Boyd, Lessig and Solomon. Gloating, Bimson said, "You're under arrest for holding an unlawful Sunday assembly."

CHAPTER 64

David stood before Abe's desk. "All our yarn is on the way for the dock," he said.

"Good. I'll wire Jacob on my way home."

"We bail Solomon out, yes? The letter of credit now is our money, yes?"

"I've done all I can for him. He's on his own."

"But he is our brother," David said. "They will beat him again."

The day after Solomon fled Abe's house, Bimson nabbed him and subjected Solomon to an intense questioning. He did not limit his interrogation to verbal harangues. Bruised and battered, Solomon almost confessed that it was Adolf who had fired the shots at William Cooke's house when Judge Caroll barged into the interrogation room and demanded the names of Bimson's witnesses to the alleged shooting. When Bimson couldn't produce any, the judge ordered Solomon's release.

"Then you bail him out," Abe said.

"You know I have no money."

"And I can't spare any of our company's capital. I need every penny."

****

Sarah answered the telephone.

"We miss you," Mary Beckworth said.

"I've been busy with the children." It had been seven weeks, but the horror of Washington still haunted her. That, coupled with the strike had kept her away from suffrage meetings.

"How is our little girl coming along?" Mary asked.

Sarah rubbed her stomach. "You're so sure it's going to be a girl?"

"Oh, yes. I could tell by the look in your eyes."

"Really," Sarah said. She hoped Mary's clairvoyance was correct. It would be nice to have a little girl running around the house challenging all the men.

The line fell silent for a long moment. Sarah thought they had been disconnected and was about to hang up when Mary said, "We're having a big rally next week. We've been challenged to a debate on the pros and cons of suffrage. I was hoping you would represent the League."

"Oh, no. Not me. I can't," Sarah said.

"We need you," Mary said. "You're our most knowledgeable member. I know you can win this for us."

"Can't you get Alice Paul? Or how about Beth Van Brunt? Or you?"

"I'm no debater. Alice is busy in Philadelphia. And you know Beth. She's too wishy-washy when it comes to speaking."

"What if the police come? They've been breaking up every strike rally they hear about. What if they think it's a strike meeting?" What Sarah really thought was, *What if I get arrested? Would Abe leave me in jail like he's leaving Solomon?*

"The police wouldn't dare interrupt this meeting. Mrs. Hobart will be there."

"Mrs. Hobart! She's dead set against woman suffrage."

"Yes,she is."

"Is she the one who challenged you?" Sarah asked.

"Yes," Mary said, her voice almost sorrowful.

"Oh, Mary. I can't debate her."

"We need you, Sarah. Please. You can do this. I know you can."

A car horn blasted. Sarah looked out the window. Her taxi had arrived. "Let me think about it."

"We're counting on you."

"I'll let you know. I have to go."

****

Sarah's taxi took her to Cecelia's apartment house. Although Abe had re-hired Ernie and told Sarah he would be available to drive her to the market, she hadn't called him to pick her up. She didn't want him telling Abe where he took her.

She hated this strike. It had made a sneak out of her. Friday she had practically emptied her pantry, giving the food to the men Solomon had sent. Now she had to sneak out of her house to meet her best friend because she was afraid her husband would go into a tirade if he found out where she went.

A sudden thought hit her. It was not the suffragists or the strike that had turned her into a sneak. It was Abe. Abe was the cause of their fights because of his refusal to acknowledge that it was time for change.

****

Cecelia sat on the shabby couch in her apartment. Her hands clutched tightly together, she cried to Sarah, "What am I going to do? I can't raise the bail money. They'll beat him again."

Sarah tugged her diamond ring from her swollen finger. She put her arm around Cecelia's trembling shoulders and handed it to her. "Take this to the *American Loan Company*. I'm sure Mr. Goldberg will give you the money you need. It's worth much more than five hundred dollars."

"But I'll never be able to redeem it."

"Don't worry. The important thing is to get Solomon out of jail."

Cecelia grabbed Sarah in a hug. "You're a life saver."

Sarah held her sister-in-law tightly and thought, *I saved your life. I hope I haven't ended mine.*

CHAPTER 65

Sarah carried two cups of coffee to the kitchen table. She put one down in front of Abe and one across from him. Returning to the counter, she picked up the tray holding the basket of breakfast rolls, jam and butter and brought them over. Slowly, she lowered herself into a chair.

He was out again last night, she thought. He said he had a mill owner's meeting. But that seemed unusual for a Saturday night. Maybe it was true this time. His clothes smelled only of cigar smoke, not that lilac perfume that had permeated them lately. She asked, "How did it go with the association?"

"Nothing's changed. There doesn't seem to be a rational man left in Paterson."

Including you, she thought.

"Neither side will yield an inch."

He sipped his coffee, drew over the sugar bowl and lifted the lid. It was almost empty.

"I'll get more," Sarah said. Rising from her chair, she winced.

"Are you okay?"

"Just a little back-ache."

He got up and massaged her shoulders and kneaded her spine down to the small of her back. "Feel better?"

"Mmmm, much," she said, closing her eyes and letting her head roll forward. She thought, *It's been too long since you've done did this to me.*

He stopped his massaging and said, "You sit. I'll get the sugar."

Sarah kept her eyes closed and let her head loll, continuing to savor the moment, despite his hands having left her.

Returning to the table with the sugar sack, Abe asked, "Why is the pantry so empty?"

Her eyes popped open and her head snapped up. Panic replaced her pleasure. "I didn't get to the market last week."

"Didn't Ernie take you Wednesday?"

Fright overtook her. If she said "yes," he caught her. If she lied he would ask Ernie and catch her. Today was Sunday. Maybe he'd forget to ask Ernie about it by tomorrow. "I went to my parents. Mother wasn't feeling well."

Abe gaped at her for a moment, whirled, and stomped out of the kitchen.

Oh God, he knew I lied. Where is he going? What's he doing?

He returned, planted himself in front of her and waved a paper in her face. "You were in the market last Wednesday. This is Mr. Shultz's bill. It says here you bought a dozen cans each of Del Monte peaches, cherries, asparagus, beans and raisins. Where are they?"

Straightening her back, she said defiantly, "Children are starving."

"You're giving food to the strikers?"

"Yes."

"How dare you? Those people are the enemy. They are trying to put me out of business. By feeding them you are helping them hold out."

"The children are not enemies. I don't know who is right and who is wrong in this strike, but I cannot stand by and let children starve."

"Then tell their parents to go back to work."

"Yes, Abe."

"From now on I'll give the order to Mr. Shultz. You'll make a list and give it to me. Do you understand?"

"Yes, Abe."

He threw the invoice on the table and grabbed his coat.

"Where are you going?" she cried. "It's Sunday. Why can't you spend today with me and the children?"

"David and I have a meeting," he growled, and stormed out.

Sarah raised her hand from her lap and stared at her empty ring-finger. How was she going to keep him from noticing she wasn't wearing it anymore? If she told him her hands were swollen and it didn't fit, would he believe her? Why should he, after the many times she had lied to him?

****

Sarah sat at the table for half an hour before she got up the nerve to do it. He said he was going with David. Was he lying? If he was, she had to know where he really went. Did she have the nerve to hire a private detective to follow him? Did she really want to know? She went to the telephone and called Leah. "Is Abe there? I forgot to tell him something."

"You just missed him. He and David went off to a meeting."

"Where?"

"In Haledon. A labor gathering I think."

Both relief and guilt swept over her. Relief to learn Abe hadn't lied to her, and guilt at thinking he had. There must be a reason for that lilac perfume odor on his clothes. Maybe some of the meetings were in a bar where there were waitresses like he had in his old place. That had to be it. After all, didn't he also have liquor on his breath?

CHAPTER 66

With David in the passenger seat, holding on for dear life, Abe drove his Cadillac wildly down Broadway, blasting his horn at horses and buggies and pedestrians.

"Where is this rally?" Abe growled.

His face contorted in fright, David blurted out, "Eighty-three Norwood Street, by Haledon. Please, not so fast."

Abe laughed, but didn't slow down.

"I cannot read the map with so much twisting back and forth."

"Yeah, yeah," Abe said and let his foot off the gas pedal. "Happy now?"

David nodded, released his death grip on the hand-holds and withdrew a map from his suit jacket pocket. "Cross the river by West Broadway. Go to Burhans Street. Turn left by Blemont to Norwood Street."

Caught behind a trolley on West Broadway, Abe had to maintain a modest speed as he headed into Haledon. Passing well kept, wood-frame two-story houses he said, "I don't know what these laborers are complaining about. Look at these nice houses."

"And look by the money your friends made. All these real estate companies are fronts by men like Lambert, yes? They earn nice profits on these houses, no?"

"That's business. If the buyers couldn't pay the price, these houses wouldn't be here."

"Let me ask you, Sarah does not work, no?"

"You know she doesn't."

"For these people to own these houses, everyone has to make a living."

"You're beginning to sound like Solomon's Socialist friends."

"You know by who owns these houses?"

"Tell me."

"The weavers, warpers, loom-fixers. The skilled, yes?"

"What's your point?"

"What for the unskilled in the apartments? Why they not allowed to own a house?"

"When they learn their skills and move up the ladder, they'll have their house."

"And if they do not learn such a skill? They have to live by squalor all their lives?"

"That's life," Abe said. "There will always be haves and have-nots. I'll be damned if some poor slob who doesn't have the brains to make something of himself will take what's mine without a fight to the finish."

"*Nu*, so that is your reason for not settling?"

"You're damn right!" Abe said. "The workers want to talk money; fine we'll talk. But we aren't talking to anyone who advocates confiscating our mills."

Abe turned left onto Norwood Street and crawled behind the laborers who had disembarked the trolley and joined the throng marching toward a house sitting all by itself on the block. When he honked his horn to try and move them out of his way, a couple of men slapped his fenders and yelled, "Go home, boss."

Abe responded with another long blast of his horn, which only solidified the crowd. They surrounded his car, yelling, "Boss, boss, boss!"

Abe slowly released the clutch. His car inched forward and bumped the men in front. They grasped onto his fenders and rocked the car.

David's face contorted in fright as he grabbed the hand-holds.

Suddenly, the crowd in front of the car parted. Four burly Pinkerton body guards, their derby hats pulled down snug on their heads, pushed through the laborers. Their coats were drawn back behind their pistols, holstered on their belts. Using their billy clubs clasped in both hands to shove men left and right, they bellowed, "Out of the way!" Reaching Abe's auto, the one acting as leader said, "We'll escort you, sir." Climbing on Abe's running boards, they twirled their night sticks by the leather straps and directed Abe to six autos parked at the curb across the street from a lone house, surrounded by lots cleared of trees waiting for a builder to begin construction.

Setting his hand brake, Abe stepped out of his auto and walked to the car in front of his. He recognized the driver's face from the mill owner's meeting last week, but could not recall the name.

"Thanks for the help," Abe said.

The driver extended his hand and said, "Paul Simpson. You're Bressler, right? You're the one we elected as our delegate to go to the Alderman's meeting next week?"

"Yes, I am."

"Come here to see the outsiders?"

"I want to hear their lies for myself so I can counter them."

"Why didn't you bring Pinkertons with you?"

"I didn't know I would need them."

"Lucky we were here, then," Simpson said.

"Why are you here?" Abe asked.

"Gathering names and faces so I know who not to re-hire when these fools come back to work."

Abe nodded. "Thanks again," he said and returned to David.

Relaxed, now that they had an escort protecting them, David said, "Give a look on all these people?"

"What did you expect after that jerk, Bimson, arrested Haywood? You were there when I told them if Bimson keeps up his arrests, he was going to unite the workers even more. He really did it this time."

CHAPTER 67

The owners of the house, Pietro Botto, his wife Maria and their four daughters, immigrated to Paterson from Biella, Piedmonte, Italy in 1892. Pietro had already served one six-year hitch in the Italian army. When they tried to draft him again he and his family fled. It took him fifteen years, working seventy hours a week as a weaver in Paterson's silk mills, to save enough money to fulfill his dream.

In 1907, Pietro bought a plot of land in Haledon, a mile from Paterson's mill district, and built his two-story stone and wood frame house, complete with bocci court and storage shed. Pietro was not a strike leader, but he was sympathetic to any cause that would increase his income. When Paterson banned Sunday meetings, he offered his house as a gathering place.

****

The size and diversity of the crowd created a little anxiety among the rally's organizers. They had expected the usual two to three thousand. But with the weather continuing warm, laborers and their families converged on Pietro Botto's house from every corner of Paterson.

Norwegians came from the Sandy Hill section of Madison, Market, and Straight Streets. The Irish from the area they nicknamed "Dublin," formed by Main, Oliver, Spruce and Clay Streets. From the Lakeview section over by Twenty-Third Avenue, Madison and Railroad came the English, German and Dutch. Syrians and Armenians came from South Paterson. The Polish came from the Bunker Hill area by the Passaic River. From Belgian Hill, near East Fifteenth, came the Belgians and French. From the ethnically-mixed Riverside area north of Van Houten came Eastern European Jews, as well as other Eastern Europeans from Lithuania, and Germans, Portuguese, Swiss and Italians. The most unskilled laborers from Southern Italy came from the Stony Road area south of Van Houten and mixed without incident with their skilled countrymen from Northern Italy who were now living in Haledon. From Ashley Heights and Prospect Park near Westervelt Avenues came the Swiss, Scots, Hungarians, Dutch and English. From Totowa came more English, German and Irish.

Standing on the second-floor balcony of Pietro's house, the organizers scanned the spreading sea of hats and faces and quickly realized it would do them no good if the assemblage could not understand the speakers. They quickly enlisted translators, and additional speakers were added to the program.

In deference to their Italian host, Carlo Tresca was the first to speak. He stepped out onto the veranda, carrying a folded banner. Holding it over his head, he let it unfold. Roars of approval rocked Haledon. The banner showed a textile loom operated by two children, their hands dangerously deep into the machinery. A fat man, dressed in a three-piece suit, sporting a bushy mustache, a cigar in his mouth, a top hat on his head, and gold fob cascading across his protruding stomach, watched the children. Bags of money encircled the boss's feet. Printed across the top of the picture in large letters was the word, "THIEF." At the bottom was the slogan, "The worst thief is he who steals play time from children. W. D. Haywood. Join the IWW and help put the thieves to work."

David chuckled.

"That's funny to you?" Abe asked.

"It looks like Weidmann, Solomon's boss, no?"

"You think what it says is true?"

"It is not totally false."

"Solomon's a fool," Abe said. "I will drag him away from those anarchists and Socialists if it's the last thing I do."

"How will you go by that?"

"I don't know yet, but I will."

"Labor is entitled to all it produces," Tresca said, mixing English and Italian. He unfurled a huge red flag and tied it on the railing next to the banner. "We will abolish the wage system, do away with Capitalism, and unite all workers under a new flag—an international red flag. Keep the red flag of Socialism flying!" he yelled, raising both hands and shaking his fists.

Abe, having learned a little Italian during the five years he owned his bar, grasped the gist of Tresca's speech and said, "They really are advocating anarchy."

"I no hear that," David replied. "I hear a plea for money. If your friends be not so greedy, this strike would end."

"Bull!" Abe blasted. "The mill owners pay their labor what the market demands, nothing less."

"I know what for the market pays. My boss knew too."

"And you weren't getting what you were worth, and now you are. It all depends on your skills and your ability."

"And by who you know."

"Some, but you need the skills and the brains to keep what you get. Let's face it, everyone is not cut from the same bolt of cloth."

"Yes, that is so. But workers still deserve to get paid a fair wage if they give a fair day's work."

"They are getting a fair wage."

"These people do not agree, yes?"

Abe motioned to the balcony. "If those outsiders weren't stirring things up, these good people wouldn't be here."

"You are wrong, Abe. This has been coming by a long time."

Acting as master of ceremonies, Elizabeth Flynn introduced a long procession of speakers. John Hagedorn from Holland spoke in Dutch, Charles Zochowsky spoke Polish, William Defendinger spoke in German. As each finished, those that understood the language cheered first, followed by spontaneous cheers from those who didn't, but who were caught up in the euphoria.

Frederick Mohl, a Socialist from New York City, spoke in English, concluding with, "America is a great country, but it is in hock, and the pawnbrokers are the international firms of Rockefeller and Morgan." He pointed to the line of autos. "If we are to live, we must break their hold on our country."

David grinned when Patrick Quinlan said, "Paterson is run by a lot of ex-prize fighters and ex-saloon keepers, and law and order does not exist here. Police Recorder Caroll has about as much knowledge of law and order as an ordinary pig in Barnum and Baily's circus has about electricity. We'll win our strike or wipe the city of Paterson off the map."

Elizabeth Flynn again took over the balcony, and said, "Now I want you to meet a man who, in his book *The Jungle*, exposed the scandal of the meat-packing bosses in Chicago for putting diseased meat, floor sweepings and putrid meat in our sausage and canned food. A man who revealed for all the world to see the horrifying conditions of our fellow stockyard workers in Chicago. A man who thought it his duty to come to Paterson to help us in our fight against the bosses. I have the great honor and privilege to present to you Mr. Upton Sinclair."

Elizabeth Flynn stepped aside and clapped loudly as Mr. Sinclair walked onto the veranda. She had never met him, but at the urging of her father she read all his writings and incorporated many of his ideas into her speeches. She was ecstatic when he agreed to speak in Paterson.

Sinclair was a thin man, about six feet tall. He had a triangular face with a wide, high forehead, narrowing down past a straight, unsmiling mouth to a small chin. At thirty-five, his hair was already thinning and receding, revealing long ears.

"I came here today to offer you encouragement in your fight against the evils of your bosses . . ."

Abe said, "It's all the same crap from every one of them. The idiots have no idea what they're talking about."

"*Nu,* you call this man an idiot?" David asked. "I read his book. If it was not by him we could all be poisoned by bad meat."

"Not us. We eat kosher."

"You know for what I mean."

"Yeah, I know, but the man is still a fool. It's one thing to go about exposing bad practices that need exposing. It's another to advocate the overthrow of the system that made this country great. Let him stick to what he knows—writing—and let the businessmen stick to what they know—running their businesses."

"What is wrong with wanting something a little better by what you have?"

"Nothing. It's advocating the taking what you want away from someone else because you're too lazy or too damn stupid to work for it yourself is what I will always fight against."

David did not answer and turned back to listen.

"Yours is the finest exhibition of solidarity ever seen in the Eastern States," Sinclair said. "Don't give up your fight. The only way you will ever get a fair deal will be for you to take over and operate the industries of the country yourself. A Socialist society—a cooperative commonwealth—that is what this country needs if it is to straighten itself out."

"See what I mean," Abe said as the crowd applauded the speaker. "He's a fool. He doesn't know what he's talking about. The reality of the world, even in his Socialist dream country is, there will always be workers and bosses, and nothing said here today will ever change that."

Stepping forward, Elizabeth Flynn vigorously shook Sinclair's hand, hugged him and gave him a kiss on the cheek. Raising her hand to bring forth another round of cheers, she yelled, "Let's hear it again for Mr. Sinclair."

She escorted her esteemed guest inside and returned to the balcony with another speaker. "Now I want you to meet a man new to our cause, Mr. John Reed."

"Ladies and gentlemen," the unimpressive young man began softly.

The crowd shifted restlessly, many questioning, "Who is he?"

"Speak up," a voice yelled from the rear of the crowd.

"Ladies and gentlemen," he began again, pushing his voice to the limit. "I have just come from a short stay in Chief Bimson's Hotel."

When the laughter subsided, Reed continued. "I have a message for you from Mr. Haywood and Mr. Lessig. They said they are willing to stay in jail a year if you will hold on and win your strike."

Hoots and hollers again interrupted him for a moment.

"I had a long talk with Mr. Haywood, and he introduced me to many of your comrades in jail. I am a writer for *Metropolitan Magazine*. Our great past President, Mr. Theodore Roosevelt, is one of my editors."

Holding up his hands to quiet the crowd's cheer at the mention of Teddy's name, Reed went on. "Mr. Roosevelt is very partial to our cause. He gave me this assignment to write about your class struggle and I am going to tell the world what is going on here in Paterson. I am going to tell them about the beatings and unjustified arrests of you gentle, brave men and women . . .

"Finally someone agrees with me," Abe said. "If I could convince Lambert to call off Bimson, I know this strike would collapse."

". . . After talking with the speakers here today, I have concluded that you peace-loving people are being exploited and persecuted by the bosses and the police, and I am going to write about you and your struggle. I am sure Miss. Flynn and Mr. Haywood would not mind if I gave them second billing to the real leaders of this strike—you wonderful people."

"Just what we need," Abe muttered. "Another Socialist rag in New York City taking up their cause. This thing is never going to end."

"Thank you, Mr. Reed," Elizabeth Flynn said.

She waited for him to leave the balcony before beginning her concluding speech. "I really thought we were going to have to hold this rally at the jail because so many of our comrades are in there." She waited a moment for the laughter to subside. "As Mr. Reed said, we are here to advise you. You don't need leaders. You are leading yourselves. We did not organize your general strike committee. You did that yourself."

She waved a piece of paper in the air. "We did not write this statement your committee chairman, Mr. Alexander Cook, just handed me; your strike committee did. Mr. Cook is going to pass out copies of this at your mill meetings tomorrow, but let me read it to you now. 'The manufacturers must realize that the improvements of machinery means something besides increasing the already swollen fortunes of a few unscrupulous and money mad barons. That the toiler who feeds and clothes the world must have a fairer and more just share of the wealth he creates. This we demand as a right, not a favor.'

"And you also have a right to strike and peacefully picket," Elizabeth Flynn added forcefully, smiling as the crowd cheered.

"Do you know the police are arresting mostly foreign-speaking pickets because they cannot talk for themselves and don't know what the judge is saying? More of you English speaking men and women must join your comrades on the picket lines.

"Boycott your enemies—those that go to work as scabs. Ostracize them. Make them pariahs in their community. Don't shake their hands, for their hands are bloody. Only the picket lines will keep the scabs out of the mills and force the manufacturers to deal with you."

Elizabeth Flynn held up her hands to cut off the yells. "Scare the life and soul out of the authorities on the picket lines. If the police arrest one of you, let two more of you take his place. Solidarity! Unity! You must show you are one if you are to defeat the boss.

"Now I must ask you a favor for your fellow workers. The strike fund needs money. Dig deep into your pockets for your fellow workers, even if it means giving your car-fare, for it is not a far walk home. I am going to pass the hat."

"I knew there was more to this than just talk," Abe said. "I'll bet she doesn't walk home."

CHAPTER 68

Abe dropped David off, but he did not head home. His anger at hearing the denunciations of the mill owners by the outsiders and their call to steal his business re-awakened his earlier ire with Sarah. As he drove downtown, he mumbled, "I should have realized it. She's a Socialist, just like her parents."

He parked his car in front of Katie's rooming house and sat for a moment. "She's going to change or . . ." He didn't finish his admonition, because like not knowing what to do about Solomon, he didn't know how he was going to break Sarah of her rebellious ways. Grabbing the gift-wrapped box, he slid out of the driver's seat and slammed the door.

****

When Abe hadn't returned home by six o'clock, Sarah telephoned Leah.

"David came in around four," Leah said.

"Was Abe with him?"

"No. He's not home?"

"No," Sarah said softly.

"Let me put David on the line."

Sarah paced the floor as far as the telephone cord would allow. She heard mumbling in the background. It sounded like David didn't want to take the phone. Leah must have prevailed.

"Do you know where Abe is?" she asked.

"He did not come home?"

"No," Sarah said, sniffling. "Where is he?"

"I . . . I . . . I do not know."

"David, don't lie to me. You know. Where is he?"

"You call by Solomon," David said, and hung up.

Sarah stared blankly at the phone. Slowly, she hung the receiver on the hook, waited a moment, lifted it off and gave the operator the number for the pay-telephone in Cecelia's apartment house. The person who answered hollered, "Wait a minute."

Sarah heard pounding, and a few minutes later Cecelia said, "Hello."

"Cecelia, it's Sarah. Is Abe there?"

"No. Why? Should he be?"

"Is Solomon home?"

"Yes. He came in an hour ago."

"Can I speak to him?"

"Of course."

Again Sarah paced. She heard a door squeak open and a voice yell, "You done mit dis telephone?"

"No. I'm getting my husband," Cecelia shouted. "Don't hang it up."

"You hurry it up."

It took almost a minute for Solomon to come on the line. "I don't know where Abe is, I'm sorry," he said to Sarah's anguished question.

Sarah collapsed into a chair in the living room. Abe hadn't wanted her in weeks and it wasn't because she was pregnant. That never stopped him. He was quite inventive when it came to seeking his pleasure.

She couldn't deny it any more. He had another woman. Solomon knew it. David knew it. She could hear it in their voices. She could smell her cheap perfume Abe brought into their house on his clothes.

Tears rolled down her cheeks. "He can't do this to me. I won't let him." Her face tightened, and she grabbed her stomach as she cried out in pain.

CHAPTER 69

Carrying a box wrapped in shiny pink paper, Abe tapped on Katie's door. She greeted him with a broad smile that stretched out the little age lines around her eyes and at the corners of her mouth. Ushering him inside, she wrapped him in her arms and gave him a passionate kiss, squirming her body as his free hand slipped under her silk robe and caressed her naked backside.

Breaking their embrace, Abe asked jokingly, "Can I take my coat off?"

"Of course, honey. Let me help you," Katie said and tossed his coat, suit jacket and vest in a heap on a chair.

"This is for you," Abe said.

"A gift. How sweet." She ripped off the paper and opened the box, exposing a vial of perfume lying in a bed of cotton. Pulling the cork from the bottle, she sniffed the aroma. "A little sweet, but nice, thanks." She replaced the cork and dropped the bottle back in the box without applying any. Putting the box on the coffee table, she picked up a pack of cigarettes and shook one out.

"You like smoking those?" Abe asked.

"They're kind of nice," she answered, and plucked a stick match from the box. Striking it against the sandpaper strip, she lit up.

Slouching onto the couch, she stretched out her legs. Her robe had split apart up to the tie around her waist, exposing her nakedness.

Abe lounged next to her, reached out and stroked her thigh, letting his pinky finger brush the softness at the crest of her legs.

"That feels good," she moaned, and flicked the ash from her cigarette onto the floor. "This is wonderful."

"Is it?"

"Oh, yes, the two of us together again."

"Uh huh. How long will you be in Paterson?"

The burning end of her cigarette neared her fingers. She leaned forward, stubbed it out in the crowded ashtray and quickly fell back to her lounging position. Draping her leg over his, she said, "Originally I was only going to stay as long as Elizabeth stayed, but now that we found each other again . . ." She smiled at him, leaving her thought unfinished.

"I'm married, remember?"

She rubbed him into an erection. "You'll leave her for me, won't you?"

Shifting to face her, he said, "Sure, Katie."

She smothered his mouth with hers and groped for the buttons on his pants.

****

Sliding off the bed and slipping her robe back on, Katie said, "I made a bunch of corned beef and cabbage and boiled potatoes for the girls. It's warming in the kitchen. Are you hungry?"

"Famished."

"I'll get it."

"You're going out like that? I can see right through your robe."

She tied the belt tighter. "Don't worry. Who's ever out there has seen it before. I'll be back in a jiff."

Abe sat on the couch. He wrinkled his nose at the odor of cigarette smoke hanging in the air. The ashtray on the coffee table had five ground-out butts. His thoughts drifted back to Sarah. When she spouted those Socialist ideas, she infuriated him. Katie was great a defusing his anger, but to replace Sarah with her? "Ha," he scoffed out loud as a vision of what his house would look like with Katie keeping it popped into his mind.

Katie returned with a tray holding wine glasses, forks and knives, and two plates piled high with plum-colored beef, shredded cabbage and white potatoes. The cabbage odor repulsed Abe. He never could stomach the way the Irish fixed cabbage. As she spread the plates out on the coffee table, he opened a window.

"Good idea. It is a little warm in here," Katie said, hustling to her bureau. She took out her silver candlesticks, fixed the candles, lit them, and placed them on the table, making sure the dented one faced away from Abe. Spreading a napkin across Abe's lap, she opened a bottle of wine he had brought her on an earlier occasion.

Abe pushed his plate away.

"Did you like it?" she asked. "You didn't eat your cabbage."

"You know it's not my favorite. But the corned beef and potatoes were good," he lied. *And Katie could never cook like Sarah*, he thought. The meat was tough and the potatoes were over-cooked. No, he'd never leave Sarah for Katie. Katie was good for one thing only and that's what he'd use her for when Sarah riled him.

****

Sarah heard him come in. She listened to him get undressed and washed. She felt him slip into bed and kiss her on the cheek. She faked sleep because she didn't want to hear more of his lies.

In moments, he was asleep and snoring, raising her ire. *How can he sleep so deeply with what he's doing to me*? She rolled her head and stared at him. Did she dare confront him? What about her baby? Every time they argued, pains erupted in her womb.

Tears welled up in her eyes and rolled down her cheeks, wetting her pillow. No, for the children's sake, she would not confront him about his indiscretion. For the love of her baby, she would suffer the embarrassment of knowing her in-laws were aware of her husband's folly. When they gave her a look of sympathy, she would present a gallant face. She was determined to go on with her life, despite his philandering.

CHAPTER 70

Though exhausted, having finally fallen asleep as the sun was rising, Sarah sat on the stage of the YMCA, the sponsor of today's suffrage debate, and stared out at the crowd of Paterson's dyers and weavers, which was at least seventy percent women. The women came voluntarily. The men came because Solomon ordered them to come. Solomon owed Sarah a big debt for her giving Cecelia her diamond ring to bail him out of jail. As a partial repayment he commandeered men from the picket lines to fill the seats. He really didn't have much trouble convincing anyone. For a few hours, the men thought they would get a laugh in this otherwise dreary strike.

Sarah's breath caught in her throat when her opponent took the podium. Abe called non-thinking people "fools." At this moment, she felt like one. Why had she let them talk her into this? Why had she let her anger with Abe overtake her rationale?

Just by her presence, Jeannie Tuttle Hobart had grasped the full attention of the audience. She may have lost out being first lady of the land, but she was without a doubt the first lady of Paterson. Her husband left her well-off and she used her money to sponsor many philanthropic causes. She was President of the Old Ladies Home, gave liberally to the Paterson Orphan Asylum, and donated the land at the corner of Hamilton and Grand Streets, on which was built the Children's Day Nursery to serve the children of the city's mill workers.

With the grace and self-confidence that came from having been at the height of Washington's social strata, Mrs. Hobart espoused her anti-suffrage views. "You do not need parades and floats and banners to state who you are. Being a homemaker is not demeaning. If you do it right, you can maintain your identity.

"When Mrs. McKinley took ill, I filled in as the President's hostess. I was not looked on as merely a wife. People greeted me with respect because I deserved it by the way I did my job.

"Your job as a homemaker is what you make it. If your home is warm and loving, you will command respect. Take pride in your work. Do it with dignity."

Turning sideways to address Sarah, Mrs. Hobart said, "My dear, with five children and one on the way, when will you find time to inform yourself about the important matters of government?"

"She's starting her own government," a man yelled, followed by hoots and hollers from his otherwise bored compatriots.

"She didn't create those six children all by herself," a woman countered.

Feet stomped and hands clapped in agreement.

Until her opponent made the debate personal, Sarah had been petrified as to how she was going to effectively rebut such a poised and distinguished speaker. Not anymore. Mrs. Hobart's condescending remark gave her strength.

Taking her place at the podium, Sarah said, "Thank you, Mrs. Hobart, for your concerns about my education."

To the gathering she asked, "How many of the women in the audience can read?"

Three-quarters of them raised their hands.

"Those of you who cannot and would like to learn, I will be happy to teach you. I'm sure the YMCA will let us hold class in their building."

Mary Beckworth jumped up from her seat behind the podium. "Those of you who would like to join the reading class, see me after the meeting."

"Thank you, Mary," Sarah said and continued. "Women are graduating high school in greater numbers than ever. We are not illiterate. My husband brings home the newspaper every night. I don't just wrap garbage in it, I read it. If I don't get a chance when he's done, I read it the next day. I am well-informed about the issues of the day, and you can be too.

"Women were not put on this earth to sacrifice for men. We are here as man's equal. We work as hard, and we deserve equal rights."

The women cheered. The men remained silent, most with their arms folded across their chests in an effort to show their bravado.

"The world is changing. Twenty-five percent of all women work outside the home. How many women here run looms?"

Two dozen hands shot up.

"Why don't you get paid the same as the man who runs the loom next to yours?"

"Yeah, why don't we?" a woman yelled out, jumping up and scowling at the man seated beside her. "I can weave as fast and as good as you, Dominick."

A hand reached up and yanked her down. "Keep quiet, Gloria."

"Boos" directed at Dominick filled the room.

Sarah went on. "Mrs. Hobart is renowned for the many children's charities she supports, and I am sure all the children she helps are very grateful to her. But there is one thing all her good deeds cannot do for them: Outlaw child labor. But the vote can.

"Voting takes but a moment's time. It will not lessen my maternal love and care for my children and my love for my husband."

She paused for a long moment. Dare she say it? She certainly was on the receiving end of it often enough from Abe.

The audience shuffled restlessly. A couple of people clapped, thinking she was done. She had but an instant more to make up her mind. Mrs. Hobart had brought up Washington. Revisiting that fiasco tilted Sarah's decision to the affirmative.

"Men have only one reason why they do not want us to vote—their ego. They cannot bear to lose their domination over us."

Howls sprang from every woman, drowning out the jeers from the badly-outnumbered men.

Sarah received the majority of the congratulatory accolades. Even Mrs. Hobart, in a private conversation with Sarah conceded, "The child labor laws might very well be changed if women voted." However she was quick to add, "I do not agree that women can balance both keeping their home and voting. We each have our own job, men and women.

When one encroaches on the other, it becomes divisive. You see how your last little comment split this gathering."

"You could be right," Sarah said. "but today women work too hard in and out of the home not to be allowed an opinion. Men must accept that if our society is to survive."

A single set of hands clapped from behind them.

Startled, Sarah turned to see Elizabeth Flynn and a beautiful redhead.

As Sarah shook hands with Elizabeth, Mrs. Hobart made a hasty retreat.

"Nice speech," Elizabeth Flynn said. "I see you've regained your fortitude; I knew it was there when I met you in jail."

The scent of lilac brought Sarah's eyes to the redhead.

"This is my friend, Katie McGuire," Elizabeth said.

As Sarah focused on Katie, Katie's eyes bored in on her. A terrifying chill engulfed Sarah. *Was this who Abe was seeing? What does she have that I don't have? She's pretty. No, she's beautiful, but there is something about her eyes*, Sarah thought. They looked worn, tired.

Forcing her eyes away from Katie and back to Elizabeth Flynn, Sarah said, "I didn't get the chance to thank you for consoling me in jail. Please accept my appreciation."

"You're welcome," Elizabeth said. "You are a persuasive speaker. Our cause could use you."

"I don't believe in your cause, Miss. Flynn. I do not want to start a revolution. I just want equal rights."

"Isn't that what a revolution is about?"

"We don't need to overthrow the government to get what we want. I think you are doing the people of Paterson a great disservice."

"By showing them how they can better their working conditions?"

"By asking for ridiculous demands. Leading them on with false hope."

"You mean like demanding a living wage and an eight-hour day?"

"Those are reasonable requests. But you're also filling their heads full of revolutionary drivel, like confiscating property. I lived in a country where property was stolen and people trampled at the whim of a dictator."

"We are not advocating dictatorship. We believe the people should own all the property and share in all the wealth."

"I read Karl Marx. His Utopia where there is no government cannot work."

"The boss system has to go . . ."

"Let me finish," Sarah said. "I also read extensively about the revolution in this country."

"Led by the elite land-owning barons."

"That is correct, Miss Flynn. Less than twenty-five percent of the colonists participated in the revolution, or even cared about a change in government. Do you know why?"

"Enlighten me."

"Because people are like sheep. They have to be led."

"Precisely my point."

"And who will lead them while we are waiting for the government to 'wither away,' as Mr. Marx professes? You? Mr. Haywood? No, Miss Flynn. This system may have its flaws, but it is far better than any other, including Mr. Marx's."

"I especially like the first line in the Declaration of Independence. 'We hold these truths to be self evident, that all MEN are created equal.'"

"Change comes slowly, but it comes when it is warranted, and without anarchy. All the people want is to be allowed to earn a decent wage for a fair day's work and then be left alone to lead their lives as they see fit. That is what I am fighting for, Miss Flynn—the right to live my life the way I desire." Sarah pointed to the departing crowd. "What is good for me is not good for him or her. We, you, me, them—we are all individuals in our wants and desires. I do not want what you want."

"But I want what you enjoy, Mrs. Bressler. And so do my people. And we will get it."

CHAPTER 71

The six hundred delegates of the strike committee—two from each of Paterson's three hundred mills—filed into the rows of seats in the high school auditorium. Milling around on the stage, waiting for the strikers to seat themselves, were the five county alderman; clergymen The Reverend Dr. Hamilton and Rabbi Manheimmer; merchant's association members Bob Conners and Harry Siegel; president of the First National Bank of Paterson, Carlton Sommers; president of the AF of L's United Textile Workers Union, John Golden; AF of L Labor Council Committee of Trades representative, Edward Thomas; State Senator Hugh Jenson; and Abraham Bressler.

Chatting with Alderman Higgens, Senator Jenson asked, "Do you believe those lousy Giants losing to the Washingtonians?"

"Yeah, some start to the season," Higgens said. "Say, did you hear, Jim Thorpe is coming to play baseball in Lakeview Park next Sunday? They're trying to put together a Paterson team to play in the New York-New Jersey League and they got Thorpe to come try out."

Overhearing the small talk, Abe shook his head in disgust. The whole town was near collapse and the only thing these politicians could talk about was baseball. He refocused his attention on the conversation between the A F of L union leaders, anxious to hear what they had to say.

Edward Thomas said to John Golden, "Did you read the latest about the trolley strike in Buffalo? Six people shot, including a woman and her child."

"A terrible tragedy," Golden said. "I hope our fellow workers here keep the lid on so the governor doesn't have an excuse to send in the troops."

Studying the two men, Abe said to himself, "Finally, some sanity." He thought, *After the meeting I'll corner them and discuss my idea.*

Alderman Quigley walked to the podium. He was a tall man, with dark hair, parted in the center of his head. To the dignitaries on stage he said, "Gentlemen, please take your seats so this meeting can come to order." To the audience he said, "Will the speakers from the striker's committee please come to the stage?"

Solomon, Louis Magnet, Ewald Koettgen, and the chairman of the strike committee, Alexander Cook, marched toward the stage to the encouraging hoots and foot stomping from their compatriots. Clasping their hands above their heads like victorious prize fighters, the strike leaders jaunted up the stairs. Their euphoria quickly collapsed when they found no chairs for them to sit on. Except for Abe nodding to Solomon, the worker's representatives received no direction or recognition. Quietly, they slinked behind the seated dignitaries and leaned against the wall.

Alderman Quigley opened the forum by announcing, "The first speaker will be the Honorable Andrew F. Mc Bride."

All heads turned toward the opening side door. Mayor Mc Bride, escorted by two armed policemen, entered the auditorium. Hisses and boos greeted him as the mayor climbed the four steps to the stage. Taking over the podium from Quigley, he stood as tall as his portly five-foot-ten inch body would allow and waited for the audience to quiet.

"Where you been, Mayor, on vacation?" a voice yelled, followed by a burst of laughter.

"A good question," Abe said to himself.

"I have been working very hard to solve this dispute," he said.

"With who, Bimson and the bosses?" a voice interrupted, evoking yet another round of jeers.

"You know I have always been a friend of the working man of this . . ." He never got the word "city" out, his voice being drowned by more rebukes.

When the crowd quieted for the fourth time, the mayor steadied himself and said sternly, "I did not come here to be ridiculed. I came to answer your questions and try to help you. If you cannot show common courtesy to the speakers, then we might as well all go home."

The harangues quieted down, leaving only a few people yelling.

"I will answer all your questions in an orderly fashion. If you sit down and raise your hand, I will call on you." He pointed to his left. "Yes, you over there."

"What are you gonna do about the police arresting strikers at the mills when they ain't caused no trouble or broke no laws, but they was arrested anyway, just because the bosses point their fingers?"

"No one will ever be arrested if no law is broken, and as long as I am around, no one will be arrested just because a mill owner says to."

"Stop around more often, Mayor, and you'll see it's happening," a faceless voice yelled, followed by howls of agreement.

The mayor held up his hands in a plea for silence and pointed to another man.

"How come when the police get to a mill, they take orders from the boss?"

"I never heard that, and it is illegal."

"Why the hell don't you get yourself out of your office and walk around? You'll see a lot of things you ain't never heard of."

Ignoring the outcry, the mayor pointed to a waving hand in the back of the room.

"Do you believe we have a right to picket the mills to keep them scabs from taking our jobs?"

"My beliefs do not count. The law is clear as to the limitations of patrolling by strikers, and the courts have further defined the laws."

"Yeah, all for the bosses," came another call, followed by loud cheers.

Alderman Quigley approached the mayor. "Gentlemen, please," he begged.

"It's all right, Thomas. We're doing fine. These people have a right to their opinions, and we will answer all the questions."

A hush fell over the audience. A few hands shot up. The mayor pointed.

"What do you think of this strike?"

"I think you should organize your own union in town. You don't need outsiders. You have enough capable men right here to be your leaders. And I believe your union should try to make a uniform deal for all the workers as to pay and hours."

A murmur of approval rolled through the crowd, followed by someone yelling out, "Finally, he said something makes sense."

A man jumped up from his seat. Without waiting to be recognized, he pronounced, "Do you really believe twenty-four thousand of us left our jobs to face starvation just 'cause some outsiders come to town?"

"I think many of you had just grievance for leaving, but some left out of fear, and others out of sympathy, and I do believe a good portion of you left because of the influence of the outside agitators."

Abe glanced back at Solomon and smirked.

Again the gathering erupted in "boos," but this time they did not last long because the mayor quickly recognized another questioner, and the crowd quieted.

"Do you believe it is right for the manufacturers of this city to desecrate the American flag the way they done in this strike?"

"I do not believe in desecration of the American flag in any way, and I strongly denounce all the praises and speeches to the red flag being made by the IWW leaders. The American flag and the red flag cannot co-exist in this country. One has to go down before the other. I am greatly saddened that the good American citizens of this city who attended the meetings in Haledon did not protest the ugly remarks made by the IWW leaders against our flag and our country."

For the first time, the rumblings approved of his comments. He let their murmurings continue for a while before selecting another questioner.

"Mayor, what do you think should be done to end this strike in a way that is agreeable to all sides?"

"I have definite opinions as to how this dispute can be resolved. Committees from both sides should meet, or the state commission on labor can appoint committees from both sides. If that is not satisfactory, you can petition the United States Department of Labor under the new law to send a fact-finding commission to our city. You must remember one thing: most of the citizens of this city are neither manufacturers nor silk workers, but they are still affected by your strike. Commissions appointed by the people of this city that are not silk workers have come to talk to me. I must tell you that the general public of our great city demands this strike be ended."

A man jumped up and pointed a finger in Abe's direction. "Tell it to him."

"You said it," another chimed in. "We're ready to talk."

Thomas Quigley returned to the mayor's side. "Thank you, Mr. Mayor." Clapping softly, he said, "Let's hear it for the mayor." He received both applause and jeers in return.

Quigley waited for the mayor to disappear through the side door before announcing the next speaker—Solomon Bressler.

Solomon walked to the podium, encouraged by the hoots and hollers of the crowd. For a full minute, Solomon did nothing to stop their cheering. Finally, he held up his hands, the frayed cuffs of his white shirt rising out of his ill-fitting suit jacket. The group quickly quieted, reacting to his non-verbal lead like a marching band reacts to the baton signal of their drum major.

"This meeting is supposed to be representative of the community, but we workers are treated like second class citizens. The mayor asked for common courtesy, but it is obvious to me that the organizers of this meeting have no respect for us.

"If I wasn't a delegate here, I would walk out of this hall in protest to the indignity they forced on us by allowing us to stand while they remain seated."

The audience jumped to their feet. As the crowd roared, Solomon glared at Quigley, whose face flushed red with embarrassment. Fleeing from his seat, Quigley motioned the other aldermen to follow him. They left the stage and returned with chairs for the labor speakers.

When his fellow strike leaders were seated, Solomon said, "In answer to the mayor, I have to say, we have always been ready to meet with the bosses to discuss a settlement." Pointing to his brother, he added, "It is they who have refused to talk to us."

Deafening shrieks erupted as people jumped to their feet.

Abe sat stone still, arms folded across his chest, taking the jeers without acknowledgement.

Solomon raised his hands. The crowd quieted and dropped back into their seats. "We have used no violence in our strike. We have put our hands in our pockets. But what do we get in return? Beatings! Arrests! Brutality!"

As a maestro brings in the cellos, violins, horns and drums at the exact moment, Solomon raised and lowered his arms to bring out the cheers and the quiet interludes right on cue.

"There are many among the bosses who believe a worker is nothing more than a piece of machinery." Hands up for quiet. "If that is so, the worker is the most important part of that machine and should be treated with utmost care."

His arms stayed down for a long moment to let the cheers roll, then he raised them for quiet.

"The worker needs a decent living if he is to operate at maximum efficiency. Our demands are simple. We want an eight-hour day, time-and-a-half for overtime, minimum wage levels for the unskilled, increases in the piece rate, and abolishment of the three and four-loom systems."

Solomon brought his hands down sharply, as if instructing the drums and cymbals to commence a loud repast. He got the same result. The stage vibrated from the clapping hands and stomping feet.

Silencing the crowd, he concluded, "The product of our labor, the precious silk we produce, is sold by the boss at huge profits. If he cannot market the product we produce for him at a fair price to give us a decent living, then he is at fault and does not know his job. We demand a living wage and decent housing."

Solomon let the thunder roll as he stood sideways, smiling at the dignitaries seated behind him. Walking back to his seat, he stopped next to Abe and said, "Top that."

Overwhelmed by the laborer's solidarity and their disdain for anyone who represented the opposition, Quigley's shoulders slumped as he motioned Abe to come forward.

Abe had expected a favorable reaction to his brother, but nothing like what he witnessed. A bit stupefied, he stood quietly at the podium, waiting for the crowd to settle down.

The crowd chanted, "Boss, boss, boss," and someone yelled, "Bring on Henry Doherty."

Abe stood quietly, surveying the men as they expended their energy at his expense. He had a prepared speech, which suddenly seemed inadequate. He tossed it away. When the noise settled to where he thought he could be heard he said, "Many of you know me." He pointed, "Joe, Pete, Salvatore. You had some great times in my place."

"Hey, Abe, how about a beer?" The interruption was followed by laughter.

"I'll meet you at the old place after we're through here." A few chuckles popped up.

"Hey, Abe, I saw your wife speak yesterday. You shoulda brought her with ya. She really put that old broad in her place."

Abe had heard about Sarah's debate. As he waited for the laughter to subside he thought *she is something*, and wondered how he was going to subdue her.

Sensing the crowd had softened and was ready to hear what he had to say, he began, "How many of you have ever known me to lie to you or not give you a fair deal? I can look any of you eye-to-eye with a clear conscience even though my eye is a little black and blue right now." He held up his hands to quiet the guffaws. "When this strike began, I wasn't a mill owner. I didn't even plan to be here today, but I opened my big mouth once too often and here I am. I've seen Miss Flynn. She seems like a nice person. It's only her philosophies and politics that I can't sanction, not her looks."

He waited for the laughter to stop. "I never met Mr. Haywood, but from what I am told, he also is probably a nice fellow. But they don't live here in Paterson and they don't know our problems. You don't need them in your strike. You have good leaders right here in Mr. Magnet, Mr. Koettgen and my brother."

For the first time, the crowd settled down to listen to an opposition speaker.

"We manufacturers and you people have the same goal. We all want to end this strike. Let's get together and settle this among ourselves like we've always done, without the outsiders."

The back door burst open and slammed against the wall.

Heads turned.

The intruder yelled, "There's been a shooting! A man has been killed!"

In less than a minute the auditorium was empty.

CHAPTER 72

Personal messengers delivered Catholina Lambert's sealed invitations, summoning the six men to a meeting at Abe's house. The location was chosen because it was far from downtown. The attendees could arrive unobserved by the bands of reporters roaming the mill district, looking for follow-up stories on the murder.

Seated comfortably in Abe's study were the leaders of the manufacturer's strike committee. Accepting Abe's offer, Lambert occupied the place of honor—Abe's overstuffed, tufted leather chair.

"This is a nice house you have here, Bressler," Lambert said.

"Thank you. It's all from jobbing."

Lambert joined the others in a forced smile.

Peter Ryle said to Lambert, "Good job in Washington last month."

"I still have some friends in Congress."

"Not for long now that Connecticut ratified the amendment for direct election of senators," Jacob Weidmann said.

"You think that's going to make much difference?" Lambert countered. "It takes money to stand for election. We'll still get what we want."

Monroe Dippel asked, "You actually got a seat in the gallery to hear Wilson's speech?"

"I was right there. It was the first time since Jefferson that a president read his State of the Union Message to the combined House and Senate. Usually, they just delivered a written report."

"Wilson's pushing hard for lower tariffs," William Skinner said. "His whole speech was on that one subject."

"Sure, he doesn't need them now that he can collect taxes on our income," Weidmann said. "First an amendment to tax income. Now direct election of senators. What's next—women voting? Country's going to hell."

"How'd you get them to leave the tariffs on silk?" Monroe Dippel asked, ignoring Weidmann's whining.

"I just explained to our congressman, what with the strike going on many of us are in a weakened position, and to drop the silk tariffs now would be devastating to us."

Skinner said, "I was in Boston last week, talking to some cotton mill owners. They think they're going to get hit hard with piece goods coming in from England now that the tax is off cotton."

Weidmann scoffed. "Wilson thinks free trade will make business more efficient. Hah! Wait until businesses start folding and the dummies who voted for him are out of work, then we'll see. He'll be begging Congress to slap those tariffs back on."

Abe served drinks and cigars and listened to the tariff discussion, but he stayed out of it. He had mended his fences with these men and didn't need to antagonize them again. Personally, he had hoped the tariffs on silk goods would be lifted. With his contacts in France through his brother, he could do a lot more business in both directions with lower duties.

"Tariffs or no tariffs, if we don't end this strike soon, half the mills will be bankrupt," Peter Ryle said. He turned to Abe, who had reseated himself in the circle. "I heard you had them eating out of the palm of your hand."

"I was getting to them, but that's past now. Anything we may have gained at the Alderman meeting went down the drain with that killing."

"Jacob, what the hell happened?" Dippel asked.

"Two of O'Brien's detectives were guarding my mill. That mob led by your brother . . ."

"Wait just a minute," Abe angrily cut in. "My brother was at the Alderman meeting."

"So he wasn't there. He's still their leader and gives the orders."

Abe scowled. "Go on."

"That band of rowdies started jeering and throwing rocks at the detectives who were escorting some workers out of my mill. The detectives got flustered and pulled their guns and fired in the air."

Abe said, "I knew this was going to happen what with those Pinkerton and O'Brien detectives being allowed to carry guns and clubs."

"It could have been a lot worse," Dippel said.

"How?" Abe asked.

"At least the guy they killed—this Modestino Valentino—wasn't a silk worker."

Abe smacked his hands on the arms of his chair. "That makes it okay? The guy was just sitting there on his porch, minding his own business, and now he's dead."

"No, it's not okay. That's not what I meant, and you know it."

"Gentlemen, please," Skinner begged. "Let's get back to the issue."

"Yeah, yeah," Abe said in frustration. "Just one more thing." He focused on Lambert. "Make sure Judge Congdon keeps those guys who did the shooting locked up until hell freezes over or there is going to be a riot in this town."

"That goes without saying. Don't worry."

"I can't help worrying. This town is ready to blow."

"What do we do now?" Weidmann asked.

"I say we keep the mills closed until July and starve them back to work," Lambert said.

"How about we bring in strike breakers from our Pennsylvania mills?" Skinner offered.

"Isn't one death enough for you?" Abe asked. "You bring in strike breakers, you'll start a war."

"What do you suggest?" Skinner said.

Abe stared Lambert in the eye. "We have to begin talking with them."

"Never! Not while those anarchists are in town. They're the ones who started this, and I am not going to surrender to them."

"I have to agree with Catholina," Ryle said. "All those people from out of town want to do is create unrest. They're devious and deceive the workers with their lies."

"You talk about murderers," Skinner said. "Haywood was tried for killing the Governor of Idaho in 1906."

"Ex-governor," Abe corrected, "and he was found not guilty."

"I still bet he did it," Skinner insisted. "He should have been hung."

"And you call *them* anarchists," Abe shot back. "Listen to yourselves. You're getting down on their level. I for one came to this country to get away from that kind of thinking where the Cossacks could ride in and arrest or kill anyone for no reason. The man had a trial. He was found innocent."

"Innocent or not, I'm still not going to negotiate with him," Lambert said. "The only way I'll talk is shop-by-shop."

"Haywood will never let the workers do that," Abe said.

"So you do think the outsiders are running this show?" Lambert asked.

"They didn't start it," Abe answered, "but they took it over."

Lambert sucked on his cigar and slowly exhaled smoke. "We'll get Bimson to pick them up and get rid of them."

"It's too late for that. They're too well guarded by the strikers and too surrounded by reporters."

"What's your plan, Bressler?" Lambert asked.

Abe was about to answer when he heard his children storming into the house, shrieking and laughing.

"How many children do you have?" Dippel asked.

"Five."

"Starting your own work force?" Ryle joked.

"Or his own union," Skinner chided.

Abe chuckled along with his guests, but inside he seethed. He had told Sarah not to bring the children back until four.

"Five children and she still has time to give speeches?" Skinner asked.

"You heard about that?" Abe asked.

"We have our spies at every labor gathering," Lambert said.

Here it comes, Abe thought, preparing himself to be lambasted about his wife's suffrage work.

"You have some woman there," Lambert added

How did he mean that? What were they thinking? I know most of them are against woman suffrage because of all the radical causes that attached themselves onto the woman's movement. They had to be thinking, I'm a fool for not keeping my wife under control.

"You said you had an idea. Let's hear it," Lambert said.

"Huh? Right," Abe said, drawing his attention back to the issue at hand. "We have to get the leadership of this strike out of the hands of the IWW and into the hands of someone we can talk to."

"What the hell does that mean?" Weidmann asked. "Who can we talk to?"

"The AF of L union."

"What can they do? Their people have been following right behind the IWW."

"Not for long," Abe replied. "After the Alderman meeting broke up, I talked to their local leader, a guy named Golden. He is as upset with the IWW as we are."

"What the hell difference does it make who runs the strike?" Lambert asked. "It'll still be a damned union."

"At least the AF of L isn't trying to change the system, and they do have a history of being reasonable."

Peter Ryle said, "I think Abe has something here."

"What's Golden's plan?" Lambert asked.

"He's going to hold a rally. He thinks he can sign up fifteen thousand strikers to the AF of L."

"Fifteen thousand!" Lambert exclaimed. "If he does that, he'll have control."

"Absolutely! Then we'll make a joint declaration that we are willing to negotiate as a group with the AF of L to end the strike. We'll have pulled the rug from under Haywood and his gang."

"I hope you gentlemen know what you're doing," Skinner said. "Haywood is not the kind to sit by and let this guy Golden steal his show. He is very popular with his followers. I heard that while he was in jail, waiting trial on that murder charge, the Socialist party nominated him for Governor of Colorado and he got sixteen thousand votes."

CHAPTER 73

The day had started out mild, but, as can happen in early May, the weather changed suddenly with a shift in the wind from the southwest to the northeast. The children were not dressed warm enough and Sarah had rushed them home from their mandated outing in the park. With the help of Chava and her maid, she hustled them into hot baths. That done, she kept them as quiet as she could until she heard Abe's guests leave. She then went to confront him.

"I hope they don't get sick. I'll not do that again," Sarah said.

"Do what?"

She stomped her foot. "This is our house too. We will not be ushered out of it because you are having some people over."

"I told you this meeting was too important to have it interrupted by the wail of screaming children throwing tantrums."

His lack of feelings for his children churned her stomach. "Oh, you men and your meetings! What have you accomplished with all those stupid meetings?"

"I'm not going to discuss it with you. It's none of your affair."

"You think I'm going to run to Cecelia and give away your secret plans?"

"The thought had occurred to me. I know what you're doing, and I won't stand for it any longer."

"What are you talking about?" Sarah asked.

"You're still sending food to the strikers, even after I forbade it."

The muscles in her neck tightened. "So what if I am?"

"You will stop it. That's an order."

She walked across the room. Slowly turning to face him again, she asked, "Don't you have any compassion?"

"Not for anyone who wants to steal my business like a damn Cossack."

"Money! Your business! That's all you care about. You don't give a damn about me or the children or anyone else."

"Don't be ridiculous."

"Who's being ridiculous? How can you talk so much about family all the time and then ignore us like we're some kind of trained seal act you take out of a cage and put back when you see fit."

He was about to respond, but Sarah's rage overpowered him. "Do you ever give me a word of gratitude for what I do around here? Like it's all so easy. And I don't understand why you wanted so many children. You yell at them if they make the slightest noise. They're afraid of you and are beginning to hide when you come home."

Abe roiled back, “Do you have any idea what kind of pressure I’m under? I have to scratch and claw every day just so we can eat. And not only do I have to worry about us, I have to worry about David and Leah too, and my mother. All I want is some peace and quiet when I get home, not jumped on by the kids. And I certainly don’t want a wife who purposefully defies my express wishes.”

She knew he was under great pressure, but so were Solomon and many other people she knew. Yet, none of them seemed to act like her husband. At this point she should have yielded, but hearing the I . . ., I . . . I from him triggered the memory of the speech she gave the other day, and her built-up ire spewed from her mouth. “It’s not this strike. The strike is just your excuse. If it wasn’t that it would have been something else.”

“What are you talking about?”

“It’s all about control. You want people who will jump to your command. Solomon won’t knuckle under to you, so he’s the bad guy. I give a little food to people I’ve known for years, friends of my family, and I’m a home-wrecker.”

Her face turned beet red and she curled her fingers into fists. Digging her fingernails into the palms of her hands to keep from shaking she said, “Well, here’s one more problem for you to solve. The mill is your domain, but I run this house. The kitchen is my factory. Unless you want to do the cooking, you keep out of it or there’s going to be a strike right here.”

Abe grabbed her hand. “Where’s your diamond ring? You haven’t worn it in weeks and it’s not in your drawers. I looked.”

Furious that he had searched through her things as if she were a thief, she jerked free, stepped back out of his reach, and said, “I sold it to bail your brother out of jail. I owed that much to Cecelia for being here for me when you weren’t.”

Abe headed for the doorway. She thought he was coming after her and quickly stepped away, smacking her side into the desk. Recovering, she ran after him, reaching the hallway as he pulled open the front door.

She screamed at his back, “Where are you going?” She almost added, “Who are you seeing, that redhead?” but she choked it back. She was petrified of the answer. She would rather not bring his philandering to a head. If he left her for good—or worse, threw her out of the house—would he demand she leave the children with him? What choice would she have? She couldn’t take them with her. How would she feed them? She could live without him, but she could not bear to lose her children. At the thought of having to live with him for the rest of her life, she broke into choking sobs. Barely able to breath, she slumped into a chair and grabbed her stomach and waited for the stabbing pain to subside.

CHAPTER 74

Abe pounded on Katie's door. When she opened it, he swept past her into her room. He didn't notice she was not in a robe, but wore a beautiful flowered silk afternoon dress with flowing sleeves and a bodice of fine lace.

"What's wrong, sweetie?" Katie asked, sniffling back tears.

"Guess," he answered, tossing his coat on the couch.

Pulling a lace-trimmed handkerchief from her sleeve, she wiped the wetness from her cheeks.

"What's the matter with you?"

"I've been reading *The Eternal Maiden.*"

"What's that?"

"A book. It's a love story."

"Since when did you start reading books?"

"I thought I'd get some education."

"You look educated enough to me. Get over here, I need you."

She went to him. Fumbling to work her buttons loose, he said, "Why are you wearing this thing?"

"You don't like it? It's what the ladies wear, isn't it?"

"You're no lady."

Her head bowed to hide new tears forming in her eyes, she unbuttoned her dress and let it drop to the floor.

"Oh, Abe, baby, that was the best," Katie said.

"Yeah," he answered.

Despite lunging into her with all the ferocity he could amass, as if he was using a stick to pound the rebelliousness out of Sarah, he was unable to quell his anger with his wife. What she said to him was unforgivable. He did care about his family.

His thoughts suddenly flashed back to what his father-in-law had said to him so long ago. "You're just like your father." That conjured up his mother's admonishment back in March. "Don't be like your father."

"I am not like my father," he told his vision of his mother. But her phantom image would not relent and answered back, *"Aren't you."*

No I'm not, his mind screamed. Your husband abdicated his responsibility, leaving you to rule the house and raise the family. I would never do that. I am the authority in my house.

Sarah is the problem, not me. Sure I want control. I deserved control. It's my money that built the house and bought the food.

Would his mother do what Sarah was doing if she didn't have to be both the head of the household and raise the children? She wouldn't, he was positive of that. His mother would have worked with charities, civic groups. That's what Aunt Sylvia, Uncle Isaac's wife, did. Why couldn't Sarah be content with those kinds of good works? That was a woman's job, not trying to usurp his authority every chance she got.

"Abe, honey?" Katie prodded.

"Huh? What?"

"Where you been?"

"What do you mean?"

"You been dreaming."

"Just thinking."

"About us?"

"Yeah, about us."

"You know, every time you come by lately, I been waiting for you. Did you ever think why?"

What the hell is she talking about, he thought, but answered her with a shrug.

"I'm not seeing other men anymore. I told Elizabeth I won't. I only want to see you."

"Terrific."

She rolled on her side and entwined her fingers in his chest hair. "Abe, honey, if your wife makes you so upset, don't you think it's time to dump her?"

He stared at Katie. She would never chastise him like Sarah did.

"Are you going to leave her?"

"As soon as the strike is over."

She swept her hand down his body between his legs. "Then we'll be together all the time."

"Absolutely."

CHAPTER 75

Abe headed for the Fifth Regiment Armory to attend the union rally organized by the American Federation of Labor. *Their coup had better work*, he thought. He, like many of the small mill men, couldn't hold out much longer. He had bills to pay, and the interest on Goldberg's loan.

Since he had made peace with Lambert, he was able to buy some yarn in Paterson and sell it in Pennsylvania, but the meager money he made in Pennsylvania was a hundred dollars a week short of covering his bills. Those operations never did more than weave broad silk from staple yarn. The fancy jacquard and ribbon weaving and all the buying and selling of quality yarn was always done in Paterson. That's where the money was, and he needed it because his capital reserves were depleting rapidly.

Abe walked through one of the open overhead doors of the armory drill shed. Dull lighting from bulbs screwed into green metal shades, hanging in neat rows above the cement floor, cast gray shadows around the stark room. Odors of sweeping compound and gun oil permeated the air.

Standing on his toes, Abe searched among the crowd of men and women for the AF of L representatives, John Golden and Mrs. Margaret Jane Conboy. Mrs. Conboy was recruited for this rally because the organizers guessed correctly that there would be many women in the crowd and they wanted a counterpart to Elizabeth Flynn. Spotting the AF of L leaders standing near the speaker's platform, Abe joined them, and together they marched up the steps to the hastily built wooden podium. Not being a speaker, Abe took up a position at the rear of the stage next to the American flag. As he stood quietly waiting for the speeches to begin, he noticed a group of rough looking men ring the stage.

Seeing their opposition on stage, Haywood, Elizabeth Flynn, Quinlan, Tresca, Koettgen, Lessig and Solomon left their circle of loyal supporters at the rear of the armory and marched toward the podium. The crowd parted like the Red Sea for the ancient Israelites. When they reached the platform, the twelve toughs guarding the stage surrounded them.

Abe moved forward and whispered in John Golden's ear, "What's going on? I thought you were going to debate them."

"No, Mr. Bressler, not debate, debase. We are not going to give them a chance to fill these people's minds with more of their lies. Tonight is our night to show them up for what they really are—thieves and liars. Before this rally is over, the people assembled here will be solidly in our camp."

Abe's eyes shifted to Haywood's enraged face. "I hope you're right, Mr. Golden."

As the IWW entourage retreated, the big bosomed, short-waisted Margaret Conboy bellowed to the crowd in her deep voice, "There he is, hiding behind Elizabeth Flynn's petticoats again, letting his woman do his work for him like he did in Lawrence."

Haywood's spine stiffened as he re-traced his steps toward the rear of the armory.

Mrs. Conboy continued, "Did you know that sixty-two thousand dollars was collected in Lawrence last year and fifty-two thousand of it disappeared? And do you know who handled the money? Miss Flynn and Mr. Haywood. They do not want to settle this strike because it is too profitable for them. But we can settle this strike so it will benefit you . . ."

"Get something for me to stand on," Haywood demanded of Koettgen.

Within a few minutes, Koettgen and five other men lugged in a large wooden crate they scavenged from the yard outside the armory building.

Climbing on the box, Haywood pulled Elizabeth up along side him. Leaning down to Solomon and the other union leaders he said, "Circulate in the crowd and turn them toward me."

As soon as faces began looking up at him, Haywood's booming voice roared. "I said it before and I'll say it again, I would rather speak for the IWW with Elizabeth Flynn at my side than next to that liar, Sam Gompers, and his Civic Federation pals any day, any time. Why did you turn to us in your struggle? Because you knew if you listened to the AF of L, they would sell you out to the bosses."

Colonel Albert A. Van Walraven perspired profusely as he observed this unexpected turn of events from the door in the hallway that ran parallel to the armory drill floor. He thought the AF of L and the IWW leaders were going to debate each other from the same podium. He did not expect the potentially explosive shouting match that developed. He was suddenly happy that he had the foresight to call out two companies of militia to stand by. Turning to his aid, Captain Halladay, he ordered, "Have the men fix bayonettes and keep their weapons at the ready."

"Have you ever heard of the National Civic Federation?" Haywood bellowed. "It is an alliance set up in 1900 by the bosses to bring what they call 'better relationships' between themselves and you. And who is the chairman of this conspiracy? Senator Mark Hanna, the owner of coal mines, railways, and industries where he oppresses labor. And who is the vice chairman? None other than Sam Gompers, the self proclaimed watchman for labor."

Mrs. Conboy saw Haywood rise above the crowd and begin talking. But because she was three hundred feet away and separated by a confused and increasingly noisy crowd, she couldn't hear what he was saying. She assumed he was countering her charges. Her ample bosom heaved as she sucked in a deep breath and screamed, "The IWW is a fraud and a bunch of crooks. All they want to do is keep this strike going so they can line their pockets with your money. They are still collecting money way out west for strikers in Little Falls, New York, and you know how long that strike has been over. The only reason they are distributing money here in Paterson is because we forced them to do it by serving them with a court order."

"The AF of L is nothing more than a gang of professional strike-breakers hired by the bosses," Haywood hollered. "They are Judas goats trying to deliver you like sheep to the silk bosses of this town so you can be slaughtered." He pointed a long arm toward the platform at the other end of the drill floor. "Look there! See that man standing on the stage next to them. You know him. He calls himself your friend. He is not your friend. He is a mill owner waiting for you to be delivered to him and his boss friends by those AF of L scabs. If he could, he would send your wives, daughters and sweethearts to the depths of degradation in his mill."

Abe saw the rear third of the room turn toward Haywood. This meeting was not going the way he had anticipated. He again walked up to John Golden. "You have to invite them up here and debate them issue-for-issue, not hurl accusations at them. These people are not stupid. They will figure out who is right."

"It's too late for that now."

Golden leaned over the stage to talk to one of the burley guards. A moment later, six of the musclemen left their position and pushed through the crowd in pairs, heading toward the other end of the armory.

Abe screamed at Golden, "Are you crazy? Do you want to start a riot?"

"And who do you think will get the blame?"

Abe stepped off toward the stairs. "You will, if I have anything to say about it!"

Golden gave a quick glance to two of the remaining guards and snapped his head toward Abe. They blocked Abe's exit and ushered him back to the rear of the stage.

Not expecting trouble from their fancy-dressed captive, the men stood casually beside him, looking out over the crowd. Abe slammed the leather heel of his shoe down on the instep of one, breaking the man's foot. Before the other could react, Abe whirled and kicked him in the shin. Jumping off the stage, he shoved his way through the crowd. Long before he was within hearing range of his brother, he yelled, "Solomon, look out!"

Colonel Van Walraven moved away from the door and shut it against the noise. He didn't know what to do. If he tried to clear the armory, a lot of people were going to get hurt. If he did nothing, he was sure a riot would break out. He decided not to risk his men against that rabble. What could that mob do in that big room? His job was to protect the rest of the armory and the military equipment behind these doors. "Captain, have your men cover this hallway. If anyone breaks through the doors, shoot."

As more and more faces turned in his direction, Haywood elevated his voice. "Why do you think your fellow workers at Dogherty's new factory left the AF of L and joined with us in the IWW? Because they knew the AF of L had sold them out. The AF of L made a deal with Dogherty to allow four looms to a weaver in his mill.

"Stick with the IWW. We are the new bosses in Paterson. We have our hands around Paterson's throat and we are going to keep them there until we get our demands. The mills are as dead as J. P. Morgan, and they will stay dead until the IWW touches the looms."

John Golden's annoyance with Abe's escape was short-lived. After a quick discussion with a couple of associates who brought news of what Haywood was saying, he took the speaker's platform.

"Use your common sense," Golden yelled. His voice wavered slightly at the sudden realization that he was looking at more backs than faces. "Don't listen to those demagogues. How can an organization that says there is no God and no church settle a strike to your satisfaction?"

Waving his arms above his head, he screamed, "Listen to us! We believe your demands are just and we know we can settle this strike for you and get you a deal that is satisfactory to everyone. Is that strike-breaking? No it is not! It is good Christian common sense. The hot air of the IWW will gain you nothing. You will never win your demands by tearing down our American Institutions. Join with the two million AF of L union members and we will get all of you a square deal. We are a union no honest man has to be ashamed of."

Elizabeth Flynn took over for Haywood. Her hat had been jostled loose in her march through the crowd, and she held it in her hand. Strands of jet black hair dangled across her cheeks. "The AF of L is not a labor union. Join the AF of L and you manacle yourself into slavery for the rest of your life."

Waving her hat toward the opposition platform, she yelled louder, "Why do the bosses love the AF of L? Because the AF of L is a bunch of separate elitist unions. Each of their craft unions is out to make it's own deal with the bosses and couldn't care less about the others. And together they couldn't care less about you or any other unskilled worker. They'll sacrifice you to the bosses so they can keep the wages of their skilled members high.

"The IWW is for all workers, skilled and unskilled, Jews, Italians, English, French, everyone united together. You can only beat the bosses by uniting in a class struggle." She flung her hat into the air and screamed, "All power with the workers world wide!"

Applause and cheers rocked the armory.

A brawny man reached out for Solomon. His right hand drawn back and clenched into a fist, the goon clamped his left hand on Solomon's shoulder and spun him around.

Abe was three steps from Solomon and two steps behind the thug. He shoved aside a man who stood between himself and his brother's assailant, hooked his hand in the crook of the thugs bent arm, and pulled. As the attacker fell backwards, Abe smashed his fist into the man's nose. The enforcer's head bounced off the cement floor and Abe finished him off with a kick to the ribs.

The other assailants turned to flee.

"Get them! They're AF of L goons," Solomon yelled.

The mob beat the five remaining thugs to the floor.

"Thanks," Solomon said.

"Despite your stubbornness, you're still my brother."

The crowd pushed and shoved around them.

"Sol, let's get out of here."

"I can't."

"Don't be a fool."

"Leave, Abe. This isn't your fight."

"And it shouldn't be yours either. Use your head. How can you align yourself with those trouble-makers?"

"We've been through this before." Solomon scanned the restless crowd. "Get out of here while you still can. In a few minutes these people are going to forget what you just did and only see you as a mill man."

Abe's face pleaded.

Solomon answered by turning away and yelling at the laborers surrounding him, "You dyers hold your ranks. We are the backbone of this strike. Without dyed and processed goods, the mills stay closed."

Seeing scuffles and mini-brawls break out between the two factions, Margret Conboy yanked the American flag-pole out of its stand. She thrust the banner high in the air and waved it back and forth. "Don't listen to them. They are liars and thieves and murderers. They will steal your strike fund. They can't get you any concessions from the silk manufacturers."

The "boos" drowned out anything else she had to say. The mob encircled the stage and shook it. Petrified, Margaret stopped talking, lowered the flag and used the pole for support, trying desperately to maintain her balance.

Haywood saw the American flag flapping back and forth above the crowd. He reached under his suit jacket and took out a folded red banner he carried in a pouch strapped to his waist. Handing one corner to Elizabeth, they held up the blood red flag and let it unfurl, exposing the huge white IWW letters sewn across it. Howls of approval reverberated throughout the armory.

Haywood pointed across the room. "There are your scabs. There are your shills from the bosses, sent here to buy your loyalty. They say you can join their scab union for free. No initiation fee. I wouldn't join their union if they gave me $150.00. Stand firm! The mills are dead and the bosses will die with them and join their capitalist ally, J. Pierpont Morgan in the grave. The only power that will bring the mills back now is our power."

Storming across the drill field outside the armory, Abe saw Chief Bimson and a hundred policemen trotting toward the building. "Damn fools!" he said and turned to run back and warn Solomon. His warning wasn't necessary. Yells of "The Police!" echoed out of the building.

Bimson and his men charged in, swinging their clubs and, pummeling anyone within their reach to the ground. Abe watched helplessly as screams—mostly of women—filled the air. Encumbered by their long dresses, many tripped and were trampled. But it was the gunfire that startled Abe the most. He jumped behind a military truck and hovered there until the stomping feet of the fleeing laborers faded into the distance.

With only the moans of the wounded now penetrating the night, Abe slowly rose and stared into the armory. Men and women staggered about, blood splattered over their clothes. The line of back doors stood open and military-clad men lay bodies in a row across the floor.

Rushing in, Abe searched the dead for Solomon. Not finding him, he sunk his head into his hands and staggered out of the building along with the walking wounded.

CHAPTER 76

The mood of the laborers on the picket lines the next day was solemn, but their resolve was as strong as ever. Solomon and his fellow strike leaders had escaped the melee unscathed. Aided by the massacre, they rallied the workers to maintain their patrolling lines around the mills. Only those in mourning, hospitalized, or jailed failed to show up to blockade the factories. As Abe walked by the picketing laborers, he wondered how these men could let themselves be led around like a bunch of sheep. He passed Gold Ribbon Mill and waved to Meyer Gold. Meyer interrupted his conversation with the policemen and waved back before pointing at two men on the picket line. Standing with arms folded, Gold watched the coppers toss the two men in the paddy wagon.

Abe saw the same scene repeated over and over again as he continued through the mill district to Irving Pincus's factory on Grand Street. *This strike is as good as over*, he thought. He was sure of it. The strikers were doomed to fail because they had no mind of their own. They let themselves be manipulated by a band of outsiders like circus lions at the crack of the lion tamer's whip. They couldn't see the only reason the outsiders wouldn't agree to talk with the mill owners was because if the strike ended, their power would be gone.

Abe glared at the pickets blocking the entrance to Pincus' mill. Without a word, he stepped toward the door, his steel blue eyes daring the men to try and stop him. Slowly the line parted and he went inside. Irving had been evasive on the telephone as to what he wanted, but Abe knew it would be in his best interests to go see his friend. Noticing Irving's shoulders seemed a bit more bent since their last meeting a few weeks ago, Abe said, "You look tired."

Irving fell back in his chair. "I am."

"It'll be over soon."

"How can you be so certain?"

"Because they're losing their power."

"It didn't look like that to me when I came in this morning. Last night's massacre seemed to bring out more pickets and more meetings than ever."

"That's all show. There's nothing under it to hold the workers up."

"I don't follow you."

"The workers are a bunch of stupid chattel. They haven't seen it yet, but they will."

"See what?"

"That both the AF of L and the IWW are only using them as pawns in a battle with each other. Soon the workers will wake up and break ranks. First one mill, then another, then another, like dominoes falling."

Irving sighed. "I think you're being optimistic. From what I hear, there isn't going to any break in the ranks. The IWW is expecting ten thousand at tomorrow's rally."

"All show. You'll see. Give them another two weeks and they'll start to collapse."

"What about your brother? He's not stupid. How do you account for his falling in so tight with them?"

"Solomon is the worst kind of stupid. He's an idealist. He's shut his mind to the real goings on and refuses to think about what this Haywood, Flynn, and the others are saying." Abe gazed trancelike at the wall. Snapping out of his bout of remorse for his brother, he said, "You hold on, Irving. You'll see I'm right."

"I'm old and tired, Abe. I can't fight them like you younger guys. That's why I asked you here. I want to sell out, and I'm offering you the first chance to buy my mill."

"Are you sure?"

"I thought about it a lot lately. Yes, I'm sure."

"How much do you want?"

"I won't kid you. Some of the machinery is old and the building needs a few repairs. You give me seventy-five thousand up front and five hundred a week for the rest of me and my wife's lives and the place is yours."

Abe nodded thoughtfully as his friend laid out the details. Buying Irving's shop would be a great opportunity for him. Combining it with his mill would make him one of the biggest operators in this town. No one—not even Lambert—could hurt him. But who could he get to run it? More important, where would he get the money? He didn't dare get in any deeper to Goldberg, and the banks weren't loaning a penny while the strike was on. The only one he could turn to was his brother Jacob in France.

Abe stood up and offered Irving his hand. "You have a deal, but I don't want to close until the strike is over. My cash flow is a little tight right now."

"I understand."

The door to the office burst open and David rushed in. "Thank God you are still here! You have to come by Solomon's apartment right away. It is an emergency."

CHAPTER 77

Taking huge strides, Abe, with David practically running to keep up, hurried down Mill Street, took a left on Curtis and a right on River Street into the Eastern European Jewish neighborhood. Every time he came to this part of the city to go to Shul or the kosher market he felt as if he had crossed back in time to a place he wanted to forget. The people continued to segregate themselves from the rest of the city, living the way they had done in the *shtetles* of Europe. And everyone spoke Yiddish, rather than English. He shook his head in disgust. No wonder they were so poor. They continued to live in the past and had no vision to see a better way of life, despite being surrounded by it every day.

Cecelia stood on the stoop of her apartment building, her children clinging to her dress. "You have to stop him," she cried.

"Has he gone crazy?" Abe asked.

"I don't know," Cecelia cried. "Please, stop him."

"Stay here with the children," Abe ordered, and took the stairs two at a time to Solomon's apartment. Crossing the living room, he shook his head in pity at the threadbare furniture. Why would he want to live like this?

Finding his brother in the children's bedroom, Abe leaned against the doorframe, and asked, "What are you doing?"

Solomon glanced quickly at Abe and continued to place clothes in a carpetbag. "What does it look like?"

"Aren't those clothes a little small for you?"

"Don't beat around the bush. I'm sure David told you. You're not going to stop me."

"I'm damn well going to try."

"They're my children. If I want to send them away with Elizabeth Flynn, I will."

Abe looked sympathetically at his brother. He really thought Solomon had gone mad. "To live with strangers? Why?"

"Because they are in danger here."

"From who?"

"Their teachers, you bosses. From everyone in Paterson poisoning them with misinformation."

"And sending them away to live with strangers will make them better off? You're a fool."

Solomon's face flushed. "Don't call me that. I'm doing what is best for my children. Once they are out of town, we can really get busy and fight you bosses."

"Is that what Flynn told you?"

"Yes. If my children stay here, they are in danger from being attacked by the boss's goons."

"Can't you see what she's doing? She used the same tactics last year in the Lawrence strike. It was a disgusting disgrace. That whole thing with sending those mill workers' children away was a ploy to get sympathy and raise money."

"That's not true!"

"Isn't it? Open your eyes. She paraded them through the streets of New York City like one of Ringling Brothers' freak shows."

"It's different here."

"It's not different. A leopard doesn't change its spots. You follow blindly behind that Flynn dame and you risk the chance of Cecelia being arrested and charged with improper guardianship. Is that what you want? Do you want your children taken away and sent to the poor farm?"

"That won't happen."

"It happened in Lawrence."

"It's different here," Solomon repeated. "This strike has been going on longer. Children are starving. Many are being cared for at the alms house."

"Maybe some are, but yours aren't. Mother, Leah and Sarah . . ." Abe stopped abruptly. Standing here, arguing with Solomon, he suddenly realized, that if it weren't for Sarah, Solomon and his family would have starved.

"I don't need their charity. I can take care of my own children."

"Is that it? You're ashamed because you think you're taking charity? End this stupid strike and get back to work and you won't need charity."

Solomon snapped the bag shut and started toward the door.

Abe pleaded once more. "If you love your children so much, send them to my house. Sarah will take care of them."

"Get out of my way."

Without warning, Abe smashed his fist into Solomon's gut, sending his brother to his knees. "I'm not letting you send my nephews away from their mother to live with strangers who will probably abuse them."

Solomon gulped in air and tried to rise, clawing at the doorpost for support. "You bastard. You, who sleeps with whores. You don't know anything about family."

Abe hit Solomon with a right to the jaw, sending him flat on the floor. "I don't abandon my children to strangers."

Grabbing the carpetbag, Abe trotted down the stairs. Handing it to David, he said, "Escort Cecelia and the children to my house. They'll be staying there for a while."

"Where is Solomon?" Cecelia asked.

"He's cooling off upstairs. He'll be all right when he comes to his senses."

CHAPTER 78

In attendance at this meeting in a room on the third floor of the Hamilton Club were the same five men who commanded all the mill owners' meetings, the same men who had been at Abe's house three weeks ago. It was Abe who asked for the meeting, or rather begged for it. After the fiasco with the AF of L at the armory, the leaders did not want to hear from him again. It was only the deal he made with Weidmann, Solomon's boss, that got Abe this hearing.

Abe had insisted on maximum security. Guards were posted outside the door and on the second floor landing to keep the press away. There were no cigars or drinks. This was all business, and planned to be brief.

"What's your brilliant idea this time?" Lambert scoffed.

"First, you have to call off Bimson," Abe said.

"Are you still harping on that? Bimson is doing a good job."

"For the strikers, not for us."

"What are you talking about?" Skinner asked. "He's arresting them as fast as he can."

"And every time he arrests some or beats some like he did at the armory, the others get more determined to resist."

"Then he'll arrest some more until he beats them all down."

"Don't be a fool, Lambert."

"There's only one fool in this room. You're the idiot who thought the AF of L could take control of this strike."

"Gentlemen, please," Weidmann intervened. "We'll get nowhere with name calling."

Abe and Lambert glared at each other for a long moment. Abe broke the strained silence first. "Beating on those poor *schnooks* won't do anything. It's like grabbing a tiger by the tail. All you do is make it madder. If it gets too mad, we'll all be in trouble."

"How?" Peter Ryle asked.

"There could be a real riot with a lot of destruction."

"Let them try," Lambert said. "It'll be a good reason to call in the militia."

"And by the time the militia gets here, half the town will be in flames. Look what happened two weeks ago at the May Day parade. Ten thousand of them marched all over this town and the police didn't do a thing to stop them. Why?"

"Suppose you tell us."

"This time the police were afraid. Half the marchers carried clubs, hoping the police would start something. They wanted revenge."

Lambert thought for a moment, then asked in a calmer tone, "Suppose we call off Bimson, then what?"

Abe had been holding the *Paterson Evening News.* He opened it with a loud snap and read, "Sweeney and Company employees meeting at Helvetia Hall Friday at three. John Haleback employees meet at Helvetia Hall Saturday afternoon. Enterprise Mill shop meeting at Schlienpfer Hall on Prospect Street Friday. Herbert Manufacturing Company employees meeting at Turn Hall tomorrow at two o'clock. It goes on and on with Paragon employees at Columbia Hall, Holms Silk Company at Institute Hall, Phoenix Silk Company at Fiesta Hall."

"So what?" Lambert said. "Those lists are in the paper every day. That damn Harry Haines can't do enough for the strikers."

"They get all their information at those meetings," Abe said. "You know how it works. They send a couple of their people from each mill to the halls to have a meeting, get their instructions, and then report back to the picket lines."

"What else is new?" Peter Ryle said.

"Suppose we close their meeting halls. They won't have a central place to find out what's going on."

"We tried that back in March, remember?" Lambert said. "It didn't work. Some judge in Newark ordered them opened again."

"That was eleven weeks ago. Things are different now. There hadn't been any shootings and a near riot then. I think the judges will be more sympathetic to our cause."

"And if they aren't?"

"Then we burn the halls down."

Lambert stood stone still and stared at Abe. "Well, well. I never thought I'd hear that from you."

"We have to get those union thugs out of town—all of them: AF of L, IWW and any others that are around. There's not one of them that's any damn good. They're all a bunch of liars."

Lambert broadened his smile. "Welcome aboard. That armory trouble hit you hard, did it?"

"And some other things."

Weidmann smiled. He already knew what was on Abe's mind.

"Once the halls are closed and the police are out of sight, we'll have our shills spread rumors saying this mill is going to open, and when they find out that isn't true, we say it about another and another, over and over again. We can even enhance the rumors by going out on the steps in front of our shops and make them individual offers to return to work."

Skinner turned from staring out the window at the street traffic. "I can't see it. So they don't meet on this side of the river. They'll go to Haledon and meet over there."

"Those meetings have always been sporadic," Abe said. "They never were as effective as the meetings here in the halls. Besides they're only allowed because the officials in Haledon invited the workers."

"Why would they stop inviting them now?" Ryle asked.

"Because we're going to have our shills disrupt those meetings with brawls."

"Now you're talking my kind of language," Lambert said. "This plan sounds like it can work."

"It will work, but only if you keep Bimson away. Nothing must be done to take their attention away from the mis-information we'll be feeding them. We must re-focus them so they'll quarrel among themselves."

"I like it," Lambert said. "When I meet with the Japanese delegation tomorrow I'm going to assure them the strike will be over soon."

"The Japanese delegation?" Abe asked.

"A group of representatives from the Japanese silk producers called me from New York and asked for a meeting to see if there is anything they can do to help us settle this strike."

"You're kidding!"

"I'm not. They're hurting as bad as we are. At least now I have something to tell them."

"I read in the paper the Japanese Emperor has pneumonia and may die," Abe said. "Don't forget to express your sympathy for him."

"Thanks, I will."

Peter Ryle said, "I hope your plan works. This strike is taking a big toll. Did you see where Ashley and Bailey Company is going into liquidation?"

"Yes," Abe said. He would have loved to buy that one too, but he already owed Jacob too much money and wasn't about to ask for more.

"One thousand looms, ten thousand spindles. It could happen to a few more of us if this thing isn't settled soon," Ryle said, beads of perspiration forming on his forehead.

Abe threw a glance at Lambert. "It will work. We just have to keep the false information flowing and Bimson quiet."

"I'll hold him off, don't worry."

As the men left the room, Abe put a hand on Weidmann's arm, delaying him for a moment. "Remember, no matter what you do or don't do about the other leaders of this strike, my brother doesn't work in this town."

Weidmann vigorously shook Abe's hand. "My pleasure."

CHAPTER 79

Sarah and Cecelia exited Abe's Cadillac in front of Cecelia's apartment building.

"Ernie, we'll be out in a few minutes," Sarah said to their driver.

As they approached the stoop, the *yentas* who were sitting there rose and stepped aside. Climbing the stairs, Sarah heard mutterings, "Slumming . . . Fancy Lady . . . Boss's wife." She grabbed Cecelia's arm and hurried her into the building.

In her bedroom, Cecelia retrieved a carpetbag from on top of the wardrobe and began to stuff clothes in it. "I miss him so much. We have never been apart."

Sarah put her arm around her sister-in-law's shoulder and set her down on the bed. "I'm sure he misses you too and he'll come by for you soon."

"He's so stubborn," Cecelia said.

Sarah nodded and thought, *That is the only thing Solomon and Abe have in common—that stubborn Bressler streak her mother-in-law mentioned.* As she consoled Cecelia, Sarah dwelled on her own plight. Solomon and Cecelia had so little, and she had so much. Yet, she'd trade everything she had for the devotion her in-laws had for each other, or at least did have before this horrid strike.

Did she dare confide in Cecelia with her greatest fear? She had agonized over that question ever since Cecelia had come to their house. Cecelia was her best friend. If she couldn't reach out to her for consolation, whom could she trust?

"Cecelia, please, you have to tell me, is Abe seeing someone?"

Startled at the abruptness of the question, Cecelia stuttered, "I . . . I mean . . . I don't know anything."

"I beg you, tell me."

"Solomon swore me to secrecy. Right here in this bedroom. I can't."

"You must. Please."

Cecelia threw her arms around Sarah. I'm so sorry."

"She's a whore, isn't she?"

"Yes."

"What if she gave him a disease? He could have given it to me." Thinking about what she said, she realized she and Abe hadn't coupled in weeks. She was pretty sure she was safe. *But what if he wanted me? If I refused him and he forced himself on me . . .* She started to cry.

"Oh, Sarah. Oh, my God!" Cecelia said and jumped up. Rushing to the dresser, she pulled open a drawer and scooped up a handful of condoms. Shoving them in Sarah's hand, she said, "You must make Abe use these."

Dabbing her eyes on her sleeve, Sarah asked, "Where did you get these? They're illegal."

"Solomon gets them. I think they're smuggled in from Europe."

"Thank you so much," Sarah said and wondered what Abe's reaction would be when she insisted he use one. "We better go."

Cecelia put the bag back on top of the wardrobe. "I'm staying here."

Sarah hugged her best friend and said, "Don't worry about the children. They're having a wonderful time with their cousins."

CHAPTER 80

Elizabeth Flynn and Bill Haywood climbed the steep stairs to the front door of Mabel Dodge's Greenwich Village townhouse. A wealthy patron of the arts, Mabel Dodge held court in her salon where Bohemian avant-garde artists and thinkers—most notably, Max Eastman, Walter Lippmann, John Reed, Emma Goldman and Margaret Sanger—gathered to debate Utopian ideas of Socialism and feminism.

Stopping on the landing, Elizabeth Flynn reiterated her apprehension. "I don't like this idea, Bill, and Carlo agrees with me."

"He would. And as long as we're on the subject of disagreement, I can't say I approve of your affair with him."

"Too bad."

Exhaling sharply in exasperation, Haywood said, "Do me a favor. Listen to John explain the show. It's his idea."

"I'll listen, but I won't like it."

****

Entering the town house, John Reed escorted them to their hostess.

"Mabel Dodge," Reed said, "meet Elizabeth Flynn and Bill Haywood."

Mabel was a tall slim woman. She wore her hair in the Bohemian fashion, cropped at her jaw line. Extending her hand, she shook Haywood's and Elizabeth Flynn's with a firm grip. "It's so nice to finally meet the two of you," she said. "I have admired your work for so long."

"Mabel has agreed to help finance our pageant," Reed said.

"Thank you, Mrs. Dodge. You won't be sorry. This pageant is going to be a great benefit to the working man."

"Please, call me Mabel."

Haywood smiled.

Reed said, "When the working people of the world rise up to overthrow their capitalist bosses, they will look to Mabel as their patron saint."

"We all have to help the poor, don't we, John?" Mabel said, sounding more like a queen presiding over her court than a saint. "Go along now and introduce Miss Flynn and Mr. Haywood to your friends."

Reed walked the guests-of-honor around the room introducing them to artists and writers. Haywood was dressed in a three piece suit and Elizabeth Flynn wore her standard black dress, high button shoes and trademark wide-brimmed hat. They looked out of place, mixing with men in turtleneck shirts and hatless women in white blouses and cotton skirts hemmed shamefully high, showing bare skin from their ankles halfway up their calves. Some women even had their feet showing, wearing only strapped sandals.

Directing his guests to the bar to get a drink, Reed said, "This pageant is going to be wonderful. With the help of the people in this room we're going to turn your strikers into a first-class theatrical company."

"If this works, it will be the first of many joint ventures for us," Haywood replied. "With your people behind us, we can unite the intellectuals who favor our cause with the workers and make a whole new America."

"This pageant will be the final impetus you need to win your strike. It will bring your story to New York City, where the press will tell it to the world."

"I still think it's a mistake," Elizabeth Flynn said. "This thing could backfire on us and create disunity among our people."

Reed shot Haywood a confused look and said to her, "What are you talking about? This pageant will unite the workers. It will publicize their cause."

"Or it will foster jealousy and split our workers. I understand only one thousand people can participate. What about the twenty-three thousand who can't?"

Haywood let his eyelid droop over his glass eye—his usual warning of disapproval when someone said something he didn't like. "All the workers will look at this pageant with pride. They'll all be participants, whether they are players or not."

"And what if it doesn't take in the thousands of dollars you think it will?"

"Are you kidding?" Reed said. "We'll pack Madison Square Garden and make a fortune."

"What's wrong with you, Elizabeth?" Haywood asked. "Are you sure you're not the one who's jealous because John thought of this idea and you didn't?"

Elizabeth Flynn glared at her mentor. "No, I'm not jealous. It's too chancy. All I see is potential discord. We need to get the word out to our people to stay the course on the picket lines. Getting the word to non-caring strangers will not help us."

"Then maybe you should stay in Paterson and direct the workers from there."

"Maybe I should. Someone has to be on the front lines while you're off playing actor." She turned and stormed out the door.

"She'll come around," Reed said. "As soon as we get this show going, she'll see its merits."

"She better."

CHAPTER 81

Abe smiled as he read Harry Haines' editorial in the *Paterson Evening News*.

"The mayor and the police commissioner ordered all the meeting halls closed because of the inflammatory speeches being made. Why now? Closing the halls now is ridiculous. The strikers will meet elsewhere, in Haledon.

Closing the halls is just an admission of weakness on the part of the mayor and the authorities and has made Paterson the laughing stock of the entire country.

The police are also drifting. There is no leadership. They are ordered to club and arrest one minute and step aside the next.

Closing the halls is a joke. The mayor should resign.

This newspaper has no sympathy for the IWW anarchists and radical principals, but it does have immense sympathy for Paterson's workers who have made a heroic sacrifice for better conditions. They should not be forced back to the mills without having reaped some benefits.

The mayor's duty is plain. Arrest the outside agitators if they break the law and incite a riot. Arrest them over and over again. But closing the halls is ludicrous. It punishes the workers not the leaders.

The thing this city needs right now is some real men with red blood in their veins and with honest courage of their convictions. Such men would be welcomed by laborers and manufacturers alike."

Abe laughed out loud as he read the last sentence.

Sarah interrupted her sewing to ask, "What's that, Abe?"

"Nothing."

She stared at him. How could he sit there as if he were the perfect husband? Worse yet, how could she sit here with him and make believe she knew nothing about his philandering? She was trapped. The only work she knew was teaching. The income from that profession was barely enough to support her, let alone five children. If she left Abe, would she have to leave her children with him to avoid having them go to work in those mills?

Her nose ran and she sniffled.

"Are you okay, dear?" he asked

Startled, her mouth dropped open. Did he actually ask how she was? He hadn't asked her that in so long it took her mind a couple of seconds to digest the question.

"Yes, I'm fine," she said.

He started to raise his paper again.

She didn't want to lose the moment. "Do you love me?" she asked.

Slowly, he set the newspaper on his lap. "Of course I love you. What a silly question."

She ached to blurt out, "Then why are you seeing that whore?" but she held it in, scared to death of how he would react. Instead, she asked, "Are you sure?"

He got up and walked over to sit next to her on the divan. Reaching out, he took her face gently in his hands and kissed her tenderly. She wanted to pull away, but didn't dare. He almost threw her out once. She couldn't take the chance he'd do it for real if she provoked him. She had to stay to protect her children from him.

"I love you," he said. "I'm sorry I haven't shown you lately. It's this strike. But it will be over soon and things will get better."

Will they? She thought as she forced herself to accept another kiss. Of course the strike must be unbearable for him, not knowing how he was going to feed his family. But it must be unbearable for Solomon, also, and he didn't run to a whore.

"Let's go to bed," Abe said.

Oh no! she fretted, scared to death of what was about to happen.

When Abe started to fondle her, she stiffened. *How can I accept his love if he's seeing someone else? Would I be no better than his whore, letting him use me whenever he wants? But how can I deny him? He is my her husband.* She reached out, opened the drawer in the bedside table and pulled out a condom. Holding it up so he could see, she said, "Abe, you have to wear this."

"What for? You're already pregnant."

She hadn't planned to confront him about his adultery this way. But was there ever going to be a good time? "I think you know why."

He snatched the condom from her hand, threw it across the room and rolled onto his side, his back to her.

Tears rolled down her cheeks as a distant memory flashed through her mind—how she had to choose between shoes and gloves for her first liaison with Abe. What an insignificant decision that was compared to the one she might have to make soon. She had made up her mind. How could she stay with a man who did not honor her, who did not love her, who would not let her lead a satisfying life? And she would fight him with every ounce of her strength to keep her children away from him. Their having to work in the mills had to be better than them growing up solely under his influence and becoming just like him.

CHAPTER 82

Haywood's face glowed with delight on this warm June day as he and Elizabeth left Adolf Lessig's house and headed for the mill district. "Did you see the stories in *The New York Times*?" he asked. "They called the pageant a 'masterpiece, a spectacular extravaganza.' I have to hand it to John Reed and his friends. Without them we couldn't have pulled it off."

"I'm glad you're happy," Elizabeth Flynn scoffed.

"You bet I'm happy. Last night New York City was a giant IWW recruiting rally. You should have been there."

"I was too busy here trying to salvage four months' work."

Haywood ignored her sarcasm and went on with his monologue. "Three thousand of us marched through the streets of Manhattan from the ferry dock to Madison Square Garden at Twenty-Sixth and Madison Avenue. When we got there, all twelve thousand spectators stood up and joined in with us in singing the *Marseilaise*. Red flags and red ribbons were everywhere. And a huge sign on top of the Garden spelled IWW in red light bulbs."

"It must have been very nice."

"It was great! We had banners draped inside and outside, showing the workers being beaten by the police. The whole thing was a huge success. It will be a rallying cry for all workers."

"Terrific! You and the Schubert Brothers get marvelous reviews in New York, but here in Paterson you're a big flop."

"What are you talking about?"

"While you and the thousand or so workers were having fun in New York City for a month preparing the pageant, the twenty-three thousand left in Paterson were wondering why they still had to march up and down the streets in front of the mills."

"Didn't you and Tresca and the others explain what we were doing for them?"

Elizabeth Flynn shook her head in disgust. "Oh, how we tried. But you had our best men in New York—the ones that always helped us rally the others. With them gone, all we had were the complainers and trouble makers that followed Boyd and Mohl."

"Are those two still around?"

"Like leeches. And they started a riot at Price Mill."

"We heard about that. What happened?"

"Price's workers don't belong to the IWW. They settled with him and wanted to get back to work. Boyd got twenty-five hundred of his pickets to surround the mill. But Price's workers were determined to get in and they had the police on their side. By the time the riot ended, over eighty of our people were arrested and Price's workers were inside.

"If that wasn't bad enough, Boyd rallied his forces and started another riot, with the police guarding Turn Hall."

"Damn!"

"Hold your profanity until you hear the rest."

"There's more?"

"A lot more."

As they turned west on Van Houten, howls of "Scab! Scab! Scab!" startled them. Looking down Van Houten toward the Phoenix Mill complex, they saw a huge crowd of laborers jostling, with an equally large contingent of police. Quickening their steps, they hurried toward the melee.

The gates to the Phoenix Mill courtyard stood open and the police were holding back a mob of laborers, while others ran through the gauntlet and over the water raceway bridge.

"Stop! Don't go in!" Haywood bellowed.

One of the workers on the ramp turned and yelled, "Get out of town, you bums!"

The minute the last man crossed into the Phoenix Mill courtyard, the gate slammed shut and the police slowly backed away from the screaming crowd, formed ranks and trotted down Ciance Street.

An unshaven laborer, a head shorter than Haywood, stepped forward. "If it ain't George M. Cohan his self. When are we going to see some of the money you raised?"

"The money is coming as soon as we tally it," Haywood answered.

"How come you got to count it? The newspapers said you got $6,500.00. Let's have it."

Haywood stared down on the man. "It's coming."

The shorter, slighter man didn't yield an inch. "It better be, and none of it better stick in your pockets."

Anxious to move on, Haywood stepped around the man. "The food is coming. We're buying it now. You'll see."

When they were out of hearing range, Elizabeth Flynn asked, "How much did the pageant make?"

"After we paid our bills, $150.00."

She stopped dead in her tracks. "What?"

"That's it."

"We're in trouble. Where are you going to get the money these people think you made?"

"Reed and his people are out soliciting it from our Socialist friends right now. He'll have it soon."

Her body sagged. "You're counting on false hopes. The New York Socialists don't want anything to do with us anymore. They're criticizing us everyday in *The Morning Call* for not settling this strike faster." She held up her hand to stop his inevitable protest. "I told you right from the beginning that Paterson was different from Lawrence. Up there we had one big mill that employed everyone. There was one boss to point our finger at. Here we have three hundred bosses and three hundred shops, and each one is different."

"We can win this strike."

"We can't. The bosses are still united, and we're falling apart."

"What's the matter with you? Are you getting scared?"

"I'm not scared; I'm being practical. We have to settle shop-by-shop now."

"I'll never settle shop-by-shop."

Abe had been watching the melee from an alleyway across the street. When he saw Flynn and Haywood approach, he plastered a big grin on his face and stepped out to confront the arguing couple. Nodding to Haywood, he tipped his hat to Elizabeth and said, "Beautiful sight, isn't it—laborers coming to their senses and returning to work?"

"Gloat now, mill man," Haywood said. "You won't be smiling when we drive you out of your mill."

Abe dropped his jovial demeanor and said, "Before I let you take one step into my mill, I'll kill you myself."

"Bill, let's go," Elizabeth said.

"That's excellent advice. You should listen to your woman and go, like that weaver said, all the way out of town while you still can move under your own power."

"The only one going is you, mill man."

"That's the first truth you said since you've been in town. I am going, into my mill and open the doors for my workers. I heard the weavers at Dexter-Lambert, Empire Silk, Paragon and my mill held a meeting last night. They're going to ask us if they can return to work today. Of course we'll let them."

"You're lying," Haywood said.

"You're through! Beaten! Leave town before we run you out on a rail."

Elizabeth pulled on Haywood's arm forcing him away from the confrontation. Abe tipped his hat to her again. "Good day to you, Miss Flynn."

When they were out of Abe's hearing, Elizabeth said, "Can't you see it? The strike is collapsing. We have to settle. We keep going like this, with your no compromise attitude, and we'll get nothing."

"No partial settlements, and that's final."

"Then it's over, Bill. We've lost. And I think we'll find we've lost more than just this strike."

"What are you talking about?"

"Your Utopia is a dream. It can never become a reality."

"What is wrong with you? I've never seen you like this. Why are you giving up?"

"Because I worry your all-or-nothing attitude will bring us to ruin. In all the strikes I have led, the workers have never expressed a desire to own the mills or the restaurants or the mines, as you say they will. All they want is a fair wage for a fair day's work. By losing this strike and not getting the workers one concession from the bosses, I fear our union will not survive."

CHAPTER 83

At the sudden *whack, thump, thump*, Abe and David flew out of the office. Their mill had come to life. They stood at the end of the aisle between the two rows of looms and watched their weavers work the machines. Like a cat stalking a mouse, the weaver's eyes and hands were everywhere. They scanned for broken threads among the thousands of warp yarns coming off the beam, passing through the reed, and into the moving harnesses of the loom, and adjusted tension and checked for evenness of their weaving.

"How do you like that sound?" Abe yelled above the whacking sound made by the picker stick smacking the shuttle that carried the bobbin of weft yarn, sending it flying through the shed of warp yarns, and the thump of the harness changing position, followed closely by a second thump as the beater pounded the weft yarns into place.

"It is the most beautiful music I have heard since I come to Paterson," David said. Pointing to the growing rolls of broad-silk fabric, he added, "And give a look at that. Is that not a beautiful sight?"

"We're one of the few companies that can do the whole job from start to finish—dye, process and weave. We're going to make a lot of money."

"You forgot only one thing. How soon will you find someone to open up Mr. Pincus's factory?"

"I have that all worked out."

"*Nu*?"

"You'll be right there when it happens, believe me."

David was about to ask, "Right where?" when he spotted a secretary coming out of the mill office and hurrying in their direction. To David she said, "Mr. Bressler, there is a telephone call for you. Your mother."

David ran for the telephone. In a moment he was back, his jacket in hand. "Leah is in labor. I am going."

"Wonderful! Go," Abe said.

Abe turned back to watch the looms work. Their rhythmic sound mesmerized him. His mental calculations of the value of the yardage coming off them so absorbed him, he didn't hear the men walk up behind him.

"You Bressler?" a voice demanded.

Startled, he turned quickly to face two men, dressed in black pants and white shirts. They had the demeanor of mill workers, but they were a little too messy for weavers and too neat for dye house laborers.

"I've got all the men I can use right now," Abe said. "Try back in a couple of weeks."

"We ain't here for no job," the one with the day's growth on his face said. "Mr. Goldberg wants to see you."

"About what?"

"He don't tell us his business."

"Fine, tell him I'll stop by tomorrow morning."

The shorter one pulled a gun from his pocket. "He wants to see you *now*."

CHAPTER 84

Sarah gently lifted her crying baby out of his crib and kissed Emanuel's hot forehead. His fever had returned. Cradling him in her arms, she waddled out of his bedroom into hers. Picking up the telephone, she called the doctor again, and again the nurse assured her, "As soon as the doctor finishes with the emergency at the dispensary he will call you back."

Sarah returned to Emanuel's room. Continuing to hold him, she used one hand to unscrew the cap of the medicine bottle. She wrinkled her nose at the strong smell of the liquid. Squeezing the black rubber bulb on top of the glass tube, she slowly let it loose, feeling it fill. Rocking Emanuel until he stopped crying, she put the glass tube in her baby's mouth and squeezed a few more drops of medicine into him.

She sat down in the rocker. Holding Emanuel on top of her swollen belly, she rocked slowly, listening to the wood groan on each backstroke and the baby's uneven breathing on the forward rock.

Frances, Sarah's maid, appeared in the doorway. She had her hands clasped so tightly her fingertips were red. "How is the little one?"

"His fever has returned."

Frances shuddered a bit and dropped her eyes to the floor. "Mrs. Bressler," she began, then stopped.

"Yes, Frances, what is it?"

Frances released her hands and wiped her palms on her white apron. "My sister come by. She is in the kitchen downstairs."

Again she hesitated, forcing Sarah to say, "Yes?"

"She tells me my father is in an accident at the mill. I must go to him."

Sarah's first instinct was to get up and comfort her maid, but she couldn't without waking Emanuel, who had finally fallen off to sleep.

"Of course you can go. I'll be all right. The doctor is coming and Mr. Bressler will be home any minute."

Forcing a smile, Frances said, "Thank you," and hurried out.

Half an hour later, despite Sarah's rocking, Emanuel woke up. Sarah carried him to her bedroom and called Abe at the mill.

"He's not here, Mrs. Bressler," a woman's voice informed her.

"Is Ernie there?" She thought he could come with the truck. She could put the children in the back and take them with her to the dispensary.

"No, ma'am. He's out with the truck picking up yarn."

She called the doctor again, receiving the same reply. *If only Chava were here to watch the children, I could take Emanuel in a cab to the dispensary.* But Chava had gone to Leah's to help with the delivery of Leah's baby.

She called the public telephone in the hallway of Cecelia's apartment building. The operator told her the line was in use.

Isidore, her oldest, came into the bedroom. "Why is Emanuel crying?" he asked.

"He is not feeling well, darling. You go back and play with your brothers."

"We're hungry."

"I'll be down in a minute to get your dinner. Go along now, and stay out of the kitchen."

Sarah watched her son walk away. She smiled as she thought how he looked so much like Abe, tall and slender. Her mind drifted to her next oldest, Samuel. A bomb couldn't move that boy. And her third, Ira, that roly-poly may not look like his father, but he sure had his father's personality. So friendly, so domineering. Always the leader of the pack. Her lips parted into a smile at the thought of Joseph. He was the most inquisitive of them all, constantly getting into things. She couldn't wait until he started school.

Her mood turned somber as her attention returned to fifteen-month-old Emanuel in her arms. There was no telling who he was going to take after. She just hoped she could get him through this fever to find out.

She reached out for her book of telephone numbers. A tear formed in her eyes as she opened it to the second from last page and read the number for Mrs. O'Neil's boarding house. Sarah had persuaded Cecelia to have Solomon find out the name of the redhead, where she lived, and for a telephone number. Solomon fought her, telling her it was better if Sarah didn't know. Only when Cecelia reminded him of everything Sarah had done for them did Solomon give in.

She didn't know what she was going to do with the information once she had it. Many times she had thought about calling Abe there to embarrass him, hurt him like he had been hurting her these many weeks. From that night when he turned away from her, Abe barely talked to her. They ate dinner in strained silence. When he didn't go out to satisfy his lust with that woman, he locked himself in his study, not coming up to bed until he thought she was asleep. Not once did he try to explain himself or act guilty about his philandering. That made her madder. But now she had to put her ire aside. Her baby needed help.

She asked the operator to ring the boarding house. "Katie McGuire, please," she said to the person who answered.

"Hold on."

A voice inside her head said, "Hang up," but Sarah fought it off. Emanuel needed his father, and she was going to do whatever she had to, no matter how painful, to bring Abe home.

"Yeah."

"Is Abraham Bressler there?" Sarah choked out.

"Who is this?"

Drawing on all her inner strength, she demanded, "Is he there?"

"No."

"I know he's there. I must speak to him. His son is very sick."

The pause was so long, Sarah thought the person had gone for Abe. But when she spoke again, Sarah's hopes faded.

"Abe isn't here. If I see him I'll give him your message."

Sarah slammed the receiver onto its hook, toppling the telephone off the dresser. Bending to pick it up, the pain that had often stabbed at her stomach struck again. She grabbed at her rounded belly, sank onto her bed and pulled Emanuel to her breast. A tear fell on his hot forehead. "Your father is never here for us, is he my darling? Not when you were born, not now when you're sick. But I'll always be here for you."

The pain having subsided, Sarah mumbled, "To hell with him! I don't need him. I don't want him. Let him try to get rid of me. I'll set his precious house on fire before I let him force me out so he can bring his whore in here."

CHAPTER 85

Entering the foyer of Goldberg's mansion on lower Broadway, Abe brushed his hand over his pants pocket, feeling the BB-filled leather sack he had carried with him since his narrow escape at the armory. He didn't know what good the sap would do him against guns, but he was glad he had it.

The thug who had pulled the gun motioned with his head toward the living room on the right and stammered, "In there."

Goldberg sat at a desk at the far end of the room. In back of him rose a ceiling-to-floor bookcase, filled with china and glass brick-a-brack.

"You better have a damn good reason for sending these *shtockers* to drag me out of my shop," Abe scowled.

"Take it easy, Bressler. Something came up and I had to see you right away."

"You don't have a telephone?"

"Relax. Sit down. Have a drink." One of the hoods had left Abe and moved to stand beside Goldberg's desk. Goldberg shifted his attention to him, and said, "Gil, fix Mr. Bressler a whiskey."

"I don't want a drink. Tell me what you want so I can get back to work."

"Okay, if that's the way you want it. I'm calling your loan."

"What? Why? You've been getting your interest payments every week right on time."

"Yeah, you've been very prompt, but I need the money."

"I don't have it right now."

Goldberg glanced at his men and said, "My boys don't like to hear that."

"No, Mr. Goldberg," they answered in unison.

Goldberg tipped his chair forward. He reached his stubby hand across his desk and picked up a piece of paper. "Lucky for you I'm a reasonable man. I have a compromise."

"What is it?"

"There are a lot of laborers in this town who liked the way I helped them with a loan during the strike. Now that those idiot outsiders have been run out of town, many mill workers want me to represent them in a strong local union."

"What do you want from me?"

"This is a contract to represent the workers in your mills. Sign it."

Abe didn't move to take the paper. "There will never be a union in my shops." He turned to leave. The muscleman drew his gun and blocked the doorway.

Goldberg's face turned threatening. "You owe me a lot of money. I want it now. But if you sign this contract, I'll give you a note allowing you five years to pay off your loan at bank interest rates, plus a percent or two." A cocky smile crossed his face. He reached into his vest pocket, pulled out a diamond ring and tossed it to Abe. "And I'll throw this in to sweeten the deal. Your sister-in-law hocked it to get your brother out of jail."

Abe recognized Sarah's ring. He put it in his pocket.

When he made no move toward the desk, Goldberg asked, "Haven't you mill men had enough labor troubles? With me in charge of the union, I'll guarantee no strikes for three years at the very least."

"In exchange for what?"

"You might have to give a slight raise to your workers now and then to help them pay their dues."

"I see."

Goldberg held out a pen. "I knew you would. Now sign."

"Over my dead body."

"If you're dead, you can't sign. But, then I guess the guy your wife sells your mill to can. Still I would rather have you sign." To his men he said, "Take Mr. Bressler to the basement and persuade him."

The hood standing by the door waved his gun and said, "This way, wise guy."

As the conversation heated up, Abe had casually cupped his hand around his blackjack, slipped it out of his pocket, clasped his hands behind his back and gripped the weapon for action. In a flash, Abe whipped his hand around and smashed the sap on the gunman's wrist. With a howl, the hood dropped the gun. Before it hit the floor, Abe whirled the blackjack against the thug's head, knocking him out. The suddenness of Abe's move froze everyone long enough for Abe to dive to the floor for the gun, raise it at Goldberg and fire.

CHAPTER 86

Sarah gathered her children in the foyer to wait for the taxi. When it honked, she hurried them down the walk, ushered the boys into the back seat and she settled into the front, cradling her sick child.

"The dispensary. Quickly," she said and threw money at the driver.

Seeing the huge fare, many times larger than he normally would receive, the driver sped off. He drove recklessly down Broadway, kicking up a trail of dust in his wake and blasting his horn at pedestrians to rush them out of his way. One frightened man froze in the middle of the street and the cab barely missed him by wheeling into the oncoming lane of traffic, heading directly at a horse and wagon. The startled teamster frantically pulled on the reins, wrestling to control his frightened animal. The driver jerked the wheel to the right, forcing another auto into the curb.

When the cab left the dirt road and smacked with a bone-jarring jolt into the raised cobblestone pavement, the baby almost flew out of Sarah's arms and she screamed in fright. Her children howled with delight as they would on a carnival ride.

"Hang on, we're almost there," the driver said.

Too frightened to reply, Sarah bobbed her head up and down.

The taxi screeched to a halt behind a truck with the word "ambulance" painted on its canvas side. The dispensary had been a mill-owner's mansion. When the industrialist moved farther east to get away from the expanding commercial district, he donated his old house to the city to be used as a hospital.

Sarah rushed her children into the foyer, now converted to a reception area. Eight women milled around the desk, babbling questions at the receptionist in Italian. With tears streaming down her cheeks, Sarah pushed her way through them and pleaded, "Please, I have to see Doctor Berger. My baby is sick."

"A boiler exploded in one of the mills," the receptionist said. "The doctor is busy with these women's husbands. He'll see you as soon as he can."

Calling upon all her strength, Sarah straightened her back and demanded, "Get Doctor Berger, *now*!"

Although most of the women she had cut off didn't understand her, Sarah's stern command caused them to pull back in fright. The shocked nurse jumped back from her desk and hurried up the stairs.

Ira, being his usual rambunctious self, starting poking his chubby brother, Samuel.

"Stop it," Samuel said.

"Children, please be good," Sarah said.

Ira poked Samuel again.

Without thinking, Sarah lashed out and slapped him across the face. Ira fell back against the desk. Afraid their mother might strike them also, the other boys cowered together. Realizing the horror of what she had done, Sarah shifted baby Emanuel into her left arm and pulled Ira to her with her right. "I'm so sorry. Please forgive me. I love you. I didn't mean it." Focusing on her other children, she pleaded, "Boys, come here."

Slowly the children approached her.

Sarah struggled to encircle them with her free arm. "I love you all so very much, but I have to tend to Emanuel right now. He is very sick. You want him to get better don't you?"

"Yes, Mother," Isidore said, and the others nodded.

"You can help Emanuel get better by being good so I can talk to the doctor." Pointing to the waiting room, she said, "Please go in there and sit quietly and wait for me."

"Sarah," a voice said from behind her.

Recognizing the voice as Dr. Berger's, Sarah turned at the same moment a stabbing pain struck her. She fell to the floor, baby Emanuel rolling from her arms.

CHAPTER 87

Abe's shot skimmed above Goldberg's head and smashed a vase on the bookshelf.

Pointing the gun at Gil, whose hand was still under his jacket, Abe slowly rose from the floor and ordered, "Drop it!"

Gil made no move to obey Abe's command.

Extending his arm for a better aim, Abe said, "I'll shoot you where you stand."

Gil looked at his boss. Goldberg nodded and Gil carefully removed his gun and dropped it.

"Now what, Bressler? Where you going to go? You can't leave town like that bum you bought the bar from. Sooner or later my boys will pick you up and break you in pieces."

Aiming the gun back at Goldberg, Abe said, "Then I guess I have no choice. I might as well kill you right now."

Goldberg pushed back in his chair and moved his head to the side.

"You—back up," Abe said to Gil. With the hood far enough away so he couldn't leap on Abe, Abe closed in on Goldberg and asked, "How long have we known each other?"

Still pressed against the back of his chair, Goldberg answered, "Eight, nine years."

"And how did we meet?"

"You know damn well—on the boat from Ireland."

"Yeah, and what did I do for you?"

"I paid off that debt."

"I don't think so. That loan you had with the guy I bought my bar from had nothing to do with me. You still owe me for tipping you off to that cheat on the boat. How much would he have taken you for if I hadn't told you he was double dealing?"

Goldberg didn't reply.

"Four, five thousand?" Abe asked.

When Goldberg still didn't answer, Abe asked, "Ten thousand?"

"Yeah."

"Here's the deal. You'll have all your money in two months if you call a truce."

"And if I don't?"

Abe picked up Gil's gun. "I'm going to keep these and give one to my brother, Solomon, along with telling him how I got it. You know who Solomon is, right?"

"Yeah."

"If anything happens to me or my family, I have no doubt he'll come after you with every man he can muster. And you know damn well he leads a big mob."

Goldberg raised his hands in defeat. "You have my word, Bressler. No one will come after you. But I want my money in two months or the deal's off."

Abe backed toward the door. "You'll have it."

CHAPTER 88

Back at his mill, Abe's secretary said, "Doctor Berger called. He sounded quite distressed. He said your wife and children are at the dispensary and you should get there as soon as you can."

On his way to the dispensary, Abe scowled and wondered what was wrong now. Why couldn't she handle this herself? If she wasn't so mixed up with those damn radical women, she could take care of the children properly. That's her job, not running off on some ridiculous crusade.

When he told the receptionist who he was, she dropped her eyes and said, "I'm sorry. Your children are in there. I'll get Doctor Berger."

Confused, Abe walked into the waiting room. The moment he saw his children, he realized something was seriously wrong. Instead of running around taunting each other, they sat somberly on the couch. Turning to Isidore, Abe asked, "What is going on?"

"Mommy is dead," Isidore choked out through his tears.

"It's my fault," Ira said sobbing. "I didn't mean it."

"What? What are you talking about?"

"She fell down and they took her away with baby Emanuel," Isidore said.

His legs felt like rubber as Abe made his way back to the front room. Doctor Berger appeared on the landing. Blood, dried to a reddish brown, splattered his white coat. Holding the banister for support, he walked slowly down the stairs.

Unable to wait for him to reach the bottom, Abe ran up and asked in a voice that almost cracked, "Sarah's dead?"

"No, she's not dead. Who told you that?"

"Thank God!"

"Don't thank God yet. Sarah's condition is serious."

"What happened?"

"She delivered a baby girl."

Abe's eyes brightened. "A girl? She wanted a girl."

"The baby was still-born, Abe."

Abe grabbed the banister. "Oh, my god!"

"It was very difficult getting her out. There was a lot of injury to Sarah."

"Where is Sarah? I have to go to her."

"She won't respond to you. She's in a deep sleep. I hope she doesn't fall into a coma."

"I don't care. Take me to her."

The doctor escorted Abe into Sarah's private room, one of the eight former bedrooms in the old house. Its stark whiteness, dearth of furniture—only the bed, a wooden chair, and a small table—and lack of any pictures made it look like a cell. Sitting beside her bed, Abe took her hand and stared at her.

Sarah's eyes popped open. She rolled her head and gazed at Abe. "My baby! Where is my baby?" she asked.

Abe leaned next to her ear. "I'm here, darling."

Sarah stared at him, seeming to not know who he was. When he finally registered to her, she said, "Get away from me. You don't love me."

Abe leaned over the bed and kissed her. "I do love you. I'm so sorry. I'll make it up to you."

"Where is my baby? Bring me my baby."

"They did everything they could, but they couldn't get her to breathe."

"One dies, one is born," Sarah said, having only heard the word "her," through the haze. "A girl? It's a girl! Please bring her to me."

"Sarah, the baby was still-born."

She seemed bewildered for a moment then screamed, "Oh my God, they're both dead! It's my fault. God is punishing me. He'll never forgive me for not wanting another baby." She broke into wracking sobs. "Why did He have to take Emanuel too?"

Abe grabbed her into his arms to quell her shaking. "No, darling. Emanuel is not dead. He's a fighter. He'll beat this." The doctor had told him he thought Emanuel might have a rheumatic heart, but he was not about to tell this to Sarah now. When she was stronger and the doctor was present, he'd tell her.

She fought to get free of his grasp. "I want to see him."

"You can't yet. The doctor is caring for him."

She fell back on the bed. "My baby! I want my baby."

"Soon, my darling."

Abe pulled her ring from his vest pocket. He lifted her limp hand and slid it on her finger. "Thank you for looking after everyone in this family."

Sarah clasped her right hand over the ring. "You're not mad at me anymore for giving it to Cecelia?"

Abe bowed his head. *What a horse's ass I've become. This is all my fault. I call everyone else a fool, but the biggest fool is me. If it weren't for Sarah, I'd have bubkes—no wife, no children, no family. She's always smoothing things out after I mess them up.*

"I love you. I'll never be mad at you again."

She curled her lips into a weak smile. "You promise?" she asked.

Abe covered her hands with his. "I've been so stupid. Can you ever forgive me?"

Her fingers fluttered. He didn't say it. If he didn't say it, it didn't mean anything. "Promise me, Abe. Please promise me."

He gently brushed her lips with his. "I promise. You'll see. It'll be better. No more nights out. No more fights."

She closed her eyes and in a moment, with a smile on her lips, she fell asleep.

He kissed her again. "I'll be back soon, my darling. I have to tend to the children."

CHAPTER 89

Abe walked his children out of the dispensary.

"We're hungry," Ira said.

"Is mother dead?" Isidore asked.

"No. She's not dead. She's a little sick. She'll have to stay with the doctor for a few days."

"Is baby Emanuel dead?"

"No, he's sick too. But the doctor will help him."

"I'm hungry," Ira said again.

"I heard you," Abe said. "I'm talking to your brother now. Don't interrupt me again."

As his rebukes had done in the past, his reprimand of Ira frightened all the children into silence. And in the rare occasions where his scolding failed to silence them, Sarah or his mother had always been there to hustle them out of his presence. Now, as he marched them to a deli in Riverside near Solomon's apartment a pang of anguish swept him. He could not recall ever being alone with his children or ever having a conversation with them.

Abe ordered brisket of beef with boiled potatoes for everyone. He fidgeted with his silverware while they waited for the food. He kept glancing from one to the other, but he didn't know what to say to them.

"I can read," Isidore said. "I like school. It's fun."

"Very good," Abe said, a sigh of relief overcoming him. "Learning is important."

"And Hebrew, too. Grandpa is teaching me after school."

"Me too," Samuel said.

"Ow," Jerry squealed and swung a fist at Ira. Ira dodged the blow and swung back. Abe intercepted Ira's small hand before it hit Jerry.

"What's going on?"

"He kicked me," Jerry said.

"Crybaby!" Ira said.

"Ira, being a bully will only end up causing you grief," Abe said, suddenly falling silent. *That's exactly what I was and look where it led me.* "You must stop hitting your brothers. If you don't, when you grow up they will abandon you."

"What does abandon mean?" Ira asked.

"They will not want to be with you. They won't have you in their house. They won't let their children play with your children. You'll be alone with no one to turn to if you need help."

"I want to abandon him now," Samuel said.

"See, Ira? It's happening already. Be good to people. If you help people like your mother does, you will always have friends who will come to your aid in a time of need, and your family will love you. Be like your mother, Ira, not like . . ." He cut himself off before he said "me." . . . "Not a bully."

"Yes, father."

****

With his children fed, Abe led them to Solomon's door.

"What do you want?" Solomon asked. "To gloat about your victory?"

"I need help."

"The great Abraham Bressler needs help? I can't wait to hear what for."

"Can we come in?"

"What are your children doing here? Where's Sarah—at David's? Leah is all right? I haven't heard anything from Cecelia."

"Sarah's at the dispensary," Abe said and told his brother what happened. "Can I leave the children with you? I have to run an errand."

"Of course."

"Thank you."

"Family, Abe. Remember."

CHAPTER 90

Walking in long strides toward Katie's rooming house, Abe dwelled on Sarah and why he had been so mad with her since he returned from Europe. *It was the strike . . . no, it wasn't the strike. It was her defiance. I'm the head of our household . . .*

His conscience fired back. But what did she do that was so wrong? Why couldn't you understand she didn't want to take over your role as head of the family? She only wanted to help you, share the household duties with you, relieve you of some of the pressure, be like your mother.

But she could do more than your mother, couldn't she? She's better educated. After she debated that woman, and everybody praised her, it made you jealous.

You were afraid if she outshined you, you'd lose control? You're so stupid you couldn't see she didn't want to control you like you wanted to control her like you tried to control everyone else in your family. She only wanted to love you and be loved back as an equal."

All you ever did was respect me, and I didn't give you the same respect in return. I thought you only needed things to make you happy. And when I filled the house with beautiful things, I couldn't understand why that wasn't enough for you. But I know now. You needed me, and I wasn't there. Just like my father, I wasn't there. Just like my father . . .

****

Katie greeted Abe, wearing a robe with feathers along the collar and down the front. After the way Abe had reacted to her new dress a few weeks ago, she said the hell with putting on airs, and threw off her clothes the minute she came home and got comfortable—and she had gone back to her lilac toilet water. She liked it better than that sweet scent of his wife's perfume.

"Don't you ever get dressed?" he asked.

"What's wrong, honey? Another fight with your wife? She called here, looking for you."

"What?" Abe exclaimed, his face contorted in horror.

"She called here. She knows about us. That's good, isn't it? It will make it easier for you to tell her you want to be with me."

Abe pushed her away. Looking around at the clothes tossed on the backs of the chairs, dirty dishes scattered over the coffee table, and the unmade bed, he said, "Why don't you clean this place up?" Waving his hand in a vain attempt to clear the gray haze that filled the room, he added, “And get a fan to blow this damn smoke and that cheap perfume out of here.”

He stared at Katie’s rouge-smeared face. *How could I ever have thought she could hold a candle to my Sarah in anything?*

Katie ignored his fit of temper. She took hold of his suit jacket and tried to remove it. “You’ve had a tough day. Let me make it better for you.”

He pulled away and shrugged his jacket back in place. “It’s over.”

“Abe, honey, I’ll wear the perfume you got me. I promise.”

For a moment he stared blankly at her. “You’re a fool, Katie. This isn’t about perfume. You’re brother was right. You and I are from different worlds. We will never be right for each other.”

Her face contorted in disbelief, she stood stone still. Recovering from the shock of his words, she threw her arms around him and said, “No, Abe, please. I know I can change. I’ll get educated. I’ll learn. I’ll convert to your religion.”

Pushing her away, he said, “I’m not going to see you anymore. It’s over.”

Weeping, she fell onto the bed and wrapped her arms around her stomach. “I’m pregnant.”

He gaped at her for a moment before asking, “Are you saying it’s mine?”

She didn’t answer fast enough.

“You don’t know whose it is, do you?”

“It could be yours.”

“And it might not be.”

Her head fell into her hands. “What am I going to do?”

Abe peeled $300.00 off his money roll. Placing it on the desk he said, “That will hold you for a few months. Leave Paterson.”

As Abe walked out the door, Katie pulled herself off the bed and screamed at his back, “You bastard! It’s yours! I know it’s yours,” and slammed the door so hard the windows rattled.

She took her fancy dress from the boudoir. Holding it in front of her, she stood before the mirror and said, “I’m not leaving this town. I’m going to be a lady, someone my son will respect.” Imagining Abe’s image in the mirror, she added, “And he’ll look just like you, boyo. When you see him around town, you’ll see yourself and be reminded of me.”

CHAPTER 91

Returning to the dispensary, Abe sought out Doctor Berger for an update.

"I'm sure Sarah will be fine," the doctor said. "Emanuel is still serious."

"What is your opinion? Will he survive?"

"I can't say."

Abe bowed his head for a long moment before saying, "I have a personal matter I would like to discuss."

When Abe didn't elaborate, the doctor said, "I'm listening."

"It's about disease?"

"What kind of disease?"

Feeling deeply embarrassed, Abe asked, "This is strictly between us?"

"Of course."

When Abe continued to hesitate, the doctor probed, "What is it, Abe? I have patients to attend to."

"It's disease from mixing with infected women."

"Venereal disease?"

"Yes."

"Abe, there's no cure. You could have infected Sarah."

"I didn't say I had it. I don't know. How can I tell?"

"Does it burn when you urinate?"

"No."

"Good. That's the most frequent sign. Do you have any chancres—sores on your penis?"

"No."

"Tired? Headache? Sore throat?"

"No."

"Excellent. Still I want to take your blood. In 1905 a microbiologist discovered the bacteria that causes syphilis. I can look at your blood and see if you have it. You better pray you don't. There's no cure."

****

Abe hired around-the-clock nurses for Sarah and Emanuel, warning them to attend to his family's every whimper. Returning to Sarah's room, he sat motionless, staring at her as she peacefully slept. At midnight the nurse insisted he go home.

****

In the morning, Abe drove to Solomon's to retrieve his children. Cecelia sat on the stoop, watching the six boys play in the street with their hoops and balls.

"How is Sarah?" Cecelia asked. "As soon as Solomon gets home, I'm going to her."

"Better," Abe said. "How is Leah?"

Her eyebrows shot up as if to say, *You care*? "She's fine. She had a baby girl."

"A girl. That's nice," Abe said sadly.

"I'm sorry, Abe," she said.

"Thank you. Where is Solomon?"

"Out trying to find work. They blacklisted him from the mills."

"Don't worry, I'll fix it."

CHAPTER 92

They devoured Sarah's birthday cake, and then she opened the presents the children had personally picked out for their mother. Abe had taken them shopping. Without commanding, he guided them to select the items he thought Sarah might like. But he hadn't given her his gift yet.

Now alone in their bedroom, Sarah sat on the bed, wearing Isidore's gift, a silk nightgown. Abe opened a dresser drawer and took out some brochures. He walked to the bed, holding them behind his back.

"What are you hiding?" she asked.

"Did you know your mother called me a *fonfer*?"

"She didn't! When?"

"Way back when I came to your apartment that first evening. And she was right. I did double-talk you. I promised you the world and I gave you nothing but *tsores*.

"Oh, no, Abe! You gave me a wonderful house and beautiful children."

"But I never gave you the world."

"I don't need the world. I just need you."

"But I promised you," he said and produced the brochures. "Next month we're taking a trip to London, Paris and Rome."

It took her a long time before the shock wore off. "What about the business?"

"David can run it. And Solomon, if you'll help me."

"Solomon! I thought he refused your offer?"

He gazed out the window at the park. The trees looked like huge black umbrellas against the full moon. "I know I can change his mind if I can just get him to talk to me."

"What can I do?"

"Help me to apologize."

"How about if we invite the family to dinner? Cecelia will make sure he comes."

"Are you sure you're up to it? It's only been six weeks since you're home."

"I need the activity to take my mind off . . . You know." Her eyes glazed over.

He kissed her. "You're wonderful. I love you."

She thought, *He has been so agreeable and attentive. Even more so than when he narrowly escaped being killed on the Titanic.* She made an instant decision to use his guilt to her advantage. "Will you do something for me if I do this for you?"

Without hesitation he said, "Name it."

"Illinois is allowing women to vote in the next presidential election. I want to also."

"How can I do anything about that? I'm not in the legislature."

"You can, Abe. There is a resolution before the New Jersey Senate to give suffrage to women. All the senators need to pass it is some coercion."

"I don't know any senators."

"But you know plenty of people who know them. Can you please ask your friends to talk to the senators about passing the resolution?"

Abe left her side and paced the floor.

She knew why he didn't respond right away. She'd asked him for another bargain. If he agreed, he'd die before he wouldn't honor it.

"I will," he said.

"And I will bring this family back together," Sarah said.

CHAPTER 93

Abe gazed at his family, seated around the dining room table. On each side of him sat two of his children. Next to them were Solomon's boys, followed by Chava and baby Emanuel. Solomon and Cecelia sat across from David and Leah. Next to Leah was the bassinette, but her baby girl was not in it. She was cradled in her Aunt Sarah's arms.

The dinner party was not turning out the way Abe had hoped. It wasn't the food that was the problem. Sarah had prepared a delicious roast. His sterling silver knife slid through it almost as easily as it did through the chopped liver appetizer. But if he had to use the same knife to cut the tension in the room, it would surely bounce off. Except for a grudging "hello" when he arrived, Solomon hadn't said a word. And his sullenness dampened everyone else's desire to talk, except for the children.

With the adults remaining stoic, Abe joined in the children's chatter. "You won't get me up in one of those contraptions," he said to Frank, Solomon's oldest.

"I can't wait to fly," Frank responded.

Beaming a broad grin at her husband for his effort to lighten the atmosphere, Sarah said, "Me neither."

"You want to fly, Aunt Sarah?" Frank asked.

"Of course."

"Your aunt is much more adventurous than I am," Abe said.

"We have toy aeroplanes in the basement," Ira said. "Want to see them?"

"Can we?" Frank asked.

"Go," Abe said, "and ask Frances for some cookies on your way through the kitchen."

"I'm going to lay Emanuel in his crib," Chava said. "I think he's getting tired."

"Thank you," Sarah said.

Leah's baby began to fuss. Leah retrieved her from Sarah and said, "I think she's hungry," and left the room to nurse her.

With the children gone, the room fell stone quiet. Determined to get Solomon talking, even if the conversation turned into an argument, Abe said, "Those IWW people are nothing but a bunch of users and thieves."

Solomon slammed his napkin on the table with a *whomp*. "They are not. They really tried to help the workers."

"Is that so? Look what that Flynn woman did with those children she took to New York City. First she marched them in a parade before she let them go to their foster homes. What do you call that if it wasn't using?"

"You'll never understand."

Sarah flashed Abe a disapproving look. He quickly broke eye contact and said to Solomon, "I understand one thing. Your IWW friends made demands and when we said we would talk about them shop-by-shop, they refused. They had no intention of ever settling. All they wanted was to start a revolution."

"Yes, we wanted a revolution. A revolution against the horrible conditions you mill owners subject us to while you get rich off our labor. Look how you live. You wear the silk we weave. You drape your house with it."

Abe started to reply, but Solomon cut him off.

"Let me finish, then you can talk all you want."

A smug look on his face, Abe acquiesced.

"What do we get from making this fabric you rich love so much? We go deaf from the noise of the looms. We get poisoned by the dyes. But we don't get to wear the garments made from our labor unless we make them ourselves from seconds. It's wrong. It has to stop. It has to change."

"I agree with you," Abe said.

Solomon threw his body against the back of his chair. "You what?"

Sarah, also stunned, stared wide-eyed at her husband.

He smiled at her and said, "I do believe the workers have rights. But they went about trying to get them the wrong way. It's one thing, striking for better pay. It's another to advocate the confiscation of private property. I don't know how you could abide by that after having lived under the Tsar. Once your IWW pals started saying that's what they really wanted, your strike was doomed to fail. You turned everyone in this town against you."

"The workers got some concessions," Solomon replied defensively, his eyes fixed on the tablecloth.

"I didn't hear of one signed contract."

"You aren't using four looms, are you? We stopped that."

"For how long?"

"Some shops are on a nine-hour schedule, and the newspapers are calling for legislation for an eight-hour day."

"That's pie in the sky. Most shops, including mine, are still working ten hours."

Solomon straightened his back and glared into Abe's eyes. "We showed you we won't be pushed around anymore."

"Big deal. Let's face it, you were on strike for five months and achieved no higher wages, no changes in hours, nothing."

"We got rid of the blacklist."

Abe raised an eyebrow. He pushed his chair back a bit, crossed his legs, folded his napkin in a neat square and placed it on his knee. "So why aren't you working in a mill instead of breaking your back digging ditches?"

"Weidmann says he's not up to full capacity yet, and when he is, he'll call me back."

"I'll give you a job right now at a hundred and fifty dollars a week to run the processing plant I bought." Abe needed Solomon badly. The foremen in each area of Pincus's mill were doing their best, but an overall manager was needed to break the bottlenecks that arose when one department was not coordinated with the others.

Solomon started to respond.

"Listen to the deal before you answer. You can pay your people whatever wage you want. You can let them work eight, nine, ten hours a day. You can do anything you want, as long as you make a profit."

All eyes shifted to Solomon.

"In other words, you want me to be a benevolent dictator?"

Cecelia started to say something, but Abe silenced her with an upraised hand. "Call it what you want. But I remember you saying last year, if you owned a mill you would treat your workers with respect and pay them a living wage. It's put up or shut up time."

"It's a wonderful thing Abe is offering," David said. "We will all be together, no?"

"Yeah," Solomon said. "Just like back in Latvia where Uncle Isaac ran the family. You may like that, but I won't."

Suddenly Chava's words flooded back to Abe. "I hope you never have to find out how it is to be beholding to your brother for everything you have. It is very hard."

"I told you months ago, I don't want to be Uncle Isaac. We will be partners. To show you I mean it, I'll give you eight percent of the stock in the company."

Solomon stared at Abe, trying to gauge his brother's sincerity. Finally he said, "You have a deal."

Cecelia's eyes filled with tears. She leaned over and hugged her husband. Glancing from Abe to Sarah, she said, "Thank you."

Abe raised his crystal wineglass. "Let's seal this bargain with a toast. To Bressler Brothers Silk Company."

With the brothers having come together and Cecelia hugging her husband, Sarah left the table and went upstairs to check on Leah. She told her sister-in-law what happened.

"You know he gave David twelve percent of the stock for co-signing that bank loan, using our house as collateral?" Leah asked.

"Yes, Abe discussed it with me. I told him I thought it was a good idea."

Sarah knew Abe's gesture to Solomon was meaningless. Giving Solomon eight percent wouldn't alter the company's power structure one bit. The swing vote rested with David's twelve percent. Abe had to give Jacob forty percent of the company's stock for the money to buy Pincus's mill. That left Abe with only forty percent. But Jacob was in France and had no say in how the company was run. Abe still maintained control.

Cecelia came into the bedroom. "It's so wonderful. I can't wait to buy a house."

"I can't wait to help you furnish it," Sarah said.

"So what are you two talking about? You seemed so serious when I came in."

"I was telling Leah that I hope David and Solomon know that Abe only wants the best for the family and he'll do anything for them, as long as they don't impugn his authority."

"Which means they aren't really partners," Cecelia said.

"They're better than partners, they're brothers," Sarah said, and wondered if Abe had really changed by the way he had goaded Solomon a moment ago.

Picking up on the trepidation in Sarah's voice, Cecelia said, "With Abe giving the orders and expecting the others to follow like Solomon said his uncle did."

When Sarah didn't answer, Cecelia asked, "What about you? How are you going to handle him when he tries to stop you from doing your suffrage work?"

"I'd like to think he understands why I need more than being a homemaker for a fulfilling life, and he won't hold me back."

"I don't understand it," Cecelia said.

"Neither do I," Leah concurred, "so I don't know how Abe will."

Sarah thought, *I guess I'll find out when we return from Europe and I remind him of his promise.*

FOOTNOTES

The resolution to allow women to vote in New Jersey passed the New Jersey Senate in 1915.

Elizabeth Flynn's fears came true. The great silk strike of 1913 was the defining moment for labor unions in America. The IWW disintegrated and the AF of L became the predominant union in the United States, merging many smaller unions into its ranks and eventually with the CIO to become the AFL-CIO.

The following are actual people who lived during the period this novel covers:

SUFFRAGISTS AND ANTI-SUFFRAGISTS:

Jeannie Tuttle Hobart
Mary Beckworth
Harriet Stanton Blatch
Carrie Chapman Catt
Lillian Ford Feickert
Dr. Anna Howard Shaw
Inez Milholland
Mrs. Champ Clark
Mrs. Burleson
Alice Paul
Rosalie Jones
Retired General John A. Johnson

PATERSONIANS:

Adolf Lessig
Monroe Dippel
Catholina Lambert
Jacob Weidmann
Mayor McBride
Chief John Bimson
Harry Haines
Thomas Quigley
Colonel Van Walraven
Ewald Koettgen
William Skinner
Henry Dogherty
Peter Ryle
Louis Magnet
Judge Congdon
Police Recorder Caroll
Pietro Botto

INDUSTRIAL WORKERS OF THE WORLD UNIONISTS:

Elizabeth Gurley Flynn
William Dudley Haywood
Frederick Boyd
Patrick Quinlan
Carlo Tresca
Frederick Mohl

AMERICAN FEDERATION OF LABOR UNIONISTS:

Margaret Jane Conboy
John Golden

ARTISTS AND WRITERS:

John Reed
Upton Sinclair
Mabel Dodge

Many of the speeches given by the strike leaders and suffragists—although condensed for dramatic effect—are actual speeches as reported in *The New York Times* and *Paterson Evening News.*